FATAL LEGACY

Also by Lindsey Davis

The Course of Honour
Rebels and Traitors
Master and God
A Cruel Fate

The Spook Who Spoke Again
Vesuvius by Night
Invitation to Die

THE FALCO SERIES

The Silver Pigs
Shadows in Bronze
Venus in Copper
The Iron Hand of Mars
Poseidon's Gold
Last Act in Palmyra
Time to Depart
A Dying Light in Corduba
Three Hands in the Fountain
Two for the Lions
One Virgin Too Many

Ode to a Banker
A Body in the Bath House
The Jupiter Myth
The Accusers
Scandal Takes a Holiday
See Delphi and Die
Saturnalia
Alexandria
Nemesis
Falco: The Official
Companion

THE FLAVIA ALBIA SERIES

The Ides of April
Enemies at Home
Deadly Election
The Graveyard of the Hesperides
The Third Nero

Pandora's Boy
A Capitol Death
The Grove of the Caesars
A Comedy of Terrors
Desperate Undertaking

FATAL LEGACY

Lindsey Davis

MINOTAUR BOOKS
NEW YORK

First published in the United States by Minotaur Books, an imprint of St. Martin's Publishing Group

FATAL LEGACY. Copyright © 2023 by Lindsey Davis. All rights reserved. Printed in the United States of America. For information, address St. Martin's Publishing Group, 120 Broadway, New York, NY 10271.

www.minotaurbooks.com

Maps by Mike Parsons

Library of Congress Cataloging-in-Publication Data

Names: Davis, Lindsey, author.
Title: Fatal legacy / Lindsey Davis.
Description: First U.S. edition. | New York : Minotaur Books, 2023. |
    Series: Flavia Albia series ; 11
Identifiers: LCCN 2023009387 | ISBN 9781250799906 (hardcover) |
    ISBN 9781250799913 (ebook)
Subjects: LCSH: Flavia Albia (Fictitious character)—Fiction. | Women
    private investigators—Rome—Fiction. | Rome—History—Domitian,
    81–96—Fiction. | LCGFT: Detective and mystery fiction. | Historical
    fiction. | Novels.
Classification: LCC PR6054.A8925 F38 2023 | DDC 823/.914—dc23/
    eng/20230301
LC record available at https://lccn.loc.gov/2023009387

Our books may be purchased in bulk for promotional, educational, or business use. Please contact your local bookseller or the Macmillan Corporate and Premium Sales Department at 1-800-221-7945, extension 5442, or by email at MacmillanSpecialMarkets@macmillan.com.

Originally published in Great Britain by Hodder & Stoughton, a Hachette UK company

First U.S. Edition: 2023

10 9 8 7 6 5 4 3 2 1

FATAL LEGACY

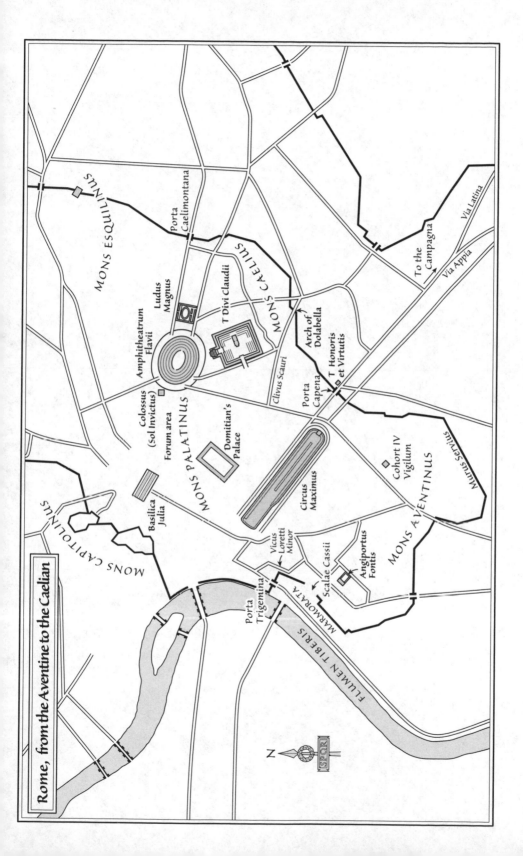

Rome, from the Aventine to the Caelian

MONS ESQUILINUS

Porta Caelimontana

MONS CAELIUS

Ludus Magnus

T Divi Claudii

Amphitheatrum Flavii

Arch of Dolabella

T Honoris et Virtutis

Clivus Scauri

Porta Capena

Colossus (Sol Invictus)

Forum area

Domitian's Palace

MONS PALATINUS

Circus Maximus

Cohort IV Vigilum

Murus Servius

MONS AVENTINUS

Basilica Julia

MONS CAPITOLINUS

Vicus Loretti Minor

Scalae Cassii

Angiportus Fontis

Porta Trigemina

FLUMEN TIBERIS

MARMORATA

To the Campagna

Via Appia

Via Latina

N

SPQR

ROME, AD 90:
AVENTINE, CAELIAN
AND FORUM ROMANUM

PLAINTIFFS AND AGENTS

Some of the Usual Suspects

Flavia Albia	honest debt collector and investigator
Tiberius Manlius	her husband, an ambiguous contractor
Gaius and Lucius	dear little nephews

Their household: Gratus the smooth steward; Dromo the dim slave; Paris the cheeky runabout; Fornix the celebrity chef; Suza the hopeful beautician; Barley the shy dog; Mercury the placid donkey; Glaphyra the diligent nurse; Rodan the seedy door-keeper

Marcia and Corellius	difficult visitors
Falco and Helena	renowned parents
Julia, Favonia and Postumus	interesting siblings
Tullius	a rich uncle
Junia	a hopeless aunt
Aelianus and Justinus	lovable uncles with specialist knowledge
Mygdonius	a wills expert

In the Catering Industry

Junillus and Apollonius	at the Stargazer (previously Flora's)
Rufus	at the Valerian (ex the Colossus)
Rumpus and the skivvy	at Nobilo's
A bunch of lying rascals	at the Comet
Thymellus	at the Little Caelian Caupona
Titus	on the Aventine bread round

At the Basilica Julia

Honorius	a legal hound
Mamillianus	a principal lawyer (not in evidence)
Hermeros	his office manager
Crispinus	a Mamillianus Associate, freely associating
Nincundio	a very angry man
Felicula	looking for a good lawyer

The Tranquilli and the Prisci	See family trees

Slaves or freedmen used as collateral, etc: Philodamus the book-keeper, Erotillus the archive clerk, Dindius the basket-seller, Dindius's son the helpful boy

Family tree of the Tranquilli

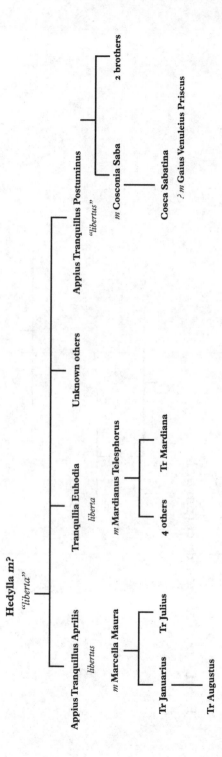

Family tree of the Prisci (partial)

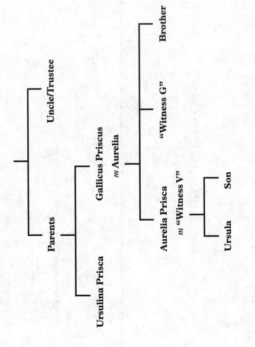

Parents
— Uncle/Trustee
— Gallicus Priscus
 m Aurelia

Ursulina Prisca

Aurelia Prisca
m "Witness V"

"Witness G"

Brother

Ursula

Son

I

According to my old note-tablets, the Tranquillus case began with Spanish rabbits. They were widely traded so there must have been money in it. That was always good news when, as a private investigator, I took on new clients.

This key item in the Roman food chain was certainly known to anyone who frequented the Stargazer. Our family's greasy spoon was managed by my aunt Junia, wife to the most boring man on the Aventine, Gaius Baebius. She used to hide rabbit bones and other inedible parts in the evening hotpots she sold over the counter to the dimmer kind of Aventine workers—those who had never realised that better bars were available. Junia's stew was no favourite, even among her crazily compliant customers. Apart from the danger of choking on unseen ribs, sometimes whole furry ears plopped out into serving bowls and splashed people's tunics. The ears could be tossed out into the street, but local laundries had started to be difficult when asked to tackle stains caused by the liquor that Junia called gravy. As was regularly pointed out, it was worse than axle grease.

People who dared challenge my aunt were few. However, it had been suggested that her stewing meat was not even rabbit, but some creature of similar size that had been offered at the back door by a rat-catcher. Nobody said this more than once. When Junia had stopped raving, they had to go and eat at the Valerian. The Valerian was to feature in my case too, along with Nobilo's, the Comet, and the Little Caelian Caupona.

My work for Aunt Junia began mundanely enough, with not a bunny in sight. One chilly lunchtime in January, two people chose to have a meet-and-eat at the Stargazer. They were a man and a woman, both married, though not to each other. The caupona waiters, Apollonius and Junillus, immediately spotted that: their customers wore wedding rings, yet the way they held hands and the intensity of their conversation gave away that they were philandering. Waiters always know.

The visiting duo ordered from the muzzy chalked board, which showed they were new customers. Whatever they had asked for, they were served hard-boiled eggs, the dish of the day. It was the only dish of every day, at lunchtime. Sometimes a few flakes of mackerel were scattered on top, generally not. Anyone who hated fish had to pick it off. The Stargazer did not confuse its customers with menu choice.

The waiters were an elderly man and a lad. It was over-staffing for their level of trade in winter, though typical for a bar that did not offer waitress service. I mean by that what my husband calls a garlicky tryst upstairs, with a dose of warts as afters. The Stargazer was so hopeless it had never managed to organise its upper rooms for such a purpose. That failure could be why our place was struggling.

The two waiters were busy—not whizzing about serving, but heads together over a geometry problem they had drawn on the counter, using lines of garum sauce. Once the new customers had been supplied with food bowls, along with their bill in a saucer, they were left to their own devices. They had not seemed to mind, as they stared into each other's eyes and barely talked.

The geometry hobby gripped our waiters. Apollonius had once been a teacher. Rome's most recent emperors were said to value education, but he had found it impossible to earn a living at his street-corner school. Ours was a rough district. Learning was a low priority; it came well after gambling and wasting money on evil-eye amulets or, if you absolutely could not avoid it, paying your rent. Reduced to pessimistic begging, Apollonius had been given work by the Stargazer's previous manager to stop him blocking the pavement in front of her bar. After twenty years of serving gut-rot here, he still mentally believed he would one day resume teaching. He disciplined the Stargazer's customers with well-tried teaching methods, like sternness and sarcasm, although he was discouraged from beating them with a stick unless they seriously misbehaved.

Nowadays he shared both serving and geometry with my cousin Junillus. Aunt Junia's eighteen-year-old son was deaf, though he tackled it cheerfully. A bright soul, he enjoyed problem-solving with Apollonius; cheeky by nature, Junillus loved the fact that mathematics was viewed as politically suspect. All our family kicked back at the government, a trait he had absorbed even though he was adopted. As a baby, he had been dumped in a skip, no doubt because of his disability; my father had found him whimpering among the building rubble and lacked the heart to walk away.

My childless aunt and her husband had then decided that it would be best if *they* took this scrap and taught him to cope with life, even though two people with less understanding of life would be hard to find. All the rest of us thought Junia and Gaius Baebius were ghastly, yet in their way they loved him, so the easy-going Junillus shrugged and truly loved them back. By some dedicated process, they had helped him to lip-read and even to talk, so I suppose they weren't all bad.

Once he was old enough, Junillus enjoyed his work at our family bar. He improved the Stargazer as much as he could, however hard Junia tried to make the place the worst takeaway on the Aventine. It only survived because it was on a good route for passing labourers; busy times were just after dawn and in the early evening. My husband and I had been known to rendezvous there during the day, but we could claim a family discount; it offered few attractions for courting couples.

Apollonius and Junillus had let the pair who came on that particular day have an inside table. Perhaps the lovers had deliberately chosen an empty caupona so they could smooch in private. They certainly hadn't come for the ambiance or conversation. They allowed themselves to be fobbed off with rubbery eggs and they poured their own nips from a very small flagon. Given the poor menu, they stayed quite a long time.

When they wanted to leave, they stood up, slid into their cloaks, then waved their bill at the "busy" waiters to indicate agreement in the traditional way—*No need to come over, we are leaving the money on the table.*

Junillus, being deaf, only noticed the gesture. Apollonius heard the chink of what he assumed to be coins rattling into the pottery saucer. But when he went to pick up the money, it was the old scam: three metal rivets.

That evening, when his mother came to cash up, Junillus confessed. Furious, Aunt Junia immediately banned these customers, who were unlikely to return in any case. She raved that there had been much too much cheating lately; all the bars were suffering after Saturnalia. Most other proprietors were lackadaisical wimps, but the queen of the Aventine planned to act. It was the second day of January, so not too late for a New Year Resolution, even a doomed one. Junia would penalise punters who left without paying—or, in other words, she would instruct Junillus and Apollonius to stop it happening. (They received her edict with hidden grins.) Undeterred, Junia hung up a notice that henceforth all defaulters would be named, shamed and prosecuted.

Who would file a court claim, especially for such a puny amount as a bar bill? She soon decided against the legal costs but remained dead set on recovery. Since her brother, the informer, was still holidaying at the coast (I knew Falco was back, but he had deliberately not told her), Junia decreed that the other investigator she knew, her niece—that was me, worse luck—must track down the two culprits.

So I, Flavia Albia, had to recover the money, did I? After stressing that the Stargazer was a family business, therefore it was my duty, Junia applied more pressure. Like Junillus, my personal history had involved being an abandoned child, discovered by Falco and his wife, who were always rescuing sad little mites. I had been about fourteen when they ran across me: unwashed, untaught and surly. In my case no one else came forward to take me in so they had to bring me up themselves. Junia now explained how I ought to be grateful that I had been adopted from hideous Britain by generous Romans, when nobody could guess how awful my origins were or how badly I might turn out. She managed not to imply I *had* turned out badly, because even Junia could produce fake tact when it affected her own interests. But she claimed this favour was the least I could do as thanks.

The people I really thanked were Falco and Helena. They took it as their reward that I was alive, sane, cheerful, useful to the community and even rather well married to a man they approved of. None of that impressed Junia. She would always see me as the dangerous product of a vile province. At my wedding to a magistrate, she had been first in the queue to complain about the catering and to prophesy that our marriage wouldn't last.

It would, dammit. He was lovely. I was determined. Anyway, we had bought a house.

Now Junia needed me. I could have said no; I should have done. But I was fond of Junillus. While his mother pressurised me, he was giving me his doe-eyed look: if the reckoning remained unpaid, he would have trouble at home . . .

I caved in. "Give me their bill and those rivets. That's evidence. I will need a fee, Auntie, though of course it goes down as an expense for you."

Junia found accountancy too complicated, despite us all explaining how to assign her deductibles. Falco had worked on the Census once so he knew all the tricks about tax. Although Junia appeared intelligent, she could not grasp that if I traced the absconders I would add my fee to their bill. Then her husband could deduct this genuine business expense from his notifiable income. Gaius Baebius would like that; he had worked in the customs service, so he was hot on withholding money from the treasury, as he had seen so many other people do.

Junia sniffed in her charmless way. She was a middle-aged woman who had never enjoyed life, even though hers had been relatively comfortable. It was too late now for her to fool around with concepts like making herself endearing. "I hope you'll get a move on, Albia. I am not intending to pay you until you bring the cash—and I don't want to hear about any of your horrible Druidic methods. My caupona has a reputation."

Too right, it had. Though not the one she pretended.

Thanks to my excellent Roman education from Falco and Helena, I knew magic was a forbidden practice. Unless you could evade arrest by hiding in a mystic cloud when the troops came for you, in Roman law the penalty was death. I needed to stop Junia shouting in that abrasive voice of hers that my work involved the occult. Being an informer caused enough confrontations with the authorities.

"I shall recover your money," I assured her patiently. Clients need you to sound confident. "It won't require a bunch of mistletoe."

I never understood why people in Rome liked thinking I was a Druid. Even back in Britannia, Druids were banned. Despite that, I had met one once: a smelly, long-haired old poseur from the west, as most were. He had said he liked little girls—then tried to back me against a log-store and interfere with me. His second sight had failed to forewarn him that I would kick him below the tunic belt and race for freedom, like a streak of moonlight.

I had been a Londinium street urchin, so I had learned a few survival tricks—but I knew no spells. Soon I would regret that. Sorting out the Tranquillus family would have been so much easier with supernatural powers. And among their complicated troubles, our unpaid bill was only the start.

II

My first need was to identify the defaulters, so I had to question the witnesses. "You were doing your puzzle on the counter," I tackled them in a professional tone, "but please try to recall what they looked like." Since they knew me, Apollonius and Junillus shuffled gormlessly, each waiting for the other to speak. "Was anybody else here who might remember these cheats?" They shook their heads. "No other customers?"

"Oh, we are always much too popular at lunchtime!" butted in Junia, to whom self-delusion came naturally. "People must have stayed away because they thought they would have a problem finding space." Junillus screwed the tip of one forefinger into his temple, the classic gesture to tell me his mother was mad. "Naughty boy!" she chided. She mouthed the words carefully, but he knew he could get away with cheek so he did not bother to look.

I pretended to put the two waiters under hypnosis. "I am taking you back . . . You are completely relaxed, feeling warm and sleepy . . ."

"This is normal for us." Apollonius must have been over seventy, but he could play-act as annoyingly as the infants he had once taught. He leaned on the counter and pretended to snooze.

"Drop it! Let us remember the scene. It is lunchtime again. A gloomy old morning, just two days into the fresh consulship of those top tribunal heroes, Domitian and Nerva, that's God-on-earth, our paranoid Emperor, and his junior colleague, widely known as Who-the-doodah-is-he? Got it now? It's Mercury day. Fine drizzle and oppressive government. Now two soppy lovers come wandering by, and as they are looking for somewhere to drool over each other, they decide this is the most romantic bar they can find."

Junillus repeated his "crackpots" gesture. Though loyal, he accepted that the Stargazer was a sorry hole. Only able to agree, I gazed around at its cracked plaster walls, the blackening spiders' webs, the emaciated cat, the counter pots where yesterday evening's congealed hot food had hardened into sludge around their chipped rims. "I suppose the hand-holding couple must have tried all the better bars on other days."

"What 'better bars'?" snapped Junia, tensing up so much her skinny ringlets bounced.

Following my rule not to fight with my client in the first few hours of being hired, I restrained myself. "The bars they can't go back to because they have already cheated the waiters once." She gave me her sniff again. "Have you got a cold, Aunty?" She hated to be called that. Her preferred address would have been "Augusta," like an empress who had impressed the Senate and won extreme honours. One who was known to poison people who crossed her.

"Junillus, buck up. Describe the man."

"I am deaf. I do not understand."

"No, you are a clever boy, goofing about." I grabbed him by the shoulders, pointing to his own features and exaggerating my words. "Marcus Baebius Junillus: you yourself are average height, brown eyes, need a haircut, stubble botched by your barber. You are wearing a short-sleeved grey tunic with part of its braid loose—you must be perished, but it's to show off these dashing wristbands—and your apron needs to go to the laundry, not tomorrow but today."

"Red cloak," he offered, batting rather beautiful lashes over big, dark brown eyes. My younger sisters were starting to adore him a little too much. "Man's. Not really red. Squashed plum. Too long."

"Very helpful. More clues, please." Even though he could lip-read, I made further arm movements to illustrate. "Tall? Brawny? Wide face? Long chin? *Bearded?*"

Junillus looked puzzled; he was putting it on.

Witnesses were often idiots, so this was nothing new. I pressed on gamely: "Foreign or from here?"

"Local," he condescended to say, this time consulting Apollonius. "Why so?"

Junillus only shrugged, while Apollonius slowly nodded. I took that to mean the non-payer had no eccentric garments or unusual features that would make him stand out on the Aventine. No help, of course, because we lived on the outsiders' hill, the one with the temples where slaves were freed; most of the liberated looked as if they had originated in some far province, although they all dressed the same as their Roman masters and mistresses because they were in their owners' cast-off clothes. Being near the wharves and the Emporium, the Aventine attracted foreign traders too. Some were swarthy, squinty-eyed, and had scars or digits missing, but so did plebeian Romans who had lived here since Romulus. (He was foreign, came from Latium, got off scot-free on both murder and rape charges: extremely dodgy character.)

Giving up on that, I tackled Apollonius about the woman. You have to try. He had never been married, and never seemed bothered by that, so I had no great hopes. Even so, he came up with "long-sleeved, straw-coloured tunic and big necklace." Apollonius thought he would remember the necklace if he saw it again. That did not mean he could describe it.

This woman probably owned more than one anyway. She was free to come out from home to meet her lover, so not someone with demanding employment. A fashionable woman might by now have changed her gold collar for silver chains, but informers cannot go into people's houses demanding to rifle through their jewellery caskets. "She's out flirting, so she needs to be careful. If her husband bought her jewellery, she won't want to tell him I grabbed it off her for a bar bill." Junillus and Apollonius had not given me enough clues—and these rascals knew it. "Try again, lads. You must have thought the couple looked respectable. Otherwise, wouldn't you have taken payment when you first put their order in front of them?" That point my witless witnesses were prepared to agree. When they weren't absorbed in geometry, they were both shrewd servers.

I tried to determine the couple's ages. "They are married, but they are having a fling. So, they were neither young nor decrepit?"

"Tooth missing," Apollonius remembered suddenly.

"Him?"

"Her."

"Front?"

"Side."

"Right?"

"Left. No—right."

It is fair to say that in Rome or any of the provinces anyone who was older than me was liable to have lost at least one tooth. Many only had one or two left.

Aunt Junia was growing bored. She would never have made an investigator. "I think that gives you plenty to work with, Flavia Albia!"

I nodded, pretended to agree, then waited until she waddled off home.

"Holy moly, I thought she'd never leave. I need a drink, fellows."

With Junia gone, their attitude perked up. Apollonius poured me a beaker, while Junillus was rootling somewhere.

"Any olives?"

No olives. Junia ordered supplies so the Stargazer regularly ran out of everything.

My cousin produced a piece of used scroll from the basket where they kept scraps for writing bills. It smelt of old fish, *extremely* old, so I lent him a note-tablet and my stylus. I knew he was artistic; I watched without interrupting as Junillus made drawings.

The first time, he scribbled two cartoon faces, one comic, one tragic, mere doodles with lunatic expressions. I sighed. He settled down. He smoothed over the wax and began again several times, until he was satisfied. He showed me a man with a square head, regular features and thick hair that came down quite low on his forehead, cut straight across.

"Was he smiling like that?" Junillus nodded. He even drew in more smile lines around the eyes and mouth. I chuckled. "He seems pleased with himself—out with his floozy, while his wife believes he is harmlessly conferring with his accountant. What about his lady-love?"

The female portrait had a long oval face, smooth hair drawn down over her ears from a centre parting and a guarded expression. Her mouth was rather tightly closed, which hid the missing tooth Apollonius had mentioned. I tapped the tablet. "Do I see nerves? She thinks her suspicious husband may roll around the corner any minute—and she's starting to feel Smiler isn't worth the risk. Can you draw in her necklace?"

No: Junillus had not noticed any jewellery. Apollonius claimed the only things he himself could draw were a trapezium or a parallelogram. When asking other people about her, I would simply have to describe her as "well-dressed."

Junillus and Apollonius finally decided to reveal a crucial fact: they knew that the couple had previously patronised the bar over the road. They had seen them coming out of the Valerian.

"Now you tell me!" I was annoyed but had to play it down. "What's this—espionage? Do you always check the Valerian's footfall?"

"It was a quiet period at the Stargazer," declared Apollonius, bravely. He knew he worked in a dump.

"Nobody came here all day, you mean?" I ragged them. "So, you were gazing across the street and you saw them. Remember when?"

"About a week ago."

"Mercury again?"

"Could be."

"That must be their assignation day. He visits his accountant, and she gets her armpits de-fuzzed at a beauty parlour. They have trained everyone at home not to notice how long they spend out of their houses." These adulterers could have been at it for years, until their secret meetings were not even exciting—although their intense hand-holding probably indicated the fling was a newer phenomenon.

I cheered up. At least the first expense I could add to the defaulters' bill would be a bowl of seafood and a beverage. Taking the tablet with my cousin's drawings, I went across the road to that well-regarded food outlet, the Valerian.

III

This was how a bar should be run. At ours, I had left Junillus and Apollonius preparing for the evening rush, a task that did not require them to hurry. At the Valerian a rush was already under way. Men in dusty tunics were leaning on their elbows. New arrivals were shouting orders to Rufus, the show-off waiter, competing for his attention; meanwhile Little Danae, his curly-haired child assistant, was applying a taper to oil-lamps' wicks as the winter dusk suddenly descended, while at the same time wiping down the counter after previous customers. She might be twelve, though she looked more like eight; two activities at once did not faze this efficient young girl. Give her a year and she'd be running the place. Even the cloth she was using looked more or less clean, though I knew it was probably someone's old loincloth.

The Valerian was not perfect. Seafood had run out. Whelks had been part-deleted from the menu board, using an elbow, judging by chalk on the waiter's tunic sleeve. Each morning Rufus toddled down to the quays for the fresh catch, but once the midday fare had all gone, that was it. Later, along with the twilight moths, a surreptitious stew arrived, illegal of course. Since Vespasian's reign, an edict said bars ought only to serve grains—as in *Yuk, what's this soppy muck?*—which Palace officials believed revolutionaries will not eat. Pulses prevent plotting, according to them. So Brutus and Cassius must have been red-meat men: neither would touch lentils or black-eyed beans, let alone hairy vetch and lupin seeds . . .

Of course, the new food edict would have failed anyway, since Brutus and Cassius were aristos, who rendezvoused in their own fancy houses. There is no record of either grabbing a bite at a bar.

The Valerian's hotpot was little better than the Stargazer's. It offered tired workers what looked like comfort food, until someone was rash enough to taste it. Quality ingredients and careful preparation were never on offer. People were best to come early too, because once casseroles cooled down in the counter pot-holes, they just congealed.

When I arrived, typical conversations were occurring: "Snakes alive! What's in this stuff, Rufus?"

"Roebuck."

"Tastes like liniment."

"He died of a cold. Do you want it or not?"

"Can I have my money back?"

"We don't do refunds."

"Well, fricassée you!"

In Rome, that was the standard even at a good bar.

Rufus liked busy times. He was a showman, in speedy juggler mode. Skinny and lithe, he raced around behind the counter, swinging his trays and flagons, then slid the dicepot along the mock-marble top to some demanding builders, pinched change from the old red gratuities crock for a departer, skirted Little Danae without knocking her over, then dealt out a shower of spoons to those starving customers who were prepared to brave the roebuck. Tossing back his long hair like a demigod, he flourished his ladle before plunging it into today's slow-simmered supper dish.

I decided now was not the time for a useful discussion. If I mentioned our cheats, Rufus would only laugh at the Stargazer's loss. I went home. That was what Rufus would tell me to do in any case.

IV

Next day my matronly duties kept me at home until halfway through the morning. As I pointed out to my husband, he was lucky I loved him (still did, after four months: good going, sweetie). Otherwise I might have been hankering for my old life as a single informer.

Until we set up home together, I had been able to control my own time. Only now did I appreciate what a luxury that was: although it had seemed right to acquire basic domestic staff, each one had brought new demands. We enjoyed elegant meals prepared by a brilliant chef, but he had already fallen out with the butcher and was suspected of a quarrel with the fishmonger too. I had found a good steward, but his latest foible was to stride around making dark remarks about the irascible chef. My young maid wanted to be a society hairdresser, not stuck here with me. My husband's body-slave was well-meaning but brainless. And the recent addition of a seedy old ex-gladiator to function as our door porter had worried everyone, even the donkey who feared Rodan had his eye on her stable. She was right too.

Tiberius Manlius, my husband, had been a magistrate when I met him. He had enjoyed that, so when his term ended at New Year he felt a restlessness, for which he had not planned. As he honestly remarked, since he had to stop hounding neighbourhood wrongdoers, he might turn disciplinarian on his own household. "This is where you find out what I'm really like, Albia!"

"A joker, I hope."

"No, I'm serious. I think I'll install a domestic fines system."

"Oh, good luck with that idea, darling!"

He had bought himself a run-down building firm around the time we were married, so that would keep him busy. I was probably due for a lifetime of him falling off inspection ladders and cursing late suppliers.

We had two recently acquired foster children. They were three and five. Even before their mother died, these little boys were known for whining. Now when they grizzled, we had to be kind to them. I found that hard. A nursemaid had been acquired from my family; she thought I was a piece of work. I wouldn't have cared, but Glaphyra told everyone I had always been difficult, so people now viewed me her way.

My cousin was staying with us; I was not even sure how that happened. Marcia Didia was a young woman with a sprightly character; she had brought her morose partner, who was recovering from an amputation. That was bad enough for him, but he had been taken off the imperial salaries list during his sick-leave and he had just found out that someone else was permanently doing his job. Thus Corellius was not only in constant pain but embittered about official ingratitude. Nobody sympathised because we all felt he should have known. Now he had found himself stuck among strangers and might have been regretting his relationship with Marcia, who did not tolerate weakness. He had a new false leg he could not get on with; at least the rest of us found that interesting. Gaius and Lucius, our fosterlings, kept creeping up and asking him to take it on and off. Corellius clearly did not like children.

"Why is he staying at our house?"

"To be looked after until he is well again."

"Why can't he be looked after at his own house?"

"Because at the moment he doesn't have a house of his own."

"When is he going to get one?"

Good question! "I don't know, darling."

Every morning—*every morning for the rest of your life, Albia*—it fell to me to soothe and organise this disparate mob.

Oh, yes? Not if I could find clients to draw me away. We needed me bringing in fees, not only to feed the hungry mouths but to pay for building supplies when our firm's work restarted after the holiday. Then we had to cover labour costs. Tiberius could only go so far in telling his men he would "treat them like family"; they were sceptical and wanted to see coins. I told him Junia's puny commission would be good practice while I waited for the desperate people with big bank boxes that every informer hopes for after Saturnalia.

The theory is that, come New Year, lawyers and private inquiry agents are always overwhelmed with new work. People have been drinking ill-advisedly with neighbours; their quarrels while pie-eyed lead to compensation claims for cracked heads and damaged goods. During the enforced closedown, many in business have finally decided to break with their inadequate partners. Family members have been closeted for too long with relatives they cannot stand; they rush into divorces, new wills, affairs, and revivals of old property arguments. Slaves have been lured away to rival homes or businesses; other slaves have run off of their own accord, so reward notices need to be drawn up and, if they are ever recaptured, formal ownership must be established; a few slaves may even be suspected of murdering their masters, though that was never a money-spinner. Girls have fallen for the wrong reveller; parents want background checks. Partying boys have made girls pregnant; someone has to arrange a fast army entry, slipping a recruiter the accepted bribe for a posting to a very remote province. Elsewhere in the military, serving soldiers have gone absent without leave, so letters must be written to commanding officers who have heard the line "He's very sorry, sir, he just lost track of time" a hundred times before. An experienced informer can help gauge how many amphorae of wine will satisfy the legate in question, then suggest whether a basic Alban will do the trick, or if the giftie had better be fully aged Caecuban, properly tagged with its original lead label, a rare survivor from the Vesuvius eruption.

I will not say my father possessed a supply of those labels, but Falco was an auctioneer, so you can guess. Available at a price, like everything.

I felt chipper. I like January. Confident that useful clients would turn up, I gave instructions at home that any petitioners should be given a time to return for an interview. So, finally, I was able to set off back to the Valerian.

The morning hubbub was over; the waiter was prepared to listen. Like the Stargazer, the Valerian traded on bluff. Rufus pretended his lunchtime crowd would be swarming in at any moment, although when

I arrived not even the bread man was requiring attention. The old delivery fellow had handed in an overflowing basket and was now sipping from a beaker on his own before he headed back to the bakery.

I showed Rufus the pictures Junillus had drawn. With a characteristic toss of his head, flipping his hair back like a self-conscious horse, Rufus said yes, he would tell me for sure: those people had *never* been in his bar because he, the world's most conscientious waiter, did not remember ever seeing them. Especially if they had been here and had bunked off without paying: then he *would* remember them because he was, as mentioned, the world's best waiter.

"You are the most conceited one!" Privately I thought he would have forgotten. He was always too busy rushing about, like a tray-carrying tornado. On the other hand, he was good, so I doubted that any of his customers escaped paying their dues.

"I was head waiter at the Colossus once. Ask anyone."

Preferring not to upset Rufus, I did not ask why the Colossus had found it necessary to dispense with his services. It was a huge, famous establishment close to where the Flavian Amphitheatre now stood, though originally named for when a towering statue of Nero had been in the grounds of his Golden House. Vespasian, a frugal emperor, had given the grounds back to the people and had the statue remodelled. "I keep waiting for the Colossus to be renamed Sol Invictus, like the statue."

"It would kill trade," Rufus disagreed. "People like a bar to be called the same as always. That was your family's big mistake with Flora's."

I told him frankly that our big mistake, after Flora died, was letting the renamed Stargazer be run by Junia. "She can't help it. She's hopeless."

"Oh, she's a legend. We have a lot of laughs at customers' miserable faces when they leave your place. Anybody died there yet?"

"Not since Junia took over."

"Amazing!" Rufus dropped his voice, faking it as the world's most discreet waiter. "Someone did die once, though?" he asked hopefully.

"I believe so, Rufus, but that was before my time. Anyway, I don't expect there is a bar in Rome that hasn't seen a fatality. Some might even have been natural causes, though I admit most times it's murder."

"Either way," said Rufus, complacently, smoothing down his locks, "anyone who dies with a drink in his hand dies happy." All waiters say that, but of course they have never tried doing it.

That was when the ancient bread man turned over his beaker and shook out any last drops, which in most Roman bars is a courtesy, to allow the waiter to reuse the cup without washing it. He came past us, taking the opportunity to stare nosily at my sketches.

"Ever seen this couple?" I asked routinely. I would have been surprised if he could see the end of his own nose; he must have been the oldest bakery boy in Rome. He still tottered about with his baskets as if he'd grown up serving wholemeal baps to noble-minded forefathers in the Republic. He was called Titus and had a nice easygoing manner. Whatever bakery he came from serviced all the bars in this enclave, even the Stargazer. That was mainly because if any other loaf-supplier tried to encroach, Titus would, in his nice easygoing way, split open their barrow boy's head.

I did not expect he would know the couple. To my surprise, after thoughtfully considering Junillus's drawings, he told me he did. He said those people were regulars at Nobilo's.

V

I knew Nobilo's, which was two streets away. Barely wide enough for three clients in a line against the counter, its distinguishing features were a one-hinge wonky shutter and no menu. Pantiles on the roof had slumped into zigzags that looked ready to collapse at any moment, almost certainly killing people. There were two shaggy horses in a stable at the back that never seemed to do anything; perhaps they were waiting to be turned into a cauldron of hash.

A metal-beating workshop next door clanged endlessly. Customers at the bar tended to be snatch-and-run types, because of the noise. As they scuttled off clutching their skinnily filled rolls, they had to be careful not to fall over piles of bowls and roped-together urns that cluttered the pavement, not only outside the workshop but along the street in both directions. Domitian had issued regulations to clear such walkway impedimenta; his agents must be leery of reprimanding the big bronze-batterers in their leather aprons, who sometimes leaned on long-handled hammers looking ugly.

They came out for a look at me. Women probably crossed the road to avoid them. I stared straight back with my "I'm from Londinium, so get lost!" expression. They slouched back indoors. They hammered away pointedly, but we knew who had won.

Nobilo's had a waiter with a squint that you couldn't take your eyes off. He was so old he'd probably served pickled walnuts to Julius Caesar. He wasn't Nobilo; everyone called him Rumpus, for some reason. He was a quiet person.

I made my pitch for information, but when I showed him my images of the culprits, Rumpus had to wander into the back and consult a hidden skivvy in the wash-up who had better sight. I helped myself to nuts from his counter-top snacking bowl. It was some chunky greyware, hardly a fancy Greek kylix, but if it was ever stolen or fell on the pavement, a replacement would cost only small change at the corner market.

Surveying the bar while I waited, I could not envisage the gloopy couple coming here. There were no indoor tables and the pavement was very public.

Rumpus doddered back, bringing the skivvy, a thin fellow whose name was never mentioned. Apparently it was enough to be known as "the skivvy at Nobilo's." Sometimes they are downtrodden but this one had an air of inbred authority. He believed that dishwashers could easily rule the world, only they didn't want to waste their time on it.

Rumpus seemed to need a permit to speak, but as soon as the skivvy nodded, all confidentiality evaporated. I was told that the man Junillus had drawn sometimes did call here but only for takeaways and not so much recently. His order would be jumbo Lucanian sausage in rye bread, with full fish pickle and all the trimmings, though no radish. When he had a companion—chortles!—he bought her egg-and-watercress in a slice of white with a dash of oil, no other dressing. The woman always waited on the other side of the road as if she wasn't with him. He would cross over, crying "Oh, hello!" in mock-surprise, and they would go off together in the direction of the Armilustrum, where it was assumed they kicked any vagrants off the bench in the enclosure, gobbled down their Nobilo's tuck, then had a bunk-up against the Altar of Mars.

"It's always a joy to kiss a man who has just put away fish pickle and all the trimmings." I was speaking from past experience, although I had higher standards nowadays. At least, I made sure Tiberius and I ate the same garlic for lunch.

"Even with no radishes," agreed the skivvy, sounding wise.

I explained that the couple seemed to have upgraded to sit-downs in bars, which must be losing Nobilo's custom for their Lucanian sausage takeaways. "I hope he always paid you?"

"You bet."

"And I assume there's no point asking whether you know the fellow's name?"

As if issuing an edict, the skivvy assured me that Rumpus would know. I did not even have to put money in the tips vase for this. Rumpus readily coughed the lot: he thought the customer was Tranquillus Januarius, a local freedman, in business as a commodity-dealer, who lived with various family members, in a respectable apartment block that had been their home for a very long time, somewhere off Sidewind Passage.

Rumpus and the skivvy knew all this because old Tranquillus Surus, the original master, a wealthy man who was well-known in the neighbourhood, used to come here. He did it for years. Whenever he was around, he arrived for his breakfast, which if anybody wants to know was green olive tapenade, spread on bread not too thickly, with a side of potted shrimps when they had any. He had been very thick with Nobilo, and Nobilo's father before him. And he loved his shrimps, did old Tranquillus.

"That wasn't all he loved!" the skivvy exclaimed. Then he turned shy and failed to elaborate, so I took it he meant drink.

"He is dead now, I imagine?"

"Oh, he passed to Elysium way back," Rumpus told me, with respect. "Must be forty years ago. What a lovely character! Nobilo kept on talking about him for a long time after. His beautiful manners and his constant optimistic outlook. Surus wasn't a young man, but we all felt he was taken from us much too soon. I still miss his cheery face of a morning; I can hear him crying out, 'Do you have any of your excellent shrimps today, my lad? I've brought a pot back for you.' We were all very sad."

"Goodness . . ."

I needed to get on. Talking about food fads is pleasant enough, but it never advances casework. I sympathised politely, as you do over strangers' deaths. Then I gathered up my note-tablets, thanking them both for their help, before I beetled off with a bounce in my heels, to start making enquiries about Tranquillus Januarius in Sidewind Passage.

VI

From then on it was easy. Once you know a street name, you simply pop along there and visit a few commercial outlets. All households have to buy food and lamp-oil. While I was there, I picked out pears for us and some candles that were on special offer after the recent festival. I would collect them later, after I'd finished with the debtors.

The Tranquilli were well-known in Sidewind Passage. I might have thought they pretty well owned it, but a uniform drabness suggested the buildings in this narrow alley were rented. Stallholders identified the right staircase; it was awkward and dark, but halfway up I found the apartment. An old plaque was labelled **AP TR SUR *NEG***, which told me Surus had been a commercial negotiator. Perhaps his descendants still were. Bankrupt negotiators were impossible to find. Such people rarely starved, unless they repeatedly invested in cargoes that were shipwrecked. So if these were any good at all, they had no need to bunk off from bars without paying.

Staff let me in. That could have been a mistake for me. I did briefly wonder if I should have left word at home about where I was going—possibly even have brought our runabout, Paris; after all, that was why we had him. I shrugged off any qualms. The door had been opened by a quiet man who looked like a responsible slave, with a younger one peering from behind him to see who it was. They had clean faces and were not belligerent. The large apartment I entered was comfortably furnished; it had an air of respectability.

Of course, implying moral decency because your inner doorways have curtains with tiebacks is an old fraud. But if I vanished here, eventually the fruit- and candle-sellers outside would tell Tiberius where they had sent me.

I was put in a reception room, where I sat on the edge of a reading couch. Another couch, another salon . . . One of scores where I had perched, waiting to start interviews. I was always a little apprehensive, though felt excitement too. Uncertainty lay easy on me. I liked to wonder what would happen.

A woman came, on her own, no escort. Sixties, dark clothes, a few long pins spearing old-fashioned hair. Not gaunt or badly lined, yet giving a faint impression that she had known hard work. She introduced herself as Tranquilla Euhodia. The second name implied she had started life as a slave; from her dress and demeanour I thought it would have been a good while ago. She was probably a freedwoman of the old potted-shrimp lover, Tranquillus Surus, or if he had died as long ago as they had said at Nobilo's, maybe he had freed one or both of her parents.

She accepted me as if unknown callers were normal. It confirmed that business was carried on here and that she was party at least to some of it. She entered the room and immediately took a seat. I had stood politely but dropped back onto the couch, sideways on so I was turned towards her, keeping my feet on the floor. "My name is Flavia Albia. I am hoping to see Tranquillus Januarius."

"Not possible." A simple enough statement. Tranquilla Euhodia was blunt, though not aggressive—or not yet. She might flare up more when she knew why I had come. "He is not here."

"Will he be at home later?"

"Out of town."

"He is a relation of yours?"

"My nephew."

Anyone who does my job will, on making first contact, try to conceal from relatives that money is owing. You need to keep the situation calm. Telling people of a debt they haven't heard about can cause hysterical upsets. In fact, once you get hold of the real defaulter, promising *not* to tell their family can be your simplest route to the cash.

I knew what to do. Even my husband sometimes sent me with the final invoice for his building firm's renovations: "Attractive one first. Plug-uglies if Albia gets seen off," he would say, grinning.

"What is the problem, Flavia Albia?"

"A matter I need to sort out."

"Money?" the woman demanded at once. Visits from creditors had happened before.

"Yes, a sum is involved." I spoke lightly enough.

"You don't look like a debt collector!"

"No, I'm not the ex-gladiator type—though if needed, I do know some."

I watched her sizing me up: neat and petite, good-quality warm winter tunic and cloak, small gold ear-hoops and wedding ring, business satchel, walking shoes. I was coming up to thirty; I had seen life, though it had left me cheerful. I felt I looked very much like a professional who could pass through the streets unnoticed by muggers, even when carrying cash for someone.

I was assessing her too. She had an armful of bangles that looked old, cheap and none too pretty, the kind someone would collect quickly when they were first on the up, as an aid to status. I had done similar myself once. You acquire such trappings to cover your inexperience, but once you grow confident, you no longer give your accessories much thought. My own bangles today were recent family presents, from last month's Saturnalia.

We were both rattling so well that no awkward social distance gaped between us. We could talk on level terms. I reinforced my earlier hint: "My principals like to send me along, rather than have your neighbours notice obvious enforcers."

I threw a glance around the room. Its furniture looked like pieces the family had always owned, well-used but in fair condition: couch, tall-backed armchair, stools, low table with animal legs. "Nice place!" If I were evaluating items that could be seized in lieu of the debt, Tranquilla heard the message. "And you seem like a sensible matriarch, Tranquilla Euhodia. Perhaps you and I can resolve my issue."

"What is it?"

"Someone left a bar without paying the bill. Nothing extreme. I am hardly accusing your nephew Januarius of extravagant living!" I produced the totting-up that Junillus and Apollonius had scribbled for the couple.

Tranquilla glanced at the total, then burst out, "Is that all?"

"To struggling waiters every loss hurts."

"Must have been accidentally overlooked." The usual excuse. People all over Rome were trotting it out to their creditors right at that moment. "Easily done."

"Could be." I smiled, but then firmed up my style. "So, what about these?" I produced the rivets and chinked the little culprits down in a line on the low table. Tranquilla's hand went out, but I swiftly took back the fake payment. "I'll be frank. Your nephew has not helped himself. To me, anyone who carries metalwork like this in his purse probably makes a habit of not settling his bar bills. If I ask around, I expect to find other disgruntled proprietors who've had military rivets passed off on them." I gave his aunt a stare. "Bad feeling about deliberate non-payers is on the rise. Complainants may join in a class action—ask for a praetor's judgment. Anything could result. You know how it is when troubles go public: I can already hear reputations collapsing . . ."

Unimpressed by the rhetoric, she simply checked facts: "Januarius was identified?"

"By various people."

"Are they reliable?"

"I trust them."

Tranquilla Euhodia looked resigned. Swiftly rising to her feet, she went to the doorway and called for someone named Philodamus, ordering him to bring the petty-cash box.

Philodamus was a standard bookkeeper. Stubble, slow walk, plain beige tunic. Fingers ink-stained in both red and black. I would not expect such a man in an ordinary domestic household, but if they ran a business he fitted.

"Januarius has dodged his dues in some bar."

Philodamus seemed unfazed. "What's the damage?"

I proffered the bill, telling him, "A gratuity on top would smooth things over. Also, I am obliged to add administration charges. It should be a deterrent in future—the on-costs have tripled the total."

"Admin charges? That's for what?"

"My fee."

"Your fee?"

"Plus expenses." I smiled, then snapped out figures at him. I had learned not to be shy about money. "I had to visit a few other bars when following up, to make sure I had the right name."

"Tranquillus Januarius?" This Philodamus was much warier than his mistress. Not yet paying out as she had asked, he clearly decided she had missed a trick with me. "You are certain? What made you think it is someone of ours?"

Being called out by a bookkeeper had not been in my plan, but I stood up to him. "The fact that no one here seems surprised is a clue. A witness has sketched the culprit's image." I fetched out my cousin's drawing, just the male absconder. I had decided not to incriminate Januarius by revealing his affair.

Tranquilla Euhodia and her man glared hard at the sketch, before she made me jump, exclaiming loudly, "Oh, no! You're wrong. Far too much hair, for one thing. That is not him."

"Really?" I disbelieved her. Januarius lost his hope of discretion: I hooked out the other picture, his presumed female lover. "This is the friend he eats out with."

The matriarch's face changed again. She sighed, then ordered quietly: "Pay the woman, Philodamus."

He paused. Something was going on between them.

"I shall deal with the debt, then speak to her," she told him.

He, too, had seen the second picture; he, too, must have recognised the female face. He began to count out cash. As soon as he had given me all I had demanded, he slid away, disappearing from the room as if running from trouble. I wrote the receipt for Tranquilla Euhodia instead.

Playing it gentle, I gathered the coins into my satchel, while I merely quirked up an eyebrow. With a dark look, she admitted, "That is Mardiana."

"You know her?"

"I should do. I gave birth to the girl." In the sketch, Mardiana looked more than a girl, at least twenty-five, probably closer to thirty. "My youngest," Euhodia continued, with what sounded like bitterness. "The others have all grown up and moved away. She's the worst and I can't budge her."

"If it really was Januarius, there's no harm in her lunching with a relative," I suggested, still linking her to my original suspect, who must be her cousin.

"It's not him," Euhodia repeated, while she looked as if she was thinking that her daughter had caused quite enough harm. "When did this happen? The unpaid bill?"

"Yesterday."

"You move fast!"

"That's my work. With practice, it's not hard. Look, I can't help professional curiosity—the waiters thought she might be married."

"Oh, she is," snorted her mother. "So we're stuck with *him* in the house as well! Mardiana is married—though, obviously, not to *this* man. Heaven help us when her husband finds out she is wandering off." Jabbing a finger at the male portrait, Euhodia's voice was rueful, rather than angry, but I would not have wanted to hear how she later quarrelled with her daughter. "Yesterday they had a tryst? Cannot have been Januarius. I told you he is out of town. He has been at our old family place on the Campagna all the past week, seeing someone about stock we rear. Your image bears only a passing resemblance . . ." I was not sure I believed that. I felt she might in fact know exactly who he was. The mother was seeming depressed, but then she altered her tone. "Flavia Albia is your name. So what exactly is the job you do?" she suddenly quizzed me.

I said I was a private informer. I did collect debts, but my primary role was to conduct searches for people who needed information. A lot of it was family work, which in the main I carried out for women.

I stood up to leave, but while she absorbed my answer, my companion had a speculative look that I found familiar. She was making up her mind to ask something. I gave her time. Tranquilla Euhodia then announced that she might have a job for me.

I assumed it was to identify her daughter's lover. But my commission would be unrelated.

VII

We might have stayed where we were, except that it was a general reception space. A member of staff opened the door, looked in, saw the matriarch, retreated apologetically. Tranquilla Euhodia decided we should decamp. Out in a corridor, she spoke to a maid as she led me to a small room, her private bower, with wool baskets and a pair of old slippers sticking out from behind a lamp table.

She closed the door firmly. "We can be comfortable here. Best not to be disturbed." We sat. The tenor of this new discussion would clearly be different: almost at once the maid appeared with a metal salver, on which sat two glass tots and a neat jug of refreshment. With a finger on her lips, Euhodia warned me to wait until the girl left; then she herself poured. She had a firm action: a woman who never relied on being served by others, one who had never learned to be waited on. "I hope you like violet wine?"

Hello! Flowery beverages are not my choice, but they have a certain place in life. Violet wine has a reputation as the liquor of ladies who plot.

This was becoming a more interesting day.

"We are a very quiet family." While I reflected drily on what that generally meant, my potential client began her brief, not waiting for any lead from me. "Forget my daughter. I shall deal with her. I want you to give a little bit of help, discreetly, to my niece."

I sipped demurely. "Would she be a sister of Tranquillus Januarius?"

"No, no!" snapped Euhodia, as if I was expected to know the family relationships. She checked herself. "Other brother's child. You may like to draw a family tree." Obediently, I took out a note-tablet, though I laid it on the lamp table alongside my tippling tot. I preferred to listen and to watch her. "I have two brothers, Flavia Albia. The elder is Tranquillus Aprilis, who is father to Januarius. Aprilis and I are very close in age. We had various siblings who have all moved on in life. We lost touch, years ago. Our last brother, Tranquillus Postuminus, was the baby in the family. He married Cosconia Saba and they had their daughter, Cosca Sabatina, very much a favourite with everyone. They never produced any others. Postuminus seemed to forget how to use his equipment. Sabatina is eighteen."

She paused. Eighteen, I thought, and she needed her aunt's aid? An only child, doted on: could be an heiress? I also wondered if she was somehow in contention with her parents. "The young lady is about to be married?" I guessed.

Euhodia clapped her hands. "I was not wrong. You are good!"

"I hope so! I imagine that you want me to investigate the bridegroom's background before you commit? Find any flaws. Is his family financially sound, or are they hoping your niece's dowry can be used to bail them out? Does the potential husband gamble, drink, consort with loose women— or screw around with men? How many scruffy little bastards is he suspected of fathering? In some inquiries I am even asked to find out if he has any brains. Personally, I would make that the first question, though surprisingly few people bother."

We shared the joke. I had identified Tranquilla Euhodia as an intelligent woman.

"That is not the problem," she said, almost ruefully, after smiling along with me. "It is our Postuminus who has come under scrutiny."

I stayed neutral. "On what grounds?"

She shied away from the direct question. "It's a huge cheek that we have been asked about him, and quite unnecessary."

"So what's the issue?"

"We need to demonstrate that he has his freedom."

At this point I knew I ought to back out, because manumitting slaves is something that happens very much within a family and there are all kinds of ramifications. Lawyers made juicy fortunes on cases where somebody's freedom was in dispute; informers were less lucky. On the other hand, I was intrigued.

I realised the potential in-laws must be questioning the young girl Cosca Sabatina's social position. The bride had to have her parentage verified by her cautious future relatives. Without the right credentials, she would be rejected.

"What is in doubt? Only your brother's status, or is it a question for all of you?"

"Not us, just baby brother. Aprilis and I can remember being given our freedom under a will. There is no question about that. We just need the situation with Postuminus to be regularised, enough to satisfy these people."

"Well," I said, while I put my thoughts in order, "if it was a simple case of a missing diploma, for instance proof of release from the army, that is something I have done before. There are official records. I am very used to searching them. As far as I know, slaves may receive the cap of liberty as a symbol, but they are not presented with certificates."

"Correct," said Tranquilla Euhodia. "We have nothing to show. Even if there had been documentation, my brother would have lost it—he has never been well-organised. The person who would have known every-thing was our mother, but she passed away."

I noted that the three siblings all had the same mother; perhaps they had had the same father as well. Who was that? Obvious suspect: the old master, Tranquillus Surus, the man who used to breakfast at Nobilo's.

"Can you sort this out for us? Is it possible to provide something official?"

She was drawing me in. I wondered if she could see how tempting any puzzle always was to me. "Tranquilla Euhodia, all I can offer is to enquire into circumstances, then write you a report."

"So long as it says what we need."

Did she want me to fake something? I shot her a reproving look. "I never do forgery!"

"Who asked for that?" Euhodia sneered, though clearly it was what she had meant.

"My reports can only include what I have discovered. My reputation depends on accuracy and fairness."

"Whatever you say," she breezed. "He is a free citizen, just like the rest of us. We just want it recognised. How much will this cost?"

I could have rapped back that there was no price on accuracy and fairness, but that never works. I named my terms, without embellishment. The commission sounded interesting, and I did not dislike her, which always mattered to me when considering clients.

She took me on, at my price. I made it plain it was a two-way contract, where I always had the option of whether to work for her. If there was any unpleasantness, such as pressure to do something illegal, I could walk away. I would decide what needed to be done, how deeply among their records I dug, and whether I really could provide what she wanted.

She seemed content. My first assessment of Tranquilla Euhodia had been that she was the family matriarch, with everything it implies. One of her brothers was older, but that did not seem to matter. Her word prevailed. She made it plain by her general attitude. She controlled the clan through blunt force of character.

She would not control me, even though I suspected she might try.

I drained my tot of violet wine. "That was very nice, thank you. As I am working, I won't have a refill. Welcome to my client list, Tranquilla Euhodia. I am expecting to be at full capacity after the New Year, but I shall try to squeeze this in for you. I shall probably take legal advice this afternoon, to check the regulations and see what we shall need to produce. But, first, I need more information, please."

Euhodia confirmed the basic background. Appius Tranquillus Surus, that old and beloved customer at Nobilo's bar, was a man of means, a businessman who operated in more than one field, a property owner in Rome and on the Campagna, and possessed of a large family of slaves. They worked in his homes and his businesses.

"What was his main line of work?"

"Spanish rabbits."

I admit I blinked.

Euhodia elaborated without a qualm: "That was how he made his first fortune. As a young man, Surus travelled to the Iberian provinces, looking for products and sources. He started with salted or smoked meat, then hit upon importing live animals in cages. That was constantly blighted by shipping risks so it struck him he could more easily breed the stock here. He built walled enclosures—we still use them. They hop around, having many babies. We only have to catch them. In his day, he supplied hundreds for the city markets. You must have seen stalls with live game—geese, ducks, pigeons, even flamingos. Originally there were never rabbits. Appius Tranquillus filled the niche. He flourished, at least until other people copied him. By then, luckily, he was in a position to diversify. We still produce the coneys but we have other interests."

Surus had died aged a little short of sixty. It was good going; most people managed less. A group of male friends gathered to open his will, which they had originally witnessed, with one man named as his executor who would fulfil all the bequests. That man, also described as an old fellow, visited the rabbit farm.

"What was his name?"

Did Euhodia blink? "We must have known it, I suppose. But people with official roles don't always explain themselves." That was true, especially when they were talking to slaves.

"Ideally I would like to talk to him, even at this late stage." If nobody remembered who he had been, that would cause problems for me, but I hid my concern. "If there was a will, who were the witnesses?"

"We were never told. I was just a young girl." Euhodia brushed it away. "I was too excited about Aprilis and me being freed to think of any other details." I still might suspect she was fudging the truth, but it seemed reasonable.

Aprilis and Euhodia had been born on the Campagna, and when Surus died they were living there, working with the rabbits; slaves' ages are not always known, but they were then around twenty. They were both freed by name in his will. The executor solemnly informed them of their new lives as free Roman citizens, explaining that they could vote but not hold office; in the next generation, their children would be allowed by law to do anything they wanted. As was the custom, they each took their liberator's family name before their original slave names. Enter Appius Tranquillus Aprilis, *libertus*, and Tranquilla Euhodia, *liberta*.

The brother and sister were informed they had been assigned a role as their late patron's agents to run his Campagna affairs. They were young, but had experience in the trade and he had trusted them. They could now conduct business, make contracts and hold money in their own right. Obligating freedmen was a very normal way to ensure the future of property and continuance of a business. I wondered if it meant they now owned everything outright, or were they merely enjoying profits while someone else had inherited the physical assets? I knew that happened, particularly where the deceased's wife was provided for; I had worked for widows who ran into problems, especially if they had greedy stepchildren. I left the question unasked, since it did not appear relevant to the slaves' fate.

"So, what about your younger brother?"

"He had not been born. In fact, he came as a complete surprise. Our mother had thought she was past all that. Then one day, after Surus died, out popped a new baby."

I could not be too delicate: "So was your mother also a slave belonging to Tranquillus Surus?"

"She was. A special one to him, clearly."

"Of course. Can I ask, had he ever been married? Were there other children?"

"Just us. Most of our siblings at the farm were given money and sent out into the world. He always treated Aprilis and me with special affection."

I managed not to say, *Yes, he left you the rabbits.* "So—what was your mother's name?"

"Hedylla."

"And was Hedylla also freed by Surus under his will?"

"Must have been," said Tranquilla. Was she sounding over-confident? "Aprilis and I were such young people when our father died, we took very little notice of the formalities. I know she believed she was his freedwoman—"

"That was what she told you?"

"Yes, of course. And when our brother came along, she named him Appius Tranquillus Postuminus, a full Roman name. The *tria nomina*. That proves everything, doesn't it?"

It could be indicative. But Hedylla might have been wrong about her position, even if she was more foolish than actually fraudulent.

Euhodia remained firm: "We have all lived as free citizens ever since then," she continued. "In due course, Aprilis and I moved up to this apartment in Rome, because the farm could manage without our constant presence. We both married and were starting families. We wanted a better life, the same as anybody. Later, our brother came to Rome too. We rented a neighbouring apartment and after Postuminus married he lived there. So we are all close together. One big happy family."

Again, I thought privately, how many times have those words been a bitter irony?

"Your brother Postuminus has never wanted to check on his status?" I asked. "Or Hedylla's?"

"Never thought it necessary. He is rather vague. Well, let's be honest, he's none too sharp," his sister admitted. "Unlike Aprilis and me he was over-mothered and led a sheltered life."

I wondered if he was simply spoiled as the baby, or had he even been damaged at birth? "Does he help you administer the businesses?"

"No. We don't need him to do that. He has his own income, from his wife's dowry and other sources. No questions were ever asked about him marrying Cosconia Saba, incidentally, and her family have been citizens for generations. So he is set up with a good way of life. He is a man of position in Rome."

Man of position or not, baby brother must be seriously dim if he had let Aprilis and Euhodia bar him from the lucrative family portfolio. I wondered—as he ought to have wondered—who would own him now, if no manumission had ever taken place.

"Euhodia, you told me your siblings went out into the world. Were other slaves on the farm freed, as well?"

"Some. They all went different ways. I couldn't tell you where they are now."

"Were any slaves *not* freed by Tranquillus Surus?"

"Yes, as far as I remember," said Euhodia, frowning as if she was trying to recall. "The executor must have sold off any he thought were superfluous or simply too far gone to be useful. The rest stayed at the farm. They worked and were looked after, just as before."

"Looked after by you and your brother, Aprilis?"

"Of course. We had taken charge. Most were ageing, so those have all died now. We have new workers. Too new to know anything about previous events."

I did wonder if Euhodia wanted me to believe nobody could tell me the truth, if it was slightly off-colour. Was she warning me away from part of the story? Clients were often menaces who asked me to uncover information whilst in fact they were busily concealing even more. They loved to make life pointlessly complicated.

I saw no reason to pry further into the rabbit farm's workforce. The only person of interest was Hedylla. Her two elder children were definitely freed. That felt like an indication of the master's intentions. According to Euhodia, the mother had been accepted as a freedwoman and her youngest son was treated as a full citizen from birth. Being a sceptic, I was bound to feel this might have been fiddled, though even if it was, perhaps the situation could be straightened out if someone like me took on the task. Many people detest having to work with documents, but I had no qualms.

"It is urgent, I am afraid," the aunt stressed anxiously. "My dear sweet little niece has committed her heart. She became set on the marriage and now that the young man's relatives have raised this issue, we need to satisfy those people quickly. It will look suspicious if we hold off too long. Can you, Flavia Albia, secure my brother's position and save Sabatina's wedding?"

I said that I was hopeful.

Proving an ex-slave's manumission was common enough. My task was to find evidence. If any existed, I knew a formal validation could then be acquired from a Board of Citizenship. It would require a fee—what doesn't? That looked to be no problem for these wealthy people. Among my contacts I knew lawyers who would argue the case if any aspect seemed tricky. All might not be lost for dear, sweet little Sabatina.

She was not all that sweet, I was to find. But that did not mean she deserved to have her love life blighted by the stigma of her father's origins. Tranquillus Surus, a kindly old fellow by all accounts, could not have wanted that for someone who was, after all, his granddaughter.

VIII

Conscious that by now there would be all kinds of domestic upsets in my own home, I was heading back for lunch. Before I left, I reacquainted myself with the bookkeeper, Philodamus, and made sure he handed over an instalment of my fee. "Payment up front is normal, Philodamus." He must have realised it depended on how I assessed each client. Given the Stargazer's unpaid bill, I wanted an advance.

He had been with the Tranquilli for the past seven years. "You seem to be well treated?" I probed: "Position of trust, decent people, good accommodation?"

He agreed he was in a position of trust. He made no comment on the rest.

Talking frankly, since we were alone at that point, I said I had noticed that when former slaves went on to owning staff, it could go one of two ways. In the pleasant version, freedmen would treat their slaves well, because they knew how miserable life could be; they felt grateful to have obtained something better so were prepared to behave generously. All too often, it was otherwise: freedmen were the worst masters, as if they thought, *We have suffered, so now it's your turn.* Philodamus, in his slow way, merely tightened the corners of his mouth, giving nothing away.

His mistress had told him to introduce me to another slave called Erotillus, who could be my point of contact. Erotillus had only been there for about three years. He wore the same kind of unbleached tunic as the bookkeeper, but had added strips of flat brown braid from shoulder to hem as a sign of refined status; on the left side he had run out of braid, so it ended too short. He was the opposite of Philodamus, bright-eyed, quick in his movements and perky. If I ever bought anyone from a slave market, those would be qualities I looked for. That would be once I had made the usual checks about disease and whether he was light-fingered. This one looked fit and managed to act reliable.

Erotillus went by the title of secretary. He was the family's archive clerk, he told me. The two slaves both laughed, because they said the Tranquilli were casual record-keepers. Erotillus confided, however, that even when he was given no instructions, he always containerised the scrolls relating to disputes, as the masters were all combative over property and business.

"Litigation?"

"Well, for preference they hang back and let the other parties sue them."

"Who wins, generally?"

"Half and half."

Philodamus chortled quietly, as if to himself. "Except when the numbskulls are wrangling with each other! Then there's never a winner." I glanced at him, but he clammed up.

It had been long before his time, but I asked Erotillus to search for any old documents left by Appius Tranquillus Surus, especially, if it still existed, his will. Meanwhile I would pursue other avenues.

Erotillus said if I needed to interview anyone I should ask him. He knew what the family were up to; he would fix appointments for me and, he joked, even make sure people turned up. We arranged that tomorrow morning I would come back to see Tranquillus Postuminus and his young daughter. I did not question the slaves about her intended marriage as I like to have some idea where my questions may lead. Besides, slave owners who hear that you have been prying can forbid further contact. Never cut off your sources too early. Keep everything open until there is nothing to lose.

I did make a joke about Tranquilla Euhodia's own daughter, after my demand for payment had exposed her lover and his rivets. "Looks as if Mardiana has been slipping out for assignations, Erotillus! Had you noticed?"

He would not admit it, but he was twinkling. Philodamus said nothing, though from his lack of reaction he saw it as old news.

"Mercury," I told them conversationally. "Isn't that the day Mardiana goes off to see her beautician?"

"Hair style, pedicure and manicure," Erotillus now confirmed gaily.

"In the morning. Then she's looking smart!" We had no need to say for what or whom she wanted to look so smart. "Do you sharp fellows know the fancy man?"

"We do not!" exclaimed Erotillus, eagerly. Philodamus made a show of pretending to be above this, but I could see he was enjoying speculation. Erotillus urged me, "Make sure you tell us if you find out, Flavia Albia."

"You shall be first to know."

We all smiled. I made a mental note that when I had familiarised myself with my assignment, I might profit from a further rendezvous with this pair. Meanwhile I asked Erotillus to arrange for me to visit Postuminus and meet his daughter the next day.

I tried to forget that my mother says when you are nobbling other people's slaves for gossip, you should always bear in mind that your own household might be giving out secrets of yours.

Helena also claims she and Falco have no secrets to reveal. That must be the biggest bluff of all time.

Even though it was nearly lunchtime, the Aventine seemed like a hill that had not finished waking up today. Saturnalia excess has that effect. Some lock-up stalls and workshops were several days late in reopening; most years there would be one or two that never again unfolded their shutters. Neighbours might never find out why. There were browning cypress boughs in some streets, though these were less likely to be signals of a death than cast-off festival greenery. On the high tops, the overall noise level was lower than usual. Skinny dogs on doorsteps could hardly rouse themselves to bark, let alone run out to menace passersby. Anywhere with a scaffold had empty platforms; I almost missed the wolf-whistles.

My own house kept up its usual liveliness. Screaming was audible from some distance away, though not due to any injury. It was only little Gaius and Lucius racing about the courtyard and balcony, yelling their heads off every time someone told them to be quiet.

I let myself in. We had a new porter, Rodan, but he had made it clear that coming out of his cubicle to open the door was too much hard work. When I delivered purchases to the cook, Fornix scolded that I should ask him another time; it was a pity I had brought home winter pears because he had already ordered in enough and he didn't want to work in a household where everyone had eaten so much fruit they all had the squits.

"Can you mash them up for perry?"

"I don't do your British muck! I'll have to pickle them."

"The master loves your pickles, Fornix."

"Oh, well . . ." Fornix knew that the master enjoyed anything that came with smoked cheese and a crusty loaf. "But he'll have to wait. I only have one pair of hands."

"For you, Tiberius Manlius will wait."

"Less of your blather, Flavia Albia!"

Hey-ho. I had shown my face. Ate lunch. Made various comments about the prevailing mania, then was given rude answers. Convinced myself my presence had calmed the atmosphere. Changed my earrings. Left hastily.

IX

Where is the body in this case?" Aulus Camillus sounded peremptory. If his grumpiness was an act, it was one he put on every morning along with his undertunic. "How many victims have been wiped out in some horrible imaginative way this week?" He must have heard about my previous, somewhat gruesome investigation. "It is very unlike you, Albia, to have no bloodied corpses!"

I smiled sweetly. "Bound to fall over one eventually."

"Then it will be *Who? By whom? When? With what?* And *Dear gods, whatever the hell was that about?*" Quintus declaimed, as if he were trying to keep a post-prandial jury awake in a stifling basilica. He was the handsome, charming one, when he bothered to play nice.

"*Cui bono?*" Both men stared at me as if they did not understand Latin.

The Camilli were Helena Justina's brothers, so officially my uncles. They might still have been a drunken student in Athens and a vague army tribune in Germany; nobody had told them that fifteen years later they were supposed to have matured. These forty-year-old perpetual lads claimed they were far too busy to advise me, then both came lolling along in unbelted tunics, with their hair uncombed, asking questions about my case and each trying to outdo the other.

They lived in adjoining houses. We had gathered in their late father's cluttered study. It was at least quiet. I had come to the Capena Gate on our donkey, since she deserved a break from being tormented by Gaius and Lucius. This house had grown suddenly peaceful because my placid beast was outside, currently surrounded by Quintus's children.

Although there were six of them, Merky was being quite nicely petted. I won't say that Claudia, their mother, had quelled the young Camilli with harsh Baetican discipline, but they were all bright buttons; they knew how to aggravate their parents by a show of unexpectedly good behaviour when visitors called. Until they poured back indoors again, romping and roaring as they forgot I was there, I could discuss tactics with the uncles. Claudia was lying down with a headache so there was no need for small-talk. I cannot say what Aulus's wife Meline might have been doing; she was something of a mystery.

The Camilli were senators, which showed how in Rome money and persistence could buy you anything. They were lawyers in the usual dilettante way, appearing in court when it suited them or when they needed to boost their cash-flow. Meanwhile in private they studied edicts and precedents with real curiosity and enjoyment. At base, they were *good* lawyers. This would always limit the clients who sought them out, because clients wanted flash, brash, dashing advocates, who loudly promised to slay the opposition and win terrific settlements. That Camillus Aelianus and Camillus Justinus would be pleasant to deal with and mostly won their cases sounded tame by comparison.

Judges liked them. Juries listened. Neither should be underestimated. The brothers would see people right. In some trouble, Legate? Bring it to the Camilli. One or the other, or if it's really knotty, push the boat out and hire both.

I worked with them sometimes. They knew I could be relied on. I trusted their legal knowledge. So, before I tackled the Tranquillus case, I laid out for my uncles my seemingly simple assignment. I thought I knew the rules, but I wanted them to refresh me.

"Find the will," commanded Aulus, immediately. Patiently, I said that was in hand.

"Long gone!" ranted Quintus. He liked to imply his brother was impatient and slapdash, while he had a deeper intellect. In reality, Aulus could be tediously pedantic, while Quintus lazily relied on natural flair. "Half a century old, Albia?"

"Dates from forty years ago. That's approximate."

"No chance, then."

Aulus leaned forwards, interrupting, "Every chance—if things were done right."

"How would that be?" I asked cautiously.

"Some old bod dies. The witnesses, or those who haven't predeceased him, assemble to certify the seals they affixed when his will was originally made."

"Do they already realise what the will says?"

"No. They didn't have to be made aware of its contents, only that what they were witnessing was the man's will."

"That was so he could hide the fact they are to get nothing!"

"Cynic. Shall I go on?"

"When you are ready."

"Thanks!" There had been tension between Aulus and me in the past; we still tended to niggle. "The wax will be sealed over linen thread that goes through a hole in the scroll," he described. "Once the testator is dead, the thread is broken, then the will opened and read. Sometimes the witnesses stamp their rings on new seals to say they were present at the opening. That's not essential. An executor is named, with substitutes in case he can't or won't accept the task. Should he take it on, he organises all the listed bequests."

"Including freedom for slaves?"

"A proportion of slaves. You know the Augustan limits: up to five if the testator owns ten, twenty-five out of a hundred, and not more than one hundred tops."

"No one bothers about that, Aulus."

"You came for advice. I am stating the law."

"I know the law sets limits, but I work with reality. Do freed slaves have to be named specifically?"

"Yes."

"But an unborn child, with the pregnancy not even suspected, will not be mentioned? It can't be."

"No, but that is unnecessary, so long as the testator frees the mother. Children, as I am sure you know, follow the condition of their mother." I certainly did know, because the question had had to be considered when I myself was taken in off the streets by Falco and Helena. Quintus was aware this was awkward for me, but Aulus carried on unfeelingly. "If their father is a free man but their mother a slave, they are slaves. But the rule you need is this: if the woman has been free at any time between conception and birth, her child is free also."

That was useful. "So there is no doubt about Postuminus if I can show that his mother Hedylla had been manumitted?"

Aulus nodded. He sounded dry, though he remained factual. "If she was such a favourite, my presumption would be that Surus freed her *before* he died in order to marry her."

Quintus had to haggle: "A more salacious presumption would be that he did *not* free her, not at any stage, because he did *not* want to marry her. We can guess that might be because he had other 'favourite' slaves squirrelled away somewhere."

I confirmed that squirrelling was possible because Tranquillus Surus had properties in the country and in Rome. "Even perhaps in Spain— where the rabbits come from." Both brothers stared at me.

Aulus took his jesting further: "Alternatively, he had a wife."

Quintus topped it: "Wives, even."

"I am assured that he never married. Please stop fantasising," I begged. "If he never freed Hedylla, then Tranquillus Postuminus and the young fiancée will be stuck—at least, she'll be dropped due to the other family's prejudice. But isn't there something that should help the young girl? Postuminus is married. His wife is a free citizen, I'm told. Descended from generations of honest citizen bakers. Doesn't Cosca Sabatina follow her own mother's status?"

"Yes," said Aulus. "She can sell loaves on any street in town. But she won't want to talk about her father while she wraps them up."

Quintus was gloomy. "As a slave, Postumius cannot marry."

"*Postuminus*. You're a typical lawyer, getting key names wrong . . . Slaves often live together as couples."

"Not relevant. He is a non-person. It would be a non-marriage."

"But he can propagate!" chortled Aulus.

"Or even procreate," niggled Quintus. "Yes, Sabatina is a free woman through her mother—but be realistic, Albia. Her father's position will count against her. If she is a slave's illegitimate by-blow, who wants her? She is the child of an unmarried mother, doomed to stay at street level. Respectable persons have questioned her history already. They insist on goods with proper title."

"Crucially," Aulus suggested, "if Postuminus is a slave, he cannot own anything. Are the groom's family hoping for a large financial contribution?"

"I suspect so."

"That will be why they are quibbling. They are afraid of being landed with a girl who has a bad history and no dowry. It's a death knell for this marriage. The Tranquilli have to deal with it. They won't pay your fee unless you can remove all taint of slavery, Albia."

"They want me to forge some kind of validation."

"They sound very sensible. Shouldn't she go along with that, Aulus?" Quintus asked his brother wickedly. "Flavia Albia, I believe your father's rule is to triple the price for fake certificates."

"I don't do creative documentation." That was true, though I was starting to see it would be the easy way out.

"Why not? Everyone else does. *We* do."

"You are lawyers. I came to you for help," I growled. "Remember, I can claim fees for you, if you manage to say anything of merit. To sum up again: the girl is free, but her father's position could be very bad news. I need to concentrate on proving whether, if and when, Tranquillus Surus awarded freedom to his slave Hedylla, and thus to her subsequent offspring."

Aulus humphed and he, too, recapitulated. "Hedylla should be named, if so. Find the will and look."

He had held the floor too long for his brother. Quintus broke in with enthusiastic derision: "And where is that going to be? I'll tell you, O trusting niece from barbarian Britannia. First, it is left lying around on a side table, in case some idiot queries the legacies. Gathers mouse droppings for a year or two, has wine spilled on it. Once all the bequests have been doled out, and after niggly Uncle Pedanticus has wittered off into oblivion even though he failed to obtain the desired south-facing section of the olive grove, then some of the scroll is torn up for laundry lists while another part acquires the sketch of a new toolshed. Finally the decrepit thing becomes kindling for a religious rite, roasting a sacrificial piglet on a portable altar. So, goodbye, will!"

Aulus raised his eyes to the ceiling. "Ignore this colourful idiot. Go back to what I said about unsealing the document: a copy should have been made, preserved safely in the family archive. A working scroll used by the heir to tick off legacies may well deteriorate or vanish, but that fair copy can always be presented in the event of queries."

"The family archive?" Pre-warned by Erotillus, I groaned. "No chance."

"Wills can also be deposited in the Atrium of Liberty."

"Overkill," scoffed Quintus. "Scroll box at the back of a cupboard should do it."

"The Tranquilli find filing too onerous." I must have sounded depressed.

"Bear up!" Aulus took on the role of helpful one. "Legacies do not have to be written down. This could be solved by recollection. Just try to find the executor or witnesses, Albia."

"No one knows who the witnesses were, and I am afraid the executor must be dead or doddering."

"No matter. Find one. He'll think you're a nice young lady. He won't notice what you're really like. Just tell him what to say. Bring him to us. We can swear out an affidavit that will do the trick."

"For a small percentage." Quintus smiled.

"Your clients will love it." Aulus smirked.

I said never mind what the clients wanted me to do, I intended to report the truth. Aulus and Quintus chuckled. They lay back on their couches and went off into debating definitions of "truth." Quintus saw this as a fluid concept; Aulus believed it was absolute and unalterable. I could see that their arguments would last until dinner, and we were now being deafened by the six raucous children who had tumbled back indoors.

I supposed my uncles had been helpful; anyway, it was good to see them. We had reached the point where their bossy wives might turn up to ask how my husband was—such a wonderful man. What a find for you, Albia! And how noble of him to have taken you on . . . I scuttled out to my donkey, ready to ride home.

Aulus stuck his head out and yelled after me: "Keep looking for a dodgy corpse. Maybe the slaves murdered the old bod!"

I gave him a derisive gesture. He waved me off cheerily.

X

Appius Tranquillus Postuminus, bearer of that thoroughly Roman *tria nomina*, lived in a duplicate apartment, one floor up from his much older brother and sister. If anything, his interior was smarter, with less of an impression that it had stayed unchanged through various generations. On the other hand, louder street noises percolated up from Sidewind Passage. In summer, when more shutters were open, I bet smells wandered in too.

Visiting next morning, I seated myself on another couch, in another salon. I wished I had brought a Greek novel to pass the time.

While I waited for Postuminus to appear, I pondered his names. (It was better than inspecting his statuette miniatures, which our family auction house would have rejected rudely.) I had an adopted brother called Postumus, a traditional choice to show he was born after his father died—supposing our sprout's natural father truly was who his mother had claimed. She, an exotic snake dancer, could hardly be relied on; although she vaguely called herself "married," it was known that a variety of lovers flitted in and out of her circus tent. My parents reckoned the real culprit was still alive and mucking out crocodiles at the Alexandria zoo.

None of this gave my brother a right to bear the *tria nomina* but he did so, because my father, who was a citizen by birth, had adopted him. In Rome, picking your way among the rules can be worrying—but all things can be fixed. I let that encourage me.

"Postuminus" sounded like something a slave girl might think was a sweet diminutive of the classic cognomen. At any rate, her orphan was a poor timekeeper. We had an early-morning appointment, fixed up by Erotillus, but that meant nothing.

Luckily I was used to this. In Rome, time had a mad logic. There were always twelve daylight hours, so they were shorter in winter and longer in summer, changing almost daily. Unless you owned a pocket sundial—and the sun was shining—you had to guess. While you were trying to figure out where north was for your sundial, if the person you were meeting had met somebody more interesting, or if he was nervous of whatever you wanted to discuss, he had every excuse to tarry else-where. Romans were never oppressed by appointments anyway.

I let my mind wander because I was trying to obliterate my uncle's corpse joke. As a young girl, I had believed I was the only person who saw that the surly Aulus Camillus Aelianus did possess a sense of hu-mour. It wasn't so funny when he broke my heart. Still, I understood his suggestion that Surus could have fallen foul of his slaves was intended to complete a friendly roundelay of wit. Being a man, Aulus imagined that if I let him tease, I must have forgiven him. *Io!* Let him dream.

I saw where the suggestion came from. My cases did tend to include a high quotient of unnatural death, although it couldn't have happened to Surus. Bonehead, Aulus: the old shrimp-lover lived for sixty years! If he was ever going to be done in, somebody would have taken him out decades earlier. Of course Aulus would say, Then look for a classic can't-wait-any-longer scenario. Someone was overkeen to get their hands on the old fellow's money.

I had once worked a case in which slaves were accused of murdering their owners. It had been messy. I was hoping to avoid another like it.

When Tranquillus Postuminus at last blundered into the room, he looked like what my husband would call a bit of a pimple, a lunk who lacked the oomph to squash a fly. I could see some facial resemblance to Euhodia, though as well as being fifteen years younger he seemed much more innocent. His face, different from his sister's except around the eyes, was pale, round, puffy and anxious. He wore a toga; I never worked out whether that was deference to me, or if he had come from an extremely formal business meeting. His commercial interests, he told me, were an apricot orchard and digestive bread.

"Digestive bread?"

"Yes." He was as nonchalant about this foodstuff as his sister had been about the Spanish rabbits.

Later, at home, Fornix enlightened me that "digestive loaves" were a fashion fad. With supposed medicinal qualities, the tiny white briquettes were sold at high cost to people who could have settled their guts more easily by guzzling plainer food and watering their wine. Fornix knew where to buy such rolls; he had served them on request when he was the head chef at Fabulo's. He could get some to try if I wanted; seeing his expression, I shook my head.

"At high cost" would be an indication of how comfortably solvent Tranquillus Postuminus was. Dim or not, I sensed he had a lot of money. A clue was his carnelian ring, with an intaglio Alexander the Great that covered his middle finger, encroaching on his knuckle and the digits either side; all his fingers were very well manicured. His daughter must be seen as a catch, at least in the dowry department—and at least if he carried no stigma of slavery.

He knew nothing about his origins. So did his insistence on wearing a toga, even at home, cover deep insecurity?

"You believe that your mother had been given her freedom?"

"Of course."

"Have you any idea if Tranquillus Surus intended to marry her?"

"I have always supposed so. They were in effect living as a couple."

It was the legal definition of marriage: two people agreed to live together. "Were they? Was that at the farm?"

"Yes."

"Your mother never came here with Surus? To the Aventine?"

"I was born at the rabbit farm."

That did not answer the question. This was hard work, given that I was trying to help him. Striving to find evidence, I asked one question that the Camilli ought to have suggested. Normally it is women who wonder this: "Tranquillus Surus was her head of household. When he died, was a guardian appointed to advise her?"

Postuminus looked blank.

I tried again. "Women, you know, are thought to be incapable of managing their affairs. So was there a tutor, as people call them, hanging around and trying to get his hands on any funds left in trust for Hedylla's maintenance? Perhaps some greasy freedman who even hoped to line his own pockets by marrying her himself?"

No, said Postuminus. There had been no one like that.

Damn. It had not only spared him being afflicted with a low-grade stepfather, but unfortunately meant there was no one I could quiz about his mother's place in society. Alternatively, I thought, it could mean Hedylla had been assigned no legal guidance precisely because she had remained a slave, legally a non-person. In that case, there was no trust fund for a financial adviser to steal.

From childhood, Postuminus had simply accepted whatever he was told. I bet he still did. His wife must have an easy time. Handling this one would be simple.

When he married her—Cosconia Saba, a well-off baker's daughter, he confirmed—nobody had queried his status. He had had a substantial windfall to bring at the time, and her brothers had been keen on that. With him already accepted in society and commerce, Cosconia must have come with the contacts who now supplied his digestive bread; perhaps her dowry even included a scroll with a secret recipe.

Their only child, of whom Postuminus spoke guardedly, was born within a year of the wedding. Now the young girl had taken it into her head to fall in love with the son of a business colleague, another orchard-owner. "Walnuts." Postuminus seemed mildly obsessed, although if there was a story to that he did not reveal it.

Sabatina had managed to engineer the youth's compliance; he said he loved her too, and that was enough to make her determined. Relatives supported them; the families were close. However, what should have been an easy, convenient match had been blighted by interference from a scribe who was drawing up the formal documents; he had pedantically raised the status issue.

I reassured the father that I was sure this would be worked out.

Postuminus, the dumb puffball, looked relieved. For a man of affairs, he was curiously compliant. I would have expected him to see through my bluff.

"Am I going to meet your daughter?"

I was. She bounced in, a stick-thin, sharp-nosed, hazel-eyed, prettified piece, who petulantly cried, "I don't want to know what any of this is about!"

"Your future, my dear," I notified her regardless.

"It's all nonsense. I am going to marry Venuleius and that's it!"

Her father was looking helpless. Surrender must be his default mode. This is so often the case in paternalist Rome, where a stern family head with so-called life-and-death authority will be trampled by self-determined offspring who don't let him get a word in. Ask most fathers.

I decided that if I failed to prove her father's citizenship, I would leave the bridegroom's family to back out, taking her lover, and show the girl how "nonsense" actually works. I was not being paid enough to give life lessons.

"So, you are looking forward to your wedding, Cosca Sabatina?"

Yes, she absolutely was, and it had absolutely better be soon. I sighed. While this one did not bother to say out loud that she could not wait to leave home, that must have been her aim. For most young women, apart from thinking they could now have sex all day and half the night, marriage seemed to offer an escape from being bullied and unfairly treated, as they generally believed they were. With that ring on, they soon learned better: they had set themselves up to be bullied and unfairly treated by their new husbands instead. Those men, if my clients' complaints were accurate, never matched up to bedroom expectations either.

I was not completely cynical. None of this was my experience. But Tiberius and I had both joined in matrimony second time around. We were mature. We had hopes, but were careful about expectations. That seemed to work for us.

Our recent wedding ceremony gave me an idea. "If you like, Sabatina, I can take you to meet my two sisters. They are a little younger than you, but extremely artistic and full of ideas. They devised some brilliant arrangements for me when I was getting married. They would love to share their expertise."

They could help me too. While chattering about chaplets of flowers, hairstyles and cake, Julia and Favonia would pose all the questions I needed. They would handle this daft chit; they still acted daft enough themselves, although as they grew older, luckily there was much more to them.

It did not seem worth asking whether her father supported me hijacking his daughter. Sabatina poutingly agreed to it. Like him, she was none too bright. She had no idea that my frolicsome pair were being set up as assistant informers. They would be keen. Naturally Julia and Favonia decried any idea of following their stuffy old parents and sister, but they always enjoyed a chance to show off their own cleverness.

I told the bride I must check when my sisters would be available. Then I would call back to pick her up, probably that afternoon. This would give me time to prime the girls. Also, since I had had a recent disagreement with my parents about a case involving friends of theirs, I had better ask Falco and Helena for permission before I employed my siblings.

"I cannot imagine why you are asking for my approval," our mother berated me in due course. She was a forthright woman; it could have been worse. "Those two will do whatever they want, Flavia Albia—anyone would think they are basing their behaviour on yours!"

I reminded her that I always tried to base my behaviour on the refined example she had set me since I came to Rome. Helena Justina, like my cook earlier, ordered me to cut the blather.

Then I told her about having violet wine yesterday; rather to my surprise, she produced some. We agreed Julia and Favonia were too young to join us, so I managed to re-establish my position as the grown-up daughter who was Mother's confidante. Winning back my father might be harder, but Falco followed the traditional role of a Roman paterfamilias: he took his lead from the matriarch.

I had always thought my family were a crazy bunch. But the Didii had nothing on what I would find when I delved deeper into the past and present lives of the Tranquilli.

XI

No will could be found. Erotillus, the secretary-archivist, told me when I dropped in on my way to collect Cosca Sabatina. He had hunted everywhere, he said, in both apartments. I asked, Could the will be out at the rabbit farm? Erotillus eagerly offered to travel there to search, because he wanted to be the first to tell Januarius how he had been mistaken for Mardiana's lover. Apparently Januarius was a very decent character—"unlike the rest of them" hovered unsaid. "He's going to rush home furious, I bet."

"Book me in for a meeting as soon as he arrives," I said. "And what about his father, Aprilis?"

"Oh, he'll be hiding out in his garum cave."

"Any reason?"

"Under his wife's thumb. She keeps him where she can see him."

"Where's the garum cave?"

"End of the alley."

Mardiana, I learned, had denied everything and locked herself in her room. Euhodia had tried to order her daughter into rural exile on the rabbit farm. So far it had proved impossible to unscrew Mardiana's claws from her perch in Rome. She also refused to name her lover. "She has to say he doesn't exist," Erotillus argued.

"He munches Lucanian sausages with fish pickle and all the trimmings," I demurred. "Sounds like a clincher to me. He exists all right—and he's either been in the army, or he goes around picking up rivets he sees in the street." There are men like that. My husband, for one, could never walk past a discarded nail. Some men have a gold coin collection;

the joy of my heart had a precious jar of items that he thought might one day come in useful. "My witnesses mentioned Mardiana wears a wedding ring?"

"Oh, you don't want to know about her husband!" groaned the archivist, in cheeky-slave mode, making me desperate for details.

"Wine? Brothels? Chariot races? Or he picks his nose and won't wash?"

"Worse, Albia! He is writing a new history of the Samnite Wars." Yes, I agreed. That was much worse. "He finished the first war, which went down a storm at his writing group, until a fight broke out over him dissing Livy."

"What's wrong with old Livy?"

"Some people say he duplicates his battles." Erotillus sounded well-informed. "I argue that's because military generals keep on making the same mistakes. Naturally their fights all follow a pattern. The point our fellow keeps missing is that Livy has written far too much already and what the public really needs is a one-scroll epitome."

"You sound as if you read," I complimented him. "Are the Tranquilli proud of having educated staff?"

"Status symbol," growled the slave. "Acquired me to show off—then doomed me to setting up a file system for these hopeless loons who chuck most things away. I am starting to suspect they deliberately won't be held to account. When people question them, it's always the old 'lost tablets' scam."

"They cheat?"

"I couldn't possibly say."

"Are they cultured? Do they have much of a literature collection?"

"No philosophy, no lyric poetry, no drama," Erotillus rattled off. "It doesn't matter to me, because I had managed to get through plenty before I came here. My last owner liked being read aloud to. He would tackle anything, so I got to share it."

"What happened to him?"

"Nothing. Under guard by his womenfolk because he's getting decrepit. They needed to settle a damages claim so they used me, hoping he wouldn't notice. Aprilis and Euhodia accepted my skills in payment."

"Bad luck."

"Life, Flavia Albia. I am a commercial commodity—one this lot didn't really need, let's face it. None of them are trying to improve their minds. Aprilis is still just a one-time rabbit breeder, who can't even read. It looks as if they have inherited whatever Tranquillus Surus left behind in this apartment, which is horrible Egyptian pornography that some other cash-strapped debtor parted with. I wouldn't call it a library, it's a bunch of junk. As an example, their set of Livy is missing *The Conquest of Italy*, and Sulla, and it only has half of *The Last Years of the Republic*."

"But it does contain *The Samnite Wars*?"

"Yes, and we are the lucky possessors of two versions, therefore. Turbo—Aurelius Turbo, that's our scribbler's name—brought his own when he and Mardiana married."

"Loving couple?"

"He thinks so—well, he did until you turned up."

"Has Mardiana locked him out of the bedroom too?"

"He never spends much time in there. I'm sure he sleeps on a bench at the writing club."

"Very conjugal! Had she already kicked him out because she had a lover, or did she have to take the lover after Turbo neglected her?"

"Bit of both, I suspect, Albia."

"Marriage of convenience?"

"Marriage of two-way nasty comments and bitter silences."

"Thrown vases?"

"Chucked manicure sets. Some men have sword scars from fencing duels. Turbo boasts a nasty ear-scoop scab."

I winced and sucked my teeth. "So tell me about his punch-up with his peers."

Erotillus happily complied. "Turbo was shy about details, except that the furious fracas had ended with dirty cloaks all round, a big repair bill for a smashed statue and a top-flight barrister laid up for weeks with a badly broken nose. It won't stop Turbo. He now has two more wars to play with, although being extremely sensitive, he is held up by his mental anguish over the Battle of the Caudine Forks. You probably know that was a big humiliation."

"Yes, I have heard teary men deploring it. Didn't the defeated Romans have to pass unarmed under an arch of spears, presumably with happy enemies jeering, *Ha, ha, who fell into our trap, you bunch of jessies? Don't go on!*" I pleaded. "That's his life? No wonder the wife strays."

"Plus he's a useless businessman," Erotillus added. "That's more important here. Last year Aurelius Turbo lost the family a huge, farmed-mullet contract, citing his research."

"Stuck at a desk, taking notes?"

"Sadly, no. He had travelled to Campagna 'in order to stand on the banks of the River Liris and inspire himself by absorbing territorial folk memory.' I ask you! At the fishponds auction, our firm was not even the underbidder. Turbo was a no-show. He didn't bother to warn anyone, just completely let them down. Aprilis and Euhodia were so angry I thought they would strangle him."

"They go in for ructions?"

"They never hold back."

"Did his wife cop for bad feeling because of him?"

"I'll say. Her mother yelled, 'Divorce him!' but he had brought too much to the bank box and Mardiana had already ordered a whole new rail of clothes, anticipating the mullet income. Her dressmaker kicked off when she reneged. There was a terrible to-do about a stole that was already pre-dyed in a colour no one else would want, with gold thread embellishments that, it was claimed, the sewing girls were unable to unpick."

"That represents quite a few barrels of fish, Erotillus."

"Large scale is this family's style."

"And do they trade in serious violence?"

Erotillus gave me a slight look, though what he remarked on was hardly bloody: "Not unless you count Mardiana swinging a bale of dress fabric at Turbo."

I giggled. "Damage him?"

"She missed."

"Bad aim?"

"Hampered. The dressmaker had grabbed one end of the bale, wanting her material back."

"All sorted?"

"Oh, no. Mardiana went for the woman with a metal jug. Dented the jug and cut her eyebrow open."

"Compensation?"

"Not even an apology."

"That's terrible—and an error of judgement, I suggest. Finding a new dressmaker can be a nightmare. The good ones all have too much work already. If they hear about ugly incidents, they don't need customers like that."

At this point, Erotillus must have decided that he had held back deferentially long enough and could turn into a normal Roman male. He made a heavy remark that I myself had a good eye for an outfit, if he might say so. I had been kitted out by Suza in a walnut-coloured gown with a creamy stole over one shoulder, both heavy enough for winter. She had waylaid me that particular morning; I had been thinking too much about testators and manumissions.

Without malice, I told Erotillus not to waste his sweet talk on me, then went to find the bride my sisters would be working over.

XII

Julia and Favonia had walked up the hill to our house. This was partly to compensate for not visiting at New Year. Maybe I should have come clean when I was working for their friends. But Falco and Helena would have bumped me off my case, which was gory but gripping. Thankfully, I solved it before I had to confess. Eventually they would come around.

"Father keeps ranting that you are barred."

"Too late. Mother let me in this morning."

"She hasn't told him yet."

"Well, Mother says the art to surviving marriage is knowing how to pick your moment. You could tell this new bride that. Let's train her properly."

We wanted to lie low until Helena had smoothed things over. So the girls, with Cosca Sabatina when she appeared, invaded our house in Lesser Laurel Street, bringing their ribbons and jingling necklaces, and enough intense perfume to make the dog sneeze. They shrieked greetings at my cousin Marcia, who quickly left, claiming she had a martial-arts class. They next badgered Fornix to make them honeyed titbits, pointedly telling him about Helena and me sharing violet wine; he countered that if he had to serve flowery cordials he would find new employment.

"No chance of a rose-petal cocktail then?" giggled Julia, wickedly.

Gratus, my suave steward, set up the three young women in a side room, where he supplied them with a brazier (and safety instructions), all our spare cushions and a pile of waxed tablets, so Sabatina could take notes. She seemed surprised by that idea. Julia and Favonia snatched styluses to make lists for her. I had warned them that if the marriage fell through, the ceremony would be cancelled, but to my sisters this was an academic exercise. They would enjoy planning it anyway.

I'd said they could tell Sabatina they knew about her difficulties. It would be an excuse to pry into her father's freedman status. What did she think? Did she remember her grandmother, Hedylla? Had she ever been to the rabbit farm? Was her branch of the Tranquillus family very rich? As for Venuleius, the sprog Sabatina yearned for, how luscious was he? Just how mean were his obstructive relatives?

I left them to it. The last I heard, Sabatina was puzzling over the ancient wedding ceremony vows of "Where I am Gaius, you are Gaia. Where I am Gaia, you are Gaius . . ." Her name was not Gaia, she complained. My sisters were patiently attempting to explain the ancient ritual. "It's symbolic. It works, you'll see. When Albia and Tiberius said their vows, we all broke down in helpless sobs—it was magic! And he hadn't even been felled by the lightning at that point—which he was afterwards."

It is a measure of Cosca Sabatina's complete self-absorption that she took no interest in my husband's dramatic story. Anybody normal would have been transfixed.

I went into my office. This small room was supposedly my private space for interviewing clients. I found Tiberius hiding up there; the dog was with him. As a result of his argument with the lightning bolt, Tiberius still suffered pain and distress; then Barley liked to loll against him comfortingly. As I appeared, they both looked guilty; the dog slid down from his couch to the floor while Tiberius feebly brushed away dust.

I had designed the room myself. The rugs were striped, the upholstery soft oatmeal. Two painters, who sometimes wandered through our house pretending to work for us, had given me frescos in a subdued palette of pale blues, watery turquoise and chalk white. A friend of theirs had executed central emblems in the panels, intricate little countryside scenes with trees, goats and shrines. You had to walk up close to see them, so they were not distracting.

"'You are Gaius, I am Gaia,'" I quoted nostalgically. Tiberius looked comfortable with it. Barley assessed our mutual affection, then wagged her tail once each way.

I seated myself quietly. My husband and I sat together, the first time we had had a chance to catch up, without other people yammering.

"Have you been on site this morning?" I tried not to make it sound as if I was being picky about dirt on couches. I hoped I never turned into that kind of housewife.

"Angling for work. I'm trying to charm the agent for that senator your father sold the old tenement to. Their new build will be too much for us, but I assured him my small expert team are just what he needs to dismantle the property first, in a neat, quiet way that won't annoy the neighbours."

"Will he bite?"

"I couldn't tell."

"But if he does, will Larcius and the men like months of carrying bricks in heavy buckets down six flights of stairs?"

Tiberius gleamed. "They will when I tell them we can have the materials."

"From *Fountain Court*? It's all rats and dirt."

He was grinning even more now. "So I assured the agent while I was offering to take them out of the way. The bricks look good; they were just thrown up on the cheap and never maintained. Even if we only get free hardcore for future jobs, I'll be happy. But I've got my eye on the stone in those steps." I was slightly bemused to find I had married a man who had looked like a cultured playboy, yet was full of plebeian wiles. "Get your bill paid?" he asked, keenly continuing this character.

"Yes. When I took her money, Junia snorted. 'If I had known it would be that easy, I could have gone myself!' I had creamed off a fee already, or she would never have paid me."

Next, Tiberius asked about the girls and Sabatina. He looked wary about the influx of loud young women.

"Fishing," I admitted. "My father, the old romantic, likes to reminisce about the lonely life that an informer is supposed to have. But he always kept good contacts. Julia and Favonia are some of mine, inquisiting a bride for me."

"And you went to see the Camillus brothers?" Was there a catch in Tiberius's voice, in case I retained a lingering affinity with Aelianus? I took his hand reassuringly. Then I explained why I had gone, giving him full details of the new commission from Tranquilla Euhodia.

As we talked, Tiberius said everyone knew the story that most slaves in the city never wore uniforms because no one wanted them to realise how many there were, in case it risked an uprising. "Nowadays it seems to me there are just as many freedmen, and their numbers are also invisible."

"So has that altered Roman society?" I asked.

Tiberius nodded. "Changed its composition entirely. It is a good Roman trait, which I suppose we should be proud of, that many people see their slaves as household members. Extended family. Nobody wants them to suffer for ever. If slaves serve their masters well—"

"And are seriously grateful!" I sniggered.

"That too," Tiberius agreed. He was a fair man, which many are, and even fair to his wife, which does cause comment. "Very large numbers of slaves are being freed."

"Yes, the Camilli reminded me that Augustus made an attempt to cap numbers. I said nobody pays any attention to the restrictions."

"Owners can be deterred by having to pay the tax each time—but Augustus hasn't stopped manumission happening. So now Rome is full of ambitious freedmen, who usually work very hard. Their contribution has been huge, especially to commerce."

I was less enthralled. "I thought freedom was not a fair reward for service, more a means to ensure the masters' names were perpetuated. Don't slaves have to take their owners' family names?"

"Generally. So, yes, it can preserve an owner's memory," Tiberius agreed. "Especially where there are no blood relatives. It is seen as inclusive, not a burden. Also, let's be honest, it fixes family assets in trusted hands; a condition is often made that the freed slaves must look after things—tombs, dependants and especially businesses. Sometimes the terms of a will specifically prevent them from selling on, to keep property together. Freedmen are thought to be the safest guardians. You have to allow for the fact, Albiola, that there is often trust and two-way affection."

"Not to mention sexual history!"

I was criticising again. Again, Tiberius accepted my quibble. "That is why so many men free their female slaves—in order to marry them. However the sexual interaction first began—"

"Even as an abuse of power?"

"Yes, even if it was forced—it has often grown into a stable relationship."

"I'd like to know how many of these wives would have *chosen* to marry their patrons."

"I can't argue."

I teased him satirically. "You could try! What happened to domestic disputatiousness? All right. I suppose people want to give their children civic rights."

Tiberius seized on it. "And so a substantial corpus of freedmen has been created: Rome's new citizens. I'd not be surprised if three-quarters of our population nowadays consists of either first-generation freed slaves, or their descendants."

I smiled at him. "Well, a lot are highly educated. That's better than the city Romulus founded using criminals and runaways!"

He smiled back. Even though he was talking freely, he was very quiet today. I knew the signs. When he came into my room to sit here by himself, he was in pain. At least this time his mind seemed calm, which was not always the case.

I would not even hug him, because nerve damage meant it could hurt him to be touched. "Do you want your medicine?"

"No, I'll try to manage."

I knew he had decided to wean himself off the poppy juice. He would succeed; he was very strong-willed. He closed his eyes and made himself endure his discomfort. It would ease. The problem was that he could never predict when these pains would recur.

I stroked the back of his hand, very lightly.

"I am sorry," he fretted. "This was not the bargain you agreed."

"I just hate to see you suffer."

It made me wonder about Appius Tranquillus Surus. If he had died at around sixty, it was a decent age. But had people in his household already detected signs of some impending illness? Was Hedylla, the favourite female slave, starting to dread that she might have to care for him, compelled to nurse him through physical decline, however long it took and however unpleasant the symptoms? How might that have affected her attitude to him—or his to her, if he became aware of any reluctance on her part? Would she have pressed a pillow to his face, or stirred poison into his drink?

"Thinking about your problem," said Tiberius, rousing himself, "given Rome's population of freedmen, it's inevitable some have acquired citizenship through a flawed process."

"Never properly manumitted at all?"

"Indeed. My guess is that very few of those will ever be exposed. They will meld in, accepted in their own circle and in their neighbourhood. They won't become a criminal rabble because their aim is to join society. They want to succeed so they will."

"If they are doing well, and contributing," I agreed, "they will be part of the human fabric of the city, until everyone has forgotten how their new lives began. If there has been a procedural error, or even intentional cheating, who cares?"

Tiberius nodded. "If that applies in your commission, then this Postuminus is extremely unlucky to have been challenged. He has been getting away with it and could have gone on for ever. He must have thought he was safe."

I agreed, but still thought a problem should have been foreseen. He could be exposed at any time. In Domitian's Rome, squealers were everywhere because the Emperor rewarded them. Someone in that family ought to have had a plan for this situation. They had me now to look for a solution, but if Mardiana and her lover had not visited the Stargazer so I came their way, would they ever have hired an investigator? I even wondered if they had had other plans for creating the kind of "proof," reputable or not, that Postuminus needed. It made me feel I should stick around, to ensure their eventual answer was a good one.

"Are you tempted," asked Tiberius, "simply to pay up to have his name added to the censor's citizen list?"

I smiled. "Perhaps. But it's a challenge to see if I can find a legitimate solution instead."

My sisters burst in on us to report. They claimed Cosca Sabatina had worn them out with her empty-headedness, which made me smile. Bright enough to catch my look and understand it, Julia tossed her head before she summed up, "She's an idiot, not just pretending to be vague. She has never had to learn to think. If her papa *knows* he is not really a free citizen—"

"Oh, he knows!" interrupted Favonia, the gruff one of the pair. "That is our verdict, Albia. He has simply closed his mind to it."

Julia made a wide balletic gesture. "So he knows! I was saying *if*. We considered both sides and have decided the wicked man is secretly living a false life, gloating at the trick he has pulled off."

"And has Sabatina spotted it?" I put in.

"She knows the truth, depend on it," said Favonia. "She could turn him in at any time herself, even though she's his own daughter. He's doomed."

Our girls were a little too gleeful. Revelation of this man's shaky status could disrupt or even destroy his family. From what I had seen, Postuminus felt himself secure, even if he ought to have been fearful.

Tranquilla Euhodia had seemingly no idea there might be any deception. It seemed odd that she didn't know, but if she did I could not square it with her hiring me. Could she really have been bluffing when she told me the problem was a failure to keep records?

If there had been deliberate fraud, she ran a risk of me exposing it. Could that even be her intention? I must be careful of any grudge between them, causing her to land Postuminus in trouble, deliberately using me as a tool for the purpose. If so, I would certainly not stand for being used in that way.

"Everything was fine until Sabatina fell for Venuleius—who sounds rather dishy," Julia told me. She added: "He's lovely to look at, hugely rich, plus he goes to the gym and everything. But that's easy for us to say—we haven't even seen him."

"And our mother taught us all to have incredibly high standards!" giggled Favonia.

"He's pretty, rich and muscly? Helena would groan," I pointed out. "She'll want to know is he kind and how good are his brains?" Not up to much, I thought, if he liked Cosca Sabatina—though many men preferred dim women.

"Even Mother would think it was *so-o-o* romantic how they met. They saw one another under an ocean of spring blossom in an orchard. The trees went on as far as anyone could see, and it was just so beautiful they fell right in love."

"Someone," I interjected cruelly, "should have told them love like that lasts from May to September—and even less in a year when blossom turns to mush with brown rot."

"Too much rain," Tiberius joined in with me, playing the country boy. "Fruit goes mouldy."

"What can be done, love?"

"Hard pruning. Hope for a decent spring next year."

"You two are sidetracking on purpose!" Favonia complained, not quite picking up the flavour of our teasing. However, she did enquire earnestly, "Tiberius Manlius, what will happen if it becomes known that Sabatina's father is still a slave?"

"He would be returned to that condition," Tiberius answered gravely.

My sisters squealed with disgust. "They would send him to their awful farm. He'd have to skin thousands of rabbits—that's what his brother and sister did for years, Sabatina told us about it. You have to peel the fur off them. They sell some rabbits alive to the markets, but that makes less profit because of needing cages and carts. So giant piles of naked bunnies' dead little bodies come rattling into Rome to meat markets."

Julia shuddered. "And, even more gruesome, he would have to kill them all first!"

"Then sort out masses of fur afterwards to be treated for sale. It would be *gross.*"

"We are never going to eat rabbit pie again."

"I bet you would if Fornix made it. Tranquillus Postuminus should escape from the family who are asking questions," I mused. "Start afresh.

He wants his girl to shut up, back out, lie low and one day be hitched to somebody meek whose relatives aren't nosy."

"But she loves Venuleius!" Favonia shrieked.

"So you tell me."

"She is utterly smitten, Albia! You absolutely have to sort this out for her."

"I can try. You've done well and I thank you, but I still need to delve further."

"Private enquiries?" Julia exclaimed blithely. "All you have to do is apply your innocent face, while you ask really simple questions. Anyone who is nutty enough to want your job could do it, Albia. I don't know why you and Father make such a fuss about informing."

I attempted to say the skill was in listening. They paid no attention but merely asked, since our cook was so good (and Falco had acquired yet another useless one), could they stay here for dinner?

XIII

The useful aide Erotillus had arranged for me to see Tranquillus Aprilis next day. He was the eldest child of the crucial slave Hedylla and, like his sister Euhodia, had been formally freed in the Tranquillus Surus will. I duly arrived at his local retail premises, which looked like the wine merchants' lock-ups on so many Roman streets. They tend to have a small entrance to control who enters, then a dim interior so nobody can read the labels.

This one was situated on Sidewind Passage at the base of the block where the family had their apartments. It belonged in a row of similar holes-in-the-wall and movable stalls, with a routine range of food shops, their fragrances fighting those of the bath-oil sellers. If you bought enough, you could even acquire a basket from a wickerwork shop to take your purchases home.

These commercial premises were the street-side layer of a four-storey block. If the Tranquilli were doing so well and had lived here so long, why didn't they buy up the property? I wondered. How many Spanish rabbits would it take to acquire a tenement?

Aprilis was not a wine merchant. He ran a fish-pickle outlet. I was surprised the neighbours stood for it, though the sauce is so popular perhaps they liked being able to collect supplies easily from his domestic trade counter. He did not manufacture on site—dear gods, there must be an edict forbidding that because garum comes from fermented fish entrails—but his produce begged for constant jokes about something around here giving off a big stink.

Once I got to him, he seemed to be a well-mannered, unobtrusive fellow, who cherished his wife and children, ran his business well and intended to die in his bed surrounded by weeping friends who loved him . . . At least, that was the face he put on. Underneath, he was probably a mean shit. Those deluded friends would get nothing when he passed on . . .

Before I could actually meet him and make this conclusion, I had to manoeuvre myself past the woman behind the man: one of those wives who stands doggedly in front. Her name was Marcella Maura. She was a hard-working sales-woman—hair in a brutal bun, big scarf wrapped around her middle, like an apron, and with her long sleeves rolled up. She obviously ran everything: the shop, the export business and definitely her husband. I could tell she stood no nonsense. Whenever nonsense showed its face in her orbit, Marcella Maura would biff it and win.

When I said I was working for Euhodia, she snorted. That was interesting: the sisters-in-law had no love lost between them. It was typical enough, and for an informer it is always worth noting. I explained how my involvement had begun with a slur being cast against Januarius, who must be this couple's son. "I was misled about him being the culprit—whom we haven't yet identified. I feel I must apologise."

"I'll forgive you!" sneered Marcella Maura. I caught a faint trace of impatience with her offspring, as if causing a debt-collector to appear, even mistakenly, was no surprise. "What else has he done?" she demanded.

"Nothing that I am aware of." I would have liked to hear what she suspected. "But it seems Euhodia's daughter has a lover." I thought Marcella would like that; her brighter expression showed she did indeed. "Had you heard?"

"Oh, no. They will want to keep that quiet!" So various Tranquilli shared the same apartment, but didn't all gather together for dinner—or, if so, last night it must have been a meal of silences.

"Januarius was identified mistakenly, if you say he is at your family farm."

"Went to see someone about the stock. We breed beasts for temple sacrifices, very high-quality ewes and rams. He'll be back. A slave has gone to collect him." His mother made it sound as if Januarius was a child needing a pedagogue to lead him about, not someone old enough to be mistaken for a man who flirted and fled from his bar bills.

"Erotillus?"

"That's the one."

Erotillus had failed to impress her as much as he impressed me, but plenty of people are indifferent to slaves, even their bright ones. Trying to assess her own status, I felt this woman had probably been born free. She was a typical female plebeian, working in a family business, knowing the product, balancing the budget, doing everything herself because she always had done. In the past they might have been struggling too much to afford staff, and right up to now she reckoned nobody else could be trusted.

A customer came to have a flagon filled with garum; Marcella Maura knew what he wanted, went to a barrel, turned a spigot, efficiently filled the receptacle, stopped at exactly the right point, twisted in a bung, checked the money, sent the customer off then shouted for her husband to emerge to see me.

When he took no notice, she waved me into his inner shrine. She left us to it. She had no interest in what we might have to say. If it was family business, that was up to the Tranquilli; she apparently despised it.

Aprilis called me through to a back store, where he was pottering among racks of amphorae. He was a mid-height portly man, with fast-receding hair, his features vaguely similar to Euhodia's; like his sister, he looked as if he had worked all his life and would not plan on retirement. He must have been in his sixties. That made him around the same age Surus had been when he died; Aprilis, too, looked fit enough to carry on, if nothing unexpected claimed him.

The amphorae were mid-height, portly things, just as he was, their pottery on the rough side; when Aprilis saw me peering at them through the gloom, he said these came with their contents from southern Spain and Lusitania. Whether I wanted it or not, he gave me a short lecture on fish sauce, going through from fine *garum sociorum*, which cost more than the gourmet dish it would be elegantly smothering, to the clear stuff called *liquamen*, which could be made from various mixtures of fish and their entrails, then the sludge from the bottom of containers that is known as *allec*. I said I assumed Surus had originally begun importing sauce while visiting the Iberian provinces, at the same time as he was having the idea of rabbits.

Aprilis agreed, but seemed unwilling to discuss his father. "You never thought my son had been out and about with Mardiana? Januarius is a good family man and has more sense."

"So I gather. You don't know the person who looks like him?"

"Could be anyone." Aprilis moved on abruptly to my mission. "I shall not be able to help you over Postuminus." His truculence sounded routine, though it could hardly be how he negotiated with people who wanted contracts for his salty products. He must have a friendlier mode.

I played obliging: "Fair enough. I assume that if you and your sister know anything definite about your brother's status, there would be no need to hire me. Are you fond of your brother?"

"He can't help being a spoiled little idiot."

"That's frank! Do you believe he really is a free citizen?"

"Why not? We are. Why shouldn't he be? So what can you do about it?" Although he was blunt, he was not unpleasant. I guessed he thought Euhodia was wasting her money. Even if they had argued about her hiring me, in the end he must have felt it was her choice.

"Well, that's my problem," I answered, still good-humouredly. "What's to be done? I shall certainly not forge documents. I hope nobody expects that." In Rome there would be people working from dark attics who did create false credentials for a fee. If I had wanted to work like that, I could have found someone. "I am just taking soundings. I understand you and your sister grew up on the famous rabbit farm before you were freed under the Surus will. Tranquilla Euhodia told me no one can remember the executor."

Perhaps Aprilis looked shifty, but it could have been the gloom of his garum cave. "Some old crony of our father's."

"Does his name come to mind?" Aprilis only shrugged. "You had not seen him before?"

"No. Never."

"Nor afterwards?" This time he did not bother to answer. "It's a shame," I pressed on, "because I really would have liked to talk to him." Aprilis still made no attempt to help. Finding the executor, even if he was still alive, would be my problem. With a feeling that things were being kept from me, I suddenly felt determined to do it.

Not showing that I had gone into stubborn-informer mode, I asked neutrally, "You would have been in your twenties?"

"Round about."

"That was very young to be given responsibility for a large commercial empire?"

"We were pretty well running the rabbit farm already. That was all we had to do at first, until we expanded. Don't forget we've been at this for forty years now. We grew into it, commerce." It might sound like clean-hands administration, but I remembered my sisters' description of the slaves' work sending rabbits to market.

"Did you make mistakes in the beginning, Aprilis, or did you start out with confidence?"

"Confidence. We were already selling the stock. We would come up to Rome with the carts and haggle like cheeky urchins. All the negotiators knew us. The only thing that changed as we grew older was our standing. Then we moved into new products, boldly enough when we saw possibilities. We had been taught to think that way."

"By Surus?"

"Yes. He told us one commodity is very like another in purchasing and shifting products. All you have to do is get your hands on something rare, convince people that they want it, then you will make your fortune."

"Surus thought you would be good at it?"

"He knew we were."

"The scale of his businesses never frightened you?"

Aprilis admitted, "We were probably too innocent to see it ought to scare us. We were young. We thought we could do anything—and luckily we were right."

"Did your mother have a role? Hedylla, wasn't she?"

"No. She worked in the house—and after Surus died, she did not have to work."

"Because he had freed her?"

"Because she was our mother and we were running the place!" Aprilis told me tetchily.

He seemed ready to grow angry, though I was unsure why. He was giving me no sense of his relationship with his mother. I suspected that as slaves they had lived on the same property yet without close personal bonds.

On a big, busy farm, Hedylla might have had to leave other people to bring up her offspring—assuming Aprilis and Euhodia had ever had any real nurturing. They must have worked hard from a very early age. They would have been out of doors slaughtering mounds of rabbits, while she lurked in the house; they might have seen her life as easier than theirs. As long as the master who favoured her was alive, no one would complain, and after he had gone, she had these two adult children who had been formally liberated and placed in charge of everyone. Presumably, there was some loyalty because of the blood relationship.

Had it been the same for Postuminus? Aprilis and Euhodia ran everything, Hedylla popped out their baby brother, then concentrated on the newborn. She could well have had a closer relationship with him than with any of her previous children. And perhaps, I thought, if she devoted herself too much to Postuminus, there might have been resentment from the older two.

"Do you share business interests with your brother?" I shot in, trying to catch Aprilis by surprise.

If he felt shifty, he hid it. "Euhodia and I take care of him. He used to help me out here in the shop but now he has his own money."

"You are much closer to Euhodia?"

"Always have been. We grew up working together."

"And what was your mother like?" I asked more sympathetically.

"Well-deserving."

As praise, that was a Roman cliché, a tombstone favourite, particularly for a woman. I had to accept it. I could not expect Hedylla's son to tell me if she was a nasty piece of work with a vile temper. Given how the staff at Nobilo's had described Surus, that seemed unlikely anyway. He enjoyed things, he knew what he wanted, he made himself pleasant and had probably collected people around him who were easy-going and companionable.

"What about Tranquillus Surus?"

"Same too. A great businessman." I noticed Aprilis did not say "a great father."

"Did you see a lot of him?"

"He came to the farm on occasions, organising production. He always took an interest in my sister and me. We thought him very jolly, and absolutely tops on the commercial side. He taught us everything we needed so we could one day run things."

"He always intended you to take over his interests? That did not come as a surprise?"

"It made sense," stated Aprilis. Was he being defensive?

"He saw you two as his natural heirs? As family? Postuminus told me Surus and Hedylla lived as man and wife."

"When he was at the farm." How often was that? Aprilis had just told me that Surus came "on occasions." I thought I saw him pull up, as if I had caught him out in the wrong emphasis.

I hid the fact I had noticed. "Of course. Do you think there is any point in me visiting the farm?"

"None at all. You will find nothing useful there. Surus ran anything official from here in Rome. Rome was his commercial base—as it is now ours."

"I understand." Drawing things to a close, I sighed. "Well, I shall do my best. Your sister says time is pressing. Rome must have a million people, so I don't think I can look through all the imperial lists of citizens, hunting for your brother's name. It does seem as if—by mistake, I suppose—Postuminus may never have been enrolled as a free man by the censor. When he was born, his father was dead and I suppose his mother may not have known how to have him registered. Women can't do it, so the formalities may just have been left undone. My aim is to find evidence to allow him to be added now."

"And will you?"

"It does happen."

"Not hopeless, then!" It did seem as if Aprilis would be pleased to see his sibling verified. At that point I detected no animosity.

As I left, he presented me with a small flask of good-quality garum, the clear, odourless variety. I saw Aprilis had a set of them in fancy glassware, ready to use as polite gifts to his contacts in commerce. "Thank you. My cook will be eager for this."

"Send him along. I can discuss his regular requirements." As his final word, Aprilis said, "We are a very quiet family."

That again! I said I had heard this pronouncement from people who had been hauled in by the Urban Cohorts after a riot. I joked that so-called quiet families were usually engaged in long court cases with those of their neighbours who were left alive after vicious brawls caused by perfidious double-dealing . . .

Tranquillus Aprilis, freedman of Appius, blinked. For a moment he looked as if he was wondering how I could have known.

I left the shop with that old informers' feeling: that I had wasted an hour talking to somebody who knew much more than he had been telling me.

XIV

While I was in Sidewind Passage, I popped up to the apartment to see if Januarius was back. Philodamus told me no; he and Erotillus would probably be home later.

"I am desperately hoping he may find the old will at the farm. I really would like to read it. There may be a clause I wouldn't have thought of." As Philodamus nodded sympathetically, I cast my eyes around the decently furnished room where we were. "I have an impression of multiple business ventures. And properties too? Does the family own this apartment? And the one above? Then what about the shops at ground level, especially the garum outlet?"

"No, they rent," said Philodamus. As the bookkeeper, he was bound to know. "They would like to possess an asset like this—but some old cove on the Caelian built the tenement, and his heirs aren't budging on ownership."

"Have the Tranquilli asked to buy them out?"

"As far as I know, they just can't fix it."

"Animosity?"

"Very litigious lot." The slave chuckled. "They don't endear themselves to the owners. Januarius likes to moan about any small maintenance issue. He'll demand compensation for 'inconvenience and disruption of tenants' use of the property.' Heaven help their landlords if ever a roof tile falls and hurts someone."

"The landlords put up with him?"

"No, they keep pointedly suggesting the Tranquilli might like to move out. Only surprise is that the freedmen have clung on here. The lessors tend to use really vicious enforcement when they want evictions."

"Doesn't that mean a building sale might be welcome? Then the tenants would assume responsibility for maintenance. Aren't the Tranquilli used to agreeing business deals? Don't they know how to make a winning approach?"

"You would think so, Flavia Albia." Philodamus had on his coy look.

"No comment? Do you arrange their rent payments?"

He loosened up again. "I do—with much muttering when I remind them. Each pays a separate share. Euhodia just gets on with it, but Aprilis tries to hide in his dark garum cave and Postuminus is always pleading poverty. According to him, he has no money because the harvest in his orchard fails most years."

"Does it?"

"All lies. He wouldn't know the truth if it arrived in a quadriga and a trumpeter formally announced it."

"Noted!" The subject of my inquiry routinely fibbed? This fitted my sisters' assessment, but if true, I could not see Postuminus ever owning up to any lies about his status. "Philodamus, who does the rent get paid to?"

"*O-o-oh*, they send someone for the money, fellow with a fast mule, stout saddlebags, bodyguard," he elaborated.

"Give me details. I am just wondering whether the original landlord might have known Surus."

Philodamus was dismissive. "Could be—forty years ago!"

I told him I was ready to follow any lead, so I asked for the Caelian address. Philodamus dug out a rent receipt with the information. The figures were nothing to do with me—but I noticed the charges for these properties were eye-watering.

I had barely finished writing down what I wanted when we were interrupted. Pushing in through one of their heavy door curtains, marched a family member I had not yet met.

"Who is this?" she demanded.

Her mother had disparaged her and mine would have criticised her manners. Suza would immediately have spotted that there had been beauty treatments; we might agree together that this woman had been wasting her money. Still, I knew that when she went out to be pampered it was partly a cover for extra-marital activity.

"I am Flavia Albia—"

"Oh, the sleuth!" She was scornful.

"Tranquilla Mardiana?" I could have waited for her to introduce herself, but I already knew who she was. I intended to establish that I had the upper hand.

She was roughly my contemporary yet looked older and, as my family would say, she was even ruder. She had a long oval face, smooth hair drawn down over her ears from a centre parting, and a guarded expression: she was recognisably the woman Junillus had drawn. Today's choice of necklace was a plainish gold chain, though it came with big round shoulder brooches and drop earrings. In this apparatus, she was a self-assured, uppity soul; I soon decided that her unhappiness came from being thwarted rather than deprived.

"Mardiana?" I repeated.

"Why do you need to know?" She spoke through barely open lips, which I knew from Apollonius might be down to self-consciousness about her missing tooth.

"Oh, I always like to meet customers from my family's bar. Lunch, wasn't it? Upgraded from a takeaway at Nobilo's. I hear it's now a sit-down for two and public canoodling . . . I landed you in trouble over your bill, I'm afraid."

She seethed, not bothering to apologise. "What are you cooking up with our slave?"

"A query."

"You won't find anything."

I merely inclined my head slightly; I remembered that this fury had thrown a jug at her dressmaker. I wouldn't want Mardiana to do anything inconsiderate to me, or I would have to knock her down and stamp on her. I was quite ready to do it. She and her fancy fellow had cheated Junillus and Apollonius. I could see she was not in the least chastened. I tipped up my chin and kept pushing. "So, Tranquilla Mardiana, who is your lover?"

"Nobody." She was like a stubborn child, refusing to admit she ate all the stuffed dates, even though she had been so sick afterwards her crime was obvious.

"Lucanian on rye, fish pickle and all the trimmings," I listed, with a thin smile. "I think he will surface eventually. All the cheated barmen on the Aventine have gone on the lookout. They want him identified. I should warn you, Januarius was fingered and it may not have been the first time. His father was vague, but when Januarius comes home, he may know who his double really is."

As I threatened her with her relatives, Mardiana made a big show of ignoring me. "Give me some cash, Philodamus. I am going to the farm to escape being hounded. I shall need spending money, though Heaven knows there is nothing to buy out there."

Her mother had won, then: it was to be rustic exile. Was the punishment to last until the daughter owned up to her affair? I wondered which of those determined women would crack first.

On the verge of flouncing out, Mardiana paused, posing. "So you met Uncle Aprilis! That must have been a delight for you. Did he give you a little garum sample, barely as big as a perfume bottle?" She was winding herself up into more vindictiveness. "Did he jump you, or was his wife on guard? Maura knows what he is like, poor woman." This tirade had a stunning climax: "Listen to me, fancy investigator. Compared to Aprilis, nothing I have ever done matters. You know his big adventure? Aprilis slept with his brother's wife-to-be, right on the night before their wedding. Ever since then, he and Postuminus have been locked in a ferocious dispute over whose child Cosca Sabatina really is!"

Amazed, Philodamus had let his jaw sag. I had worked for warring families before, so downplayed it smoothly. "Well, that sounds nice and traditional!"

I managed to remain unmoved, until Mardiana gathered her skirts then bitterly stormed off.

"Charybdis!"

"And six-headed Scylla! Did you know about that, Philodamus?"

"Twenty years ago? Before my time and they have clearly been keeping it dark."

I was thinking fast. This revelation put my case in doubt. If the young girl's father was her uncle, at least Aprilis was a free citizen—and a seduction on the night before a wedding was sinful but not strictly adultery. Still, coercing a virgin could be a dramatic claim in court. Venuleius and his picky family would be seriously unimpressed. Even if I could prove that Postuminus was a genuine freedman, he was now revealed as a betrayed bridegroom in a tangle, verging on incest, that no respectable in-laws would appreciate. His wife did the dirty and their daughter might be anyone's? Stop the new marriage! I could feel my commission dwindling away.

"Do you think Euhodia knows?" Surely not! Or, I wondered, was her attempt to help her niece through me intended as atonement for family guilt?

"Euhodia knows most things. Eve of the wedding? Such timing!" exclaimed Philodamus, still revelling in it.

"Yes, and so caring of the dear little brother! Was there existing antagonism? Did the older pair see Baby as a cuckoo in the nest? I'd love to know how it all came out," I said. "Someone must have let the story slip to Postuminus. Is he popular, or did everyone have a belly laugh at his expense? Why has he never divorced Cosconia Saba? Don't tell me— profits from her family's bakery are part of her dowry, not to mention the recipe for that sought-after digestive bread!"

I asked Philodamus (in confidence, of course) whether this scandal could be the reason why Postuminus and his wife had never had any more children. Philodamus suggested (in confidence) that could well be so. In his time here they had slept in separate rooms and had as little as possible to do with one another.

Was that also true of Tranquillus Aprilis and Marcella Maura? No. Whatever Aprilis had done, Marcella Maura was the kind of woman who made sure she obtained her rights.

Fired up so he abandoned his normal reticence, the slave told me Cosconia Saba had a reputation of her own. She might have been distant from her husband, but it was said no good-looking dough-kneader at the family bakery was safe in her vicinity.

"Even prior to her marriage?"

"Who knows? She used to go back to see her brothers from here, and come home with a basket of rolls, looking very much happier."

Privately, I did not blame her. Being, at a young age, married to a wimp on account of a bread recipe, seduced by an older man who had apparently had plenty of practice, then probably blamed by everyone, first while she was pregnant, then for the rest of her life? It cannot have been easy. Cosconia Saba would have needed to find consolation while she toughed it out.

She was the mother of the daft young girl I was supposed to help. "Was she a good mother?"

"A bit remote. They used nannies."

"Can I meet her?"

Not possible, Philodamus said regretfully. She had died about five years ago. A female ailment, causing terrible wasting and agony. "The cruel ones all saw it as her just reward. You might have liked her, Flavia Albia. She was charming and witty, even when I knew her."

I gathered that before her illness, Cosconia Saba had also looked splendid, after a lifetime of eating only digestive bread.

I was annoyed. This old story might upset things. Plenty of brides enjoy a final fling in the last desperate hours before they are publicly shackled to a man they may have doubts about. Most don't land me in a position where their escapade could lose me fees.

And now I felt sorry for Postuminus, so I was stuck with my responsibility to him.

XV

I went home. The best way to deal with a shock like that was to withdraw and consider options. Would Mardiana tell anyone she had blurted out the secret? If not, should I admit to other family members that I knew? How far did they acknowledge it, even among themselves? I would prefer to keep quiet, though I might not have any choice.

If one of the house slaves had told me, I knew how it would have resolved itself: when tackled, my client would deny the story; next time I visited, I would find that slave had disappeared, moved elsewhere or even been sold off.

As it was, the scandal had been revealed by a relative, one who was alive when the incident happened. Mardiana must have been about ten, no doubt excited by her uncle's imminent wedding. I could imagine her as the sly kind of child who would be all ears while a quarrel was raging. The fascinated little girl would have listened in, old enough to understand what had caused all the door-slamming and wild accusations.

Denial of this story now remained a possibility because Mardiana was herself in disgrace. The rest could pretend she had made it up out of spite—especially spite against me after I publicised her love affair. Then I would look stupid; I would probably lose my commission for accepting what they could pretend was a pack of lies.

I did accept it. The story sounded true—it was too extreme not to be. So, where did that place me? Was Mardiana going to broadcast this to a wider audience? If the Venuleius family ever found out, would there be any point in continuing my commission? Until someone stopped me, I decided to carry on. My own people at home would snigger, but the revelation was too strange to ignore.

Where did this situation place the people involved? Did Tranquilla Euhodia, my client, know? I presumed she did. She lived with her brothers. I wondered whether the liaison had become open knowledge straight away, or if the truth had crept out some time later. Either way, she could not have missed the bitterness between Aprilis and Postuminus; any debate over which was the real father of Sabatina must have been visible. When relatives insist on occupying close living quarters, fights tend to spill out onto the communal stairs. Everyone in Sidewind Passage probably knew. True paternity, of course, could never be proved, so the aggravation would continue.

Was this why Postuminus lived apart upstairs? How had that come about? Was it for space and privacy, a demand from his wife, or had he refused to share with his brother once he discovered the betrayal? Had he always wanted distance from his siblings? Had there always been antipathy?

What about his wife? I could imagine she had not wanted to share an apartment with Aprilis. Mardiana had not specified whether Aprilis seduced the bride or assaulted her, whether Cosconia Saba had been attracted to him and, if so, how deeply. At the very least it was embarrassing. Then once the wedding had gone ahead, all parties needed to avoid actual adultery or any festering suspicion of it.

Aprilis had his own marriage to protect. Did Marcella Maura know what he had done? Did she hate it or condone it? Did he and she have children, other than Januarius?

Then there was Sabatina. Did Postuminus accept her as his child when she was first born, which could mean he only learned what his brother had done much later? Why didn't he then move even further away? He seemed to have enough money to choose for himself. Or was he so vindictive that he stayed in the same building in order to keep picking at the sore—sniping at his brother whenever a chance arose? In that case, Aprilis might enjoy seeing little brother laid low now.

Whatever the truth, their sister must have hired me while hoping the scandal could be kept secret. It would be fatal if the Venuleii found out. She had fixed her mind on me proving Postuminus was a citizen, his wife had been compliant, his daughter was legitimate. All respectable. Never mind the almost-incest. That had obviously been swept under a floor rug years ago and Euhodia meant it to stay there. She had decided we would strictly take the line that Sabatina *was* the child of Tranquillus Postuminus and he an upright Roman.

She might be his. The fact he and Cosconia Saba had had an empty marriage for a long time need not mean they had never consummated their relationship in the heat of young desire. Cosconia was said to have been promiscuous later—though perhaps that was a direct result of what had happened earlier. In the interests of good taste, no one need mention that. The poor woman was dead. Perhaps she had been glad to go. She would never have a chance to explain or excuse herself; at least her behaviour could be erased. No doubt, like Hedylla, she now had a memorial stone that informed the world Cosconia Saba worked in wool and was quiet of conversation, an all-round Roman matron who was "well-deserving" of her husband.

She had left him a single parent. She had stuck him with a child he could not want or love. Would the put-upon Postuminus go along with what their daughter needed from him? Perhaps he viewed her marriage as his way of shedding a tainted responsibility. Pass Sabatina on to Venuleius, then forget his own tragedy.

It was interesting that when I saw them together there had been no sign of this problem. He was a downtrodden father; she was a self-willed child. That was all I had noticed—and I had been looking carefully. He was a wimp while she was spoiled, but that was so typical it was virtually enshrined in Roman law. Remembering that scene, I came to the conclusion that Cosca Sabatina had no idea her mother and her uncle had had a prenuptial fling.

No idea so far, anyway. Out of pity, I must be careful that my stirring up of these past woes did not lead to someone telling the poor girl the truth. Or it had better not be my fault if, at the wedding banquet,

Postuminus drank so much wine he warbled to Venuleius, his spanking new son-in-law, "Let's hope she hasn't done to you what that evil bitch her mother did to me . . ."

Even at that point I felt doubtful. If Sabatina's wedding banquet ever happened, it would be some achievement.

XVI

I approached my own house, telling myself wryly that nothing so extreme affected us . . .

For once, Rodan opened the door for me. He scuttled back into his side room like a cockroach fleeing lamplight, plainly up to something hideous. I left him to fester. Instead, I was drawn through the atrium and into the courtyard by a worrying stillness. Only one person was there. Enduring this solitude, I found Gaius Corellius Musa, my cousin's partner.

Polite, intelligent, very much ex-military, he would be known for the rest of his life as "one-legged Corellius." He had fallen off a horse; that was the cover story. I knew from my father that legionary scouts led dangerous, surreptitious lives, skulking in places where they should not be. His accident had ended this man's army career and now seemed set to end his civilian one too. Marcia and he had been running a government safe-house, observing foreign diplomats who were being entertained officially. It was trusted, interesting work that they had enjoyed, with a compelling palace salary. In that post, Corellius had limped about until he could no longer bear his discomfort. But while on sick leave he had been replaced, edged out permanently, he suspected.

Marcia Didia was one of those young women who horrify satirical poets. Martial and Juvenal would love shrieking about her outrageous behaviour; she really did exercise at Glaucus's gym on the Vicus Tuscus; Glaucus accepted only serious clients. She had offered to visit the house where they had worked and punch the lights out of the replacement steward. Corellius furiously told her not to interfere. Marcia retorted that if he was going to talk to her like that, she might punch *his* lights out instead.

Their relationship had sprung into being very fast and not long ago, so this suggestion seemed reasonable to her. She had knocked him floorwards at least once, though the first time he had been unaware of the boxing so he had not seen it coming. I was there when she did it. Marcia would not give him a hand up. He was tough; he didn't want it. But now he was an invalid: not so tough, and no longer sure what he wanted. He could not cope; nor could she.

Neither of them had anywhere to stay except at our house, so I had had to play the peace-maker; that duty had never suited me. On arrival home today, I greeted Corellius warily, yet not so warily as he greeted me. He probably knew I would have liked to shed my warring house guests.

Corellius had used his savings to commission a first-class false leg in moulded bronze, only to find it hurt him too much to use. It was the right size, of striking design and beautiful workmanship. (A description that fitted Marcia; Corellius had taste.) When I brought in a doctor for Tiberius, my husband refused to cooperate so he pushed the medic on to our other patient. The verdict was, his stump was too recently healed. We kept saying Corellius must be patient, everything would improve in time, he would be able to walk eventually. But he despaired. He had once been active, self-sufficient and courageous. He had thought the amputation would set him free from pain. Now he had to use a crutch. In between, he was stuck in a chair, still suffering, sickly, bored, probably losing his girlfriend and definitely his confidence.

Worse: our two little boys, Gaius and Lucius, became fascinated by the one-legged man. They were constantly plaguing him.

My instinct was to leave him on his own in the courtyard. Before I could sneak past to my room, guilt stopped me.

I sat down with him. Gratus must have built him a small fire, onto which the patient was chucking occasional sticks, looking as despondent as if the doctor had told him he had only three hours to live. A bad atmosphere was haunting the courtyard. While I was out, things must have been very lively. Corellius said Tiberius had carried off the children to visit his uncle (taking the dog); the chef had gone to see his brother (taking the donkey); all the staff were on an outing to the baths (not taking Rodan, who was scared of water).

"Dare I ask, what about Marcia?"

"Stormed off."

"Oh?" I asked, carefully.

"We had a tough exchange of views."

"Well, that keeps a relationship fresh!" It had better not be terminal. What were we supposed to do with Corellius if my ridiculous cousin dumped him?

Possessing a dark intelligence, he saw my anxiety and muttered, "She will be coming back."

"Thanks for that!" A proper hostess would be polite, but I was Flavia Albia: I thought it was time to start being frank.

Desperate to engage the man somehow, I asked if he wanted to hear about my case. He didn't, but I would not let him off. My house: my items of interest. I needed to summarise progress; all he had to do was poke his fire and listen. On legionary campsites, hearing tall tales for hours must be standard when the beer has run out, the legate has "gone to see his uncle" and there is nothing else to do until the next barbarian ambush. It may even have its own section in the army's training manual. The rulebook can't all be methods of signalling or how to build a pontoon bridge.

I was succinct. After I had finished, Corellius sat quiet. The scandalous elements in my story failed to excite him. His concerns, as a scout and then a spy, had been political; his responses to that were coldly logistical. The madder side of human nature left him cold.

I rummaged in the fire with a stick, thinking to myself that exploring the madness was precisely why I did my job.

When Corellius did speak, his suggestion was interesting: "You do not like these people?"

I accepted it as a fair question. "I thought I liked Euhodia, or I would not have taken the case. I don't particularly dislike them—and in my work it can be best to avoid bonding. Stay neutral and just take the money."

"But will they pay you?"

"It's done. I took a lump upfront."

Corellius was clearly surprised. He had worked for miserly emperors and sestertius-pinching secretariats. They make the rules. They pay poorly; they pay late. Even to question counts as disloyalty to the divine. Nobody argues unless they want an order to commit suicide. Either cut your own wrists to save the budget, or a tribune with a sword can be supplied . . .

Having gained his interest, I kept going. "At the moment, I am not surprised by the mess: clients often engage me to tackle one question, yet once I start, their real beef is different. The trickiest element is working out what they are really after. Half the time they don't know themselves—then they won't easily accept what I tell them."

Corellius liked his missions cut and dried. Whether it was skirmishing tribes or a devious delegation wearing funny turbans, he wanted to find out what the bastards were planning, then submit a well-written report. Once he sent his briefing up the line, he was finished. Someone else had to decide what to do—or not do. He had an inbuilt cynicism about that: he did all the work, but the idiots up top were too inept to act upon his research.

That is how bureaucracy works, of course: the stubborn submission of good advice that will only be buried. Truth is too awkward. Action too risky. Corellius could have been a happier man if he accepted that. In fact, it seemed to me his striving against the system might have been what had really led to him being replaced.

"I suppose," he said suddenly, "these slaves must have murdered Tranquillus Surus?"

I confirmed that a crime had already been suggested. "I don't feel it," I objected. "If they did, then hiring me was a stupid move."

"Singularly ham-fisted! How old were the first two when they inherited his business interests?"

"Young, but just about adult."

"Surely it's incredible they should have been left in charge?"

"At that stage, it was just a farm full of thumping rabbits. The slaves had worked there since they were infants. They knew the ropes and had the capacity to become successful entrepreneurs. Surus knew what he was doing. Besides," I contended, "suppose they really had conspired against him, and perhaps even did him in, why this stuff about only some of them being formally freed in his will? Why not bash him, steal his business, then pretend they were *all* set free by Surus?"

Corellius did not like a woman who argued with him. (This was why, although Marcia was gorgeous and spirited, they could never have a life of roses.) Refusing to agree my point, he shifted to a new one: "Do you trust the matriarch?"

"Tranquilla Euhodia? It may not last, but so far I do."

"She is the person paying you?"

"She is." Had my attitude towards her shifted since I started? "She did assure me her two brothers were on good terms, yet I found out they have been quarrelling for at least twenty years. So she has lied, and I do have to get to the back of it."

"No, you don't. I see exactly what it is," Corellius decided for me. "Aprilis would not share their patrimony with a third sibling." He was too dogmatic, but he might have been right; I did not protest. Sitting in this courtyard, I was the *domina*; my role was to encourage harmony and to do so I must let men pronounce. Anyway, I was tired. "He and his sister were close in age so he accepts her," Corellius duly pontificated.

"Besides, she is a forceful woman."

"If you say so. When another brother was born unexpectedly, Aprilis decided to exclude him. He would share with Euhodia, if he must, but this new intruder was out."

"Postuminus was never pushed out," I disagreed. "He lives with them—well, he lives upstairs. He looks as wealthy as the other two, so money came to him from somewhere. His bakery interests were acquired with his wife, but he owns an orchard too."

"Where did that come from?" Corellius demanded, not ready to give way. "Do you know for sure it was bequeathed by Surus?"

"No." I was being fair, though my companion showed no appreciation. "I do not know, and that is an excellent point, Gaius Corellius." I continued this flattery because he was depressed, with good reason; in my house he would be shown kindness, whether he was grateful to us or not. "Surus won't have left a bequest to his youngest, because he was unaware Hedylla was pregnant. A menopause surprise, Euhodia described it." I gathered myself to go upstairs. "Thank you for the lead. I shall have to trace the history of Postuminus and his beloved orchard."

If it had been spring, I might have suggested Corellius and Marcia travel out to look at it for me, hoping that the gorgeous acres of blossom would restore their rocky friendship. An expedition in early January to stare at dormant trees on the cold Campagna was more likely to finish them. I did not want the invalid to catch a chill in his stump, nor to be abandoned in open country by Marcia.

Corellius thought he was controlling my case for me. "You are missing the obvious, Flavia Albia!" he called after me, still quite aggressive in setting me straight. "It's staring right at you. Surus was *not* the father of the youngest child. The other two know it. The mother—Hedylla?—must have invented this story. The other two can't prove it. But, trust me, that's why Euhodia and Aprilis have it in for Postuminus. If they could have hired you to prove who his real father was and then be permanently rid of him, they would have done that."

"Juno, I hope not," I answered fervently. By then I was leaning over the balcony banister. "What you say sounds very reasonable, but if Hedylla was popular with the workforce and enjoying herself while the master's back was turned, she might never even have known which rabbit-rancher was responsible. Proving who a slave on a farm slept with over forty years ago has to be impossible. If she did, Postuminus could be anyone's."

That was a terrible idea. For me, he had to have been fathered by Surus.

Still, all was not lost. At least seeing someone else in a state of frustration thrilled my house guest. When everyone started to filter home, they found Corellius taking a turn on his crutch and his false leg, cheerier than we had ever seen him.

XVII

After members of my household returned for lunch, they were notice-ably quiet. I said nothing. Mother would have been proud of me.

It was clear that my husband had given his nephews a talking-to about bothering Corellius. Since they were so young, I was prepared to believe they were simply fascinated by his prosthetic. Be fair: so were all the rest of us, but we adults never let him see us staring. It was a very fine false leg, though for a man who had been in the army, he seemed oddly hapless at using his specialist equipment. Still, he polished the metal like a trooper. Now he was having a good hop around after, as he saw it, solving my case. Gaius and Lucius sat together, simply watching him.

I wondered at what age Aprilis and Euhodia had been put to work on the rabbit farm. Three and five, like ours, would be considered suitable for slaves to start toddling about with easy household tasks—though surely not wringing creatures' necks? However harsh the regime on the farm was, they must have been let off that because their baby hands were not strong enough.

Ours were spoiled by comparison. Even I could not wish serious labour onto this unhappy pair. They still cried for their dead mother and worried about what their future held, even though their worst struggle would only be learning their alphabets and numbers. Gaius and Lucius, these solemn tots in smart green and blue tunics, would have the best life we could give them. Even if I had been prepared to say I did not like these children (something I would never again be able to admit now they lived here), children they were. Gaius and Lucius might be taken along to a building site by their uncle, but it would be as a treat. Tiberius would grip their tiny hands and keep them out of harm's way. At six or seven, I myself had been piling cabbages on a crude stall, but no one had expected me to stack the vegetables neatly, let alone to engage with customers; mainly I tumbled among the dogs and watched the world go by.

I was a foundling but never a slave—thank you, gods of Rome and Britannia—yet I had lived in a poor provincial community where nobody wanted me. That meant I could imagine Aprilis and Euhodia being neglected, shouted at and lonely. I had no doubt that, sent up to Rome routinely with cargoes of rabbits, those urchins would have been beaten if they had let animals escape or were cheated by market traders. They would have had to learn fast. Recollection of their troubled infancy would be alive in them today, even now they were approaching old age. If Gaius and Lucius were subdued merely by words from Tiberius, which I knew would have been gentle, how much worse would it have been for two very young agricultural labourers in the unsentimental environment of farming for profit?

And how hard would they have found it to watch a much younger child being brought up in a different way?

Tiberius and the boys had cadged lunch at his uncle's house. They had brought home a packet of spiced cake, a peace offering for Corellius. In the absence of Fornix, other people foraged; those who went to the baths were moaning about the water not being hot enough, but had satisfied themselves with sausages from hawkers with trays.

I dived into my private room, because an unexpected character had been brought for me to interview. Suza fetched bread rolls and cheese for us, after Tiberius whispered why I had been supplied with this strange man: Uncle Tullius was rewriting his will. Considering he could manage that alone, he had sent over his testament expert.

"I shall just pick at an olive," the expert claimed, nonetheless plunging into the bread basket as if this was his first meal all week. "I'm always well supplied all day, when I'm with Tullius Icilius."

He was a weaselly, sneezing, toggle-cloaked, knitted-hat specimen. He had a thin face with a pointy nose and dark eyes that were evaluating the furniture. I supposed he must be used to setting probate values. He looked like a filing clerk, one who knew only the first half of the alphabet because his colleague controlled the other letters and you must stick to demarcation lines, mustn't you?

He was called Mygdonius. He could have been born in a mansion or a palace, but from his name he was child to a floor-washer. His mother was probably imported from the north. He was free now, a self-employed paralegal with special knowledge. Probing his personal manumission experience would be impolite. He had come to talk about wills, which were his passion, so we stuck with that.

Easing into conversation, I asked whether Uncle Tullius had decided on an upgrade after Tiberius's sister died, to make new provisions for her boys—of whom there were actually three, although only two lived here. Mygdonius said no: Tullius changed his will every few months. He had always done so.

"He loves it. He calls me up to the house in case of technical queries, but he disappears on his own with a stylus. I never have to get mine out. Afterwards he holds a happy gathering for his new set of witnesses. I get to join in, if I pick my moment."

Mygdonius helped me out with my cheese in case Suza had brought too much. Through mouthfuls, he then imparted Roman testamentary lore. "I can see you are an intelligent lady." He must have meant I was too dumb to spot him pinching half my lunch. "You have to bear in mind that, when writing his will, a Roman is finally free to reveal his true character. No need to skirt issues or hide his opinions—he'll be dead when they become public, so he can speak out."

"Yes, I have heard the joke that it's the one time in his life that a Roman tells the truth!"

Mygdonius showed no reaction; he wanted to make any jokes himself. "He can say what he likes and the world will expect honesty. It can start right at the first sentence. Never mind 'Titius, be you my heir'— Titius is a hypothetical name we use, you know, when discussing precedents. The legator can get right in there with 'Titius, since I can find no one else, curse it, I shall have to name you as my heir.' I have seen that, even where Titius immediately looks at the snotty debts that will land on him so he does a bunk. That's a bugger. If nobody takes, as we call it, the dead fellow is declared intestate. Which is a bowl of shit. Any pious man sorts his affairs. It's his duty. Intestacy is a filthy crime that puts stuff in the wrong hands."

"Wrong hands?"

"Women, for instance." The expert shuddered. I grabbed back the cheese comport. Women do have rights, even in a paternalist society. That was what my mother taught me. While I was asserting my right of possession, he elaborated. "Nephews who have murdered their brothers-in-law. Dear little grandsons only twelve months old, who are being shamelessly preyed on by crooks and their mothers."

"The crooks' mothers or their own?" I was feeling satirical.

"Either. Worst case, both!" Mygdonius joined in, grinning.

I said I had heard of something called an unduteous will. In Roman tradition, there was an assumption that people close to the deceased, especially blood relatives, should expect to be looked after. "He can still leave them out," Mygdonius explained. "But he'd better say why."

"Why?"

He brightened as he invented witty suggestions: "Take your set-up here. If Tullius Icilius were to exclude your husband, he'd have to scrawl, 'I leave absolutely nothing to my nephew Tiberius Manlius, because he is a foul-mouthed brute who insults me every time we meet, he poisoned my dog and he stole my silver. Anyway, I hate the idiot's face.' That would do it."

"I don't think so," I answered mildly. "I would be able to swear that Tiberius Manlius is exceptionally kind to dogs." Barley, who was in the room with us, looked up at me and wagged her tail.

"He gave you the puppy?" Mygdonius guessed.

"No. She came in off the streets of her own accord—but he encouraged me to let her stay. He deals with fleas. He built her kennel."

"Lawyers would love it." Mygdonius chortled. "Keep them happy for years. But if you ever got a court to see it your way, being excluded by Tullius Icilius would be unduteous to the aedile."

"Then what happens?"

"Will is not valid. Tullius is intestate."

"So the rules kick in?" I did know something about wills.

"Dodgy," Mygdonius disagreed. "Tullius has no sons, grandsons or brothers: bit of a predicament, if you are old school. No agnates—that's no descendants through a male line."

"Tiberius Manlius is a nephew."

"Sister's son. A hard-liner would say your doggie-lover gets nothing under the rules."

"Him and, I assume, the three little ducklings, the great-nephews?"

"All cognates—blood relatives via Grandpa only. Grandpa's gone?" I nodded. "They lose out. Tullius has missed a trick. A man should ensure he has brothers!"

"And if not?"

"A praetor would have to adjudicate. Eight of those. Two civil, the rest assigned to special courts. Depends. The one you get *might* say he cannot change the law. They all love doing that. Cognates are viewed askance. Can be done, but many think including descendants through a female line is to be deplored."

"You're our expert. What do you think?"

Mygdonius forced himself to be cheerful: "I think, unless your husband showed up behaving like a foul-mouthed brute, then—with a hefty fee, of course—a praetor might be induced to decree favourably that this is what Tullius Icilius should rightly have done, so give the sister's son the loot."

"Very nice."

"Until a stream of wine merchants arrive with their unpaid bills." Uncle Tullius was a warehouse owner, a deeply canny businessman. There would be creditors, because he always delayed settling up as long as possible, yet I thought he would leave enough in the bank box to pay people off.

"What about the three kiddywinkles?"

"Descendants through his *sister* and her *daughter*? Oooh—horrible! The boys have no rights to anything unless Tullius specifies a reasonable gift because he's kind-hearted. Or if he adopts them. Then they would become his agnates."

"He won't. He thinks they whine too much." So did I, yet I could see Gaius and Lucius ending up as our own snivelling agnates. Their father was a liability; I was pretty sure Tiberius wanted to take full responsibility for at least our two, out of love for his dead sister. "Could Tullius adopt the aedile?"

"Too old. Only allowed with a minor."

I shrugged. "Well, we're not expecting the dear old uncle to pop off yet. So why all today's fuss, Mygdonius?"

"His way of life."

"His way of death, you mean?" I chimed in.

"You're a charmer! Some men love to pore over their memoirs, their army life, travels and love affairs. Others write their wills. Tullius Icilius enjoys deciding who he hates this month. Then he raps out a codicil obliterating them: 'Odoriferus is an arsehole.'"

"Is Odoriferus another hypothetical name?"

"Like Titius? No, he's pure Mygdonius. So: 'this codicil,' Tullius will rant in fury, 'overturns every previous bequest.' Sometimes he'll be feeling clever, so he'll go the whole way: 'I leave that piece of filth Odoriferus my sole bequest: a rope to hang himself.' I always encourage specifics. When people are weeping while a will is read, a little joke keeps the mood light. Either way, Odoriferus gets the bum's rush."

"Until the next revision supersedes the overturning?"

"Could be, but once Tullius falls out with somebody, the bile tends to linger."

"I must tell my husband to be careful!"

"Oh, he's safe. Old Tullius always says the same about the aedile: 'He's a double-dyed devout tight-arse who broke my heart with his divorce, but he's all I've got. He keeps coming around looking hopeful. I'd better stick him with a bit.' Don't ask how much. The witnesses roll up trying to sneak a peek, but he never shows anyone his real intentions."

Tiberius Manlius did *not* keep visiting his uncle in the hope of gain. I knew he stayed close out of dogged affection—even though Tullius had long ago gathered the family finances so tightly into his own hands that Tiberius could lose everything. At risk was even his inheritance from his parents, which Tullius had shamelessly grabbed, claiming that at sixteen Tiberius had been "too young to look after money," and had never handed back.

Last year, the supposedly feckless nephew had been given cash to buy and renovate our house when we were married, but Tullius always made out it was a gift, practically with loan status, extracted from him by a trick. He liked to imply I was a gold-digger, who had put Tiberius up to it.

I suspected that my devious father, Falco, had helped nudge the uncle. When two very different families are cobbled together because of a love match, there is bound to be jostling. Luckily, Tullius and Falco had each aimed to look more generous towards us than the other. "It's your choice," mine had said, not noticeably joking. "You can have it now, or when I croak."

"*Now*, Papa!" I whipped back. "In case you throw it all away on gambling and loose women." My father rarely gambled; he said he was no good at it. I never dared to speculate about the other temptation, for which he always implied he had a lot of talent.

I could have made myself anxious about this new will, but too many families are destroyed in that way; in the long run, there is nothing you can do about it. Instead, I wondered who might have laid claims on the leavings of Appius Tranquillus Surus. When he died, how many possible hangers-on had lined up? And how good was his executor at dealing with them?

"Mygdonius, I can't find out who an executor was."

"Be in the will."

"Nobody has the will."

"Oh, you're stuck, then!"

My meeting ended when Gratus collected the empty tray. Mygdonius then lost interest. I took him to the door, in case Rodan was too busy to let him out properly.

Since I had told him about my case, the expert felt obliged to bestow wise words upon me: "Never you mind looking for the will in your case," he counselled. "You want to find the poisonous pile of codicils. Pick out any that look forged. They'll have a lot to tell you. If a will ever does turn up, check whether any scribe wrote in a clause to give a big treat to himself. That sort of fiddle gets slotted into many wills. But the codicils are bound to hold your answer, Flavia Albia!"

XVIII

If the Tranquilli could not find the main will, I supposed there was no chance of turning up codicils either, but I might as well suggest they looked.

We had hit the lull just after lunch. Either nobody would be at home, or people might lurk at the apartment, thinking they were safe from me because I had a family to supervise. Any family of mine had to get by without me. I left the boys with their nursemaid, Corellius with Marcia, the steward making a dinner menu for the absent cook.

I suggested Dromo should brush the donkey, but my husband, like me, was going out. He took both the donkey and Dromo. This fell short of a full escort but was a larger signal of status than he normally bothered with. I raised my eyebrows, so he had to explain.

When he visited Uncle Tullius that morning, he had learned that his ex-brother-in-law, "the ridiculous twerp," would be rebuilding a warehouse that had burned down at Saturnalia during a vigiles drinks party—as fire-brigade venues often did. Tiberius was hoping to acquire the rebuilding contract; he planned to fleece the twerp through some wriggle (as he called it) that involved Fountain Court; this presumed that Trajan's agent could first be smooched into awarding Tiberius the Eagle Building's demolition contract, with its free reusable bricks . . .

I had married a Roman. He had looked upright and reverent, but his love of tradition included ancient business practices. I ought to have expected this.

"The agent comes from Spain, darling?" That might make the man ignorant of Roman scams.

"No, Umbria. Everyone thinks the big noise Trajanus is Spanish. He was born in Baetica, but only because his family had gone out there to 'help exploit neglected local assets.' The Ulpii are rooted in the bedrock of northern Italy. But they can recognise an exploitable asset in a provincial situation. Baetica has gorgeous produce—olive oil, grain, honey, wine, fish sauce, fish, esparto grass, cinnabar, precious metals—"

"And rabbits!" I carolled merrily. It was inevitable that get-rich-quick ex-pats with senatorial ambitions (let alone imperial ideas, as we learned later) had left people of inferior rank to develop such things as rabbit supply lines—even though their own future route to the high life in Rome would hardly be superior, if it was via a house on the none-too-desirable Aventine.

Tiberius and I went our ways to different parts of the hill. I took the now familiar route to Sidewind Passage, where I was soon gazing at the tolerable tenement that had originally been rented by Tranquillus Surus. Before I went in, I mooched among the street-level shops, making myself agreeable. I stayed out of the garum cave, but acquired useful provisions elsewhere. Fornix might not thank me, but in the pottery shop I was lured into buying one of those cute pastry moulds: a rabbit with his paws stretched out. I am rarely a soppy woman, but those pie shapes are irresistible.

Now that I knew the kind of questions to ask, information flowed freely. Once I'd got the pot-seller talking, others clustered around us, happy to enlighten me. I asked if anyone could remember Surus; all those I spoke to that day were too young or had arrived after he was gone. But they readily talked about the current occupiers.

Life was not free of friction between the retailers and the upstairs tenants. The Tranquilli were not quite the neighbours from Hades, but people described them as pernickety diddlers, all out for themselves. They hogged the water-carrier. They never swept the pavement. Contention over a sponge-merchant's barking dog rankled bitterly. Arguments about carts flared on a daily basis; delivery problems were a fact of life for shop-owners, with inevitable noise and donkey droppings, though it seemed the worst offenders were those who brought in goods for Aprilis. The rest were reticent about this, but the basket-seller muttered that a heavy amphora cart had run someone over once. "Horrible sight!" The others stopped him, as if still shocked and unwilling to talk about it.

Instead, I encouraged them to bad-mouth individuals. They happily responded. Euhodia was pushy (which they almost admired), her sister-in-law Marcella Maura kept herself to herself (reckoned to be rude), the two brothers were at each other's throats.

"Why is that?" I asked innocently.

"Old scores!" they said, grinning salaciously. I could tell everyone knew about the seduction of Cosconia Saba.

No one ever saw much of Aprilis's son Januarius, who was nice enough, but always off in court.

"What's he done?"

"He's the plaintiff usually. He'll sue anyone for anything."

"I thought he was the decent one."

"Not if you leave a bucket where he can fall over it. He has a brother who's a lawyer. Used to tell him how to claim for broken bones—whether he actually had them or not."

"Handy."

"Was, until the brother ran away."

"What had he done?"

Noses were tapped. They implied more unmentionable scandal.

"Januarius's son is off the scene too."

"Bad parenting?"

"Nice lad but never had ideas of his own. When his uncle did a flit, he must have copied him. Similar types if you know what we mean."

"No reason for the bunk?"

"No one says. Secretive lot."

"Oh, so there are secrets?" Everyone chortled.

People in the alley were fully aware of Mardiana's affair. They were all waiting for her husband to find out. Aurelius Turbo, derided as a dim dupe, would cling to her, refusing to believe anything bad of his wife. People were waiting enthusiastically to watch him face it. "He thinks she's a cracker—he needs to get his eyes looked at."

Nobody could give the mystery lover's identity. Some, who bought snacks at Nobilo's, reckoned to have seen him there, but if they were right, Mardiana's squeeze was a younger man, much better-looking. Besides, sometimes she sneaked out while Januarius was on his frequent visits away because of the sheep breeding, or pushing writs in court, so it couldn't be him. I said gravely that I was intrigued by how thoroughly people here kept notes. They assured me they never took any interest in their neighbours' troubles. We all laughed.

The late Cosconia Saba had been a pleasant woman, people agreed, though her two brothers, sinister bakers who came on the scene occasionally, were hard men, whom nobody wanted to cross. For me, the most interesting thing to come out was that the bride whose position I was to safeguard, Cosca Sabatina, was viewed as a sneak with dangerous intentions.

"*Dangerous?*" I couldn't believe them.

"That minx is plotting a mountain of trouble. Everyone thinks she is a honey and hard done by, but it's all a wicked front. She's cold and she's devious. One day it will come out that she's a madwoman."

I wondered what my sisters would say about that.

Before I could seek more details, a small commotion in the roadway caused the shopkeepers to melt back to their premises. They served any customers with one hand, while leaning their elbows on counters to look out. In Sidewind Passage, being nosy was the way of life.

Beasts of burden were being loaded. I retreated to the pottery stall until the owner told me the man on the stairs to the Tranquillus apartments was Mardiana's husband. Wearing a big cloak and slightly ridiculous hat as he checked out his luggage, he was carrying a cylindrical scroll case under one arm, which, remembering he was a historian, I assumed was a convenient container for research material while he was travelling.

Aurelius Turbo must be leaving town. Rather than let him slip away unexamined, I nipped over and introduced myself.

XIX

Greetings. My name is Flavia Albia. I investigate family problems. You may have been told that I am assisting the Tranquilli with their status issues."

Perhaps because he knew so much history, the scholar faced the world uncertainly, with an attempted half-smile and simultaneously furrowed brow. His face was a very long triangle, with a high forehead, topped by crinkled brown hair. He had the thin frame of a man who was too busy with the magnitude of thought to remember to eat. If he did, he wouldn't be able to choose whether he wanted a damson tart or a raisin biscuit. Although he was making efforts to say which mule was to carry which of his bundles of property, the muleteers were ignoring his instructions. He might be a devotee of the political past, but this man had not studied life enough to know that is what muleteers have always done.

They would take his stuff. They would drop some in the road, let everything be rained on and steal small items, but most packages would arrive at their destination, perhaps even at around the same time as their owner. The unevenness of the bundles and bales, with occasional things sticking out, said this was not a trade consignment. That would be more regular, and better packed.

All I wanted to know was where he intended to take his baggage train. "I hope, Aurelius Turbo, you are not leaving your wife?" I really hoped he had not been told I was responsible for their fatal rift.

"Certainly not!" His response was crotchety, as if many other people had badgered him with the same question. "My wife has gone to the

Campagna so, of course, I am going after her." I flexed an eyebrow, not commenting. He could not bring himself to say the word "affair" but declared, "I know all about it."

If that was true, then legally he ought to be divorcing her. In a family that everyone called litigious, a notice of separation should have winged its way to her at the rabbit farm, or even have been delivered to her personally before she went. Again, I said nothing.

"I forgive her!" he declaimed.

He was not allowed to. Adultery—I mean adultery by women, though of course not men, since this was Rome—is a final act. Husbands have no discretion. Wives are damned. Our current emperor, Domitian, was extremely keen on censorial rectitude; once, when he had convinced himself his wife had been unfaithful with an actor, he banished her but soon recalled her "because he missed her." This sweet option was never available to other people.

"You forgive her? That's generous. But does Tranquilla Mardiana want to be forgiven?" Thinking of what I had been told about their supposedly distant relationship, I suspected she really hankered for a virile boyfriend.

"I shall persuade her to come back to me."

"Do you really expect that, Turbo?"

"Must happen. We were made for each other. We were irresistibly drawn together the moment we met. She may try to leave, but Mardiana knows she has to come back to me."

"That's romantic."

"No, it's a fact."

I could not see her being so compliant. I gave due consideration to the proposition that, despite her irresistible soul-mate (one who could so enliven the breakfast table with Rome's territorial disputes against the land-grabbing Samnites), Mardiana had regularly slipped out of doors to another, who bought her egg-and-cress and perhaps gave her a quick bunk-up in the Armilustrium. She might even have found it exciting that he took her to that stunning bar, the Stargazer, then brazenly left without paying.

How, too, could someone who wanted to impress with his elegant erudition feel darkly tied to a termagant who had thrown a jug at her dressmaker?

All right. Humans are sensitive. "I can see you love her very much," I said. It was not meant unkindly.

Turbo looked shocked by the word "love," but he had too much in-built politeness to guffaw. "Fate!" he responded gloomily.

"Oh, I see." Fate gets the blame for many events, especially those that are really caused by human selfishness and lack of conscience. "Well, it seems cruel to be fated to live on a rabbit farm. Gazing across endless pie-meat enclosures is a harsh punishment for a woman who has strayed, perhaps foolishly." I risked the key question: "Do you happen to know *who* has been luring your wife into the wrong arms?"

"I don't care who he is. The man is irrelevant." Wrong: that man's adventures with Mardiana might lead to disgrace, financial penalties and exile. If her behaviour was ever formally exposed, exile would be much worse than the rabbit farm: the law said she would have to take herself to a barren island and, as quickly as possible, die there.

I did a mental risk assessment, then owned up that I had been the messenger who brought news of his marital tragedy. Hardening my heart, I assured Turbo I was prepared to keep quiet publicly, but in return for my silence I had questions.

He was no use. I should have known. I might as well have tackled a brick wall. One with rising damp in its foundations.

He knew nothing about the status of Postuminus. Mardiana was fifteen years younger, born when Tranquillus Surus had been long dead. Turbo and his supposed soul-mate had made their vows after Postuminus and Cosconia Saba were already married; Sabatina was already a small, noisy child, with that family living upstairs.

I asked about Hedylla. Turbo told me she had never visited the Aventine, even after she had three children living there.

"Was Hedylla still alive when you married Mardiana?"

"Yes."

"Did she come to your wedding?"

"Hedylla? No."

"Had Euhodia, your mother-in-law, invited her?"

"I presume not."

"Hedylla was her mother. Your bride's grandmother."

"I suppose so."

"Then why was she barred? Didn't Euhodia and Aprilis get on with her?"

"It seemed they had grown up without ever being close."

"Did people in the family see Hedylla as a slave still?"

"Nobody talked about her."

"Why was that?"

"She never seemed to feature in their lives."

Turbo did say that when Hedylla was annoyed, she had quite a temper. Judging by his own wife, aggression ran in the family. Erotillus had told me Mardiana had once carved a lump out of Turbo using an ear scoop as a missile, though I couldn't see the scar. Maybe her volatility enhanced their magnetic attraction.

"Did your wife even know her grandmother?"

"She knew who she was. They would meet if my wife visited the farm."

"What about Postuminus and his mother?"

"He had been very much closer to Hedylla."

"Could that have been because when Postuminus was born Hedylla had been freed by Surus, so she was able to look after him but not the others, children she had had as a slave?"

Turbo only shrugged.

"Did you see *him* as a slave?"

"No. When I met him, after my marriage, he was living here as a freedman, like Euhodia and Aprilis." As if it were an afterthought he told me, "Hedylla never even came to Rome to visit Postuminus and Cosconia, didn't want to see the granddaughter, didn't make the journey even for her precious youngest."

"*Was* he precious to her?"

"Oh, yes."

I said I presumed Turbo himself had never met the woman. He came out with the fact that his own family owned property adjoining the rabbit farm; it was how he and Mardiana first met. He claimed he could not remember Hedylla any more than any other rural slaves Tranquillus

Surus had owned—but since his family were such near neighbours, and Turbo as a boy had spent a lot of time on the wrong side of their boundary, stealing rabbits, he had probably known Hedylla for much of his life.

That still did not help me. She was a slave. A rural slave, which was generally worse than being a city domestic. She would have been a possession not a person, barely a face among many anonymous workers. As the freeborn son of well-off property-owning parents, Turbo could not be expected to remember her.

There was more to it, however—once the lofty intellectual bestirred himself: "She did turn up in Rome, of course. She came to look after the darling one, after his wife died."

"Oh!" No one else had mentioned that. "I understand Cosconia Saba suffered badly in her final years. Did Hedylla come to help during her illness?"

"Not her. She always had a down on the daughter-in-law."

"Because . . ."

"There were stories."

"Aprilis?"

"Aprilis." Turbo sounded as if he knew of the seduction, yet he made no comment. "Hedylla wouldn't speak to Cosconia Saba. She only appeared after the funeral."

"That was about five years ago, I understand?"

"Yes, but Hedylla herself died too, oh, barely eighteen months later."

Even now Turbo did not think she mattered. I would have liked to ask what Hedylla died from, but all he wanted to talk about was being magically drawn to Mardiana when she was a young girl visiting the farm from Rome and how he had declared his attraction on one viscerally exciting day until, in the teeth of family opposition on both sides, they were married. I gathered that in any conflict about the pair uniting, Mardiana had never thought of lining up her granny to support her. Hedylla cannot have been viewed as a classic materfamilias.

"Why did your family disapprove, Turbo?"

"Why indeed!" he exclaimed wryly. "Well, it was only some of them." He chose to say no more. Possibly it was because he was a citizen and Mardiana a freedwoman's daughter.

Now their irresistible love-match had been plunged into disrepair. To me it was no surprise. And I had worked as a private investigator long enough to feel this was exactly the kind of stupid situation in which, probably in a haze of unplanned drunken sex, the parties were liable to rekindle their relationship.

Well, they might try. Some other informer might do well out of it later, when one of them suspected the other had yet again given them cause for divorce.

A carrying chair had appeared in the alley. It was lopsided and battered, with a pair of chairmen who were still picking lunch crumbs from between their gnarled teeth; it would probably only take its passenger to a stables on the city boundary where he could pick up wheeled transport for a more effective run out to the country. The mule train was ready to move off as Turbo jumped inside his chair and slammed the half-door, without formally ending our conversation. He had barely latched the handle when he ordered the bearers to go.

Only after the men had swung into motion did he lean out and yell back at me: "Forget the farm. The rabbits don't matter. It's the orchard everyone fights over." I had to suppose that a scholar who was in the process of documenting the causes of three Samnite Wars was well able to evaluate a tribal dispute. So, that was intriguing. "All the trouble," he bawled to me, and anyone else in Sidewind Passage, "has always been caused by the apricot trees!"

XX

I was not ready to broach Postuminus about his orchard. He owned it, he had assured me—yet Erotillus had accused him of being a regular liar. My sisters had reached a similar conclusion about him from his daughter. Given the awkward stories about his wife, I wanted to be sure of my ground before I next spoke to him.

Without approaching the upper apartment, I went into the main family rooms on the floor below. I had hoped to see Philodamus, the bookkeeper, who might know about any orchard dispute. However, my prophecy that a slave who spoke out of turn might be swiftly disappeared by his owners was brutally accurate. Philodamus had seemed such a respected servant, with charge of day-to-day bills and the petty-cash box, yet he had gone. A shifty lad let slip that he had been returned to his previous owner; this boy clearly regretted telling me, so I knew he had been instructed not to. Philodamus, who had come here as repayment for a debt, had now been ruthlessly pushed on his way again.

I guessed Mardiana was behind it. She had seemed angry when she found me chatting with Philodamus. She might now regret announcing the scandal of Aprilis and his brother's bride while the bookkeeper was listening. I could envisage her spitefully complaining to her mother that he was telling me too many family secrets. That would have provided cover for her own shocking outburst.

I had revealed her affair. This was to pay me back.

Luckily, the staff never tried to bar me. It had been known on other cases. I made sure not to question the admissions lad too closely; instead I tried to talk to Erotillus. He was still in service there, but I was told he was busy. Again, the lad wavered as he told me. I understood. All I could do next was gravely request a meeting with Tranquillus Januarius, saying quickly, "I had mentioned that I would like to speak to him when he returned from the farm. Just to complete my introductions to family members."

It sounded legitimate. I was placed alone in their general reception room, where eventually he joined me. A small nondescript slave followed him, then squatted near the door. Januarius confidently strode in and fell onto a couch.

It seemed a long time since my cousin had drawn his picture of the Stargazer's non-payer. I could just about see why those at Nobilo's had identified Januarius as the culprit. In his mid-forties, he did have a square head and regular features, with hair cut straightish, though no heavy fringe on his forehead, as the man in the sketch had because this man's hairline was receding like his father's. During introductory remarks, I asked if he realised he had a double who was going around the Aventine in a dark red cloak, up to no good.

He laughed and said he had heard something like that. "Is it right that he has been having an entanglement with Mardiana? He must be cracked." Januarius had a hearty baritone guffaw, full of easy joy; it confirmed what people said, that even though he was litigious, he was the most likeable of the Tranquilli.

I went quickly to my main question, but he could not help: Januarius was about the same age as Postuminus, so he, too, was too young to remember Tranquillus Surus, and knew nothing about the old will.

"In that case, I don't suppose you ever heard who his executor was? The old friend who came to the farm to arrange bequests?"

Januarius shrugged. I had no sense of him dodging the question, though he turned to the slave by the door, demanding refreshments. "Let's have a decent tray of stuff, boy. I've been travelling all day." If it was a distraction, it was smoothly done. I abandoned the will issue and waited while the slave quickly brought snack bowls and mulsum tots. Then I toyed demurely with almonds, while Januarius lounged on a couch, tucking in, with one slipper tapping a footstool. That could have been nerves, but he looked at ease.

I asked him about Hedylla, his grandmother. He had known her, but he claimed only slightly. Hedylla's role had obviously not extended to telling long stories of the family's past or giving wise advice to the young generation. Clearly this grandma never doted on her little ones, never gave them toys or secret sweets nor came up with pets their parents had already refused. Januarius could only confirm that when he knew her she always acted like a freedwoman. His parents, Aprilis and Marcella Maura, had assumed so. Januarius had always assumed it was true of his uncle Postuminus as well. "Bit of a pickle if that's wrong!" He sounded intrigued, not positively gloating.

Januarius could not remember Hedylla ever talking about Tranquillus Surus. "Postuminus told me Surus and Hedylla lived as man and wife—though your father did say 'when he was at the farm' as a qualification."

"Oh, you've met my father?"

"I talked to both your parents."

Januarius dived into a nicknackeroony crock of olives, neither commenting nor seeming disturbed by the thought.

I said, "I suppose when he wasn't at the farm, Surus was living here in Rome, in this apartment."

"Or at his house across town."

"Oh!" That was the first I had heard of a house across town. Januarius seemed to think I would know. "What happened to that?" I asked quickly. "Who lives there now?"

Januarius looked up, pausing his olive consumption. "Maybe he only rented?" he suggested, which in Rome was always likely.

"Otherwise when he died he must have left it to someone. None of you?"

"None of us," he agreed calmly. While I pushed away the almond saucer, he added, in the same civilised tone, "All a long time ago."

I dropped the subject. That was perhaps as he meant me to.

I did not ask about his father sleeping with his uncle's wife-to-be. I could see no easy way into that subject; this jovial man, relaxing at home after his winter trip onto the Campagna, might not appreciate the enquiry. His own mother, Marcella Maura, must have conceived him at around the same time, so it was tricky to probe. Marcella might even have been pregnant with him while Aprilis deflowered Cosconia Saba.

Some fathers-to-be stray precisely because they lose their bedroom rights when their wives are uncomfortably pregnant. Most don't do it with a brother's bride.

I still thought that if I could learn more about the two brothers' relationship, it might provide a clue, but I would not upset Januarius, easygoing though he seemed. Instead I took a new tack, delving into the suggestion that the apricot trees were contentious. "I met Aurelius Turbo." Januarius pulled a slight face. I saw he assumed I shared his view that the historian was cranky. "He told me to ask about the orchard."

"He told you to ask *me*?" asked his cousin-in-law in surprise.

"He wasn't specific. Who owns it?" I pressed.

There was a sudden change that made me jump. "Oh, no! Flavia Albia, do not ask me that!"

I was amazed by the fierce reaction. Tranquillus Januarius banged his small glass on a side table. His little slave looked scared.

He leaped up from the couch. Standing upright, he threw back his head and, to my astonishment, laughed loudly as if this was the best joke ever. The roar of amusement went on so long, with such gusto, I could only sit waiting for his explanation, with a faint polite smile.

When he quietened down, he began mopping his eyes and coughing, as if my innocent question had choked him.

"I am sorry," I ventured, as he resumed his seat, much more slumped than before. "Why was that the wrong question?"

"You don't know? You really do not know?"

"I do not. Postuminus told me the orchard was his."

"He would!"

"Not right?"

Januarius was losing his amusement. His mood became closer to despair. "Laying claim to the orchard is that numbskull's life's work. I think he'd jump in a bath and slit his veins if there was ever a settlement."

"Settlement? So someone disagrees about ownership?"

"Someone—and someone else—and practically everyone who has ever had any connection with the pestiferous place."

"Who exactly?"

"Everyone!"

I plunged straight in: "So what about you, Januarius? Do you think it is yours?"

Januarius barked with more caustic mirth. "I don't have to consider that—not yet. My father claims it whenever he wants a row with Postuminus—which is most of the time." I immediately saw that this orchard dispute might give me an explanation of the feud between Aprilis and Postuminus. It was the kind of fight that might rankle. Before I could ask, Januarius careered on, full of passion. "Let him argue—but he's not handing it on to me! When the pater passes, I will refuse being his heir if he tries to land me with the bloody orchard claim. It's poison. He knows I think that."

Given how much money can be acquired through fish pickle, I was startled. "You would give up the garum just to avoid the fruit?"

"The garum stinks." The old joke seemed to calm Januarius down.

"I have been told you enjoy judiciary arguments?"

"Not that one!" He became more earnest. "Listen. What I don't want, Flavia Albia, is endless years of legal action. Raging rows every dinner time. Pernicious scrolls piled in all the rooms of the house. Fees that would make your eyes water. Day after day taken up. No peace, no respite, no normal quiet family life. There are scores of those old apricot trees—and I hate every single bloody one of them."

"I hear they look wonderful at blossom time. But if you have abdicated from the argument, how are you involved?"

"I am not." A sudden new mood of depression swept Januarius. He crooned miserably, "I am not. Not now. I am never going to touch it."

"You have lost me."

"Never again."

"Explain, please," I insisted. "'Not now'? What happened before?"

"Those trees have done damage to my bloodline. I have lost enough through this—it has to stop. I'll do the damned rabbits. I'll breed sheep for sacrifice. I'll put my name to noxious sauce. I'll organise transports,

I'll haggle with hoary negotiators, I'll plead with indifferent customers, I'll load ballast into the stinking bowels of rotten ships with my own hands if I must, but I will never, ever involve myself in 'Who owns the orchard?'"

Januarius picked up his glass again. He filled it from the flagon, then tossed back the contents. He poured himself a rapid refill. Although he offered me another, I shook my head.

"Wise girl! Anyone who gets tipsy talking about that orchard could end up senseless in a gutter with a broken heart."

He quaffed and re-poured, shaking the now empty flagon at his slave, so he would run for another full one. I realised I had better squeeze this story out of Januarius while he still had control. "Tell me what exactly you have lost," I suggested, speaking quietly.

He gazed at me. It was a challenge. The cheery man who came into the room in the first place had now completely altered. His energy had faded. Sweat gleamed on his high forehead. He had the haunted look of someone who intended to share phenomenal grief. I felt myself brace as Januarius began.

XXI

By the time he finished, I would have come to the conclusion there were worse things in the world, though not if you were a participant. All anybody had to do with this dispute was walk away fast. Januarius knew that, though he had learned it too late. To live with the situation for year upon year must have been worse than stressful.

There had been a lawsuit over the apricot orchard for half a lifetime. I suspected I was not even being told the full version.

The land had been bought in the first place by Appius Tranquillus Surus. Januarius said that was the only point on which no one ever quibbled: Surus bought the land.

During his lifetime he was vaguely intending to do something with it, but Surus was no tree planter. His businesses covered meat or fish products. He had no interest in trees, which he saw as too slow an investment, with too many natural risks. So, at the time of his death, the land in question merely formed one packet of his general property, an asset he had never taken seriously.

Even so, that meant Surus must have left the land as a bequest in his will. So to whom? I might well ask, grumbled Januarius. Three generations had been arguing about ownership for over forty years.

My uncles, the Camilli, would say that looked an attractive case—but they would never touch it. In my head, I could hear Quintus muttering it was the kind of monster that would only wear them to ribbons. They'd spend all their fees on apothecary powders to dull the agony.

———

The Campagna is a low-lying, partly marshy, sometimes malarial agricultural area around Rome. It has a long historic past. Bordered by mountains on the horizon in three directions, and by the Tyrrhenian Sea to the west, it long ago became closely tied to the city, with market gardens producing vital fresh produce to feed Rome. It is fertile, but there are salt marshes. My father had relatives who lived there; he always spoke of them as hopeless losers trying to grow vegetables that hated wet feet. Their crops died all too frequently. Father thought dying would be the best solution for his relatives, too. He said it explained why Uncle Fulvius, the intelligent one, ran away to an eastern castration cult, then lived notoriously in Alexandria.

As Rome developed, the Campagna had grown into a desirable place for people with wealth to build second homes. It was close enough to the city to travel easily out to their estates, returning to Rome in a day whenever business in town or boredom with the country required. It was a good retirement area or a political retreat. Persons of leisure could imagine its misty mornings were romantic. Great names, and freed slaves who had once been the property of those great names—imperial nurses, wardrobe organisers and the like—had large villas there.

Grains and vegetables predominate but there are vines, with olive, apple and fig trees. Somebody near the Surus rabbit farm had decided to try more refined fruit. When Tranquillus Surus bought his extensive tract of land, it contained straggly, end-of-life cherry trees; they had produced barely a few bowls for consumption at the home farm. The cherries were now long gone. Around twenty years ago, apricots were planted as something more unusual. These could be harvested as fresh fruit for cooking or eating, or else dried for keeping. My home chef, Fornix, used apricots in many recipes.

I asked who planted the apricot trees, but Januarius was in full flow. He said Postuminus claimed the orchard through his mother, coming into possession after Hedylla died.

"That was only three or four years ago?" I managed to squeeze in. "Did she leave a will?" Free female citizens with property were allowed to do that. Slaves could not.

"You have seized on that because it argues that Hedylla must have been a freedwoman," Januarius agreed. "Of course, if she was *not* free, any so-called will would fail."

"Has that been an element in any legal arguments?"

"Partly."

"So those who say her will is valid must believe she was a free woman. She was able to call herself a wife to Surus, with the orchard left to support her in widowhood?"

"That would be so."

"Or, if not, who else claims the orchard?"

"Well, my father for one."

"Is his claim on the orchard why he quarrels with Postuminus?"

"No, he always has picked on him."

"Why?"

"Brotherly love."

"I see! So go back to the orchard please: up until Hedylla died, did she enjoy its produce without any problem?"

"No, not at all. You are talking about my family! There have always been problems, especially over who could pick the fruit."

I hate a fruit-picking controversy. You can never really solve them. Whatever the proper rights in the case, people just go along with baskets and help themselves.

The dispute was on several fronts, Januarius told me, including a quarrel about a neighbour's boundary fence that had actually turned violent. As a result, the Tranquilli had to contest a bitter compensation claim for a broken shoulder.

"Someone hit the neighbour?"

"It was complicated," muttered Januarius.

"Surprise me!"

"I was not present myself. Postuminus was on the scene, and had probably started the war of words on our family's behalf. He never knows when to keep his mouth shut. Even so, from what I can gather, Hedylla struck the first blow."

"Hedylla!"

"Nobody ever messed with her. Our neighbour fired up and came back at her. That was ridiculously brave! Hedylla was strong enough to pull calves out of their birthing mothers when the farmhands couldn't manage it. However, his shoulder was actually broken by Telesphorus. In his defence, Telesphorus was trying to hold the combatants apart. He was being whacked with a fence post for his trouble, so he decided to put a stop to that. Telesphorus never had much sense."

"Who," I squeezed in resolutely, "is Telesphorus?"

"Mardianus Telesphorus. Husband to my aunt, Euhodia. Father of five, four of them now serenely creating very pleasant families of their own a long way from here—plus the famous Mardiana. Not so pleasant. Surprising, in fact, that you revealed she has a lover!"

"Afraid so. Your double. Nobody has mentioned Telesphorus."

"No?" Januarius acted out genteel surprise. "Well, he was fairly forgettable. Anyway, he died."

"Not because of the fence fight?"

"Cannot be proved."

"Really?"

"He was overweight and had a heart attack. It could have been stress—or the physical effort. He collapsed not long after the incident, though the other side's lawyer would never agree he was a victim of the physical debacle."

"Who was the other side's lawyer?"

"Some basilica hound called Honorius."

I knew somebody of that name so I pricked up my ears. I might be able to get the inside story here. "Did this Honorius make any counterclaim?"

"Provocation, mainly. And he tried saying our action was time-expired. Euhodia wasn't too troubled—the marriage had more or less run its course. They were too young. I understand my father told them so at the time—no one knows how they stuck together for so long . . . Even so, when Telesphorus copped it, my aunt thought she ought to make the effort. Wifely responsibility. Demonstrate respect to the father of her family, or at least show thanks for his years of putting up with her and for giving her at least some likeable offspring."

"How did the suit end?"

Januarius sighed. "I suppose it did end. Our side was paid off by the neighbours with cash and goods. We dropped our claim against them, to shut them up about the broken shoulder. There must have been blame on both sides."

I nodded. "Like most litigation, the futile demands for justice had little chance of satisfaction?"

"No real point," agreed Januarius.

"And I suppose it has been very expensive? No one can now afford to pay compensation anyway, because all their money has been guzzled away in legal fees. If you have sons," I concluded, "train them as lawyers!"

"I don't need the advice," said Tranquillus Januarius in a hollow voice. "I have both a brother and a son in that profession."

This, it turned out, was why earlier he had spoken so dramatically of damage to his bloodline.

His younger brother, who was called Julius, had been trained in law during the period when the Surus freedmen were establishing themselves. While starting out on his career, Julius was asked to represent Euhodia; it was a kind offer for her promising young relative but also, of course, made to him because he came cheap. Trouble with the neighbours was already rumbling. Years before the claim for Telesphorus's death there had been trouble with dogs getting in. "We realised later who must have been involved." Then another row about rabbits escaping. A counterclaim was made for intentional damage to rabbits. The boundary fence dispute happened later. Julius became entwined in that. At first he believed he had fallen on his feet; it looked like a really good opening, a big case that might establish his reputation at the Basilica Julia. As ramifications draggled on interminably, Julius saw that even a much more experienced lawyer, with less of a conscience about never solving anything, might have been swamped. It preyed on his mind; he became deeply troubled.

Januarius had never grasped everything since his brother was reluctant to discuss the embroilment. After a valiant struggle, Julius finally gave up on the Telesphorus suit. New arguments were about to be presented by the other side, which, to his despair, made all his previous work pointless; he was also terrified that his own reputation would be traduced because of something Euhodia and Aprilis had made him do. He upped sticks, left home with mutters and sheep-shearing and vanished. When it became obvious he might never return, his wife considered dying of grief but instead divorced him.

I did not ask about the wife. She had returned to her family, I had enough to contend with.

Januarius also had a son, called Augustus. I remembered that the street traders called him "the dopey one." He had begged to be a lawyer too, convinced he could succeed where his uncle had failed. Yes, Augustus was one sardine short of a full creel.

Januarius had reluctantly agreed, since Augustus easily forgot all he had witnessed his uncle Julius enduring and announced that the law was his route to wealth, women, wine and fame. Nobody could argue because the same reasons had been initially given to Julius when, as a freedman's child, he was actively encouraged to take up a legal career. So Januarius had had to cave in, though he stipulated Augustus must not involve himself in his own family's complex affairs. "I told him I would pay for his training with a glad heart, but he must promise never, ever to touch the litigation that destroyed my poor brother."

"Has it worked?" I asked, already in trepidation.

"Of course not," replied Januarius, quickly becoming satirical. "My son will always be a trouble to me—for many reasons. I can only hope we can keep his situation quiet, unlike his uncle's. Julius may have seemed to disappear out of the blue, but rumours have been surfacing. He has been accused of bestiality with a goat, a charge he only escaped by fleeing to Belgica, funding himself with money he had stolen from three of his clients."

By now I was running out of ways to look sympathetic.

Januarius then told me his brother had a fine mind and a good heart, "but was betrayed by his innocent over-enthusiasm."

I was beginning to believe none of this family was innocent of anything. "I am sure it will all turn out to be a mistake," I murmured, to encourage the downcast relative.

The poor sap said he hoped so. Screwing a goat was just about acceptable, but Belgica would take some living down.

XXII

To spare Januarius, I left him alone. I was not sure I believed his stories, but they did illustrate genuine misery as a son, brother and father. I could only applaud how he endured this, yet stalwartly managed to clear a row of snack bowls. He had emptied them all one-handed, while gripping his wine so tightly his knuckles whitened and I feared for the beaker.

His small nervous slave showed me out. I did not question him.

After the apartment door shut behind me, I had much to contemplate. I took the steps down slowly because the staircase was dark, steep and treacherous; in Sidewind Passage I paused. Needing to collect my pie mould, I went across to the stall, where I then stood staring back at the Tranquillus tenement.

"Want a dormouse-fattening pot?"

"No, thanks. My cook would rebel."

Just as the seller was parcelling my rabbit mould, our attention was caught by a short, loud bout of filthy language up above.

My father says, when things grow too quiet, expect a madman to burst in through a door waving a very sharp knife. What happened next was certainly unexpected. There were actually two madmen in the building I had just left; fortunately, neither had weapons.

The bawling stopped, replaced by sounds of unnatural activity. A series of agitated bumps and bangs came down the staircase that served all the apartments. With a final crash, a pair of bodies locked in a crazy hold flew out through the narrow entrance.

"Oh, not again!" grumbled the ceramics man. A nearby colleague who sold baskets actually pulled down his shutters with a look of disgust.

The first combatant, a heavy bruiser, fell into the alley backwards. I winced as his head cracked on the ground. The other was being physically towed by him; that man had snatched at the door lintel as they tumbled through, but his hands failed to take hold, so he was pulled face-down on top of his assailant, who was half throttling him. At least it was a softer fall. The first still refused to let go of the second's clothing, his big fists tightly gripping the shoulder folds of a twisted toga, so they lay there temporarily, tangled together, until the one who had fallen backwards abruptly went limp.

Everyone in the alley stopped what they were doing. No one ran to help.

There was a stunned pause.

"One of the bakers," the ceramics seller enlightened me. "Elder Cosconius. If he croaks, his brother will definitely not like this!"

I would have moved forwards, but a couple of attendant types who had been standing lower down the street came to life and rushed up. Dressed in flour-dusted tunics and with strong arms from dough-kneading, they seemed to belong to the unconscious man; they began urgently assisting, so the crock-seller and I remained by his counter, watching.

The contestant who had sprawled on top flailed, freed himself, edged off his dead-to-the-world playmate, then crawled to a house wall where he managed to pull himself upright. Groaning theatrically, it was Postuminus. He had a black eye, a split lip and after his tumble down four flights he was filthy and woozy; otherwise he looked unhurt.

More footsteps, lighter ones, pounded downstairs. Two women jostled irritably as they pushed out through the entrance arch. First came Cosca Sabatina, the bride-to-be, wailing, then Tranquilla Euhodia, my client, tight-lipped.

If young Sabatina had been involved in the fracas upstairs, she had managed to remain completely neat, not a fold of her wheat-coloured gown looked out of place, not a rich girl's earring had been lost. She adopted an attitude of concern. Fingertip to her lips, like a shame-faced innocent, she simpered at Postuminus, "I never meant this to happen!"

Her aunt rounded on her. Remembering how Euhodia had hired me saying that this young girl was loved by everyone, her asperity intrigued me: "Oh, don't you worry, precious. Nobody will blame you!" No one hearing this would know Tranquilla Euhodia had once claimed she wanted to help her niece. She was now a judgemental family matriarch who could barely contain her fury.

Sabatina kept her poise. "What could I do? Uncle Lucius came asking about progress on the wedding. He wanted to know what the hold-up is. I had to tell him everything."

"How they want your father's status regularised?"

"Not only that . . ."

"What?"

Sabatina sounded much too meek. "It somehow slipped out that I had overheard you shouting at Philodamus because he'd been gossiping about my mother and Aprilis."

"You stupid girl!" Euhodia exploded. "You shouldn't have been listening and you shouldn't have passed it on. You knew what would happen. Nothing ever needed to be said to Lucius Cosconius. Get back indoors. Take your father up and look after him."

"He says he may not be my father!"

"Oh, this one is your father, all right. You both have the same stubborn wickedness."

Although covered with bruises after a brawl, Postuminus didn't look bad enough to squash a spider, not even a scary fast-moving one. "He wanted to kill me!" he complained ineffectively.

"Pity he failed!" snapped the matriarch. "You're still in one piece. Stop whimpering." Euhodia was my kind of older sister. Gone was all trace of the woman who had entertained me with violet wine. Not only was she standing for no nonsense, her scorching tone had hints of pent-up violence. She switched her attention to the man on the ground. "Is he dead?"

"Not quite."

"That's a shame!"

The concussed uncle had begun to rouse himself blearily. A retainer ventured to tell Euhodia, "He's going to sue you to Hades and back for this . . ." Incongruously, the accuser concluded with a lame salutation of ". . . *Domina*."

"Come one, come all!" Euhodia scornfully spurned the threat. "But if he wants to see the girl married, he won't upset the Venuleii with this kind of stupidity. Let's pray they don't hear about it. The brothers know damn well we have to behave impeccably. Carry him home, put a poultice on his head, then make him rest up. I don't want to see the Cosconii here again until we are ready. I shall send word when people can turn up in wedding outfits."

Euhodia stomped back indoors, shooing her brother and his daughter ahead of her. Postuminus was heavily limping. Sabatina was screwing her fingers into her eyes, though in my opinion not genuinely crying.

Business in the street resumed at once, as if such altercations happened all the time. The one door that had remained firmly closed throughout was that of the garum shop run by Aprilis, but it probably had a security squint that anyone could have been looking out of to watch the fracas.

I went up and banged on the first apartment door, wanting to see Euhodia in private. Nobody would answer. I took the extra flight to where Postuminus lived: same result.

On the whole this was probably as well. Now I had seen and heard how bloodthirsty they could be, I preferred not to ask aggravating questions, in case some member of this wild family broke my new rabbit pie mould.

XXIII

Fornix was unimpressed by my cute crock. I warned him the same stall-holder sold dormouse pots. He said if I wanted to eat vermin, I should never have hired a chef. A doctor would have been more useful.

His speciality was fish—or it had been, until his falling out with our fishmonger.

"Any sight of a peace treaty yet, Fornix?"

"The man is a vile cheat."

"No pan-fried little picarels then?"

"I don't bugger about with whitebait. I have brought home a sea bass," snarled Fornix, smoothing his apron. "Why do you think I went to see my brother?"

"To get away from people here quarrelling?"

"I have worked at the legendary Fabulo's!" the cook reminded me pompously. "After all my years of that clientele, I know how to close my kitchen door and ignore any idiots outside."

His brother on the Esquiline, who was also a family cook, must have his own supplier under control. The bass was a beautiful piece of fish. Fornix gave it to us baked in his small home oven, with a semi-tart sauce that contained anise and chopped pears, the pears I had over-bought two days ago. If only my investigation was coming together so well.

After the home altercations earlier, everyone remained subdued. They ate their dinner quietly, while I watched over the proceedings like a cockatrice who could slay with her mere breath. The mother-goddess might have left them to their devices all day, but now everyone had better mind their manners or be turned to stone. By the time we reached

126

the grapes and cinnamon biscuits, my house resembled a *Teach Yourself* book on etiquette.

Marcia and Corellius slunk off upstairs at the first opportunity. Dromo laid out his sleeping-mat, huffing loudly. Fornix was standing at the kitchen door, brawny arms folded, counting in food bowls; he would match up any leftovers to whichever guilty parties had sent them back, then march out to interrogate them on whether they had lost their appetites or were they suggesting there was something wrong with the food. Luckily tonight he was satisfied. Some bowls had even been licked.

We were rewarded with tiny cassia bark treats. Fornix brought them out from his den on a silver comport. He had held it back until he saw we were grateful enough for the previous courses.

Left to ourselves, Tiberius Manlius favoured me with a huge grin. He knew I had been controlling the crowd like a tyrant. While topping up his own beaker modestly, he made a great play of flavouring a new drink for me with three cloves and a scratch off the top of the honey pot, stirring them in with the end of a spoon and a delicate gesture.

"Thank you, Faustus, dearest. Now stop pretending to be terrorised."

We chinked. We sipped. We smiled lazily as we settled back into each other's company. Married life had its moments.

I asked about his day, then brought him up to date with mine. I said the Tranquilli needed to sit down together more, with a good dinner, the way we did; my feeling was that none of them appreciated either the warm social intercourse we encouraged or the excellence of our table.

Since Tiberius claimed to have been brought up a country boy, I questioned him about birthing calves. He pulled a face. "If she helped with that, Hedylla must have been a strong woman."

"Apparently so, and they say she had a temper too."

Tiberius reached over to neaten the collection of bangles on my arm; I could rarely be bothered to fiddle with them, as some women do, so as usual they were askew. I let him line them up as a kind of caress. "So," he asked, smiling, "do you think Hedylla beat old Surus to death, and did it with a milking stool?"

"She worked in the house."

"Distaff then?"

"Could be. Falco and you must be so glad Mother and I have forbidden the traditional spinning nonsense in our homes. Upset us, and we won't own any dangerous equipment."

"I don't relax, Albia. I never forget that you know where the mallets are kept."

"I think I'd choose the big club hammer," I decided. "Stun you quickly. I wouldn't want to cause a man of mine unnecessary suffering . . ."

I told him about the fight I had seen. "Postuminus and one of his brothers-in-law scrapping. I would try to see Lucius Cosconius tomorrow for a talk about it, but from the look of him, it will be some while before he is capable of speech. Maybe I ought to confront Euhodia, question why she has been lying about relationships between her brothers."

Tiberius disagreed. "From what you say, she won't tell you."

"You're right. She's more likely to shove me off the case. I don't really know why she hired me."

"You just happened along, bearing Junia's unpaid bill. Spur of the moment."

"And now she regrets it?"

"How could anyone regret you?" Under the easy small-talk, Tiberius was thinking. "Listen! If Julius and Augustus have both gone their own ways, there has to be a lawyer somewhere, applying himself to all that litigation."

He was right. "How can I find out? Without telling the family?"

Tiberius had an answer: "Go to the basilica, shout, 'Who handles the Tranquillus case?' then watch all the other lawyers screaming with laughter."

I told him that would be an unseemly way for a woman to behave, and he chortled so when had that stopped me?

XXIV

Contacts: a good informer needs contacts. Next day, I managed to acquire what I needed, picking up my lead from a man I knew already.

I had decided to ask Honorius. Januarius had mentioned him; if it was the same person, he was a basically competent legalist my father sometimes had dealings with. My family first met him the year I came from Britain. Pa had been risking his bank box in suing people, then being sued himself.

Honorius had been a junior to Silius Italicus, a grandee in the courts and in politics. That big beast was a powerful, unscrupulous, dangerous senator, a consul and provincial governor with a dirty past he was quite open about and a filthy future ahead of him. Silius had called himself an informer once, but he was the kind who divvied up false prosecutions for crooked emperors. A deviant who created a bad reputation for the whole profession, the word "corrupt" had been invented for him. It remained unclear how much had rubbed off on Honorius, but training under Silius Italicus certainly gave him presence. Father kept up with him. Falco always loved the piquant thrill of working with people he despised. Even I had filed his name in my memory, just in case I ever needed a basilica prowler's input.

Short and neat, Honorius had looked about eighteen originally; he still did, even though he, too, was a senator, albeit one who could never pay his way up the full *cursus honorum*. Instead of holding flashy posts, he had acquired fifteen years' solo experience in law, and must be around forty now.

Helena Justina had always thought he was a mother's boy. His tender mama must have died by now. His crinkled hair had receded and gone partially grey; it was now a tad too long as if no one reminded him when he needed a barber. He imagined himself taller, sharper and handsomer than he really was; otherwise I could not fault him. Though lean, he kept fit and had always been good-looking; certainly at fourteen I had noticed him.

Now I was twice that age and a married woman, one who did not feel it necessary to mention Honorius to her husband. Tiberius had rushed breakfast, off on a site visit to a temple restoration. I had been persuading little Lucius not to throw goat's cheese around. There was no reason for secrecy. My plans for the morning simply never came up.

It was one of the few days in the month when legal action was permitted. I had come down from the Aventine into the main Forum Romanum, where I pulled my stole over my hair, tripped up the shallow steps where the board games are scratched, and trotted into the Basilica Julia trying to look like a simple-minded widow who wanted a hack to hire.

The enormous spaces would daunt anyone nervous. There was a huge main hall with a polychrome floor where I knew from experience you could easily slip on the well-trodden marble; it was surrounded by white marble side aisles, with a public gallery above. Since the building housed not only a mix of courts, but administrative offices and even shops, finding one man in the throng required luck and a professional instinct. I wasted time in one of the aisles, but was then drawn to the right area. At least I knew what my quarry looked like. Nobody would have pointed him out.

Honorius was hanging around, eyeing up his rivals, while they all loafed in the post-Saturnalia lull, pretending to be swamped with sestertius-rich plaintiffs. None seemed to have any. Luckily, instead of serving writs they could waste their past earnings on trinkets for their mistresses, slim scrolls of epic poetry (even one by Silius Italicus, now venturing grandly into vanity publishing) and, like everywhere else, snacks.

130

I found Honorius beside a food stall, applying his fine legal mind to the merits of stuffed vine leaves versus fried curd-cheese balls. He asked my opinion. I said it depended on his gall bladder. For me, *globuli* would be tastier but if he was prone to heartburn, the fat was a killer. On the other hand, if they softened their vine leaves with vinegar before piling in the minced ingredients, he might find the acid too much.

He acknowledged that I was not simply queuing for a portion. "Were you looking for me?"

"My name is Albia. Flavia Albia." He did not remember me. "Falco's daughter."

"The unforgettable Didius! Does he have a task for me?"

"No."

"Your husband, then?" Honorius had immediately sized up my wedding ring. I don't hide it. At that point I had been married only four months and we had an honest arrangement. Both of us had rejected the other contenders and intended to stick at this union.

"No, not him either. I came on my own behalf."

"You need legal advice?"

"Information."

"Are you paying?"

"No fear. I am Falco's daughter. You know the score. I'll be calling in favours you don't realise you owe. Insulting you with stinginess. Picking your brains for nothing—though if you're any good, I will say a nice thank-you."

"Right."

"Helena Justina brought me up."

"At least that's encouraging!"

Honorius acquired a downcast air, thinking about the Didius rules of engagement. While he upset himself, we watched a fracas: a man screaming that he had been ruined suddenly ran up to an advocate and attacked him with a dagger. Ushers hauled him away as if they did it all the time.

"Nincundio." Honorius named him, showing no surprise.

The legalist who must have upset this Nincundio nonchalantly straightened his toga, mopping a small bloody scratch with its hem, then carried on talking to his companion. Judging by their animation, a chariot race was under hot discussion, with big money riding on it. Gambling was illegal; practising lawyers would be aware of that.

Unable to decide which snack had a better case, Honorius had purchased both, perhaps hoping they would cancel out each other on the way down his digestive tract; I suspected he would end up with double burps. While he munched, I summed up my inquiry, saying he could have the full scroll version if he was mad enough. "I'm told you have had a hand in this," I mentioned crisply, aware that I sounded like my father ordering a forum punk to cough facts and make it quick.

Honorius gave way with a hand gesture, as if surrendering to an opposing advocate. "Proving status? You will need the will."

"He wasn't born. Anyway, long-lost document."

"Give up, then!"

"Pessimist."

"Your father used to consult a testaments man—was he Scorpus?"

I remembered. "Old Fungibles, they called him. Grey weasel, worked from a hole-in-the-wall, acted for the worthy poor. Can't ask. He died."

"Fell off a roof or jumped down a well?" asked Honorius, naming two of the most common deaths in Rome. As an associate of my father, he was bound to go off into fantasies about the world we worked in.

I patiently went along with it. "Neither. Slipped on an oily patch at the baths, cracked his head on the rim of a huge marble basin."

Honorius demanded, "How did the bathhouse managers excuse that?"

"You are thinking failure in their duty of care?" I suggested. "No good. The floor-moppers were there and lifted up Scorpus, sent him home on their fuel donkey, dried him nicely first and found his tunic, even combed his hair over the enormous bump and gave him a packet of hot sausages from the trayman, gratis. Scorpus revived sufficiently at home to guzzle his free gift. Then, while chomping the last sausage, he choked to death on a piece of gristle."

"Trayman long gone?" Under my father's teaching, Honorius had turned into a realist.

"Scuttled to hide in somebody's backyard—then *he* fell down a well."

We sighed. Life was a bastard, Fate a bitch. Work, for any freelancer, was as elusive as Tiber mist.

"Your case," mused Honorius, finally addressing it, "sounds hideously familiar. Endless pleas and counter-pleas, involving a woman's estranged brother. Falco once told me she was half crazy. He said he could have coped with that—most of his clients were. 'But she talked a torrent, she smelt of cats and she drank . . .' Was her name Ursulina Prisca?"

"Juno!" I remembered Ursulina. "She'd been a midwife once. By the time we met her, she was just trouble. Whenever that old biddy came to our house, Father would sneak out the back way while Mother and I had to shoo her off. My task was to run in shouting, 'There's a fire on the roof! Mama, you must come at once!' Wasn't the brother a soldier, so he was permanently away from Rome? Letters took half a year to reach him, then he never answered anyway."

"Priscus the legionary," confirmed Honorius, darkly. "Where was he located? Cappadocia, Cilicia, Commagene? Some bloody unreachable outfit, starting with a C for Crap." Clearly it was a bad memory. "He's dead now. Falco said he would have sent the man a poisoned shirt much earlier, if only he had thought of it."

Honorius wiped his greasy hands on his toga. Like all togas in daily use, his garment showed signs of having been used as a napkin before. The great Cicero might rarely have had fish-pickle staining his purple status bands, but most men I knew thought if they were forced to wear national dress, its folds were convenient rags to soak up anything from spilled lamp oil to toupee glue. Wool washes well. That's what they all think, though I had heard Lenia at the old Eagle Laundry reckon you can never get out sealing wax.

"Priscus!" repeated Honorius, sounding as glum as a woodlouse under someone's boot. "Yes, I knew Gallicus Priscus. Priscus and his awful old sister. Your father beguiled me into taking that on. Falco was utterly slapdash—he called Ursulina a widow, though unusually she had never been married. He got her age wrong—he even said it was all about her brother's will, when they were really fighting over their father's. The damned brother was still alive when I got lumbered."

"I am sorry," I pretended.

"Lying is not pretty!" Honorius reproved me. "I can still hear your father blithely announcing that his own mother had palled up with Ursulina, and *her* advice was that the valuer had underestimated a walnut crop and I wasn't to trust the freedman with a limp . . . I do not know or care what stage this fiasco has reached nowadays—though some poor drudge will be handling it still, you can depend on it."

"Didn't the issue die with the soldier?"

"No—because he had *issue!*" That was his idea of a joke.

"Ursulina's brother had children? But soldiers cannot be married. It's deliberate. Their offspring are illegitimate foreigners who can be left behind in the provinces without any claim on the army or the soldiers who screwed their mothers . . ." Tactfully, I added, "Surely?"

"Discharged," said Honorius. "He was possibly cashiered for crime in the crappy province. Anyway, a little wife had popped up, with a daughter whose status had to be ratified, plus I believe some other infants—at least Falco had done the necessary on that aspect. My impression was that the soldier's diploma might not have been entirely legit. Aurelia—the wife's name, I recall—was provided with some suitable document, so Falco claimed what he passed to me was all straightforward . . . Bloody nightmare," Honorius reminisced, not holding back. "Angry women and crooked men romping all over the show. I'm just glad to be out of it."

"Poor you!"

"The little wife died eventually. Children became adults. Sprogs of their own now."

"Good to know," I purred.

Honorius became more excited: "You mentioned a disputed property—my ghastly project, I believe. Ursulina Prisca thought she ought to be getting benefits. The centurion reckoned he was a man with bills to pay so he should inherit. A completely different family, it turned out, had actual possession and were claiming squatters' rights. They were all grappling over both the land and a usufruct."

"Usufruct? Right to harvest the fruit? Was this about the apricot orchard?"

"Correct! Your father assured me it was just a few disputed punnets—then he buggered off abroad somewhere."

"Greece. Greece, then Alexandria," I was able to fill in. "I had arrived in Rome. They took me with them. What sileage had Falco dumped on you?"

"You sound like your mother," Honorius commented.

"I take that as a compliment."

I told him to buck up and describe the rotting mound of legal muleshit and any relevant law. The Twelve Tables on the duties and rights of citizens, lists as old as the republic and as clear as Tiber silt, had been giving this city a daily diet of failed conciliation for centuries; the man we had watched knifing his lawyer was a classic result. But I could not see how a litigious old lady and her brother, now both deceased and silenced, both urban free citizens, could tie in to my investigation of the Tranquilli, a still-active family of rural freed slaves. All I had come to find out was, after Julius ran away to Belgica, who was acting for them as legal adviser in his place?

Honorius sniffed. "The Tranquilli? Their name makes me shudder even now. My clients of yesterday owned the orchard where your clients of today had been given the usufruct. In the end, yours came to mine with written evidence that they claimed would change the situation: they presented us with a codicil."

Something clonked into place. A codicil? Mygdonius had been right to tell me to look for one. "Did you keep it? Can I see?"

"No. Their lawyer snatched it back in the end, nervous he would be accused of duplicitously writing it."

XXV

"W as it real?"

"It was false."

"Prove it?"

"I would have done."

"What was wrong?"

"Papyrus too new, ink not faded enough, wrong witnesses, iffy wording, smudged date, spelling error in the testator's name, all amateur but—"

"What?"

"They had used his seal."

"Whose seal?"

"The testator's."

"Don't mess me about, Honorius."

"I am so sorry," he apologised sincerely. "I must have worked alongside your jokey father for too long."

"He would say, 'Spill, Honorius!'"

"He would indeed—just before passing me the bill for his drink at the bar."

"Spill, then!"

"They were his freed slaves; they must have got hold of his signet ring. The counterfeit was alleged to be a revised bequest, written by a deceased party you have heard of: Appius Tranquillus Surus."

XXVI

The meet

Since Honorius had mentioned drinking with my father, I led him to a stall I knew, on the promise of a tot. He was not expecting a watery camomile infusion. I ruthlessly stressed its digestive benefits after eating snacks. The stallholder praised my product-placement but failed to offer me a free flatbread. I pointedly failed to tip him.

Honorius and I became two classic informers: squatting on uncomfortable stools in a dark corner, aiming to escape being trodden on by the public while we swapped depressing notes. All the scene needed was a drunken beggar and a rootling rat.

The catch-up

This was growing serious. To start at the beginning, we had to wade through formalities while our tea cooled. I trotted out my adoption, training by Falco and recent marriage to a magistrate.

Honorius had always been hoping to re-establish relations with his ex-wife. "She is still hitched to that other fellow she married when she left me. They have nine children, so I suppose I must start believing it is going to last."

"Fifteen years is a long cooling-off period. She's gone. Start a new life, Honorius!"

The sideways intro

Sipping our drinks, we could now ease into business. I explained how I had acquired my case after the Stargazer's unpaid bill. I even showed the sketch, which I was still carrying about.

Surprisingly, Honorius thought he had met Mardiana's lover among younger relatives of Ursulina Prisca and her brother. Without a clerk to jog his memory, he could not remember which. He only remembered two family members he called Witless G and Witless V.

"*Witless?*"

"Witness, then."

"Working with Pa made you frivolous! The rivets left in the saucer at our bar were military, but you can't be fingering the centurion. He died."

"Only about three years ago," Honorius reminded me.

"Tranquilla Mardiana is not a woman to have an affair with a ghost. If it were possible to punch ectoplasm, she would knock any spirit to oblivion."

Honorius agreed. "Not Priscus—though he would have pocketfuls of rivets. No legionary leaves with just a faded red tunic and a good word from their commander. They are given a diploma and maybe a chestload of thank-you medals, but they all reckon to retire loaded up with military paraphernalia. Ballista bolts, spades, non-standard daggers, boots, items that have walked from the stores . . ."

"You're sounding like Father again. So Gallicus Priscus bequeathed his eager heirs a crammed lean-to?"

"He was," said Honorius, heavily, "generally viewed as 'handy.' He must have left behind many jars of junk."

"I love a man who is handy!"

"You wouldn't love this one. The family used him as an enforcer in their property management. He had a terrible reputation. He threatened to use fortress nails to fix bad tenants down until they paid." Honorius shuddered fastidiously. "So I dare say he had horrible uses for rivets."

"When he passed on, Ursulina made you scrutinise his will?"

"Brutal: 'I leave my only sister a basket stall, so she may always have free cat baskets.' He did it too, the spiteful swine. He had fitted out premises specifically and installed a freedman to sell the wicker."

I groaned. "By this, he had demonstrated his intent, so his sister could claim nothing else. Don't look surprised, Honorius. I have already consulted a wills expert. Who inherited the bulk?"

"Must have been Witness G, the agnate."

"His son, as normal people would say?"

"I am following my client, Albia. Ursulina always called her brother 'the thieving agnate' and all his children 'the agnate's brats.'"

"If the agnate acquired the rivets, is your money on him for adultery with Mardiana?"

"Probably. As your father would say, I hate his haircut. But anyone could go into the shed and collect a handful of metal."

"All the family joined in the orchard dispute?"

"Half of them. Some of the women looked reasonable, but reasonable women don't often come my way."

"Working with my father definitely rubbed off on you! Right, better talk about this orchard some more. Give me what you know."

The warning notice

First Honorius appended a health-and-safety overview: "Flavia Albia, do not attempt to follow what I am about to tell you. You are entering a pitch-dark labyrinth where terrifying monsters lurk. No clue of thread can be long enough to guide you through."

"Dead ends and double-backs?"

"More loops than an eastern carpet." Despondently he added, "More fleas too."

"All right. I am itching," I hinted, "to hear how whatever you had to do for Ursulina Prisca touches my current investigation."

Crunch time

Honorius ran his hands through his crinkled hair. "It looked straightforward," he told me sadly. Even slumped in gloom, he was good-looking. Passing women stared, though in the basilica they were few. "The late Ursulina and her brother were, for years prior to their demise, striving to take possession of this piece of land."

"The orchard from Tranquillus Surus?"

"It had been left in trust to their uncle for them."

"Ursulina and her brother?"

"Ursulina *or* her brother. One of many issues they quarrelled over."

"When could one or both acquire it?"

"After the old uncle died."

"Did he ever die?"

"Must have done." Honorius immediately looked doubtful. "Nobody bothered to pass any details to me, of course! The siblings were themselves not young, even when I knew them. He must have been decrepit."

"And what was he to Surus?"

"No idea. Leaving him the orchard could have been payment for a debt—or the two men may simply have been friends."

"Could the uncle have been the missing executor in the Surus will?" I sounded hopeful. Honorius shook his head vigorously. I was glad he had no dandruff in that crinkled hair.

"Don't waste time pursuing it, Albia. I knew only that her uncle was holding this orchard for Ursulina. Or for her brother, her brother maintained."

"You never met him, this old uncle?"

"Never had a need."

"Oh! Didn't my father train you to be thorough?"

"Falco had bunked off abroad. I used my judgement."

"Fine. Get on. The orchard comes to the nunc after Surus dies—"

"And the two beneficiaries immediately start arguing. There wasn't much point. The land alone was of no real benefit. Any produce arising had been bequeathed to some freed slaves—your clients, we have established—an extra complication."

"Was that usual?"

"Freedmen tend to be looked after."

"And Surus, I'm told, was a nice man who would do that. So why the arguments? Was it just brother and sister?" I asked.

"No, Ursulina and Priscus were aggrieved at the freedmen, whom they wanted to clear off the land. The freedmen refused to go. But my side were also in conflict with each other. Priscus didn't want his sister to inherit anything." I made a rude noise. Not counting that as a proper rejoinder, Honorius continued pompously, "Ursulina Prisca insisted their uncle had assured her it would give her some security."

"Did he write that down?"

"Foolishly, no."

"Poor deluded old girl, then!"

"Another factor," Honorius continued, unmoved by his past client's plight, "was that the bequest had been named by Surus as 'my land with the old cherry trees.' Only it doesn't have cherry trees any longer, due to the centurion. After twenty years of remote agitating against his sister, Priscus turned up back in Rome. I presume he must have served his term."

"Yes, that's twenty years, Honorius—though unless he was wounded, he ought to have done five more in the reserves."

"Your finagling father helped him out."

"What? Falco wangled a fake military discharge?" I pretended to be shocked.

"Doesn't Falco know someone who can provide 'copies' of documents?"

"Falco always knows someone, that's true. All strictly legit, he would tell you."

Honorius smiled tiredly. "Anyway, Priscus was in Rome and ready for trouble. He sneaked to the Campagna where he dug out the cherry trees. By that time they can only have been cankered stumps—the original dispute had already gone on for two decades. He called it husbandry. After all, it was on land he was claiming as his own. Two years later, he replanted with new trees, not cherries. He said this was to benefit a new grandchild of his. Ursulina, who had no children, threw up a fit of the horrors, shrieking he had stolen the property."

"Surely she was right, if the orchard was in trust for both of them?"

"Agnates," answered Honorius, in a hollow voice. "Male descent, said Priscus."

"That stinks! What did the Surus will say?"

"Ursulina never managed to get her hands on it."

"Priscus prevented her seeing it?"

"He was a high-handed, aggressive character. But, according to him, he had never possessed the document. Only the uncle had ever had it, so Priscus could not hand it over when I asked."

"You asked Priscus? Why didn't you ask the uncle?" I demanded.

Honorius slid into his extremely-busy-lawyer act: "Time, pressure of work, never thought there was a chance of persuading him to hand over such an ancient document, but mainly I didn't know where he was or if he was alive. Frankly I had had enough. Priscus first argued that the freedmen no longer had rights because the original bequest had been specific about the fruit. Cherries, remember. Different trees altered the legator's intention. The new fruit, Priscus said, would be outwith the scope of the usufruct."

"Outwith!" I exclaimed admiringly. "What trees, *outwith the intention*, did nasty Priscus plant?"

"Some exotic type from the crappy province?"

I helped him out: "His new trees were apricots."

Honorius, no botanist, only shrugged. "In his view—and I was inclined to agree—the exact species did not matter. For the usufruct to revert, it had only to be something new." He gathered his toga around him, as if huddling within its folds for protection or comfort. "Then more trouble occurred: there nearly was no other fruit. Animals got in and damaged the new saplings—slips, Priscus called them."

"Animals? Would it be rabbits?" I hardly needed to ask.

"Yes. Witnesses saw them hopping about. It caused a rare moment of harmony between Ursulina and Priscus, as they made a joint complaint for the damage. They believed the rabbits had been released into the orchard maliciously."

"True?"

"A reasonable deduction."

"Win the case?"

"Lost it. Counterclaim, after wild dogs invaded and rabbits were poisoned."

"*Poisoned?* Retaliation?"

"Sound suggestion! The farmed creatures were generally deemed to be exceedingly healthy. I read one very touching document about how lovingly they were looked after." I imagined Honorius scornfully regaling a jury with this affecting tale, had things gone to court. "Fresh water. Feeding regime. Stroked kindly, if any bunny was a little bit off-colour."

"Weep, Muses! Counterclaim failed?"

"No, compensation agreed." Proving how the rabbits had got into the orchard would have been difficult, Honorius said, but the poisoning incident had been crude and, unfortunately, someone among the Tranquilli had even overheard Priscus plotting to do it.

"A *dumb* centurion? What next, Honorius?"

"The freedmen, your clients, brought along a forged codicil." Honorius perked up. "New evidence. Suddenly discovered after twenty years, according to them. Nice try, but unbelievable. Ursulina and her brother got together to fight them on that, so for a brief ghastly period, I represented both."

I asked gently, "Hideous experience?"

Honorius could only nod. He braced himself: "Using the old fallen-down-the-side-of-a-couch excuse, your clients' brief, a man with obvious mental problems in my opinion, was purporting that before he died Surus had amended his bequest. The alleged codicil instructed that the use of the fruit should continue for his freedmen even if the trees were replanted."

I chortled. "An obvious fiddle?"

"Blatant fix: no dice."

"Winning rebuttal?"

"Watertight."

"How was it resolved?"

"It never was." Honorius seemed bitterly aggrieved. "I was holding out for the codicil being fraudulent. I had lined up a specialist to declare it was a recent forgery. I intended to accuse their lawyer of writing it. I even suggested referral to a praetor, no matter how much that cost. Then, about a year into negotiations, they all unexpectedly dropped the matter. Both sides backed off. Something had happened. No one told me what. I was summarily bumped from the case."

I snorted. "I know that scenario!"

"Clients can be so irresponsible," Honorius griped back. "Still, for all I knew, these people had simply run out of money. It certainly took long enough to extract my fees afterwards! Must have been a record four or five years before they coughed up. I had debt collectors on a permanent retainer pursuing them."

"I am weeping for you, my friend . . . Why were you bumped?"

"I would love to know! They were cagey. I had no reason to persist. Who cared anyway? I was a free man again. I was walking on air. I did have the impression some dubious resolution had been agreed, probably one I would have advised against."

"So was that the end?"

"No." Honorius laughed. He had been holding his camomile tea beaker, but now he drained any last dregs, firmly wiped his mouth and tossed the beaker over to the stall-holder. He had a good aim; he must do throwing games at his gym. "Startling news! The dispute has revived. I was told recently that even the apricot trees are nearing the end of their useful lives and someone is wanting to replace them yet again. Cannot be Priscus, so his heirs must be taking it up. Three years since he died would be about the right time to decide to start an action."

"I thought people rushed blindly into suing?" I exclaimed. "This is your Witness G again, plus Witness V, or wife thereof?" He looked impressed by my recall, though in fact I had made notes. "Who told you the case was live again, Honorius?"

"A young colleague came to ask my advice after he was offered it. The landholders are attempting yet again to squeeze out the usufruct beneficiaries. Nothing changes. Those freedmen have never stopped collecting the produce but the Prisci keep turning up with grapplers and baskets themselves. Then it ends in becoming physical."

"And with ruined fruit!" I chortled. "These freed slaves were Tranquillus Aprilis and Tranquilla Euhodia?"

Honorius made a drama of shuddering. "Etched into my memory."

"My client and her brother. The rabbit farmers. In the past they had their mother weighing in too. Any mention of another sibling, younger, called Tranquillus Postuminus?"

"Rings no bells."

"Well, this is my case, really. I have to prove he was given his liberty. Somehow he gained possession of this orchard, so somebody thinks he is allowed to own property. Why did people on your side give it over to him, Honorius?"

He shrugged. "Can't say. Not my action."

"All right," I clarified, for myself at least, "the first two freed slaves inherited the harvest of an unproductive piece of land, which subsequently was replanted by another party. It became much more valuable, so mine fought your clients for the right to the fruit and profits. Since then, their own brother has grabbed the orchard, we know not how or why. According to the accepted facts, Postuminus is one person who had *no* rights. Yet he, rather than his brother and sister, gained possession. Your side want to grab it back again? So what has changed? And what happens now? With Ursulina and the soldier both deceased, the current petitioners can only be the soldier's descendants. How do 'the agnates' brats' get on together?"

"Badly, I presume." Honorius grinned.

"What about the grandchild, the one the apricots were planted for?"

"Again, no idea. By now, there are more than one, I think. Witness V, the centurion's son-in-law, fathered them so he considers he has an interest. He is a typical husband-making-trouble, that well-known species—unsubtle mentions of dowry, heavy hints about patriarchal rights, 'We must have justice for our children!' He'll be nastily triumphal if *he* ever gets hold of those trees."

"The sister, his wife, has a brother?"

"She has two," said Honorius. "One in the background, one pushy. A new generation, very fresh and keen. But I will never again let myself be involved in their affairs."

I agreed he was wise. "And what of your colleague who came for advice?"

"Poor beggar! I advised him to flee to the hills. He has what he calls a cottage on the shores of Lake Albanus where he lives as a couple with his 'close friend,' another man. Delightfully bosky. Fabulous views. They frolic like very frisky Greeks, and even keep sheep. Merry shearing japes."

"Baa!"

"The 'cottage,'" Honorius mouthed, sounding jealous, "has old imperial connections. Enormous square footage. Gigantic candelabra, statuary pinched from Greece and a huge bathhouse with silver taps."

"Affluent plush? I see!"

"I haven't met the boyfriend, but I gather both come from well-off families who fund them. Nice people, almost civilised by today's standards. The young lawyer doesn't need this work, so he listened to me and ran for home."

"Someone else will take it on for the Prisci," I replied gloomily. "Someone always does." That left my original question. "So, Honorius, I believe the original lawyer for the Tranquilli ran off to Belgica under a cloud. Can you tell me on the sly who acts for my clients since he fled?"

He came up with what I needed: "If it's the same as it always was, that will be Mamillianus."

"Oh, sulphurous gods of the underworld, not him!" I was smitten by despair.

For his part, Honorius twinkled mischievously, heightening his handsome look. "Ah, you have encountered the eminent professor?"

I kicked out my feet in their stout walking shoes. I was so angry I had to use my core to remain balanced on my stool. "I met a young man who studied at his very expensive lecture series. Apparently the prof teaches well, with a cynical edge to his theories. He is unusually honest about the dishonesty of the law."

"Oh, come!" Honorius blushed. He had always been an innocent.

"I met Mamillianus in person," I grouched. "He claims to have retired from active practice. He has no need to slog away at trusts and probate—he is rolling in loot. He puts it about that he earned his reputation acting for the authorities, prosecuting gangsters. Instead, he has been corrupted and takes a retainer from the worst crime family on the Esquiline."

"I didn't know that!" Honorius seemed surprised, perhaps considering how to fix up a similar sinecure for himself.

"He keeps it quiet. The kind of clients who use Lucius Mamillianus shun publicity. They like their representative to jump when they call and play discreet." Honorius was lapping up the gossip. "Why is the noble Mamillianus slumming it, handling low-grade pleas over an orchard?"

Honorius explained: in so far as a group of his associates, ex-students of his law academy who had failed to find other employment, did all the work for him. Mamillianus only put his name on the fee invoices. Honorius reckoned the freshman who would be struggling with writs

146

for the Tranquilli nowadays was called Crispinus, although he advised me to talk to the office clerk, Hermeros.

This suggestion proved Honorius had been schooled in business practices by Falco.

The afterthought

As I left him, he called out, "You have access to the Camillus brothers, don't you? What do they think?"

"They advised me on manumission. Helpful, if theoretical. Do you ever work with them, Honorius?"

"On occasions—but they are bit too cerebral for me . . ." That was a new word for my uncles. Then Honorius quizzed, "Don't I remember your father ranting that a Camillus had messed about one of his daughters?"

"I know nothing of that," I lied robustly. "Camillus Aelianus reckons I am bound to discover that Surus was murdered for his money by the slaves."

"Sounds plausible. Aelianus is very bright."

Honorius said it as if he thought the same as me: not bright enough, in this instance.

XXVII

I went to the basilica rooms where the Mamillianus Associates sweated. I should have known better. They were all out to lunch. Crispinus had even left a note with the classic line that he had gone to his grandmother's funeral.

"Again!" muttered the clerk. Left alone to mind the office, he was becoming rebellious.

Hermeros was a thin-faced starveling in a green tunic that had been made for someone more generously built. Balding and despondent, he was the trodden-upon menial who really ran the business here. He knew where all the scrolls were filed, which clients brought in the most money, who Mamillianus had taken into the firm because his father was popular and powerful, and which lazy young advocate was cheating on Mamillianus. Whenever a sad face came in through the door, it was Hermeros who would soothingly tell the client he had seen it all before so he was sure there was a remedy. He never mentioned that it would take six years and all their money.

"Gran's funeral?" I queried scathingly. "The poor old lady dies a lot?"

"Enters Hades about once a month. That's every time," grumbled Hermeros, "the group of them swans off to lunch on an upper-crust hill."

"The Esquiline? I know that's where Mamillianus has his private base. Doesn't he live in a swish apartment near the Temple of Jupiter the Victor?"

The associates would not have been to their principal's private home, the clerk exclaimed, and Mamillianus was also kept in the dark about their out-of-office activities. That was quite easy, since he only showed up at the basilica to collect the income they toiled for. They would know when he was coming. Then they all had clean faces and looked busy.

"So where do your young men go out?"

"Confidential."

"Why? Why keep their lunching quiet?" I had never heard of such a ban in the famously sociable legal profession.

"They get drunk."

"Well, they are lawyers."

"All right, we expect that . . . Sensitive meetings." Had Hermeros been less stroppy over being left alone in the office, he would never have admitted this.

"Conflict of interest? They eat out with advocates on the other side?" I raised a genteel eyebrow.

"No comment."

"Advocates *or even plaintiffs*?"

"No comment doubled."

"I hope this isn't my case, the one I came to ask about. For the Tranquilli? Locking horns for years with Ursulina Prisca and her military brother? Is it their heirs your men are lunching with? You can say all you like to me," I assured the glum fellow. "I am a woman, I don't count. Come on, Hermeros, I know fraternisation happens. If a client ever quibbles, your young men will say they are conducting informal negotiations."

"Shadowing the opposition," the clerk agreed.

"Oh, yes—oiled along by music and dancing girls. So is it yours who pay the bill?"

"I never see much evidence of the other side sharing costs!" Hermeros was still grumpy about them going out. "I have to go along to the Comet with the cash box and settle up next morning. Luckily, Mamillianus believes we use a lot of office equipment and stationery."

"Don't the expenses get passed on to your clients?"

"The Tranquilli have been our clients for so long, they have a book-keeper who triple-checks our bills. He hates being presented with claims for working lunches."

"Philodamus? I think you will find he has moved on," I mentioned kindly. "Still, at least your bills do get paid!" I then told him about the man who defrauded the Stargazer.

"We can assist, if you want to take the matter further. A few strong letters?"

"No need. I myself handled the matter."

Hermeros humphed. "Amateurs like you are the bane of professionals like us!"

"People like my family can afford neither your time charges nor how long you take, Hermeros. I do my job. For a set fee, I find those to blame and retrieve the cash from them. Everybody moves on."

The clerk shifted his attitude. He gave me the company line that Mamillianus and Associates had unrivalled expertise in family and commercial law; they were hard-working specialists in supportive community engagement. They employed their own team of medical experts for personal injuries, plus the best loss adjuster in Rome for dispute resolution, a field in which they were regarded as the best.

I replied: not in that fight over the apricot orchard, surely? He let out a savage belch.

We settled that he would tell me where the associates' lunching cronies lived, which was the official "meeting place"; then I would get out of his hair. If anybody ever asked, I would say I acquired my information from a beggar on the Vicus Tuscus, one whose name I did not know.

"You have done this before, Flavia Albia!"

"Yes. I would give you my business address for future use, but I have met Lucius Mamillianus. I will not work for him."

"He has retired."

"Like hell he has. He still turns up breathing brimstone and paying the bribes, whenever the vicious Rabirii need one of their foot-soldiers plucked from a jail cell."

Acknowledging that, Hermeros told me what I needed to know. I wrote the address neatly in a note-tablet. It was not on the Esquiline but an elegant part of the Caelian. At least that was nearer.

XXVIII

Tiberius and I knew people who lived on the Caelian. Once densely populated by ordinary citizens, a devastating fire had cleared out the working classes, as fires so conveniently do; wealthier types, who needed more space and air for their fine way of life, were able to move in on the two elegant peaks. One was dominated by the massive Temple of Claudius, with its square formal grounds, overlooking an extraordinary nymphaeum that splashed and tinkled away, filled from an aqueduct. Vespasian, whom Claudius had patronised, had restored this memorial complex; since completion, it verged on grotesque. From the fancy folks' point of view, at least it meant nobody would colonise the area with smelly or noisy industry.

Spreading manicured gardens contained secluded homes that were invisible from the pleasant lanes running between them. Occasionally sinister men emerged to take guard dogs for walks. The householders were often absent at their seaside villas, lakeside leisure palaces or mountain retreats. Teams of staff kept their homes looking neat until the owners returned for occasional festivals. Whether they were here or not today, snooty persons on fat donkeys were delivering small packets of upmarket foodstuffs in expensive baskets.

I felt out of place. In a district like this I was meant to. It was one rare occasion when I became acutely aware of my British background. Around here, merely coming from Londinium would need to be disguised. Anyone who thought I looked suspicious might send for the Urban Cohorts to check me out. I didn't want that.

A few roads wandered through the herbage. Caelian streets had swept pavements, with clean-running gutters and shops selling shiny items or artefacts made from unusual woods, often trimmed with tufts of fur. A few tenements had survived, though they were properly groomed; they looked architect-built, following all known building regulations. No loose flowerpots would tumble from those balconies; no slipped tiles would crash from roofs. No beggars dared to squat in their doorways either.

There were houses—big, single-owner premises, upmarket exteriors, window grilles, huge doorknobs. One was my destination. It looked discreet, but very substantial. On the outside, it spoke of significant age, a historic shell that perhaps went back a hundred years, into the reign of Augustus, probably not quite Republican. The interior felt newer, though not modern.

The owners were property magnates. They had been successful landlords for several generations, building up a portfolio large enough for their door porter to have no idea how large "large" was when I asked him.

After being admitted, I was seen by the man who assessed visitors. He was the face-to-face contact for tenants, whether prospective (to have viewings arranged) or aggrieved (to be shunted off with advice to send in a letter). Family friends might stroll past him, though he did write down the name of anyone who entered the house, then ticked them off after they left. People came and went here, but a distinct effort was made to keep track. Not many places I visited were so strictly organised; still, this had once been the home of a retired centurion.

The chamberlain, or whatever he called himself, was quite an elderly man; he looked as if he had been there a long time. He had good Latin and a laundered tunic; he was clean-shaven and treated everyone as equals, with a friendly manner. He never mentioned his name; if you had business here, you were assumed to know.

As an informer, I stumped him. While he was deciding what to do about me, a woman, my age or slightly younger, came into the atrium with her sleeves rolled up; he called out to her, naming her quite informally as Ursula. Was she the soldier's grandchild? Did Gallicus Priscus plant the apricot trees for her?

Ursula was fresh-faced, bouncy, cheerful and accessible. Bright brown eyes, hair screwed back. Although she wore no jewellery, at least not around the house, her yellow gown was of good material, covered up for protection by a large apron because, she explained, that morning she was helping to clear out a store cupboard. Despite mucking in with the household task, there was no doubt she was a full member of the property-owning family. She slipped off the apron and said nobody else was at home so I had better come along and explain my enquiry to her.

There was other activity. A girl with a tray appeared, telling my companion she was trying to tempt someone's appetite with a cinnamon custard. Approving this, Ursula said she would be along soon. "Do you need me right now?"

"No, your mother's sitting with him." I worked out that "nobody else at home" meant nobody male; this invalid was exempt from business due to old age, presumably.

As we moved out of the atrium Ursula told me the house had three storeys: an uncle lived on the top floor with his wife, enjoying the best views, while her parents, her brother (when he bothered to be home), her husband and she occupied the next level down. Here on the ground floor lived an elderly relative who needed looking after; she did not specify his relationship. The custard girl, a neat unflustered type, was his nurse.

I said I was sorry to drag Ursula away from her duties. "I don't want to cause any nuisance, but it is rather complicated," I apologised.

"We need rose-petal wine then!" returned Ursula, brightly. I blinked. This case seemed to involve an unusual number of sweet tipples.

She had led me to an interior garden, just beyond the atrium, saying that as I had my cloak and she was burning up after her pantry exertions, we could manage there. I decided it was a subtle placement: a person of my status could enjoy the air, while not permitted entrance to an inside room.

From our position we could hear voices: I recognised the nurse, being firm but not unkind, answered by fainter mumbles from the old person she was looking after. This peristyle garden was a fashionable space with topiary, a small fountain and low hedges. My companion perched on a licheny stone bench. I was brought a folding stool. That came with a portable table, along with a glass flagon and cups on a silver tray. The slave half filled the dainty cups, then left us.

I told Ursula I was an informer, on the trail of a document that clients needed. I said I had come from Honorius, whom I believed had worked for her own family in times past. She seemed to know nothing about that. I held back that he never wanted their business again.

"I need to see a lawyer called Crispinus. I hope you don't mind, but to speed things up, the office clerk told me I might find Crispinus here this morning. Some kind of case conference? If he can help me, well and good, though if he has nothing to tell me, at least that will save me hanging on in hope. I am running around rather, as you can gather."

"They all went out to lunch," answered Ursula. I could not tell whether her tone showed disapproval. Would the men come home so pie-eyed they were sick in the atrium pool? "You missed them, I'm afraid. I know it's still early."

I smiled. "Long walk to their chosen eatery? 'They' would be . . . ?"

"My uncle primarily. He is negotiating something with the Crispinus you mentioned. They meet up regularly for men's talk. Utterly boring, we would say! My father goes out with them usually, and I think my brother took the chance to tag along today. He doesn't always. He has a friend he stays with, so on the whole he isn't here."

"Do you know where they were heading?"

"No idea," she said, so promptly that she sounded like someone who had been instructed never to say. I guessed that would be to ensure the men were not interrupted, during the castanet work from their hired dancing girls.

"A place called the Comet was mentioned," I nudged.

"Sorry, I don't know where it is. Why did you want Crispinus, Flavia Albia?"

"Just a quick word. Crispinus is acting for the family I am working with, the Tranquilli." Without seeming to watch Ursula, of course I was doing so. She gave no reaction, however. I would never have known that the Tranquilli had been in contention with her family for decades, surely sometimes discussed in her hearing. "I need confirmation of land ownership. Crispinus may be able to help."

With a sudden gesture, Ursula tossed back her rose-petal wine, like a soak. "Don't tell me! This has to do with that terrible orchard!"

I inclined my head. I sipped cautiously, not ready to reveal that I wanted to know about any claim Postuminus had, and how he had obtained his property from these people. They presumably believed he was a free citizen. In all the disputatiousness, I had not lost sight of my basic brief. "You have heard about the orchard troubles?" I asked, as if in mild surprise.

"I try not to know. My family owns a few problematic properties, as you are bound to in a large portfolio, but that one is a horror."

It gave me a lead to ask what her position in the family was. She confirmed that the soldier, Priscus, was her grandfather. Her grandmother had been his wife Aurelia. So Ursula's mother, called Aurelia Priscilla, must have been one of the offspring whose legitimacy my father had proved and, according to Honorius, either Ursula or the brother she had mentioned had been intended by their grandfather to benefit from the apricot trees.

"Good heavens, what a coincidence!" I expressed amazement. "Your great-aunt, Ursulina Prisca, was a client of my father for a very long time. I believe I even met her!" As I tinkled with fake laughter over this link, I wondered privately if the cordial that Ursulina had drunk so much of was this rose-petal wine. I would enjoy sharing that idea with my parents.

I was surprised at how I was feeling. My father had known Ursulina Prisca, even if he was always trying to dodge her, but I found I had an interesting conflict: I couldn't quite like the fact that Ursula was descended from the quarrelsome brother, whom I now felt had done Ursulina down.

Perhaps Ursula also felt that the orchard had positioned us on different sides. I had admitted the Tranquilli were clients of mine. If she and her own brother were involved in new legal proceedings against them, she would not want to talk to me. She might be a pleasant woman, but I represented the opposition.

There was still scented wine in the glass flagon, but she jumped up and claimed she really must return to her domestic tasks. I had to abandon the conversation.

XXIX

I walked slowly to the exit on my own, absorbing how well-appointed the house was. Their atrium was four times as large as ours, floored with black and white marble in a geometric pattern, complete with mosaic borders and floor mats. Its pool looked clean—at least, I joked to myself, until the men came home drunk and fell into it. There were fresh flowers in a large niche lararium. Walls were painted in the eccentric style made fashionable in Nero's Golden House, with mock marble dados in dull reds and smudgy greys below painted picture galleries. I had no time to admire the illusionistic art with its mythologies and still-lifes, because the chamberlain hobbled up to tick me off his list; he saw to it that I departed.

At some time in the past, money had been thrown at this house. Their decorator had been extremely happy. Thirty years ago? What had happened to the family then to bring an influx of cash and the energy to beautify? Everything I knew about them seemed either to be longer ago or much more recent.

Outside in the quiet street, I stood, thinking.

Suddenly the door through which I had emerged opened again; someone else came out behind me. I was amazed to see a familiar figure. "Philodamus!"

I had the faint impression that if he had known I was there he would have lurked indoors until I moved away. Even so, he greeted me amiably enough. He had smartened his stubble slightly but wore the same beige tunic, had the same wary expression and slow movements. From the ink stains on his fingers, I guessed he was doing the same job as at the Tranquillus apartment, still acting as a bookkeeper. He told me he was on his way to pick up cash from a banker in the Forum, which confirmed it. I suggested he walk along with me and tell me what had been happening to him. He had intended to turn right through the Forum Romanum and I would have been going left around the Circus Maximus, so we compromised by taking a gentle stroll through the gardens of the Temple of Claudius. On the way, we could chat.

I apologised if my enquiries had been responsible for his abrupt relocation, though I was puzzled. Philodamus told me the Caelian was in fact his *old* location. He had been passed to the Tranquilli seven years ago, and they had now returned him to his previous owners. "I don't mind at all. To be honest, I never felt happy with the other set. This was like coming home."

"What debts are you getting handed around for?"

"Can't tell you. I am just the collateral."

I was sure he was lying. He had always seemed honest before, but he was a bookkeeper so he ought to be well up on the finances of both families. I made a mental note—but let it go, given what had happened the last time I asked too much of him. There is a well-established Roman custom of yelling at slaves, whether they are yours or not. I had to be more cautious. I needed information from Philodamus, though his duty was to be loyal to whoever owned him. One wrong move on my part, and nobody would blame him if he beetled back to the house and made a complaint.

I admitted how I had come to the Caelian in search of Crispinus. I wanted enlightenment about the apricot orchard and now saw it as urgent. Philodamus pretended the issue was too complicated for him.

I called him disingenuous. "Stop faddling. You were with the Tranquilli, so you must know. How did Postuminus obtain that orchard?"

"Have you asked him?" That was a sensible question but again Philodamus was uncharacteristically playing the dumb slave.

I acted disingenuous. "I am trying to avoid offending anyone. That was why I was hoping to speak to the man privately. Still, I should have known—a lawyer was bound to have gone to lunch! Frankly, though, I was surprised he mingles so freely with the opposition." Philodamus received that in silence, so I admitted, "Even if *he* does, perhaps I ought not to have gone in there myself. But I can call up a family link to Ursulina Prisca. Did you ever come across her?"

"Before my time," Philodamus reminisced. "And the centurion would never let her into the house. Fortunately, his family always owned property, so he never actually made her homeless. He could always find somewhere to shunt her and her menagerie of horrid pets."

"Yes, I've heard about a legacy of cat baskets." I laughed, but it got no reaction. "My father did some work for Ursulina—until Papa was called abroad. I even met her, back then. I had a little smile over that, with the young woman I was talking to today, the one called Ursula. So," I murmured, "would her uncle, who has gone out to lunch with Crispinus, be the person I have been hearing about, called 'Witness G' in legal papers?"

"Another Gallicus," agreed Philodamus. "Like his father, Priscus, who brought me into the family."

"Oh! Did the centurion buy you when he came back to Rome?"

"No, I was born in the east. He bought me on the docks at Alexandria. Priscus and his wife Aurelia had a household there, a private home he set up off-base after he was promoted. I was part of their establishment. The centurion had me trained up to keep his personal accounts."

"Alexandria?" This was not what Honorius had told me. "I heard Priscus was stationed in one of the more remote provinces."

Philodamus seemed surprised. "No. He spent all of his career with the Third Cyrenaican legion in Egypt."

Compared with the dangerous frontier provinces, Egypt was regarded as a cushy posting. To have clung on there in the same legion throughout his career, engaged in imperial administration rather than fighting, was quite a feat. "Your master knew how to stay comfortable!"

"He did have to go to Armenia at one point," the bookkeeper demurred. He sounded defensive. "A squadron from the Third was assigned by Nero to serve under Domitius Corbulo. It was a horrible posting."

"Corbulo was a brute, by reputation! That was on detachment, so temporary?"

"Yes, but it came right at the end of my master's full term. He was already looking to the future as a veteran so he sent Aurelia and the children back to live in Rome, in anticipation. We packed up everything and I came with them."

"To the house I visited today?"

"Yes. Old family home. It had been built many years ago for my master's mother on her marriage. After she was widowed, she stayed until she passed away. On leaving Armenia, the centurion joined us here. Kicked his sister out—"

"Ursulina?"

"He wanted the house for his own family, now he was in Rome. A sister he had never got on with did not feature in his plans."

"Well, sisters don't count for much!" I felt much more sympathy towards Ursulina Prisca now. Her feud with this brother began to make sense. I had an uneasy feeling that because she came across as bothersome, my father and Honorius might have failed to help her when her need was genuine.

"I didn't know her." Philodamus gave me a wary look, then changed tack. "The centurion hated Armenia. Corbulo was a terrible commander. Too much discipline, bleak life in camp, notoriously brutal training. Priscus was then supposed to serve five years in the reserves, but he got out of that. Medical reasons. Lost some toes to frostbite. It was famously cold on the Corbulo campaign—they had soldiers actually freeze to death."

I wondered if my father had suggested the centurion hacked off a few digits so he could claim it prevented him marching. The diploma Falco deployed on behalf of the centurion's children, legitimising them, might have been as fake as Honorius had suggested.

"Ursulina Prisca was a great-aunt to the young woman at the house. Was Ursula named as a gesture of respect?" I was wondering if her parents had hoped for a legacy from the childless spinster. Or was it an apology for the centurion shoving Ursulina out of house and home? A pitiful compensation for an old lady whom I remembered fretting about her insecurity. "Such a small world! I need to draw a family tree." I pretended to be concocting it. "We have Ursulina Prisca and her brother, Gallicus Priscus. *He* married an Aurelia. Their daughter has the same name."

"Aurelia Priscilla," Philodamus filled in.

"She was at the house today, although I did not meet her. Sitting with their invalid."

"She's very good with him." Before I could check the frail person's position, Philodamus continued, "Well, they all are. I like these people, Flavia Albia. Aurelia Priscilla, the centurion's eldest, married and still lives in the house. You were talking to *their* daughter, very pleasant young lady. She is Venuleia Ursula, after her father, Venuleius."

I stared at him. I was sure he had not realised that the detail was a stunner. It was the name of the young man who wanted to marry Cosca Sabatina.

"These people are the *Venuleii*? Now that is a twist!"

I was shocked. Today, I had been enjoying light conversation and refreshments in the elegant home of the very people who had caused me to be hired; this was the family who had asked awkward questions about manumission. "Are you telling me that you now live and work with the young hunk who fell for Sabatina? The one whose upcoming wedding I am supposed to facilitate? The very family who want to know whether Postuminus is a slave?"

"Yes, of course," said Philodamus, not turning a hair. "Sabatina's intended is the grandson of my old master. He is Ursula's brother. Venuleius Priscus."

What a turn-up. The lovelorn Venuleius Priscus had gone out to lunch today with his father, his uncle—and a group of advocates who were representing his fiancée's writ-torn relatives. I had missed my chance for the time being. But I would track down this intriguing youth and hope to pick his brains.

I really would have liked the chance to talk to him. My first thought was to wonder how genuinely lovelorn he might be. My second, what exactly were that group of men up to?

XXX

I did not want to land a slave in trouble. I left him to complete his errand. Now I knew where he was, I might try to pick his brains another time. I would have to be careful about going back to the house, though.

I needed to reorganise my thoughts. First, it was time to visit Tranquilla Euhodia. I would challenge her with lack of frankness and explain that underhand business could be threatening her niece's plans. If the bridegroom's relatives were consorting with her own lawyers, Euhodia would need to be warned of possible treachery. However, she and Aprilis must be pretty sharp so I did suspect that any coup the Venuleii were intending might be roundly knocked back.

I went home and had a quiet lunch myself, not as disreputable as the meal that the lawyers and their cronies must have been having. We had no dancing girls in Lesser Laurel Street. Everything seemed so peaceful that I felt safe to leave people to their afternoon. Tiberius was out on site somewhere.

In Sidewind Passage, that afternoon, everything was quiet too. I raised a hand to various stallholders as I passed. I noticed the garum shop seemed to be closed, but perhaps Aprilis and his wife took a siesta in the afternoon. When I went up to the apartment there was no evidence they were at home but Euhodia, playing the matriarch as usual, soon appeared.

She wore her usual dark, unexciting dress and gave a quick rattle of her cheap-looking bangles as if annoyed that I was bothering her. Some clients press for reports; others can hardly bear to see you once they have poured out their woes and sent you off to work. This time, I was kept in the main room, not taken to the private bower.

I said I needed to assess my initial findings; she received this with a frown. I related that I had unearthed large amounts of material since we last met, mostly hearsay, and that it had not taken me very much further with the critical issue of Postuminus being liberated. I admitted, "I have to be honest, no helpful documents have come to light. I have only acquired a picture of your brother and his life with his mother. Postuminus was very much a favoured child with Hedylla?"

Euhodia nodded. Her expression was frosty, a reaction to the subject, I felt, not personal against me.

"Hedylla seems to have been quite distant with you and Aprilis, yet I am told she did come to Rome and lived here after your brother's wife died. Was that to look after him?" Another nod led me to challenge Euhodia herself. "She, as your mother, had never supported you in that way, when your own husband passed away?" Given no answer, I commented quietly, "I imagine that you can look after yourself."

"My elder brother gave me strength."

"But later Hedylla thought the two of you were not enough to console Postuminus? Oh, I remember. You said he lacks worldliness."

"He lives in a dream!" Euhodia was drawn to exclaim. Then she made an acknowledgement I was not expecting from her: "It was different for me, when poor old Telesphorus dropped off his twig. Hedylla had been involved in a stressful incident that led to his death." Honorius had said the cause of death was unprovable, but I could see Euhodia believed, or chose to believe, she could assign blame.

"A fight, literally, over a boundary dispute?" I saw no point in pretending nobody had mentioned it.

Euhodia looked wary, though she rallied. "It was better that Hedylla stayed out of Rome afterwards. We were involved in a complaint against the other parties. Lawyers advised us to do nothing to inflame the situation."

It was my turn to nod. Lawyers always say that.

"Turbo, your son-in-law, told me your husband had weighed into the fight, but he thought Hedylla had struck the first blow."

"Turbo is a troublemaker," Euhodia said matter-of-factly. "His mother is a very old friend of mine, but I should never have brought that clown into our family. He was keen on my daughter and I let myself be influenced. Her other son would have been more suitable. Still, it's too late now."

"Turbo seems to believe Mardiana and he were made for one another."

"Ha!" Euhodia would not even discuss it.

I decided not to mention the incident when Turbo had lost the lucrative mullet contract, so I asked instead, "Was it difficult to prove that your husband, Telesphorus, had died as a direct result of the fight?"

"We won compensation," Euhodia exclaimed proudly. "Not enough to cover the loss of my children's father, but it showed we had right on our side. Mind you, we only saw part in cash. The rest was in kind, which never feels as good."

I congratulated her on the persistence it must have taken, law being what law often is. Then I sprang on her gently that I had heard someone else in the fracas had had his shoulder broken. Who was that? And did *he* want reparation?

"All his own fault!" snapped Euhodia, still avidly indignant. "He had deliberately put himself in the wrong. He was stealing what was rightfully ours. Wanting compensation after he caused the row was a real cheek. We never paid him a copper."

As she gloated, I slid into my main concern: "I am asking about that orchard, Euhodia, because Postuminus told me very definitely that he owns it."

"Is this important?" Her defensiveness hinted she wanted to put me off.

"I can make a case that land ownership demonstrates his free status."

"He does own it," stated Euhodia, baldly.

"I may have to ask him for proof . . ." Although on the surface she was unfazed, possibly Euhodia stiffened. She certainly bridled when I asked, "I believe you and Aprilis had a usufruct? Do you still stand by your right to pick the fruit?"

She was angered by the question. "No, we gave it up. Aprilis rants, but it's right that our brother now benefits from the crops."

"So, tell me," I probed, playing the puzzled investigator, "how exactly did Postuminus manage to acquire the orchard?"

It was the key question. Being suspicious of them all now, I half expected Euhodia to brush it aside. Instead, she tossed her head slightly, as if impatient with the query. "He was given it."

"By whom?"

"The landowners."

"When was that?"

"After his mother died."

"Recently, then?"

"We lost her three years ago. The other people must have had a conscience somewhere. They decided at last to relieve themselves of the property."

"The arguments had gone on too long, you mean?"

"Forty years is long enough!"

"I should think so. It had been very contentious. Were you surprised the landowners agreed?"

"Nothing those people do surprises me! They were running out of cash to pay lawyers. They shed the stupid thing. Dumped it on us. They knew the trees were ready to be grubbed up."

"You mean the centurion's apricots? Have they too now reached the end of their productive life? That shows how long your two families have been competing for ownership!"

Euhodia smirked ruefully. "Indeed!" At this point she began to spill more freely: "Gallicus Priscus was a nasty, vicious man. He thought being in the legions made him master of everyone. Trouble over the fruit went on for decades—not that there was much to argue about originally, with the wizened old cherry trees. I remember them. Piteous. Then Priscus came back from the army, full of himself. The bumptious bully had the cherries felled without notice, and planted new saplings—after which he had the gall to claim that some of our rabbits had escaped and nibbled at his little green slips. We would have got him on that—it was nonsense. Minor damage, anyone could see. He had constructed a new boundary fence the size of a frontier to keep out barbarians, never mind a few hungry little bunnies. Next thing he got into our property one dark night. In the morning we found half of our stock dead."

"That must have been terrible!"

Euhodia was contemptuous. "Seen worse with foxes. The man was an idiot. Postuminus actually heard him telling his overseer what he was planning to do."

"Oh, wonderful!"

"Yes, even Aprilis had to admit little brother came good that time—and it was the making of him. Postuminus is a loner and he was out strolling by himself at twilight. Heard the soldier and one of his people. They had got onto our access road and Priscus was talking about slinging poisoned bait into our enclosures. It took us several years to screw compensation out of the soldier, but once he got his hands on his discharge money, we relieved him of most of it."

"He cannot have liked that!" I marvelled.

"Don't feel sorry for him. He had had three thousand denarii plus a block of land in Egypt, which he managed to sell somehow." Euhodia sounded envious of the centurion's manoeuvre. "Veterans are supposed to take their land grant, then live in the provinces as farmers. Pin down the natives with their friendly Roman presence . . . It would have been good riddance if Gallicus had done that, but back he came to Rome, ready to cause decades' more trouble."

"But he did pay up for the poisoned rabbits?"

"Had to." I saw Euhodia's expression close. "We knew more about Gallicus bloody Priscus than he wanted to be public! To this day, we still have his bloody son tied down just where we want him." She did not specify what they knew. I could not help remembering how Honorius had hinted at something fishy with a discharge diploma. Since my father had been involved, I felt safest not asking. "We used his gold to reward Postuminus," Euhodia continued. "Set him up, brought him to Rome with us, funded his marriage. Fixed it nicely with the Cosconius brothers—another tribe who don't deserve their success," she threw in.

"Not even for developing digestive bread?" I shifted position on my seat, then whipped in a new question: "Was the poisoned-rabbit settlement also how Postuminus gained the orchard?"

"No. No, that happened later, years afterwards. Years."

"More aggravation on the farm?"

"No." Euhodia was short. Her face darkened, showing her age. "Nothing like that."

I waited, but she refused to elaborate. "Let me ask you something else, then. Is it true that a codicil about who could harvest fruit was found?" I wondered whether she would own up that it had been a forgery. "I would like sight of that, should it still exist."

"I heard some talk of a codicil," Euhodia agreed vaguely. "Maybe the lawyers still have it. Postuminus, as I have always told you, cannot organise himself. He certainly won't have kept it."

"Why would he have it anyway? I thought the original will from Tranquillus Surus awarded the fruit to you and Aprilis?"

"Oh . . ." Unconvincingly, Euhodia pretended to be vague. "Who cares? It's all in the family!"

I jumped back to the main question: "And Postuminus has no documents explaining how the orchard was gifted to him?"

"He got it. That's all that matters to him."

"If I were him," I said, "I'd want a deed to prove it. Are you sure nobody will raise questions in future over his ownership?"

Euhodia gave me a smile. "Oh, no! They would never risk what might come out."

I gave her back a thoughtful stare. "About the centurion?"

"Him and his son. We sorted them. Don't ask."

"Well! I can't force you . . ." I would have tried, but could see she was adamant. Time to raise the other issue then: "There is something else I must discuss. Tranquilla Euhodia, you have a family lawyer called Crispinus?"

Euhodia leaned forwards slightly, expectantly. "Does that matter?"

I leaned towards her myself. There was nobody else in the room with us, but outside the curtained doorway, people might be able to overhear. "I have discovered something rather unpleasant. This probably affects your niece's wedding. Do you know, Euhodia, that your lawyer, Crispinus, is unprofessionally close to the Venuleii?"

I saw her lips tighten. "How?"

"Surviving members of the centurion's family regularly lunch with him and others in his team—and Crispinus pays. He provides the full works. Music and dancing girls."

Euhodia did not like this situation any more than I did, but her response was awkward. I helped her out: "I smell dirty dealings. Is there anything Crispinus may know about Postuminus? Anything to your brother's disadvantage?" She began to catch on. "For instance," I spelled out, "did Crispinus arrange that gift of the orchard to your brother? Does he know the reason for it?"

Euhodia shook her head. "We kept the lawyers out. It was a private transaction." Did this indicate some unhealthy secret? They seemed to use lawyers for other things often enough.

Yet again, she clearly would not tell me, so I decided to spring a tougher challenge: "Worse ideas are being hawked around. Go back in time much longer. It is being suggested that Surus, your old master, might have been pushed into his grave before his time. Helped along by somebody who wanted his wealth."

Euhodia fired up. "Absolute nonsense. Whoever told you that? It's a wicked suggestion—it's slander!" I had a bad moment thinking the Tranquilli might sue my uncle, although I knew Aelianus could talk his way out of it. Euhodia stiffened, full of indignant dismissal: "Appius Tranquillus Surus died at peace in his bed after a short illness."

That rusty old tale from so many scandals! The ritual lie that is given out in public when the true facts are eye-watering. The whole point will be that everyone *knows* what really happened to the victim. If they don't, the words "died at peace" are shorthand, a clue that sends them running to the Forum to read the *Daily Gazette* scandal column.

"Well, then," I went on doggedly, "might Crispinus know the unfortunate truth: that Hedylla, and therefore Postuminus, had never been manumitted formally by Surus?"

"I told you—"

"You told me your brother was a freedman. You said it only needed to be proved—which was my task. If Crispinus knows something about it, then I must be given whatever information he holds. After that, if your lawyer is crooked, you must face it. It looks to have been him behind the

Venuleii asking that difficult question about your brother . . . Do you pay Crispinus a lot?"

"Too much."

Everyone says that about their lawyers.

Euhodia sat up straight. "Are the Venuleii paying him too? Backhanders?"

"I don't know." I thought it likely. If they had been picking up bills for those friendly lunches, I would have been sure, but for some reason Crispinus was funding the entertainment.

"Find out, if you can! What should I do?" Euhodia asked me brusquely.

"Be very careful."

"I shall terminate his work for us."

"Not immediately. My advice would be to keep quiet, act normally, then watch him. He won't know I have told you this. Don't use him for the wedding—dowry contracts, for example."

Euhodia still wanted to shed him. "There are other associates in the firm."

I pulled a face. "According to my information, several of those associates fraternise with the Venuleii. If I were you, I would not in future use that firm at all."

"We have always used them!" This is the terrible justification people use: *We have always trusted them, so that means they must be honest.*

"You can always stop," I disagreed bluntly.

"But Mamillianus has a fine reputation—"

"Like many a crook. Listen. He works for organised criminals, but please don't tell anyone I said that. It could have repercussions. I don't use bodyguards, and I have a young family. But you are my client, so it is my duty to warn you of any adverse information I discover."

She thanked me.

Watching her, I thought she had lost her former vim. At that moment, Tranquilla Euhodia was a woman, no longer young, widowed and with most of her children far away, who must sense that her grip on the family's affairs was beginning to falter. Even her long and close commercial relationship with her brother Aprilis might start crumbling as he, too, was ageing. His wife, Marcella Maura, a notably strong woman, had spoken of Euhodia with a lack of empathy. I foresaw trouble.

I said that, in view of the long-running legal feuds, I understood why a marriage between Cosca Sabatina and Venuleius Priscus might be unwelcome to relatives on both sides.

"Nonsense!" retorted the matriarch, with a flash of her old fire. She reiterated, "His mother and I have been friends for years. Aurelia Priscilla and I agree: the young people have fallen in love and that is wonderful. It could be just what is wanted to put an end to all those squabbles for good!"

No chance, I thought.

Still, since Euhodia was my client, I refrained from saying so.

XXXI

Next morning I had a good idea, or so it seemed when it first struck me.

I went back to the Basilica Julia, wrapped in a different cloak from yesterday. I hung around near the Mamillianus offices until Hermeros, the clerk, came to open up. Then I waited in the big basilica side aisle until he reappeared, hung with a cross-body satchel. I presumed he was heading out to pay for lunch with the Venuleii, on behalf of Crispinus.

I followed discreetly. He trotted along to the end of the Forum, as far as the new Amphitheatre. He went past Domitian's arena training school. Gladiators were already bashing noisily inside, but the usual bawdy, boozy audience, who liked to throng and cheer, had not yet gathered, so I managed to get past without any bruising harassment. I would not normally take that route, but I could not lose my quarry. He bought himself something at a bar he must have favoured, but it was not his destination.

He doubled back away from the Amphitheatre. The Comet turned out to be a large eatery on that street of seedy entertainment places, the Vicus Capitis Africae; it was up past the halls where imperial slaves are trained. On its signboard a celestial manifestation was wizened, its hairy tail just a squiggle falling off the left-hand edge. With lamps and a few garlands, the place probably believed it had a highly convivial atmosphere, though any joy must be brought in by customers. Emptied, it looked basic and austere.

Once Hermeros had been inside and left again, I entered myself. Several staff members were moving brooms about or wiping down surfaces with minimal effort. I could hear the chink of beakers being washed in the back area and smell cloying after-effects of what must have been a

170

busy late night, following what I knew to have been a long day of entertainment yesterday.

I spoke to an unappealing waiter, who claimed his memory could not reach back as far as the previous lunchtime, even though presumably he had just allowed Hermeros to pay for some of it. I was too late. It was clear the Comet's proprietor and lacklustre staff had been told to keep their mouths shut if an informer called. No doubt Hermeros had handed over a larger tip than usual. Nothing I had would match it.

I picked up a rather sparkly shoe that someone had dropped behind a bench, gave it a knowing scrutiny, then placed the dancer's footwear on the counter where it had just been sponged down. I felt no guilt; the half-hearted clean had left behind gleams of salad oil. Nobody had ever taught the staff to get down low and look along the marble for stubborn smears.

With a bright smile and thank you very much, I left the whey-faced lags to their clearing up. I had been an informer long enough to know a good idea will generally let you down. I'd even had to stand outside in the street, watching, at the precise moment Hermeros thwarted me.

I hoped Hermeros had not known I had tailed him. I thought not. But he had obviously worked out that sooner or later I would arrive asking questions. Even if the associates annoyed him when they went on the razzle, he was a good enough clerk to protect them and their firm. For all I knew, lunching out with the opposition was company policy. It would certainly fit what I knew about the ethics of their principal, Mamillianus.

Now I had another good idea: brunch at my parental home. Coming back along the Circus Maximus into my own district, I stayed at river level, mooching along the Marble Embankment to our town house. Being winter, it had a slight smell of mould, due to the nearby Tiber's old flooding. My parents had never solved the after-effects of repeated damp in my grandfather's time. He had never bothered; he would just move his furniture upstairs and wait for spring.

They were in. They had finished breakfast. My mother was supervising the tutor as he attempted lessons. As soon as I arrived, my brother, aged twelve, raised a peremptory finger like a potentate: the tutor gave up. So did Mother. My sisters were out seeing a friend. I assumed that meant shopping.

At least my father had not gone off to the family antiques business. With no auction that day, he was lounging at home, a sturdy, curly-haired plebeian who, however long he feigned his role as a pillar of the Aventine community, still harboured a dangerous aura. His genial expression hid uncomfortable thoughts; those twinkly eyes had regularly seen bad events. Didius Falco had a past. He kept it well-contained these days, but what he had experienced would never leave him.

He knew the Comet. He said he never went there because it was full of stinking lawyers and their abominable clients. I asked about musicians and dancing girls but, with my mother listening quietly, he claimed to have no knowledge of such creatures. "As you know, Tiddles, I spend very little time in rowdy bars."

"Don't call me Tiddles."

"Sorry, Flavia!"

"And don't call me Flavia."

Ignoring the warm blanket of family humour, I mentioned Ursulina Prisca; that drew groans on all sides. Passing on the news from Honorius that she had finally died cheered them up. Father proclaimed majestically that a dark veil of terror had cleared. He could have been a chief priest pronouncing release from a natural catastrophe, though in general he had no time for priests.

I asked about Ursulina's brother, the centurion. Falco remembered him. He first pretended not to, but that was another father-daughter game. Even Helena knew nothing of Priscus, whose commission was one Falco had undertaken after he himself had returned from the army. He had set himself up as a struggling investigator, a raw bachelor still scarred by brutal experiences in Britain. He was offering to find lost documents for the feckless members of the public. "What's new?" I snorted, with feeling. "Will the public ever organise a decent filing system?"

"Better not, or we'll be out of work."

Pa admitted he had been hired for a diploma diddle. Private informers routinely carried out such work for military veterans who either never had or who casually lost their discharge tablets. I did it myself, though gnarled veterans generally thought I was there to be assaulted so I preferred being hired by women.

Apparently, the discharge that Gallicus Priscus had brought home to Rome with him had been completed incorrectly by his commanding officer or, in truth, by the commander's clerk. Priscus had been serving with a vexillation that was traumatised by assisting Domitius Corbulo, a general who, upon landing at Corinth from Armenia, was famously ordered by Nero to commit suicide as his punishment for too much success. It was understandable that in the chaos at Corinth, attached to a dead general and far from their home province, mistakes might have crept into the Third Legion's otherwise meticulous issue of documents. So said Falco.

"I suppose the clerk would never have got this wrong while comfortable in Alexandria, with nobody falling on swords and everyone just watching the crocodoodles basking on the Nile?" I said.

It was a bureaucratic error that could readily be corrected, stated my father, grinning broadly.

"How?"

"Don't ask."

"Right."

"He had completed his twenty years."

"And did he dodge the reserves?"

"Medical questions were at one point asked, I dimly remember. The verdict went against him."

"Sad!"

"Priscus was desolate. Dedicated soldier: couldn't face rejection as unfit. I organised a certificate to say the poor man was on the verge of a mental breakdown over his disappointment."

"Really, Pa? I haven't heard him described as soft! People picture him as brutal. Anyway, he returned to Rome—is it true he had to sacrifice toes for the privilege?"

"Doubting child, whoever told you that?"

"Honest Father, I presume you advised him to do it." I could hear my mother sniggering with muffled amusement. As Helena Justina refixed a bone pin into her flopping chignon, still managing to look elegant however much her slippery hair strayed, Honest Father applied a mask of baffled innocence.

"Priscus ended up with copious legal bills," I dropped in nonchalantly. "Some involved compensation he had to pay for poisoning rabbits."

"Rabbits!" That made Falco sit up.

"Yes, poor little murdered ones."

"News to me!"

"Shows what he was like, though. Look, if Gallicus Priscus had dodged the reserves, did he still get his full military leaving premium?"

"Who says he dodged?" chortled Father. "I lined up the Urban Cohorts for him, where, should they ever have called him up in a city crisis, he wouldn't have had to march far on his damaged feet."

"You hate the Urbans!"

"Yes, because people like him are on the complement."

"So," I recapped, "he limped home on his chopped-off toes. Although he was a legionary, so banned from marriage, he had nevertheless produced two children who, subsequent to his discharge, were legalised—with a chit to prove it, smart-looking chits being the Falco speciality."

"Wrong!" chipped back Falco.

"Why?"

"Gallicus Priscus had *three* children."

"Pedantry."

"True, though. Girl, born even before he signed up, long gap before his wife went out to live with him in Egypt, then two boys. One of the boys was a nasty blighter. I blamed the father."

"All three have chits?"

"Each was fitted up with a fully executed, officially endorsed, signed, stamped and sealed docket of retrospective legitimisation."

I glared at him. "Are they real or fake?"

"I," announced my father, M. Didius Falco, "am the best private informer in Rome. Trust me, they look real."

In fairness, he had once acquired similar documents for me. Mine look real too.

XXXII

This conversation almost persuaded me that I could follow in ancestral footsteps and fit up Postuminus with documentation. With my mother's eye on me, I havered over the ethics. I was still hoping for a mid-morning snacks tray. Knowing their habits, I hung around. Knowing I was doing so, they forgot to summon anything.

My father explained how he had ended up beset by Ursulina Prisca, fully ten years after his successful work for her brother. The centurion's wife Aurelia, grateful for Father's validation of her children, sent the old biddy along to him, even though Ursulina was deep in an argument with her own husband. Was there special marital discord at the time, or did Aurelia not mind whether she alienated Priscus?

"She must have heard I was good," proposed Father.

"Really? Maybe she agreed with my conclusion that Priscus was a vile brother, stealing from his bullied sister. So Ursulina was right to protest," I ventured, even though everyone here used to view her as a menace. "All along we should have pitied her, not scarpered if she knocked at the door."

"She was crazy."

"Anyone can be both right and crazy," my mother corrected. I saw my brother write that down in his note-tablet, where he kept "good facts." The tutor rolled his eyes, knowing it would be resurrected at some inconvenient moment.

Since they were still holding out on having a snacks tray, I punished them by describing at length my meeting with Honorius. "I know you see him as a protégé and want the gossip."

"Sock us with it. Has his wife had him back yet?"

"Nine children with her new man, but Honorius lives in hope."

"Ha! Was he any use to you?"

"Yes and no."

"Ever Honorius. Always sees both sides of a case."

I chortled. "He would call it good law. I mentioned to him that Uncle Aulus believes I shall discover that the slaves in my case couldn't wait any longer, so they did in Surus for his loot. Honorius expressed no opinion, but he covered himself by saying, 'Aelianus is very bright.'"

Helena, who probably thought Uncle Quintus had more intelligence than his stolid brother, commented, "Your father taught Honorius everything he knows. No wonder he can obfuscate . . ."

Falco looked proud of his teaching skills. "So, Albia, have you found any evidence for these crude suspicions?"

"None. Everyone says Surus was delightful, loved by all and, even though it seemed a little early, he died naturally. It's quite disappointing."

My father, who had been involved with many a murder, reckoned if people said that, the old man must have been a vicious swine; he guaranteed foul play had taken place. I only had to find it.

As a family, we spent pleasant time discussing ways in which you could murder a rich, elderly person who was reluctant to die of his own accord. Since Tranquillus Surus had been such a potted-shrimp lover, belladonna in his breakfast takeaway was our favoured method. Helena said no one would ever query the notion of shellfish being off. Falco agreed. Also, the waiters at Nobilo's could not be accused of carelessness or a cover-up, provided other customers had eaten the same and survived. Barflies tended to have iron stomachs; they had to. Waiters could be blamed for many disasters, but their lives were hard so we would not wish injustice upon them. Not, anyway, unless Rumpus and the skivvy had come in for unexpected legacies from the dead man.

I pointed out that if they had, they would not be stuck with their horrible jobs in the bar.

They would have spent it all by now, disagreed my father.

Or they are frugal savers, suggested Mother. She decided that the next time I was passing the bar I should pop to the counter and ask whether old Nobilo, who for so many years had been pally with Surus, had ever inherited a large sum from his much-loved customer. We all agreed that if Nobilo had, it would prove our poisoned-shrimp theory, with Nobilo firmly implicated in supplying the belladonna.

With our merry theories solved, I decided to leave. Immediately, the house erupted with the noise of my sisters' return, clamouring for refreshments, which still failed to appear. I finally remembered there had been talk of a new, even more hopeless cook. The girls bounced in, full of affection for everyone, though somewhat miffed at seeing me.

"What are you doing here? We went to your house to find you. They said you had gone to a bar! Ugh! We asked Tiberius Manlius which one, so we could find you, but he just smiled annoyingly and claimed you never tell him anything. He went off to a building site as if he didn't care at all. What kind of disreputable wife are you, Albia?"

I thought it was useful this pair had not discovered that yesterday I spent most of the morning with handsome Honorius, even if it was in a public place where many witnesses could verify that he had been eating morsel food, then we both had camomile tea.

"A wife who works. Julia Junilla, be spokeswoman. Why were you looking for me?"

Julia, the taller, mercurial one who most resembled Helena, shot a quick look at Favonia, the stumpier, brusquer one who was most like Falco. They were in league; I recognised the game. Whatever they had to tell me, they would string me along, keeping it to themselves for as long as possible.

I resisted. "If you are intent on withholding, I am off home to feed the dog."

That was too much for them. "Don't go! You absolutely have to know this!"

"But you aren't going to like it."

"Try me."

"She's run away with him!"

Experienced in sister-management, I stayed calm. "Who? With whom? Why? Where to? And what do I care?"

I did care. I worked it out before they told me: Cosca Sabatina and the junior Venuleius had eloped.

XXXIII

Heads together, my sweet sisters were watching me. "This is so exciting!"

"Does it mean there won't be a wedding and it's all over with your case then, Albia?"

No, I growled. It only meant my client and her relatives, not to mention *his* relatives, might have to hire me to find the missing couple.

"They will," observed our mother, "once you turn up to explain that is what they need!" She knew I worked just like Falco.

I squared up to the girls. They were sitting on the same couch, the only one left spare. I was acutely aware of my parents, watching slyly to see how I dealt with this. Neither intended to help, partly because they were still annoyed about my case with those old friends of theirs. Also, they loved to tease.

My sisters would need careful handling. All of my father's training in interrogating witnesses was on the line here—with added tension, because the parents would never allow me to question these two ditsy creatures cruelly, or even pretend I was going to. Luckily, although I was a lot older and had left home some years ago, as daughters of the house we three still had a special camaraderie.

Julia and Favonia, seventeen and fifteen, both stared back at me with big, dark, utterly innocent brown eyes. They were dressed for parading with another young girl: too many scarves and home-created curls, too much colour, too little restraint in their choice of jingly bracelets. It was January, yet they both showed their bare pink toes through strappy sandals. At least Favonia had given up and was burying her perished little feet under a cushion.

I thought they were showing very slight apprehension. Had they been involved? "Better own up, you two, if this was your crackpot idea." That scared them. It was still possible to frighten these girls, though they were learning fast. "Better tell me, even if it is Sabatina's own plan and you only helped with details . . . Now, look, I am going to let you help me get ahead with this." I hoped the attempted blackmail did not sound like pleading.

"We don't know anything!" Julia rapped back.

"And it is not our fault," added Favonia.

"Of course, darlings! I cannot imagine you were ever in the know." I could easily imagine it, in fact. "But, note, I am treating you like adults here—if you have been to see Cosca Sabatina today and found her missing, let's not mess about, shall we? It would be *so* useful if you told me quickly what your visit was meant to be about."

They considered this, trying not to look at each other. "Wedding plans."

"Of course! Would it be silly of me to suppose an elopement came as a surprise?"

Favonia reached a decision, finding a way to make it sound good: "She had mentioned something. She talked wildly about running off instead of waiting for the ceremony. But we thought she would never do it."

"Too soppy," Julia elaborated their version. "We were sure she had no idea how to make plans."

"Let alone actually do it, before anybody realised and stopped her."

"And in January—which is so cold and horrible." Clever touch, Julia!

Everyone in the room knew that if one of our pair decided to run away with the butcher's boy their scheming would be immaculate. We would never catch up. They would have triplets and a flourishing charcuterie before anyone discovered them.

"So, just let me get this clear, what were you expecting to do today with Sabatina?"

"Plan her wedding!" they chorused again, reproving me.

"Right. Was she still at the apartment when you arrived?"

"No. The stupid girl knew we were coming but she could not be found, so the people there told us."

"They were milling around in a pickle about it, which they would not admit. A slave called Erotillus whispered to tell you she had vanished from her room this morning, not taking anything, except her jewel box."

"Forethought!"

"She has a lot of stuff. We've seen it all." They must have cosied up to Sabatina fast. Still, a couple of days was enough for this pair to become best friends with anyone. Mind you, they could dump people just as rapidly. "She was given all the jewels when her mother died. Some pieces are quite nice—though not as lovely as yours," they hinted to Helena, who turned deaf ears. She was a generous mother, though very strong-willed when pressurised.

"Sabatina has skipped by herself?" I persisted. "Escaped her chaperone?" My sisters rolled their eyes. "Look, you know that when a girl of her age leaves home without permission, it is extremely serious. Anything could happen to her."

Julia assured me, "Oh, she is not by herself! No respectable person," she continued self-righteously, "goes out alone. She was jealous of us, because we can always be escorts for each other. So we are safe and we look respectable." My parents groaned. They had fought this out on many occasions, generally losing the battle.

"She had told us that if they ever did go away together," Favonia carried on blithely, "Gaius Venuleius would come with a chair to fetch her. Of course, we asked about that where those scruffy stallholders hang out in the alley. You have probably noticed them." While the stallholders were no scruffier than the norm, I would never have said it was safe, or would look respectable, for two nicely spoken teenagers in fancy scarves to question them. My parents were giving me sceptical looks, so I had to gesture that this was no fault of mine.

Ignoring us, Julia took up the tale. "A chair arrived. They told us Sabatina must have been expecting it, so she skipped out into the alley in a big cloak with the hood right up, looking pleased—well, as far as they could see. Then off the bearers scuttled with all the curtains closed."

"Which direction?" My father could not help weighing in.

"Sidewind Passage is a dead end," I told him. "It's very narrow. When the chair reached the road, no one in the alley behind could have seen which way it turned."

Mother had a go. "Was her young man there, instructing the bearers?"

"Nobody mentioned him."

I took back the command as best I could. "What is their destination? Come clean. Didn't Sabatina tell you where they are intending to go?"

"No, I don't think she did." The girls openly consulted each other this time.

Julia was wary, but Favonia said, "When she was talking to us, it sounded as if they hadn't decided. He has a friend who lives out of town, but she had told us he couldn't take her there."

"Why not? Is the friend too sensible?" I chortled. "Afraid of trouble for himself if he helps abduct a virgin? Or did he tell the pair not to be such idiots because at the very least they might lose their marriage settlement?"

My sisters giggled, more likely at the mention of virginity than my practical allusion to money.

I prophesied sternly that *he* would be shoved into the army, like his nasty grandfather, while *she* could end up skinning rabbits by the thousand on that farm in the Campagna.

"Oh, no, they won't have to worry about that," Favonia assured me. Occasionally lacking humour, she sounded single-minded, very much in earnest. "She told us everything will be fixed up for them the way they want. They are going to get the apricot orchard."

"The one where they met each other, under the heavenly blossom," sighed Julia. "Albia, isn't it just too, too romantic?"

XXXIV

I made my way up the Aventine from the Embankment, marvelling at how those fruit trees caused so many different upsets in the lives of two different families. How could Cosca Sabatina and her hunk believe that her father—who had already told her he might not even be her father—would simply hand over a property that meant so much to him? Stick a tail on a centaur! I saw no hope of it ever happening.

If the apricot trees had aged until their crops were degenerating, what was the point? The young people were unlikely to have the resources to plant anew; even if they did there would be several years to wait before the next generation became established and fruitful. I was not a country girl, yet I understood that. Sabatina and Venuleius both came from families who owned land on the Campagna, with orchards, so unless they were extremely dim they must have heard discussions about horticulture and should know better.

Being too dim seemed entirely possible. On the other hand, people had told me that Sabatina was a devious schemer. I'd seen a little of that when she stirred up her uncle, Lucius Cosconius. One of the stallholders had suggested her plotting could become extreme. Was this new situation part of that?

I had no information about Gaius Venuleius, except that he was Ursula's younger brother, of whom she had spoken as if he was fairly casual. He spent a lot of his time with a male friend, she said. However, it seemed he was not too casual to arrange an early-morning flit. Even if Sabatina pushed him into it, he had organised the carrying chair, as expected. He was a reliable time-keeper. How many women can say that about their lovers? I could, although I knew my mother had had a lifetime of never knowing where her husband was, when she might see him again or what state he would be in when delivered home.

I stopped at my house where I picked up Paris, our runabout. He enjoyed excursions and made reliable back-up when things grew lively. I was teaching him to help when I needed observations done or there was some suspect to chase around.

He wanted to know if he could come with a cudgel, but I assured him that for an elopement it was city rules.

"Not tooled up?"

"No, dear. Just thumbs in your belt and a nasty expression."

The dog wanted to come, but we sneaked out while she was not looking. After the door closed, I heard her whining. I hardened my heart. This promised to be a complicated day.

At the Tranquillus apartments, I went first to see Euhodia. As soon as I knocked, the entrance door was whipped open by a slave, who looked excitedly bright-eyed. I could sense the tension. From time to time I heard a brief burst of running feet; once a room door slammed in the distance.

Paris and I were led to the usual reception room, where Euhodia swiftly joined us. Even her brother Aprilis poked his head in to see who had arrived, though he did not stay. "I'll be down in the shop, if anyone needs me." He was hiding from the disaster among his garum jars. For a man who had once caused a family scandal, he seemed quite nervy.

"Flavia Albia! I take it you have heard?" Euhodia did not mess about. "She is a silly little snippet, no better than her mother was. They are both going to regret this. In my view we should simply let them fly away and make the best they can of the mess they have created."

"You know what will happen," I disagreed mildly. "Let them go, and they will be back before the year is out. By then they will have quarrelled bitterly. He will have run through their money and she will be expecting a baby. He will slink away to his family, who won't want to help yours. You will be stuck with the bulge and its petulant, unmarriageable mother. That would not be a problem for a family with your wealth, if people loved Sabatina, but let us be honest, most people don't."

The matriarch listened and nodded. Whatever had been said among the Tranquilli before I arrived today, she was seeing my point.

Euhodia threw herself lengthways on a couch. She punched cushions intermittently. "For heaven's sake, the Cosconii must never know about this!" She reiterated that the brothers had been intending to help the couple, using bakery money. She seemed pretty spiky about it and clearly thought little of them, yet did not want the brothers to cut off any promised funds.

I was sympathetic. "It would be best to ascertain the full situation before her uncles are informed. I can help you, if you want?"

"And how much will that cost?" demanded Euhodia, like a woman who had already lost a fortune here. The crisis was making her exaggeratedly angry. Surely it was Postuminus who would pay any penalties, not Aprilis and her? However, she calmed down and as an explanation mentioned loss of face, which she said would affect all their businesses.

I said I could try to find the lovers, for which I would charge my usual rates. "You need to bring them back quickly, before anything happens."

"Sex, you mean?"

"Primarily. Plus loss of family valuables. I hear the young girl took her jewellery."

"*What?*" Euhodia had not been told. I made sure to conceal that my information came from Erotillus. While she sent someone to enquire upstairs, I asked how Postuminus was taking the idea that the two lovers intended to live off his orchard. That was news as well. Euhodia despatched a second slave to order him to come down. "Tell the daft lump I want him here straight away."

After a short delay, Postuminus shambled in. The bruises from his fight with Lucius Cosconius had coloured up well. They were showing below short sleeves on his tunic; his one acknowledgement of the domestic alarums was leaving off his toga. Otherwise, for a father whose only child had run off, he seemed unusually cool—though, as we all knew, perhaps she was not his child. Maybe he was glad she had gone, yet he managed to make a suitable comment that it was regrettable. I could not tell whether he and his sister had already discussed the escapade.

Unsurprisingly, he, too, had no idea of the couple's plan for him to hand over his treasured apricots. That visibly rankled.

"Perhaps they are going to send you a ransom note!" I speculated drily. "It sounds as if they have decided they can blackmail you—and I see two possibilities." Now I briskly lectured the brother and sister. "One: they are daydreaming. This is a fantasy the pair have concocted, a scheme that will never work, though the wide-eyed wonders think it will. Or two: they have some genuine reason to believe they can force you, Postuminus, to part with your trees." Taking my lead from the way his sister treated him, I even pointed a stern finger. "This is no time to gibber. We need you to come clean. What threat can these young people hold over you?"

Of course he denied there could be any threat. The more he did so, the more convinced I became that he was telling lies.

Euhodia instructed Postuminus to return to his own apartment. He was no use, she said, mooning about under her feet here. She would organise the attempt to retrieve the lovers, with my help. She would pay me; Postuminus would pay her. The abandoned father had best start counting his spare cash, ready for more unplanned expenses.

I sent Paris downstairs to re-interview the stallholders. My sisters had talked to people in the alley almost as soon as Sabatina left, which was good, but they might have missed something Paris could extract, using his greater experience. While he did that, Euhodia had her brother's slaves brought one at a time from his apartment and we interviewed them. She did allow me to conduct the first examination, while she watched. After that she took over; I let her. She learned quickly; she was following my lead in her own questioning.

There was nothing more to find. For months, Cosca Sabatina had been burbling about her wedding, wishing it could be sooner. If she had been intending to run off, no one had spotted any signals. The only thing her personal maid let slip was that her young mistress had a complex personality. People underestimated her. The maid agreed with my theory that in this elopement Sabatina was the driving force: she would have pushed Venuleius into it.

Before I left, I had a last discussion with Euhodia. Yes, the two young people had met and fallen in love, perhaps with more intensity on the girl's side. Well, that was normal. Euhodia did not know who introduced them.

That they could marry had been agreed by the girl's aunt and the bridegroom's mother; male involvement, as in so many situations, came later. The men had to arrange things financially, though both families would have been expecting that anyway. Each young person was of marriageable age now.

Tranquilla Euhodia had first met Aurelia Priscilla, the centurion's daughter, when Euhodia and Aprilis came to live in Rome. Aurelia had been kind to her, making the new arrival feel at home in the city. The two women had remained friends ever since and had agreed to negotiate this marriage with a hope of ending the squabbles between their families.

"So would Postuminus have included his orchard in the settlement?"

"Oh, no!" Euhodia was horrified. "He would have established the girl nicely, with her uncles from the bakery. Her own mother's dowry would have been used. Between Postuminus and the Cosconius brothers, it was amicable enough. Both Cosconii are very fond of her, like us all . . ." She was tailing off because, now I knew more about the family, that sounded lame. And Lucius Cosconius had been furious when Sabatina revealed that his sister had been seduced by Aprilis long ago. Euhodia carried on gamely: "The orchard is an important source of income. Postuminus had wanted it for a long time and he won't let it go. Anyway, it would be far too much to give to that ridiculous girl."

"In that case," I spoke mildly enough, though I was ready to bring everything out into the open now, "I suspect there is only one reason the couple believe they can force your brother's hand."

"Which is?" Her voice sounded level, but Euhodia's eyes narrowed in anticipation.

"They have discovered his secret."

"What secret?"

"That Postuminus has *never* been granted his freedom," I announced. "He must be terrified of someone informing on him to the authorities. His daughter, unfortunately, seems a girl who would do it. You know the position: if somebody denounces him, he will lose everything and be returned to slavery. I am supposing that proof of the position exists—and that these lovers have it."

Exposure would be disastrous for Postuminus, especially after a lifetime of believing he was free. For the rest of them, too, such a scandal might be serious. Euhodia had already spoken about loss of face; in the business community their reputation would be shredded. Like me, she could probably hear the coming jokes in her head. She and Aprilis might cope with having a relative who was a slave, especially since they came from slavery themselves, but being publicly shamed by a "respectable" brother who was put back into shackles would be very different. "Where's your brother today?" would be the least jibe cackled at them in their commercial haunts. Crueller comments would follow.

The ribaldry would be coarsest in outlets for digestive bread, I suspected. Nobody likes to pay through the nose for a ludicrously expensive product when the seller is subsequently exposed as a confidence trickster.

Euhodia briefly trembled. Even though she had hired me in the first place precisely to investigate this, she denied what I had said. She was the matriarch; she would take the lead. The family needed to keep up their pretence. I urged her to be honest. I was feeling tied in by my commission, so much so that I was ready to work on her brother's behalf against anyone attacking his status. If he really was a slave, I wanted to help them find a way to extricate him.

The poor woman repeatedly insisted to me that nobody could possibly hold them hostage over this. As I looked at her face and the strain in her expression, I was now certain that, like her brother, Tranquilla Euhodia was lying.

I could have walked away. But I was committed now. I had to help them.

XXXV

There were no running footsteps or slamming doors at the fine house on the Caelian: the Venuleii had not yet realised their boy had run off. It would be my task to notify them.

I had asked to see Ursula because we had already met. The smart old chamberlain who monitored visitors immediately picked up the gravity of the situation, though I did not explain what had happened. By this time, I knew from talking to Paris as we walked there, that people working in Sidewind Passage had overheard more than Julia and Favonia knew.

"The young couple were being pretty lax, Flavia Albia," Paris had told me, on the way. "A right pair of idiots, in fact. The girl came wandering down from upstairs and merely stood by the chair arguing with the lover—and, yes, he was there. They should have jumped in and hurried straight off. It sounded as if they had still not even decided where to go."

"Madness!"

Paris nodded. "Local people seem a nosy crowd. Very useful. They said Venuleius, if that's his name, was jumping about and insisting they would not be welcome at some place outside Rome where he usually stays. Then the girl squealed that they couldn't disappear to the rabbit farm, or even his family's place near by it, because Mardiana and Turbo were there and would snitch on them. In the end, he ordered the bearers over to the Caelian to a bar he knew. Then they were going to decide what to do."

"Well, that should help us catch up and stop them . . ."

Assuming the bar might be the Comet, I had given Paris directions while I came on alone to the house. He could be trusted to find the place. If he caught sight of the lovers, he was to observe the situation or, if he had to, intervene and stop them going off anywhere else. Paris could manage those dithering amateurs single-handed.

As soon as I told Ursula what was afoot, she sent some staff along too, with orders to collar the couple and escort them back here. I had instructed Paris that he should concentrate on securing the girl; the young man was of no interest to me. Let the Prisci deal with him. I guessed if he saw they'd been intercepted, he would leave her to face the music on her own. My aim was to take her home.

I had met Ursula in the same peristyle as last time. I wanted to find out if she knew why the youngsters were so confident about that orchard. As she and I began talking, an older woman joined us: mid-forties, short, stout and soon anxious-looking. She was Aurelia Priscilla, the centurion's daughter and mother to Ursula and the eloping bridegroom. She confirmed to me that she and Tranquilla Euhodia often met up away from their relatives for violet wine or lunch with gossip.

I mentioned that my father had once carried out work for hers. She looked surprised, and perhaps apprehensive. Falco has that effect.

News of a crisis must have run around the household, even though it still seemed calmer than the Tranquillus apartment had been. I was aware of staff walking around the upper balcony or edging into the garden's colonnade, pretending to be about their business yet surreptitiously listening. A third woman hurried out to the garden. This arrival was perhaps ten years younger than Aurelia Priscilla, maybe ten years older than Ursula. They introduced her as wife to a brother of Aurelia, the one who still lived there; he, I knew, had been in the group who went to lunch with the lawyers.

"Oh, himself will be thrilled!" his wife scoffed, when she was told of the elopement. "Upsetting the Tranquilli? He'll love it."

Her name was Julia Laronia. She was a thin, nervy type, wearing an olive green gown that did not suit her complexion, with a girdle she kept twitching as if it failed to sit comfortably. Intriguingly, she added, "I thought you were going to tell me he had been up to another of his games."

What games could those be? She clammed up. I had to deal with the matter in hand, but I did not forget her remark.

I now began to see polarised attitudes in this family. The women spoke supportively of the young people's marriage, yet the men did not liaise with the women any more than they had to. I presumed it was the men who were putting together contract terms and financial plans, during which they had come up with the status query for Postuminus. Was that conceived during their lunches at the Comet? If so, what contribution had the potential bridegroom made? Were the senior Prisci pushing him about? Was the elopement concocted by them all, or was it simply his rebellion against his male relatives?

I asked his mother's opinion, telling Aurelia: "I only know what Cosca Sabatina has said, that the couple are equally in love. Both have pressed their families to let them marry, according to her. But young women tend to misread situations when their hearts are involved. Is your son truly as eager as she is?"

For a beat of time, I felt Aurelia Priscilla hesitated. I almost believed I saw a glance pass between young Ursula and Julia Laronia too. None confirmed any doubts, however. Aurelia assured me Venuleius junior was deeply smitten. The intended linkage of the two families was a joy. She and Euhodia—as Euhodia must already have told me—could not have been happier. Everyone was looking forward to cementing new friendships, with the dear couple embarking on a long and fruitful partnership.

She made play with her arm bangles. Finally she burst out with, "My son needs to be married at his age!"

That rather spoiled the sentimental story she had given me. It turned the marriage into a practical necessity. Romance died. This time I saw for certain that Julia Laronia, the young man's aunt by marriage, was surreptitiously scoffing. I deduced there was some problem with the young man.

"So tell me why," I continued with the mother gravely, "these young people believe that the orchard, which I know has been the subject of great contention, will now be freely gifted to them?"

All three women made a show of looking blank; they failed to convince me. I let them hear my scepticism. "The apricot trees came into the possession of Tranquillus Postuminus but I see a huge question mark over how and why. And why ever should the couple suppose they can manipulate him into giving it away?" I hardened my tone. "I am assuming blackmail. Ladies, can you shed any light?"

Julia Laronia must have been a born troublemaker. Informers love such witnesses. Unable to contain herself any longer, she rounded on Aurelia Prisca. "I told you! I told you at the time! The little minx must have found something."

My companions were inexperienced in investigations of the type I carried out. Aurelia looked flustered. She struck me as one of those women who are perfectly competent; they run a home and raise a family, maybe even assist with a business—but, although they should be full of spirit, they lack self-confidence. I wondered if in her case it came from the centurion's bullying.

She drew in breath, seeming obliged to explain. She could have refused—in fact, she could have had me thrown out of her house. Instead she answered her sister-in-law first: "She did, Julia. I do know she did. My brother may never have told you—we hoped nothing would come of it. He was certain the whole thing would just go away."

I sat quiet and let the conversation roll.

"You are so right. The scoundrel kept it to himself!" Julia Laronia said in a tight voice. I gathered that in front of his sister and niece she kept up a front, but her husband was difficult to live with and she might easily have called him something worse than "scoundrel." I even suspected she wanted to divorce him, except that Aurelia and the others were loyal to him so would never support her. She herself might have no family to take her back. "Aurelia, tell us! What did the girl discover— and what has she done about it?"

Laronia was bright-eyed and imperative. Ursula, meanwhile, kept her hands tightly folded, remaining still, as if dreading whatever was to come. I could not detect whether she had known in advance, although I suspected she had.

More troubled than ever, Aurelia Priscilla turned to me. Her manner was apologetic. In some homes I would have been irritated, though I found I liked all the women there. I only wanted to encourage her. Aurelia said, "Something happened when my father died."

"The centurion?"

"Yes. You told us your own father worked for him?"

"A long time ago. But he remembers. He would, I am sure, want me to express his condolences." *Bad girl, Albia!* Falco had called Gallicus Priscus brutal. However, I fell back on conventional sympathy: "I am so sorry. Had your mother died before him?" Aurelia nodded mournfully, the type who almost enjoyed bereavements. If you had lunch with her, the conversation would be bound to dwell on anybody who had died, from the imperial family to a server in a shop down the street. "And, Aurelia, were you close to your father?"

"I admired him." Interesting verb. I noticed that Julia Laronia humphed quietly.

Despite initial awkwardness, Aurelia then told her tale: she had been deeply upset when her father died three years ago. He was a force in the family; when his great personality vanished from the house, his absence had affected her badly. After the funeral she had spent time remembering how she and her mother went out to live with him in Alexandria, where as a small child she had suddenly obtained the father she had not known before. She had loved Egypt, which was so colourful and strange, and she had loved learning that she had a handsome, boisterous papa who ran everything around him in a lively fashion.

"Some people found him rather tiring!" Julia Laronia mentioned to me drily, barely bothering to use an undertone. She had made her own assessment of my attitude, and I did like her cutting style. But I only smiled slightly, not wanting her to interrupt Aurelia's story.

Because Aurelia was grieving so hard, her good friend Euhodia had come to sit with her. Euhodia had brought her niece, Cosca Sabatina, a motherless girl who needed to be introduced into female society and taught how to give genteel comfort to sad acquaintances. She was around fifteen at the time. Her character was as shallow then as now. "Euhodia has her own girls. She did a good job with them—well, mostly. We don't talk about Mardiana. She was trying her best with her niece after the mother passed away so cruelly. Yet Cosca Sabatina always seems unreachable . . ."

"She wants to be!" interjected Julia Laronia.

Sabatina had soon grown bored in a roomful of hushed, solemn women with their heads veiled. She was told she could look around the house, since she had never been there before. She wandered off on her own.

One of Aurelia's brothers had been sorting through their father's old documents. At the end of her visit, Sabatina was discovered in a library, where the newly inherited scrolls were laid out. She was reading this private material with much too much interest. Still, everything looked in order, so she was simply ordered not to be so rude and told to come away. After she and Euhodia had gone home, Aurelia and her brother had discussed it. They hoped that the girl was curious and bad-mannered, but no more. Only later did they realise paperwork was missing.

A silence fell. I had to ask what the missing material was.

Aurelia Priscilla needed to brace herself again, but once she started she did not hesitate. That might have been because she still felt maternal indignation. "We don't like to talk about it, but I will tell you. It was correspondence from a long time ago, Flavia Albia. When my son was about twelve years old, he used to attend a gymnasium. He was always very sporty. His grandfather encouraged that. He went by himself to his practice sessions, with only his pedagogue. That young man was a good companion in many ways, but he did not immediately report to us what was happening. Gaius Venuleius was good-looking, as are all the men in our family. He was young, a nice boy, perhaps too naïve and trusting, especially with people his parents knew—and we did know the man involved. Eventually, we learned the truth. When he went to the gym, he had been assaulted."

I looked at her.

His mother blushed. "Yes, in the Greek way, Flavia Albia."

"I am sorry. He must have been very upset. But you found out who was responsible?"

"A considerably older man. He was one of the Tranquillus family."

XXXVI

This was not Greece. Rome had plenty of *palaestra* prowlers. Young boys were warned about pests, how to avoid them, always come straight home and tell someone if you have been bothered . . .

I knew more about rape than the women would have realised, but I tried to sound gentle, following what Helena Justina had once told me. "It is unfortunate, but we all know it can happen. If it cannot be forgiven, it is still best to forget and never let it ruin a life. Otherwise, the abuser wins. My own brother is twelve," I told the women. "We have given him the stern lecture so many times, he even jokes about it. But he would still be shocked and terrified if anything ever happened to him. We know he is more innocent than he thinks." I sighed. "Even so, you cannot keep them locked up. You can only be vigilant."

Aurelia was surprisingly reasonable as she agreed. "Find out and put a stop to it. That was what we did, Flavia Albia. As far as we could, anyway . . ." I wondered what she meant by that. "My husband was furious, but he thought it better to play down what had happened, as you suggest, so our boy would not be permanently affected."

Julia Laronia said to me, "Venuleius was right, for once. Give him credit. It ought to have been handled quietly, as he and Aurelia had decided, but the centurion was so angry, with the victim being his grandson, that he overruled everyone and created havoc."

Aurelia nodded. "Then my husband let himself be influenced by my father. He had a change of heart and went along with the fuss, after all—his only son, you can imagine . . . Unfortunately, we were at the time deeply embroiled in a legal dispute—"

I started hasty time-scale calculations, but without notes I could not work out quickly enough when this was. I had to ask Aurelia what, in the complex history of these two battling families, had been going on: the orchard wars, of course. Specifically, the occasion when the neighbours had had their physical fight on the boundary. Someone's shoulder was broken; Euhodia's husband had collapsed and died; she sued for compensation. It was during the same era of tireless litigation that the Tranquilli had produced their fake codicil to the Surus will, prepared by Julius, their young lawyer. Then, as I already knew, out of the blue the codicil was dropped and all action terminated; Honorius was abruptly dismissed.

Honorius had said new evidence had surfaced. Was it this? One of the Tranquilli stupidly assaulted a young boy, giving the Prisci good cause to challenge everything? Presumably young Gaius Venuleius and his pedagogue were witnesses, credible ones. Other people at the boy's gymnasium might also have seen what had happened. The Tranquillus family must have been sure they were about to lose any claim against them.

Mentally, I trawled through the male Tranquilli to decide who had done the damage: the aggressor was twenty years older than the boy at the time? Aprilis was a generation older, so not him. Could it be the much younger Postuminus? Hard to believe. He was too lacking in positivity to jump on anyone, even if he liked young boys; I'd seen no sign that he did. I suspected my contacts among their indiscreet slaves or their neighbours would have commented, if so. Januarius seemed genuinely too careful and too straightforward to have hidden such a leaning from his sharp-eyed wife. Euhodia, I knew, had sons as well as daughters among those four children who had all left Rome, but they were spoken well of. Mardiana's husband, Turbo, I had met; at around thirty now and maybe twenty then, no one would have called him "a considerably older man."

"Who was it, Aurelia?" Well done, Flavia Albia. Why not simply ask?

"We would rather not say." That's why: asking rarely works.

"Your son is in a different pickle now. Anything about his background may help to resolve this caper with Sabatina," I urged.

Aurelia refused to have that. "It was a long time ago," she demurred.

"Yes, of course."

"But you think I should tell you?" she quavered. Her daughter and sister-in-law were looking edgy, perhaps because of Aurelia's unease. They had not yet been defensive of her, but I could sense it was close. "Speaking out can cause such unhappiness."

I tried to be kind, but I had to persist. "Secrets do more harm. Please say. If I don't feel the man is important, I can ignore all this."

Just my luck: we hit a point when Aurelia Priscilla discovered her self-confidence. "No. Euhodia and I are trying so hard to reconcile our families. No harm has been done in the long term. Gaius is very sure of what he wants in life, but he has agreed to be married. I think it is better to let past matters die down quietly."

Sanitising the past would be fine—except that these women clearly thought Cosca Sabatina had discovered the old story and meant to use it somehow. There was no dying down quietly there. *She* thought the situation was so bad she believed her father would buy the couple's silence with a whole orchard.

Her lover had been the victim. Presumably that would add colour to their bribery note. The girl knew he had been assaulted and she must also know her family wanted the story smothered. Was she rousing her bridegroom to protest about his past? Or had Sabatina not yet told Venuleius what she intended to do?

I had to wonder yet again whether Postuminus had been the perpetrator. Yet I still could not see him in the role. For one thing, although people regularly insulted him, nobody had ever suggested he was a sex pest.

In Rome, that was the kind of easy slur anyone would happily throw if they had the slightest grounds. Read any salacious imperial biography and you will find youthful male seduction thrown into accusations of bad character. Mistresses don't count. It is masculine activity that will be portrayed as damning, even years later. Any satirist was quick to pounce on (or invent) such stories; historians, too, loved sneering at what princes did, or were said to do, either with their peers or with slave-boys or dwarfs. Even Domitian, our moral censor for life, had had this trotted out against him. He was supposed to have been seduced by Cocceius Nerva, who this year was sharing the consulship with him.

Homosexuality was not illegal, but nor was it traditional clean living. Ambitious Romans could ignore the accusation, but best to prevent such rumours arising. Had Postuminus been a slave, he might well have been used by men—that was one thing he escaped by being a freedman. But it was unlikely that he would have approached a young boy from a respectable home.

Well, not unless given encouragement.

This was a tricky subject to pursue with a mother who had been keenly furthering her son's marriage. I chickened out.

XXXVII

I did have ways of screwing facts out of nervous witnesses. My methods need not involve applying red-hot brands or pulling out fingernails. I had found that by looking respectable and putting people at their ease, I could often guide them slyly into revealing their most private knowledge. Laughing along with them was good. Pretending I knew the truth anyway had been known to work. Mentioning that I might inadvertently alert someone's mother, offering to break certain news to a husband, or shock a child, or enlighten a powerful employer were all good tricks. In this case I intended to use my faithful favourite: let the question drop, then unexpectedly ask them again later.

Ask one of them, in fact, when the others were no longer present. I knew which one I would prefer, but any would do if the chance arose.

But, first, something else happened.

Noise erupted out in the atrium as the staff Ursula had sent out to look for her brother came home. Along with them came her uncle, who had apparently been breakfasting late at the Comet. So now I met him.

He was loud, in a way he must have learned from his father; he immediately gave the impression he was a bully too. As soon as this bombast marched through the atrium and burst in among our group, I realised who he was: the cheat who had reneged on his Stargazer bill. The purse where this specimen carried the dinks for his rivet trick was a heavy leather item hung on his wide, showy belt. I decided at once he had not failed to pay because he forgot, or had no money with him, but because he thought he could get away with it and that amused him.

I was carrying his portrait, still in my satchel, though I kept it there temporarily and said nothing. Our waiters had been right: he was married. Now I knew why Julia Laronia openly spoke unhappily of her husband. Did she know about his meetings with another woman? Did she know who it was?

Mardiana's lover possessed, as Junillus had shown him, a square head, regular features and thick hair that came down quite low on his forehead, cut straight across his bushy eyebrows. His hair was so dark I was speculating whether he used dye. In his middle thirties, he fitted Aurelia's boast that the men in this family were good-looking. I could tell he thought himself a cracker—at least he had physique and swagger. At Nobilo's they had said his order was Lucanian sausage and fish pickle with all the trimmings. He came into our space escorted by poorly digested gusts of his chosen food. He must really soak his breakfast rolls in garum.

He noticed me. I knew the type. "Who's this?" He was waiting to find out, before deciding whether to waylay me later in some dead-end corridor.

I was introduced. I nodded quietly. The women called him Gallicus, and listed his relationships to them: husband, brother, uncle.

The no-chance chancer had riled me without doing much. Well, he had a thick gold neck chain. That is usually indicative—he was no caring intellectual who read elegiac poetry. His main fashion accessories were wristbands. His signet ring was a chalcedony eagle, a chunk of bling so big you could have weighed out onions using it. The big winter ones that have no flavour.

You can guess: I, Flavia Albia, was determined not to like him.

He came up and shook my hand. His grip was bone-breaking. I hate people who do that. They must know they are hurting you. One day I shall bend a perpetrator's wrist back and snap it in retaliation.

"Greetings!" he cried, as I rubbed my sore paw. "I heard that the canny Tranquilli are employing a delightful young lady to assemble documentation for Postuminus. Please don't mind us asking about him. We have to be careful. There are so many tricksters around these days." The rivet-dispenser would know all about that! "Dare we ask if you are making progress?" He was trying to be charming. You know what your mother would tell you: same as mine. Never trust charm.

I flung my riposte at him: "Documents are my speciality. I was winning—until your foolish young man ditched the regular procedures. That changes everything. Unless the bride is collected up and sent home fast, I believe their wedding has to go ahead, whether your contracts are ready or not. Her pure reputation is at stake. Sabatina's mother was a free citizen. Her daughter has full legal protection." Gallicus wanted to interject, but I carried on regardless. "Sabatina's mother has some very hot-tempered brothers. Looked at from your position, this morning's work by your nephew has all the allure of a dead mouse in a lady's cosmetics case."

He blinked. Then he pretended to jump back in mock alarm from my imagery.

I was being tough with the man in a way I had not been with the women. He expected me to be respectful—but, unknown to him, I knew about the Stargazer.

Time to tell him. "How does your credit stand at the Comet?" I asked him quietly. "I hope you paid up for your breakfast today. It's so easy to walk away from a bar and forget the reckoning, but I do debt-collecting too. If somebody dodges a bill with three military rivets, for instance, that is a challenge I shall love more than any straightforward proof-of-manumission enquiry."

Gallicus dodged my accusation. "*Is* Tranquillus Postuminus a straight-forward case?"

"Oh, I think so." I can bluff. It is one of my basic services to clients. "What is not so clear is why your boy and Cosca Sabatina have run away—but if there is a simple explanation, I shall find it."

"My nephew is youthful and impetuous. He must find what he's done very exciting. Do you have any ideas?" enquired Gallicus, maintaining his friendly manner but watching me narrowly.

"One or two," I hedged.

"Such as?"

"Oh, I think I should discuss theories with my clients first, don't you?" I plunged into direct questioning: "So! Are you going to tell me why the fleeing youngsters believe they can commandeer that orchard?"

"I don't believe I am!" Gallicus retorted, smiling the smile he probably used to attract women. His sister and niece looked indulgent, his wife less so.

I managed not to sniff. "Tell me, then. You came back from the Comet with your household staff, but not with the girl and Gaius Venuleius. Have they been at the bar this morning?"

"I never saw them," he replied lightly. "Somebody said they were heading there—well, it's a place he is very familiar with, from eating out with family." That made the Comet sound like a festival venue, where you could take toddlers and your ancient auntie for someone's birthday feast. "I told the waiters to let us know if they turn up, then brought our people home again. No point in slaves wandering about the streets."

"The couple never came? That's disappointing," I commiserated, staying dry.

I had noticed that although Gallicus had brought their people with him my own was missing. Paris, my runabout, must still have been out on the loose on the Caelian. Since he had not appeared to report to me, I reckoned he must be following a trail.

I saw little to gain by dallying among a family I did not work for, so I made a pretence that we should all liaise over the runaways. Neither they nor I seriously intended to do so. Then I prepared to take my leave.

I was crossing the atrium, nodding myself out with the chamberlain. Light footsteps followed me rapidly. Unless you suspect it is someone with a knife, this sound is a joy to an informer.

XXXVIII

It was Julia Laronia. Looking over her shoulder to ensure she had not been followed, she made a pacifying gesture to the waiting chamberlain as she pulled me into a side room. This was fitted out as a small domestic library; it was unlike anywhere in the orbit of the Tranquilli, where Erotillus had bemoaned their lack of culture. Here, neat scroll collections were lined up in pigeonholes, looking as if all the sets were complete. It was peaceful, well-lit by high windows and had that wonderful library aroma of cedar oil.

I was tempted to wander around peering at title tabs, but Laronia was too urgent. "What was the crack about rivets?" she demanded, though she had clearly taken in the gist.

I produced the artwork by Junillus, while I outlined the incident. "Is this your husband?"

Quickly glancing at the male portrait, Julia Laronia tossed aside the waxed board in disgust. However, she started when she saw the female, clearly recognising Mardiana. "Oh, yes, it's him—and I know that tramp as well! How long have they been messing about?" she grated.

I said, truthfully, I did not know. "I hope I haven't upset you?" I apologised. "I wanted him to know he has been identified for ducking his debts."

"Don't worry, I know what he's like!" Although his wife brushed it off, I could see she was smarting.

"I am sorry."

"Not your fault. Not even mine. I had some idea when I married him."

"Why did you?"

"You have to marry somebody!" I thought that was debatable, but her sister-in-law had said similar about Gaius Venuleius, so that must have been their attitude. Laronia explained: "The family are very rich. Mine had been once, but they were struggling."

"Does money help?"

"It takes away the pain."

"Do you have children?"

"No." She sat down on an X-framed reading chair. She must have been around my age and she took care of herself, so the question was relevant. Having met Gallicus, I presumed he had continued bedroom relations with his wife, even after he found a mistress. Mardiana was probably not the first. "He wants heirs, of course," Laronia growled. "Stopping it happening is one way to punish him!"

I made sure not to ask more: Rome was ambivalent about birth control. "He can come across as charming," I commented ruefully.

Julia Laronia pursed her lips. "When he wants. I never push him—I don't care enough to bother. Really, he can be dangerous."

"Has he ever harmed you?"

"No, but I watch his temper. I am not a wife who goads. Other people challenge him—a very bad idea. There are horrible things I could tell you . . ."

When she tailed off, I knew I might never have another chance; she had only come after me today because of his affair with Mardiana. I took a seat myself. "May I ask you some questions, Julia Laronia?" We had a table between us where scrolls might be laid out. I dropped a hand onto the table top and asked quickly, "Is this where Cosca Sabatina found the documents she is holding to ransom?"

Laronia nodded. "Laid out in plain sight, waiting for that thieving girl to come along. Gallicus was so full of inheriting a share in the house, he never considered privacy."

"A share?"

"Equal with his brother and sister. Their old grandfather had left it in trust to his wife in her lifetime, but eventually she died. The indomitable Ursulina should have inherited part, but the centurion completely shoved her out. He got a praetor's ruling that he needed a home for his family. That's men for you! In his own will afterwards, his three children shared this place equally. The business empire stayed separate, though. He couldn't change that. So his sister kept her share of it."

"Ursulina Prisca was a rich woman, in fact?"

"Very. When their father died, she inherited half of all the business properties, though naturally the men still ran them and she was cheated out of rental income. That's going to stop, because she made Ursula her own heir."

"Good heavens!" No wonder Venuleia Ursula was such a pleasant young woman. She had a monster inheritance. "Ursula's brother may feel he has losses to recoup?"

"If he does, it's nonsense. He'll one day end up with plenty. Ask me what you want," Laronia offered abruptly. "I'll either tell you the answer, or tell you no. Remember, though, I live with this family. Aurelia Priscilla is a good person, and Ursula is a sweetheart. But carry on. No one knows we are in here. The chamberlain won't tell on us."

Sometimes when I was closeted with a fresh witness, they lost their nerve and began fluttering like a trapped moth. Not Julia Laronia. If there were beans to be spilled, she would scatter freely. We might be there for some time.

Setting aside inheritance issues, I set off with a neutral question: "Do you know Aurelia Priscilla's friend, Euhodia?"

"We have met. And I can't avoid Mardiana either."

"Why is that?"

"Isn't it obvious? Because," Laronia told me heavily, "Euhodia's tramp daughter is married to my husband's brother."

Ouch! I never saw that coming.

"Of course." I managed to pick up the thread. "He is *Aurelius* Turbo. Silly me!"

So the table on which we were conveniently leaning had been used for intense study of the Samnite Wars. It was a pleasant piece—rectangular, animal-paw feet, triple candelabra standing at each end, inkwells and pens. Knowing what I now did about the two combative families, it seemed neat that Turbo had once used this library to engross himself in long-running tribal wars.

"Yes. Aurelius Turbo, ridiculous husband to the slut Mardiana!" Julia Laronia gleamed with mischief. "Misjudged marriages did not start with the latest fiasco, Flavia Albia. Gaius and Sabatina weren't the first. Aurelia and Euhodia thought everything would be rosy if they hitched that other pair."

"As a reconciliation, it failed!"

"Yes, and their new scheme will too—spectacularly!"

I remembered that while Euhodia and I were discussing Mardiana's affair, she had complained she took on Turbo misguidedly, pushed into it by Aurelia Priscilla. "Mardiana has been trysting with your husband—yet Turbo claims he and she are eternal soul-mates."

"Turbo is just pig-headed."

"Yes, I wasn't much taken with him," I agreed. "Whatever he studies, it doesn't include human nature—well, not his wife's. But he did seem harmless."

"He is a fine academic, I believe," Laronia told me, with no audible sarcasm. "They should have left him alone to do what he wanted. Oddly enough, he has always got on with Gallicus, even though they are diametric opposites. It was after Turbo had been married off, and he moved out, that Gallicus felt lonely. My husband is the type who always needs company. I believe there was talk of him going over to the Aventine to live near Turbo. He tried to get hold of an apartment in the same building, but the tenants had rights and they refused to budge."

I sat up. "Do the Prisci own property in Sidewind Passage, then?"

"I think the whole street is theirs." Oh! "So Gallicus married too." Laronia continued with her own story. "I arrived here a little later. If Turbo had made a home with his own people, instead of with them on the Aventine, who knows?"

"So you came—" I pondered dates again "—during the orchard tussle?"

"I had that pleasure." She was tart. "The famous fence fight had occurred, so they were all locked in litigation. I was shocked by their intensity. At first, they made out with me that the incident was simple horseplay, after they had innocently gone to pick fruit. Later I realised. Harvesting the fruit was a deliberate slight. The centurion had encouraged Gallicus to escalate the conflict."

"Do you know whose shoulder was broken?"

"My husband's."

"Ah! He was in the fight?"

"If there's ever a fight in his vicinity, Gallicus will be there. And ousting people is in his blood. He carried out commercial-property evictions on his father's orders. His touch is never gentle and he hasn't let the shoulder hold him back. His father brought him up to deal very harshly with tenants."

"The centurion was a stern landlord?"

"Vicious," Laronia grunted. She was fiddling with her girdle again, as if mentioning him made her nerves jangle. I wondered how her father-in-law had been with her. She might be skinny, but her face was attractive. Most centurions won't miss a chance to misbehave.

"You didn't get on with him?"

"No. Gallicus is bad enough. His father was *seriously* rough."

"Out of control?" In my time I had encountered the worst kind of military men.

"No, the opposite. The kind of hard professional who always knew *exactly* what he was doing. He would attack before anyone had even thought of annoying him. My husband tended to follow his lead, and the two together were lethal." Again Laronia seemed on the verge of telling me something, but sheered off.

"Yet Aurelia Priscilla told me she admired him!" I marvelled.

Laronia reprised the look she had given to Aurelia, but said, "Why not? He was a wonderful father to her. When the mother took her out to Alexandria, Aurelia would have been a delightful little tot, all curls and adoring big brown eyes. Love at first sight on both sides."

"How was he with the boys?"

"Born out in Egypt and controlled from babyhood. They were definitely *his* boys, to be moulded in his image. The younger boy perhaps less so. Their mother favoured Turbo, fought to get him an education because she saw he was clever. I think the centurion gave way over Turbo's learning and his obscure interests, because he always had Gallicus to be tough like himself and share his purposes."

"Tough but charming," I suggested.

"Don't be fooled by the charm."

I risked saying, "Mardiana clearly is."

"Her mistake. Her husband knows his brother's past. If Turbo wants, he can enlighten her about Gallicus. The sentimental fool really is devoted to her. He will try to persuade her to stay with him. But old history could be about to rear a very ugly head."

"History?" I queried.

Unfortunately, Laronia had limits to her indiscretion. "Gallicus is a maniac. But do not ask."

She stood up, so her chair scraped backwards with some force. She thought she was ending our interview, but I kept my seat, looking up at her. Drawn either by a love of gossip or a need to unburden herself, she did pause.

"Tell me," I continued, "Gallicus had his shoulder broken by Euhodia's husband. Do you know if any reparation was paid by Telesphorus or by the family?"

Laronia shook her head. "Happened before I was married—though I certainly heard about it. We had to wait until that shoulder healed, which took a long time, before our wedding went ahead. Gallicus is a traditionalist, you see, and I could not have been physically carried over the threshold until his bones mended."

I smiled as I imagined it. "But there was no compensation?" I repeated.

"No. For one thing, Telesphorus dropped dead. Euhodia started agitating about that. I think he had been pushed and shoved around—by Gallicus, who I told you is aggressive when he's riled. Needless to say, the lawyers were arguing happily on both sides. A slave and some money did change hands in respect of Telesphorus. But it was all around the same time as that other trouble, what Aurelia was telling you about."

"The incident with her son?" I was finding it hard to see logic in this. "But didn't that mean the Prisci had another claim against the others?"

"Yes, but *their* argument in return was that the boy had encouraged what happened."

"Goodness! Did he?"

"I never knew the whole story." Laronia was still standing, her hands tightly gripping the back of the chair she had previously occupied.

"He *wanted* it?" I pulled a slight face, openly doubting her. "This family accepted a version where the boy was complicit?"

Laronia prevaricated: "I agree, it does sound as though someone got off extremely lightly. As I understood it, all the legal issues just collapsed."

"Why?" I would like to find out for Honorius the reason he was paid off.

Laronia was still trying to wriggle. "Oh . . . there had been a document, something that our side proved was a brazen forgery." That would have been Honorius, lining up his experts. "The Tranquilli were about to be shown up very badly."

"So they backed away?"

"No, they had to drop their action; they lost the main man in their legal team."

"Lost him? Dead, dumb or simply careless?"

"Did a bunk, Albia," explained Laronia, laughing. She seemed to have relaxed again.

"Why was that?"

"First," she confirmed, still with a great deal of amusement, "the lawyer himself had created that forgery, so he was about to be exposed. All the Basilica Julia knew. It was an attempt to change a will to benefit someone in his own family, I believe." I sat up straighter. That was nothing to her next revelation: "And then—you won't believe this, Albia—it was their *lawyer* who had been playing about with Gaius Venuleius."

I took a breath. "Name?"

"The lawyer? Didn't Aurelia decide not to tell you . . . ?" she teased. I flashed a pleading look. Laronia was soon havering. "Of course, it was public knowledge that he absconded . . ."

I smiled back blandly. "So what's the harm? Let's have it."

"It was Julius."

"*Julius?*" I had forgotten about him. The brother of Januarius, the one Januarius had told me was devastated by stress, among other things. "Tranquillus Julius—who scampered off to Belgica?"

"There was talk of unspeakable deeds with a donkey," Laronia agreed, pretending shock.

"I heard it was a goat! More importantly," I rapped back, "even his father says that Julius was embezzling—in the full sense of stealing from his clients. Not from you, I take it?"

"Not us. He never did any work for the Prisci." Laronia might only be related to them through her marriage, but she was revelling in this juicy gossip. "Flavia Albia, do not be taken in by any false story the Tranquilli give out that Julius is lost in Belgica. We know exactly where he is. They are keeping him on their Campagna farm."

"Oh? Fenced up like an animal in an imperial menagerie?"

"Comfortable retirement, I believe." Laronia sighed regretfully. "But he does have to share his retreat with their ghastly rabbits. Hop, hop!" she murmured.

To which I answered gently, "Hop, hoppity, hop!"

XXXIX

More scandal might have followed, but Aurelia Priscilla entered the library. It was so small, only a couple of single-height bays, that she almost stumbled over us. "He wants to be read to," she murmured, scanning pigeonholes distractedly.

"Need my help?" asked Laronia, not explaining why we two were huddled there together.

"No, I just have to find the next scroll, because he remembers what we had been reading last time . . ." She took one and left, still without comment on us.

"The old fellow?" I clarified with her sister-in-law. "Is he a relative?"

"Not directly." Laronia was being oblique, on purpose I realised afterwards. "But we look after him."

She clammed up. Aurelia passing through might have made her feel uncomfortable, even though the other woman had shown no disapproval, nor did she even seem to spot that Laronia was giving me information.

Nobody in my own family was so easy-going. They were all alert for conspiracy. You couldn't sneeze without some nosy observer supposing it was a signal about a secret plot. This was generally right too: the Didii harboured more plots than there were fleas on a rat.

Laronia had such an air of finality it would have been rude not to leave. I rose and slowly put on my cloak, while I thanked her for her frankness. Once again, I said I was sorry about her husband, but again she said she knew what he was like. "A man who takes his breakfast at a neighbouring bar!" I summed him up.

"Oh, they all do that from time to time," Laronia informed me airily, leading the way from the library. I presumed she meant men in this family, and that eating out was to cover their conniving. "At least it saves on the bakery bill," she finished blithely.

"Does Gallicus renege on household accounts?" I pressed her, as we re-entered the atrium. Plenty of men in Rome did. Getting paid was any tradesman's nightmare. "Do your fishmonger and olive-oil merchant suffer?" She could probably tell I would never let go of the rivets trick at the Stargazer—not now I had seen the comfortable home Gallicus lived in. What he had done was despicable. It continued to offend me.

"No, we pay our way." Laronia soothed, exonerating the swine even though we had established he was a dreadful husband. "Aurelia Priscilla controls the budget, as her mother did. We also have an excellent book-keeper."

"Philodamus." My statement made Laronia look surprised. Even the old chamberlain, ready to sign me out on his tablet, was taking notice. "I have been wondering," I went on. "When Philodamus was passed across to the Tranquilli, around seven years ago, was that as reparation for Telesphorus?" I saw no likely reason to revisit this house, so I might as well cover all my puzzles.

Julia Laronia would have been living there at the time, though as a new bride, so I gazed pointedly at the chamberlain. I had noticed before, he was an older man than staff were in most households. He was smart, yet I could not tell whether he was a slave or a freedman. Nor, when he looked to Laronia, could I detect if he was merely ascertaining whether he should answer me. Or could some hidden factor be worrying him?

Laronia nodded permission, so the polite factotum told me: "Philo-damus was indeed given over as part-payment 'for suffering endured,' when Mardianus Telesphorus died after an accident in our orchard." I noticed he called it an accident and said "our" orchard.

With nothing to lose, I pressed on: "But now the Tranquilli have no further use for his wonderful bookkeeping?"

"They always suspected Philodamus spied on them." The chamberlain managed to imply elegant regret at this. In proper houses, nobody spies.

I smiled, as I admitted ruefully, "I may have had something to do with that recently! Still, Philodamus seems happy to have returned to a place he sees as home." I wrapped my cloak around me, to reassure them I would be leaving at any moment. "You look as if you have been here a long time and probably know everyone. Do you mind if I ask you one more question?"

As before, the man double-checked with Julia Laronia. She made no objection, though nor did she walk away and leave me with him. She stood where she was, her arms folded, waiting and listening.

"You mentioned the orchard." I kept it light. "I know it belonged originally to a man called Appius Tranquillus Surus. I also know he died a very long time ago, so questions I need to ask in my work can no longer be answered. You don't happen to remember, I suppose, what Surus died of?"

"Pneumonia." The chamberlain did not hesitate. This time he only glanced back to Laronia after he had spoken. He said it firmly. He looked surprised that I had asked.

"The old man's friend, proverbially!" I took a chance: "Though I have been told some people felt Surus died before his time. Even worse, this sounds astonishing, but I have actually fielded hints of foul play. There is quite a strong undercurrent that he did not die of natural causes. Do you have anything to say about that? Was it really pneumonia—or could somebody have helped him on his way, presumably for financial gain?"

The chamberlain was astounded. "That is rubbish!" he exclaimed, letting slip his urbane persona. He sounded angry and even upset. Recovering smoothly, he added to his first answer: "I was a young man at the time, but I remember clearly. Surus died of pneumonia after he was soaked through in a very heavy shower of rain."

"You knew him?"

"At a distance."

"People seem to have liked him," I remarked.

"People did." The chamberlain, outraged by my suggestion of murder, was fretting at my continued questions. He flexed his note-tablet; he wanted rid of me.

"He was certainly known to the family here," I persisted. "He left that orchard to old Ursulina Prisca and her brother."

"Yes, *Domina*. He was known here!" The man's tone was oddly arch, as he delivered what was intended to be his final comment.

He and Julia Laronia exchanged a glance, excluding me. They were amused. They were also not intending to reveal whatever joke was being shared at my expense. Later, when I understood, I realised they must have thought me an idiot.

If this had been a Greek adventure novel, I might have wondered if the pair of them secretly knew that Appius Tranquillus Surus had simply disappeared for some reason and was not dead at all. Mind you, if my figures were right, that would have meant by now he was at least a hundred.

Settle down, Albia.

XL

Paris was waiting outside the house. "Progress! But I thought I'd see you in private, Albia."

We walked away from the Priscus dwelling at a brisk pace. If the chamberlain or anybody else had been looking out after us, they could have told from our pace we had something to discuss and were heading for a known destination. On the wandering Clivus Scaurus, we turned before the Temple of Claudius, so we were heading along its final stretch towards the Porta Caelimontana. The Comet lay just the other side of the old gate in the ancient Servian Walls.

As I had hoped, Paris had seen the lovers arrive at the bar. He had watched them have their chair parked a few doors along, after a waiter made gestures about blocking access to his counter. They walked up the pavement, Sabatina tottering on girlie shoes. It was just when Paris reached the bar. Being a strange face, not yet known to those involved, he stationed himself at the outside counter discreetly and ordered a custard slice as cover.

"It looked as if they were expected—at least the boy was."

"Is he a boy? Paris, I thought he was twenty, or twenty plus."

"Well, he behaves like a boy. Pretty looks, shows off his gym muscles, no manners, no damned idea."

"Luscious, as Julia and Favonia would say! Go on, then. Who was expecting this demigod and his girlfriend? Was it the man from the Stargazer?" I dug out the sketch, even though Paris had seen it before at our house. "Straight-cut hair and an attitude. I've met him now. A turd they call Gallicus."

The runabout nodded. So Gallicus had lied when he said he never saw the couple. "Him—and another, older," said Paris. "The men had been eating, looking casual, as if they were filling time while they were waiting for the young pair."

"Number two was a similar type?"

"The same. Forties. Burly, bossy, fast talker, knows it all and wants nobody's opinion. I never saw whether he paid his bar bill!" Paris jokily referred to the rivets incident. "He stayed on there with the couple. I thought I could safely leave them chomping and quickly find you."

"Chomping?"

"The dear young things had begun to niggle, so the bosspot was organising food bowls for them. It looked just like a father taking two children out for a festival. Constant need to fill them up. Next thing they'll be complaining they are bored, then just at the wrong moment they will be desperate for a toilet."

I could not help laughing. "Let's hope the infants like whatever he gives them, or they will be hurling those food bowls onto the floor in a screaming tantrum . . . Who do you think the provider is?"

"Something about the way he was with the young fellow, and how the young fellow behaved with him, I wondered if he really was the father."

"Venuleius Senior," I said. "That fits. This is starting to make sense." It was, but with an unpleasant tang. "What else happened, Paris? Some slaves from the house must have turned up?"

"Yes. The man from your sketch demanded why they had come, as if he didn't like it. He gathered the slaves together and, I guess, returned them here."

"He did." Gallicus didn't want them? I felt an interesting sensation now, the crawling ants of realisation. "So had those slaves seen the young couple at the bar?"

"Yes. They let out a gusty cheer as they arrived, so the girl looked confused and the boy looked shifty."

Paris and I were descending the slope to the ancient Caelimontana Gate, which had been remodelled into the Arch of Dolabella. Before we emerged and reached the bar in the Vicus Capitis Africae, I fired off,

"The slaves made no attempt to apprehend the couple? They had been told to grab the runaways."

"No. The two men seemed happy just to send the slaves home again," Paris said. "The couple were not trying to escape."

Now I had it. "They were all happy together? Nobody was agitated?"

"No."

"Paris, you see what this is?"

"No, Albia—but, knowing you, I dare say you are about to tell me." Paris and I had a teasing relationship.

"It's not an elopement at all," I announced to him. "This is a family conspiracy."

XLI

At the Comet, the group was breaking up.

Gallicus had left before, of course. I identified two remaining men from the descriptions Paris gave: a paternal type was settling up with the waiter, so here was one person who properly paid his reckoning. A young buck was waiting for Cosca Sabatina to reappear, pulling a face after using the facilities; then he braved the backyard toilet too. The older and younger men were in similar brown tunics, with belts they had bought at the same market and cloaks from the family tailor. Their style matched that of the absent Gallicus, with big accessories; their body-weight and manners confirmed they were of one family. You could tell they had wealth. Self-assurance poured from them like too much shaving unguent. They probably reeked of unguent too, but I was keeping well back in case the girl saw me.

While the waiter found change, the older man told Sabatina to go on ahead, out to the chair. Gaius Venuleius hung back with his father, not feeling bound to escort his lady in a street she might not know. He was well-built and very good-looking, though in manner he hovered on the weedy side of affable. I might have let him move sacks from a cart into a store, though I wouldn't have trusted him to build the pile neatly.

I muttered quick instructions to Paris, who followed the girl; her progress was slow due to footwear she had chosen for show, not pavement-friendliness. When I first set up as an informer, Helena and Falco had advised me to forget fashion and always to be in walking shoes. I'd say that goes for elopement too. You never know when you may need to sprint away—either escaping pursuit or after realising you have picked a shoddy boyfriend you need to lose.

Eventually the moppet fell into her conveyance; it had closed curtains so she never saw what happened next. As the bearers bestirred themselves from sitting on the kerb telling dirty stories, Paris marched up. Pretending he worked for the Prisci, he put on a surreptitious air and announced quietly, "Change of plan! We're taking the woman ahead for now, then sonny will follow. I'm coming to show you the place . . ."

The chair had been parked so that instead of impeding the Comet's counter it blocked the doorway of a local grocery; the shop's het-up owner was giving grief over losing her chickpea sales. Paris urged haste before she sent for the vigiles. In fact she had gone in for a besom to sweep them off her frontage herself.

Like many last-minute plans, ours worked much better than schemes people have endlessly chewed over. The chairmen trotted away around a corner out of view, with Paris loping alongside.

Excellent. Cosca Sabatina had been kidnapped from her own elopement.

A few moments later, Gaius Venuleius wandered out from the bar, then stood outside, looking puzzled because he could not see his bride. His father joined him and instantly picked up that something bad had happened.

I leaned on the bar counter, while the two men had a hot exchange. They finally turned in my direction; both were still scanning the street as if they hoped the chair had just taken a turn around the block to avoid the grocer's aggravation. I was a woman. They ignored me.

I raised one hand, to give them a pointed little wave. At last they took notice. I smiled sweetly. "Greetings! You must be the Venuleii." Senior, at least, detected trouble. "My name is Flavia Albia. Someone has probably told you, I am an agent for your future relatives, the Tranquilli." These two were trying not to glare. As far as my clients knew so far, the marriage was still supposedly planned, so the Venuleii had to pretend. "Cosca

Sabatina asked me to apologise. She has rushed off to an appointment she suddenly remembered."

I waited courteously, while they worked this out: the girl had vanished; I worked for the other side; their plot had gone awry; I had had something to do with it . . .

I toughened up. "Time for truth-telling. I'd like to hear whatever today's antics are about."

"Where is the girl?" the father demanded.

"Don't worry about the girl."

"Where is she?" wailed her future bridegroom, supposedly lovelorn. From his face, he was fearing he would get the blame for this.

"I shall be looking after her. I expect," I spoke as if I were still working out what to do, "at some point Sabatina will be returned to her family. I am sure that is what they will want, and it may be the best solution. Meanwhile, she will stay at a safe house until things have been explained to her."

"What are you talking about?" The father became threatening, but I stood my ground.

"My task," I told him, as calmly as an accountant announcing bankruptcy to people who have brought it on themselves, "is to enlighten that poor girl. I shall have to explain what your scheme was and why her wedding will not happen. I shall do so away from her relatives to give her privacy. They will have to be told, of course. And I cannot shield her from painful disillusionment."

"You're talking rubbish," snapped the father, though he knew what I meant.

"No, I'm talking sense."

"You know nothing!"

"I concede that I don't yet know everything. However, I can see enough. I have identified a very determined conspiracy. Your wife," I tackled Senior sternly, "and her friend Euhodia may genuinely desire friendship between your stricken families. I shall enlighten Euhodia. If your wife has been given no idea what her male relatives intended, then, Venuleius, you must square it with her yourself."

He rejected that.

I continued: "I have no doubt, no doubt at all, that even if a wedding had taken place, the union would have been a sham." I faced up to the young man, letting him see my distaste. "Own up, Gaius! You do not love Sabatina, as she believes! You have never loved her." He blustered, yet did not deny me.

"He likes her," the father remonstrated feebly.

"Does he? Or, like all young men his age, does Gaius Venuleius like the idea of freedom from the family home? I know he has certain friends outside who are pulling him another way. But his mother says he has reached the age where he needs a wife, so he meekly goes along with that. Lovely mother, loving son! He wants to be set up for life, with ample resources. To get it, he might even have tolerated the girl, at least until she wanted more of him than he can ever give."

"We both agreed," Junior protested. "We were going to be happy." He had a way of sounding sincere, while not meeting anyone's eyes. This might have convinced an inexperienced girl. To me he was like a dog who had knocked a cake plate off a table and downed the lot. "We want our wedding."

"So you tell me! Not for the good wishes and augury! Does Sabatina understand *why* you wanted it?"

"I don't know what you mean."

"Promises must have been made to you—so how much have you been influenced by family pressure? *Do this and we shall see you all right* . . . What were you expecting if you cosied up to Cosca Sabatina? Tempt her with a celebrity wedding, get her away from her family, gifts no doubt? Your apricot-blossom proposal was a good touch! Who arranged that sweet introduction, by the way?"

"My uncle Gallicus." The young man seemed honestly puzzled by the implications. I was prepared to believe his older relatives had been using him, probably confessing only half of the true story.

"The one who wants his orchard back?" Deliberately ignoring the father, I made a more crucial check on the son: "He is using you to grab his trees? I think you have had calls from elsewhere, calls not to do it.

Gaius Venuleius, are you still in communication with the lawyer Tranquillus Julius?"

"I haven't seen him for years!" The young man rapped that at me so quickly I had to back off. He did not look effeminate, but I had been wondering whether he might be. He coloured; his father stiffened. I sensed an atmosphere.

"We heard he went abroad," said Venuleius Senior, baldly bluffing.

"No, he is on the Campagna shearing flocks. Forget the Belgica story."

"He breeds animals for temple sacrifices." Venuleius clearly knew more than anyone had told me.

I turned on him: "Doesn't your son spend time away from home? Is it on a farm?"

"It's by a lake!" inserted Junior, indignantly. He seemed to think better of this outburst and fell silent.

"A lake? Rustic and no doubt *very* private!" Neither made any more protest. Our location was public and the public were listening eagerly. "Suppose, Gaius Venuleius, that despite lakeside attractions, you had willingly married Cosca Sabatina."

"Of course! She is a wonderful person."

"All right. You think so," I conceded, though not believing him. "To me, Sabatina is an enigma—either hideously dim, or wickedly bright. I don't believe she has any idea about you, Gaius. I do hold you responsible. Whatever part you played in setting up your romance, it was a grim deception perpetrated on an impressionable soul. She thinks you love her. That is what she desperately *wants* to think. You may convince yourself that she should have paid more attention. I say her betrayal is cruelty. I also say it was deliberate. Her charm for your family is that she belongs to the Tranquilli and her father is in a difficult situation that means one way or another he can be brow-beaten."

"That's nonsense," Gaius disagreed, though his own father was remaining silent; Senior had seen the game was up.

"No!" I accused the spurious bridegroom. "You have conspired with your father and uncle's greed. A talismanic property has been given away but they want it back, and without recourse to law. So your engagement was a fraud. Your marriage would have been the same. Your elopement must have been arranged today to push things forward. It all derives from years of legal wrangles. Nothing has changed. The endless strife drags ever on. The gain your relatives are pursuing carries its own smell. In all this," I said gently, "what I detect is the subtle perfume of apricots."

XLII

Confrontations happen while people are standing outside a bar, but it is never an ideal venue: too many passersby shoving in their elbows, too many witnesses adding their own points to your conversation, too much pigeon poo, too much noise. In January you soon feel the cold. I huddled tighter in my cloak and realised I wanted this to end.

While I was at the Priscus house with the women, the Comet must have filled and then emptied of its urgent lunchtime crowd; now, with early winter end of day, it began attracting home-goers. The outdoor temperature dropped. The light held up but was sinking towards evening. Customers who wanted to take supper home were calling for counter service. A few pushed past us to go indoors before the evening tables were taken; someone demanded a dice pot. Everyone was tired, soon irritated that we, who were talking instead of buying or eating, occupied space that they needed for normal caupona purposes. The waiters had sharpened up from the lethargy I had witnessed only that morning; they said nothing, because the Venuleii must be prized regulars, but they gave us ugly stares and swung flagons around wildly.

There was no chance of me being invited back to the Priscus house for a civilised discussion on reading couches. Venuleius Senior made his move: he shouted angrily that he didn't need to talk to me. The noise level had increased at the bar as the street grew busier, so I signalled that I would let father and son go; I had no way to detain them. I was not the kind of informer who would trail along behind them, calling out pleas and risking blows.

There were no goodbyes. I would set off for home, although before I turned away, I glimpsed Venuleius Senior muttering to his son. Junior was being instructed to follow me.

Let him. Well, let him try. I knew how to lose him.

Head up and mind busy, I started walking. I need not debate the conspiracy any further with the Prisci. All I had to do was report to Tranquilla Euhodia that she and hers had been seduced by a bogus proposal: the Priscus men were set on clawing back that blighted orchard. I guessed they had first tried asking for it as part of the marriage settlement, but Postuminus would not play; Euhodia herself had roundly told me it was too much to give to the young couple. After that, advised by Crispinus, the Prisci had cruelly raised the issue of slavery; that would mean Postuminus could not own property. When it took too long, or even perhaps because they heard I was working to rescue their victim, they grabbed the bride and tried to force his hand. Sabatina might have believed she had coordinated her elopement, but she had been tricked. Time would tell where her lover stood in the murky business, though I thought he had been duped too.

If her love for him was real, she now faced heartbreak. I had known that pain once, when I was much more down-to-earth and resilient than this young woman. I pitied her disillusionment. I even pitied her father, though he might seem gormless. He had been pushed around enough to make me want to set things straight for him. People had made me see Postuminus as a victim: that was enough for me.

Lost in these thoughts, I was so set-faced I never even noticed any hassle by Domitian's new Gladiating School. If there were cat-calls, I missed them, which was one way to cope. Coming to, I marched around the Flavian Amphitheatre and straight down to the Circus Maximus. I remembered I was being tailed by Gaius Venuleius. A check identified him, still sloping behind me. He had not been trained to use doorways, find cover behind other walkers or criss-cross the street. Coming alone was not best practice anyway: decent shadowing needs two people. It was a cynical pleasure to be tailed by such an amateur.

My father would have stopped suddenly and pounced on him, with fragrant invective or a sucker punch. I could not be bothered. I was going home. Anyone could have found out where I lived, without this incompetence. He should have tapped me on the shoulder and asked for a note with my business address.

In Lesser Laurel Street, when I reached home, I ran into Corellius, taking exercise. He was leading our donkey; he said Tiberius had promised he could borrow her on a daily basis. Corellius would take walks along the Vicus Armilustrium as far as he could on his bronze leg, trying to increase the distance every time. When he could stagger no further, he would swing himself up and ride back. Merky, a tolerant beast who had been given to me by a grateful client, looked happy, though Corellius was as despondent as usual.

I gave Merky a pat, then watched them leave. I had been intending to use the donkey myself for more work this evening. I was tired enough that, instead of being annoyed, I took it as Nature's way of excusing me from duty. Going indoors, I ordered Rodan to step outside and if he saw a feeble young man to bellow at him to get lost.

For once, the porter obliged. I heard him shouting crudely. He wandered back in, decided that was enough work for the day, and slunk to his hut in the building yard. He was supposed to lock the doors and stay on guard at night, but he had a lurid collection of excuses for never doing it. We thought Rodan might be afraid of the dark. Tiberius always went around slamming home the night bolts.

The children were playing in the courtyard with their automaton crocodile, making bloodthirsty jaw-snap sounds. Their nurse, Glaphyra, had her eye on them, but was gossiping with my steward. Gratus called, "Your mother came! She is not very pleased with you. You had better trot down to theirs tonight, ready to grovel."

I knew why she had come. I was sure I could leave Helena to cope until I had time for an apology. If they were seriously annoyed, Father would come striding up the hill full of fury, but today's misdemeanour could be explained away. He would probably bring a flagon to share with Tiberius. By the time it was empty, Falco would have dropped whatever he was supposed to say to me.

I went upstairs to rest until dinner. The evening darkened. Gratus walked around with lamps. Gaius and Lucius were making a routine din, as Glaphyra collected their toys and cleaned them up.

Tiberius came home from the baths, where he had been with Dromo. I could hear Dromo whining his perennial complaint that he had not been allowed a pastry. Making no comment, Tiberius joined me in our room. Kicking off his shoes and throwing his belt aside, he flopped onto the bed. We kissed cheeks, a formality we liked to follow. We had time and opportunity for love-making but were both too weary. We just lay there together, not even talking.

An hour later we were still there; it was so comfortable and quiet, I had fallen asleep. Tiberius was holding me in one arm, with my head on his shoulder, probably worrying about when he ought to wake me for dinner. I was not fully unconscious; I knew he was silently considering the predicament. He ought to be aware I was never a woman who required primping and perfuming before a meal in her own home. I would wash my hands and find slippers, but the master would be lucky if I even threw on a necklace for him. Of course I might do so, if only to outrage Suza by choosing an incorrect accessory . . .

Something else woke me.

Downstairs in the courtyard, the heart of our happy household, little boys squealed, someone else screamed shrilly, then strange voices began violently shouting.

XLIII

Tiberius and I both jumped up so fast we tangled in the doorway.
"Sorry!"

"Shove out of my way then."

From up on the balcony, we could see a group who must have been fetched here by Gaius Venuleius. He, his aggressive uncle Gallicus and several slaves were powering around the courtyard, menacing our people. There was no sign of Rodan. Gallicus must have broken in. As a tenancy enforcer, he was bound to be adept with latch-lifters. Clearly he had neither respect for property nor for people. He was wearing a long dark red cloak now, as Junillus had described at the Stargazer.

Little Gaius and Lucius were standing on a stone bench, screaming. A dropped bowl and towels showed where Glaphyra must have been washing their hands and faces for dinner. She was now being violently grappled by Gallicus. He was very strong, but she was a round, well-stuffed package, who had had years of dealing with the male race. So she was fighting off his assault quite well, even though Gallicus had somehow dragged her across the courtyard and partly up the steps, where he appeared intent on hurling her down again. Glaphyra grabbed onto the handrail with the unbudgeable grip she used on violent children. They continued to struggle as I started down towards them.

Three or four other men wove about below. Gratus, my steward, was having fisticuffs with one, placing blows as precisely as if he were positioning pictures. His blows were hard, however; Gratus was suave, yet he sometimes let slip a phrase that told of a rough past. Suza, a top-heavy girl who had come to us from a fish farm, danced tauntingly around another fellow, gurning as he failed to catch her. Young Venuleius had least luck. Fornix had emerged from his kitchen, a bold man with the solidity of a chef who ate his own food; he rolled out brandishing a huge cleaver. He kept half a biscuit between his teeth as he backed the bridegroom against a wall, while Dromo capered and shouted excitedly, "Cut his ears off, Fornix!"

From memory it was ears. Or maybe not. Fornix was a Roman cook; he would not shrink from slicing intimate organs. Dromo was a Roman slave; he was an expert in obscene ideas.

Tiberius surveyed the fracas in his usual restrained way, then assumed an orator's pose for a moment and formally let out a bellow. Our house had been invaded before, so he was partly enraged that his newest security measures had failed. Barefoot and weaponless, he was at a disadvantage, though soon hopping on one leg as he pulled on a shoe. At his roar, the action slowed; the noise wavered. "You tell them, Aedile!" Fornix responded, nonchalantly finishing his biscuit as he waved his butchering blade.

He then abandoned Venuleius, because a retainer had grabbed Suza; the cook turned to rescue her, swinging himself around like a laden barge on a full tide. On the staircase, Glaphyra bit Gallicus. He tried not to lose his hold, but she swung her big hips into him and stumbled away while the sideswiped man fell against the rail, cursing. I stepped over him; he made a grab; I snatched free, kicked him and followed Glaphyra, who had rushed to the boys. Young Venuleius, no longer threatened by Fornix, had knocked Dromo to the ground and made a run towards Gaius and Lucius. Luckily, he drew up short. Glaphyra enveloped her charges. She whisked them to safety in our dining room, while I held up a hand to him, palm out, as a warning signal. "Ooh—careful!"

Venuleius had halted of his own accord, almost with his heels smoking. All at once he stood desperately still.

Tiberius, now shod, had been descending the stairs. He stopped and I heard him whistle gently, through his teeth. All the noise fell away to nothing. Into that dead silence a new voice spoke, taking charge.

"Nobody move. Nobody speak. Listen to what will happen. All you burgling bastards, let go of the aedile's staff and family. Go onto your knees, then guts on the grit. Put your faces on the ground and stay there. Hands behind your backs where I can see them. Even a finger twitches, and your boy goes straight to Hades."

This man had walked in from the builder's yard. He stepped up behind Venuleius, seized him, stopped him dead and pulled back his head by the hair. His free hand positioned a slim, glinting dagger right against the young man's throat. He ought to have been on a cavalry horse, but otherwise it was classic: a competent Roman soldier was about to behead a conquered barbarian. Venuleius was trying to stop himself shuddering.

I wondered facetiously where the emergency stiletto had been hidden. I could guess. Down his bronze thigh. He had probably had a special secret compartment made for it.

No longer depressed, he was in charge and cheery. When he ordered, "None of you move or I'll slash him!" everyone believed him.

The man was our visitor: legionary veteran, army scout, imperial spy, Corellius Musa.

XLIV

One benefit of living beside a builder's yard is that you will always have rope for when a bunch of marauders is lying at the foot of your climbing jasmine, waiting to be tied up. While they moaned, Tiberius fetched his rope.

Rodan appeared, shouldering a horrible spear he loved. He must have hidden until the danger had passed. We let him point his precious weapon at the prisoners, like the victorious gladiator he had never been. The prisoners were not to know this unpleasant vision with the nose drip was a coward. A poke in the backside with sharp metal tends to subdue anyone.

When the racket kicked off, Corellius must just have returned from his walk; from next door, stabling the donkey, he had heard the screams. Merky, still untethered, now trotted into the courtyard and began nuzzling Fornix for a carrot. He fetched one. At least he took that huge cleaver safely out of the way.

Tiberius roped Venuleius and the captured slaves around the arms, standing them up one by one, ready to walk. He identified Gallicus as the ringleader, so hog-tied him, telling the slaves they would have to carry him. "Rodan here is trained in combat, so beware. He will march you all down the Clivus Publicius to the Circus Max. You can loose yourselves there and give him back our rope. I might have let you keep it and invoiced you, but I know at least one of you never pays his bills."

The men, who had heard Tiberius called by his courtesy title "aedile," listened meekly. Corellius had limped to the bench and sat down;

he tossed his slim dagger from hand to hand, sneering at them as they stood in their bonds obediently. Gaius and Lucius escaped from their nurse, ran across and scrambled onto the bench, one at either side of him. Their hero: they would adore him from now on. Fortunately, as they snuggled up, he stopped playing with the blade.

"My uncle and I are citizens! You cannot lay hands on us!" young Venuleius attempted. At least in a crisis he did not simply fade. Perhaps there was hope for him.

"Your uncle and you," returned Tiberius calmly, "have enticed away an unmarried young girl, broken into my house and laid hands on my faithful staff. I shall do what I like. You can either put up with it, or my colleague on the bench can slit your throats after all. I don't mind if he does. We shall offer the home-invasion self-defence plea if it ever comes to court. Better than that: you can tell me now what exactly you and your debt-dodging uncle thought you were doing, barging in here."

"I am trying to find my girlfriend!"

Tiberius looked my way, playing the patient man of the house. "Flavia Albia, why does every inquiry of yours involve lowlifes climbing over our yard wall to tell me they are looking for lost women?"

"I am sorry, love. The women who hire me have ridiculous men who can't even use a door-knocker. This lot are landlords. They will have used skeleton keys."

"Oh!" Tiberius at once started to search Gallicus, since skeleton keys are useful tools for a building contractor.

While he confiscated the gadget gleefully, I turned a stern gaze on young Gaius Venuleius. "Cosca Sabatina is not here."

That was true. Paris had taken her to my parents' town house. Unlike ours, you could only gain entrance through the front door (unless you knew how to access the back by crossing other people's properties); Paris had stayed there as a bodyguard. That was why Helena Justina, who considered the girl a liability (and a bad influence on my sisters), had come here earlier for an exchange of views with me.

"Where is she?" pouted the one-time fiancé, like a boy who had lost his spinning-top. I feared that was all she meant to him.

"Cosca Sabatina has been placed with trusted people in a safe place. I am done with her. Her family can decide what to do about her falling in love with a two-timing toad. Venuleius Junior: Sabatina is not running away with you today. Nor will you ever marry her."

"I am not a two-timing—"

"Yes, you are," I said. "Whenever you crawl out from under your stone, it's off to that so-called cottage, I believe?" Our eyes met. He subsided.

The group he had come with were being shooed through our atrium towards the street door. I kept young Venuleius back so I could talk to him privately. "I gather your special friend refused to condone the elopement plan by letting you take Sabatina to your Lake Albanus love-nest. I dare say he loathed the whole marriage scam?"

Venuleius nodded miserably.

"Let me give you some advice, then. You should stick with him. Say you are sorry you were leaned on. First thing tomorrow, return there, accept his forgiveness, then lead the life you two have chosen. In your own place, on your own terms. I heard that you have already been set up by your families with giant candelabra and silver plumbing. That sounds like acceptance. I doubt if the Prisci will cut you off, Gaius, once they grasp that you won't be deployed again for wicked purposes."

"They can't force me," he said immediately. "I have some property that was left in a legacy."

"Oh?"

"My great-aunt."

"Ursulina Prisca?" *Ursulina, the drinking cat lady?* "I thought she left everything she could to your sister, Ursula?"

"She did," he admitted. "But she stipulated that as long as I was unmarried, Ursula must look after me. Ursula and I have always been on good terms."

I commented wryly how unusual that was in the families I dealt with.

It was the opposite of how their great-aunt had been with her own brother. I wanted to believe it was reconciliation, yet I suspected Ursulina Prisca had known what kind of life young Gaius yearned for; she was stirring up trouble. The centurion would have been a typical military bigot; he must have loathed having a masculine partnership openly carried on by one of his grandchildren. His son Gallicus sounded similar. They both probably wanted Gaius castrated and exiled.

As we stood on the threshold of our street door, watching the rest being marshalled for their trip down the hill, I asked sadly, "Gaius Venuleius, what will happen to you now?"

He remained calm. "Nothing," he said. He was a young man; he could withstand a reverse.

"No more marriage proposals?"

"No. I shall live quietly with my companion."

"I think he must be the young lawyer my colleague Honorius has met? Will you tell me his name? He is not the broken-down Julius Tranquillus?"

"No, no. It's Augustus. We are about the same age. His uncle used to bring him to the gymnasium I went to. Augustus refused his advances and made friends with me instead. We have been friends ever since."

"Ah! And he is a lawyer so he will never lack work. You don't feel the need to find an occupation yourself?"

"I shall have one," said the young man, almost surprised I had asked. I felt surprised too: I was turning into Mother, who wanted everyone to have lives that were settled, harmonious and of value to the community. Helena Justina did realise you cannot help some people, most in fact. She always said so long as you have a conscience and time on your hands, you had to try. Even if you failed, the chaos and infamy people chose for themselves were more comfortable to live with than an itchy rash.

So I persisted with young Venuleius. Under the dumb behaviour, he was brighter than he looked; he had a confident plan for his future. "My sister and I have two uncles, Gallicus and Turbo, neither of whom have children to inherit from them. That means we are their heirs. One day, Ursula and I will be joint curators of an enormous business empire." He sounded realistic. "You asked about an occupation: I shall have to become a businessman. Of course we shall be kindly landlords, so people will cheat us, and we may see our fortune slipping through our fingers. Ursula and I won't want to evict tenants with violence. Never!" He seemed definite about that, as if some horror haunted him.

I said he should ask the family slave Philodamus to teach him book-keeping. Seeming pleased, he promised to acquire the basics. That should help, and one day Philodamus would make a good freedman running the family empire.

Of course it might not happen that way. Young Venuleius should consider that his two uncles both had unsatisfactory marriages. It did not take a prophetess to envisage breakups, then separations generally lead to further unions. Many lives have been altered—or some would say ruined—by stepmothers and -fathers. Many men father babies even very late in life. Nobody could be sure those two uncles would remain permanently childless.

Assuming, of course, that they currently were.

I bet there were hidden offspring yet to be discovered. It seemed to me that the Priscus family must have more secrets lurking. I thought that, even before I had any idea of the big surprise that awaited these embattled people.

Tiberius and I stood in the porch with our arms folded, watching Rodan shepherd the home invaders along to the corner, where they would take the Clivus Publicius down into the ancient valley of the Circus Maximus. Once we had seen them out of sight, we had to turn back indoors where our hysterical household needed calming. Normality must be restored. Corellius had to be thanked, so he could be grumpy about his heroics. In the atrium, I snorted at our verdigrised little household gods, as usual wasting their time in pointy-toed dancing, instead of usefully protecting us. Tiberius, ever a pious man, nevertheless saluted them. Then the other exhausting rituals of domesticity had to be gone through: dinner, bedtime stories, tucking up the donkey and the dog in their stable and kennel, checking locks and dousing lamps.

Eventually peace reigned. Our house lay in darkness, with barely a sound. Outside on the Aventine delivery carts were rattling, their drivers cursing incomprehensibly, a nightly performance that was so regular we were hardly aware it was happening. Even that rumpus came to an end finally. Tiberius and I, keyed up by our evening's excitements, lay together simply listening to the rain on the roof.

Then, just as we were falling off to sleep, he murmured, "Darling, if I am to take an interest in your case, I shall need you to explain something."

XLV

A moon would have been useful. You can go wrong discussing your work in darkness; it's always best to see the other person's expression and calculate accordingly. Tiberius and his men were restoring a porch on a small temple, but I would never have asked him whether its foundations needed shoring up more than he'd anticipated, unless I could gauge from his face that it was the right moment. Not, for instance, when he had just redone the figures and realised he had badly underestimated, so the increased materials would swallow all his profit.

I had spent a lot of time advising people on the edge of divorce. Half the time the problem was caused by someone's irritating questions. *Who were you with last night? How much are you telling me you drank? When is your bloody mother going home? Do you think I'm a raving maniac? Well, if you want to walk out on your children, why don't you pack your bags and go right now? What do you mean, I can keep your mangy dog?*

Judge your moment. Whenever possible, keep your mouth shut.

Of course it was never like that in our house. Unless we count the incident when he was struck by lightning, Tiberius managed to behave like a reasonable husband. I, naturally, was beyond reproach. This meant we shared love and anxiety in a balanced way. We were creating a home and building our businesses jointly. I knew about his renovation contracts; he took an interest in my caseload. We were a typical, up-and-coming, middle-rank Roman couple. We knew our place in society, even if it was wobbly. One day there would be a memorial painted of us, side by side in party clothes, me seeming apprehensive and him shifty, as if somebody had just muttered, "I thought you were going to have a shave!" or "I wanted you to wear the other earrings." I would be nursing a note-tablet of unreliable witness statements while he held a scroll with bills-of-quantities for some wheedled tender.

In the meantime, Tiberius was suggesting that my current commission was hard to follow. When a husband with a brain like a whetted knife tells you that, you are in trouble. If he felt he had to express his concern at the dead of night when there were several better things to do, including sleep, I felt compelled to wake up and take notice.

Struggling for possession of a blanket, I summarised for him.

A man had failed to pay a bill. I had sorted that out, though it was indicative of bad character. He was bedding his sister-in-law while trying to cheat her family out of an orchard her uncle had acquired, in my view illegally. Previously, the defaulter had had his shoulder broken by her father, who had died of over-exertion or possibly violence. Her cousin had been fingered as the adulterer, falsely. The cousin had a brother who had seduced the adulterer/defaulter's nephew, who was now living with the cousin's son.

Tiberius adjusted his pillow under his head. "Perhaps this is simpler than I thought."

I had always loved his irony. "To sum up: the nephew almost married a female cousin of the adulteress, who is either the child of the orchard-possessor or of his brother, who is also the brother of the family matriarch, who is my client."

"Thank you. It's all perfectly clear now."

I snuggled up against him, taking his warmth. Too few women seem to appreciate this is what husbands are for, especially in winter. "So what puzzles you, dear one?"

For a moment Tiberius was silent and thoughtful. Then he said, "There are two families, right?"

"Two families. One tribe of commercial entrepreneurs, one coven of property owners. As a matter of fact, the Prisci own the building where the Tranquillus freedmen live. It can never have helped."

"Two families. Not linked?"

"Well, only by adultery, secretive male friendships, scheming females knocking back violet wine at every chance, punch-ups in orchards and endless legal pleas."

He lay silent again. I knew better than to drift off into sleep. I nudged him, though I kept it gentle. "So why the queries?"

"Oh . . . I learned something while we were out in the street, waiting for you to finish giving Venuleius motherly advice."

"His mother is a good woman, but she probably listens to his father. The father may not be entirely obnoxious but Gaius needed help. He could be a nice boy if he escaped from his relatives. Indeed, Honorius says he and his partner are a delightful couple."

"Honorius knows them? Is Honorius . . ."

"He can't be. Honorius desperately wants his ex-wife back."

"Means nothing. The world is full of women that men in public life are using as their cover for masculine affairs. He may be bisexual anyway."

"What do you know about bisexual men?" I snorted.

"I observe them at the baths. From a distance, of course."

"I hope so! Honorius is simply daft. He always has been. And this is not about him."

Tiberius conceded that.

He then double-checked with me that the uncle with the straight-cut fringe was one of the Priscus family. He revealed that he had jokily told the uncle that they should exchange details, just in case Gallicus decided to sue him for being hog-tied. "Although I stressed again how suing would be ill-advised."

"Good. So what happened?"

"I duly announced myself as Tiberius Manlius Faustus. For a man hanging in the arms of slaves with his feet roped to his wrists behind his back, he took it all most courteously. Indeed, while physically helpless, he acquired much better manners. He too introduced himself to me. He gave me his full three names."

I waited.

"Ask me."

"No, you tell me."

The bridegroom's uncle, the centurion's son, the defaulter from the Stargazer, was a full citizen and bore a full Roman *tria nomina*. He was called Appius Gallicus Tranquillinus.

"Go to sleep," murmured Tiberius. "You can decide whatever you make of it tomorrow."

XLVI

Sleep was a remote hope, at least for me. Having delivered himself of his conundrum, the paterfamilias went out like a light.

I spent a disturbed night of a kind that is familiar to informers. Walls cracked. Doors rattled. Shutters creaked. Out on the dark Aventine, after several hours of light rain, a restive wind bustled down the empty streets; its inconsistent gusts were strong enough that an occasional flower trough or lamp crashed down. There were the usual unexplained cries in the far distance. It was too wet for wildlife so I heard neither owls nor foxes. Nor was there any sign that the vigiles were on patrol. No one had parties breaking up with music and drunken loudness, but beggars would be shuffling and burglars never give up.

This was Rome, mostly asleep. Temples were locked, shops closed, shipping moored on the sluggish, silt-heavy river. Somewhere soldiers would be stamping cold feet in clammy boots. In the bowels of the palace, clerks were already at their ceaseless interference in the Empire's well-being; the dour Emperor for whom they had to toil was probably awake.

And I lay awake too. I had only known that man as Gallicus. Praenomen *Appius*? Cognomen *Tranquillinus*? What could that mean?

I knew that among the interminable conflict between those two families, friendships existed. Tranquilla Euhodia and Aurelia Priscilla were an example. Being cynical, I could say that, despite their individual marriages, Mardiana and Gallicus Tranquillinus must have enjoyed camaraderie.

I did now wonder, however, if all along Tranquillinus had been pretending attachment to Mardiana as a ploy, to further his real lust for the orchard. Did he at least sound her out on what her family were planning? He had been one of the party who went there defiantly to pick fruit, resulting in his own shoulder break and her father's death by misadventure. Had either he or Mardiana been married to others when that fight happened? Were they sleeping together already? Did it matter? Would it matter now, assuming that after exposure they were forced to stop seeing each other?

I knew of one other friendship: old Surus and the uncle of Ursulina Prisca and the centurion. Those two men must have known one another sufficiently well that, forty years ago, Surus had left the uncle to hold his orchard in trust. Was it purely as a gesture of gratitude that the centurion had later named his elder son after Surus? It would be nice etiquette. Gallicus Priscus being the man he was, it could also have emphasised that *he* had to support a wife and children. His sister, poor Ursulina, should be pushed aside. He considered that orchard a gift to his own descendants: he said he replanted the fruit trees for his grandchild. Probably he meant the male: young Gaius Venuleius. Almost certainly that was long before the centurion realised his grandson would one day be living with another man as his partner.

Perhaps he never knew that. Perhaps it had been kept secret from him. Alternatively, perhaps when he wanted to sue Julius for the alleged assault, he was deterred by having his grandson's orientation spelled out to him. If so, I was startled that there had been no talk of disinheritance.

If Appius Gallicus Tranquillinus had been older, I might even have wondered about old Surus: had he put himself about in Rome and actually fathered a child who was then given names so close to his? I thought not. However much everyone liked Surus, it would be an odd family that acknowledged someone's by-blow in that way. Another, better, solution could be that since Surus had not married, he might have wanted to adopt an heir.

But it would not work. Tranquillinus was at least five years too young. Surus could have been aware of his sister Aurelia Priscilla when she was a baby, but he would never have known about the centurion's two sons.

Tranquillinus was born in Egypt. The unpleasant centurion had been taking his ease with the pampered Third Cyrenaican legion at the other end of the ocean in Alexandria. So why would a soldier name his first male child after a rabbit-farming entrepreneur who had died five years before and who, anyway, had lived more than a thousand miles away?

XLVII

I managed to sleep. Almost immediately, or so it felt, morning struck, with the usual shock that the selfish dawn goddess dumps on you when your body has turned to sludge.

The informer's curse is having to force down a beaker of lukewarm drink, then leave behind a half-eaten stale bread roll because some urgent task is calling. I had to collect Cosca Sabatina from my parents' house. They were all sick of her. A slave had been sent to fetch me to fetch her, no excuses allowed. I stuffed my head under my pillow, but Gaius and Lucius came outside my bedroom door, banging their toy drum. They thought it was hilarious. When I crawled out, the Didius slave was grinning too. One of Grandpa's leavings: time he was despatched to Hades after his master. That morning I would have handed over the ferryman's copper myself, if it rid me of his happy, jeering face.

At least down at the town house, my mother always arranged breakfast as a rolling buffet of meats, cold fish and goat's cheese, with olives and generous pickles. At one time she had had four children, all wandering from bed at different times, or five she said, if my father was counted. Breakfast would only be cleared when it became essential to sponge down the serving table for lunch.

I dragged myself down the hill, protesting at the slave, who was hard of hearing so that made it difficult to get a rise out of him. My parents had bread delivered daily. On waking, my sisters would accept only thyme-infused Greek honey with exceedingly fresh morning rolls. I won't say they were spoiled, they just knew how to look cute and get what they wanted. So, on the home doorstep, I arrived just as that morning's basket turned up, lodged insecurely on one arthritic hip of the easy-going bakeryman, the ancient Titus. This was the same Titus who brought supplies to all the Aventine bars, then took his morning reward at the Valerian.

"Greetings, Titus!" I cried, diving in for a still-warm soft bap, while the slave who was escorting me grabbed the basket. He ran indoors to stop me raiding it.

"Ever find that fellow you wanted?" asked Titus, while he waited to recover his wickerwork. I praised him for remembering my quest for the debtor, then thanked him for his tip about Nobilo's. "Oh, that's all right. I give good tips."

"You do! Got any more for me?" I joked, through chewing.

"What are you after?"

"Oh . . . What's the real gen on Appius Tranquillus Surus?" I threw this in out of devilment. "Everyone at Nobilo's thought he was a lovely man."

"Everyone at Nobilo's needs his head examined!"

"You knew him?" Now I was surprised.

"I know all the world, if I deliver their bread."

I grabbed hold of Titus and pulled him indoors. He cannot ever have been across the threshold before; he squinted at the faded, smudged old frescos while sniffing the winter odour. The house stood only twenty feet from the river, which, before improvements, used to wash across the Embankment and come in for a look around. The family still mainly lived upstairs.

"You never said you were after old Surus," Titus complained.

"I couldn't. I knew nothing about him, until they mentioned his name at Nobilo's." Nobilo's seemed a long time ago. "According to Rumpus and the skivvy, he had beautiful manners and loved potted shrimps. What did you think?"

"He was polite enough," agreed Titus. He took the weight off his bones, perching on a wooden hall chest that was antiquated yet looked younger than him. "He could be nice when he wanted to, or he could get up your nose. He didn't cross my path too much. I never heard anything about him eating shrimps."

I said not to worry: I didn't expect Titus to have intimate diet knowledge. He informed me, with no trace of humour, he only knew people by what bread they liked; however, he knew a lot about them from that. Surus might have set himself up as a seafood gourmet at Nobilo's, but Titus reckoned his taste in loaves was unoriginal.

"How's that, Titus? Was he your customer? His freedmen live in Sidewind Passage. They have rented the same apartment for a long time. Do you deliver to them?"

"Sidewind? Of course. I do all those places. Man and boy. At that apartment—middle floor, watch yourself coming down the stairs—it was Surus at first, when he ever bothered to be there. Then it was his two freed slaves after they came to Rome. Later on they had families, which made my basket very heavy, and all topped off by Postuminus one floor up. He doesn't have to pay anything."

"Why doesn't he pay? Is this a special deal?"

"Family go free!" Titus reproved me for not knowing. "Ever since he married in. He's one of ours now, worse luck for me. That young girl of his can't ever make up her mind whether she wants sesame topping or poppy seeds."

"Oh! You must work for the Cosconius brothers?" I belatedly realised.

"Man and boy," he repeated. "They are lovely people." I held back that I had heard the Cosconii were fighting thugs. I had even seen one falling down a staircase while saying he wanted to kill Postuminus. Their deliveryman himself had a reputation for seeing off any competition so presumably the obstreperous brothers had trained him in their ways.

He rambled on, reminiscing. "That Surus! I hated him. He was a nightmare. Coming and going, never letting on when he was going to be there or not, and what he wanted ordered. I'd turn up and it was either too much or too little for that day. Then I had to go to and fro again. Everything was better after Euhodia arrived. She just gives me a list for next time."

"Why," I pondered, "was Tranquillus Surus always coming and going? Was he off visiting his rabbit farm?"

"Yes, he did go there." Titus rubbed his nose. He sounded doubtful, as if this might not be the right answer to my question. "He went to look at his rabbits, sure enough. We used to joke about it. People thought he was like a rabbit himself, breeding on his country slaves. He was quite open. He said every new little slaveling he fathered was an investment. If he didn't need them on the farm, once they were old enough, he could sell them."

"That's harsh," I commented. "Though it's a common attitude. So did he spend a lot of time in the Campagna, 'boosting his investments'? How often was he actually at the apartment?"

"On and off."

"Half and half?"

"Less."

"Once a month?"

"About. I knew, because I had to allow for it: I needed to bring good eight-segment loaves whenever he was in residence or, if not, drop it down to a few burned buns for any slaves he left there. Yes, he was ruthless," Titus argued, stuck in the previous conversation. "But he was good to those he trusted. Look at Euhodia and Aprilis. And haven't they done all right!"

"Yes, and I suppose, if he'd known, he would have made arrangements for Postuminus too." I was still trying to define the younger brother's social position, as I had been hired to do.

Titus had little time for Postuminus. "Or sold the little blighter off! Him and his airs. He owed it all to doing them a favour and then getting a good dowry out if it. It was a lucky break, that favour—whatever it was."

"I think he overheard someone planning to poison their rabbits."

"Oh, yes? Still, who was he fooling? He had nothing going for him otherwise. Even when he came to Rome, he just worked in his brother's shop, heaving garum about when told to, and being cursed by everyone. She was a lovely girl, of course, the wife I mean. Cosconia. One of ours. We all loved her. And miss her. Her poor brothers never got over it. Terrible it was, the way she died with all that pain. She didn't deserve it. Well, nobody does, do they?"

No, I answered gloomily.

"The Fates!" declared Titus.

On a whim, I told him someone had suggested that, unlike poor

Cosconia Saba, Surus might have died because somebody twisted a Fate's thread-cutting hand.

Titus chortled with delight. "Not likely! The silly old blighter caught a cold, Albia."

So that confirmed it. "In a storm? The wet and wind-chill finished him?"

"About right." The breadman was losing interest, but came back with a sudden rethink. "Of course," he said. I loved the way he said "of course" then sprang an unexpected detail on me. "Whoever thinks he copped it early, they could be thinking about the other time." I tried to look bright and encouraging. "I mean," the deliveryman informed me, "the time that woman appeared out of nowhere and beat Surus up."

"Beat him up! A lovely fellow that everyone at Nobilo's adored?"

"Well, it didn't happen at Nobilo's, it was in his own apartment," Titus solemnly assured me, with his own logic. "He lost half his ear before the staff managed to drag her off him. She must have bitten him—he could have caught rabies. He wasn't as badly hurt as he thought, but ears can be tricky and he lost a lot of blood. Well, his ear was half gone so never looked the same again. She was taken right away somewhere, straight after, but he never forgave what she did to him. Old Surus, he was absolutely livid. He swore he was going to punish her."

"Did he?"

"I don't know. She was never on my bread round."

When I asked what had caused this violence, Titus suddenly went coy on me. My mother had appeared at the top of the stairs, breakfast napkin in hand, a tall figure playing reasonable, as she came to see what was delaying me.

Throwing a nervous glance up at Helena, Titus gabbled that he had to run. With a quick don't-nag-me-I'm-coming wave for Mother—a gesture she knew all too well because her children all copied it from Father—I followed the deliveryman to the front door. Looking back anxiously, he muttered, "It was kept really quiet. All I can think is, that woman must have come here to see him without him expecting her. Then his people at the apartment must have maddened her by telling her about his other place."

"What place?" I demanded.

"I told you he was always in and out. Of course, the big reason for it was that the Sidewind apartment was his hideaway. Don't ask me what he was hiding from. It can't have worked—that woman found him. But in Rome, he spent most of his time at a great big house he had. He owned it and that was where he really lived. I think it was over on the Caelian."

Now I remembered that Januarius had mentioned Surus might have had "a house across town." He had belittled it, implying the house was only rented and saying it was "all a long time ago." He had probably referred to it accidentally, then wished he had kept his mouth shut. He and his family must have known all along about this other place but they had ignored its existence whenever they discussed Surus with me. Perhaps they liked to forget what that house said about Tranquillus Surus and his real life. As implications crowded in, I knew I had been misled deliberately.

I gave the deliveryman instructions to go up to see my cook. He could tell Fornix we would always buy our bread from the Cosconii from now on, and the excellent Titus would deliver it.

XLVIII

I felt more alive now. A new twist in any case sets me thrumming. I badly wanted to pursue what Titus had told me, but first I had to deal with the disconsolate bride. I bounded upstairs as if I were a teenager again to hurl myself at the breakfast spread.

"Flavia Albia. How good of you to drop in, darling!"

My sisters were in another room, keeping Sabatina away from Mother, while they did and redid the girl's face paint and jewellery. She liked that: no surprise. Our two had enjoyed the game to start with. Their attentions had kept her occupied most of yesterday, but I was told Julia and Favonia had whispered this morning that they were growing *so-o-o-o* bored.

Splitting a roll for chickpea paste, then dotting on mad quantities of sliced olives, I kissed my mother's cheek. She had her clean scent of rosemary hair-wash; it took me back to when she first rescued me in Britannia and began the long process of cleaning me up to be civilised— which she might say was an ongoing project.

Since I was here to remove Cosca Sabatina, she relaxed, though she did list appalling behaviour from the young woman, who had never been taught to be an acceptable guest. "Mind you, she doesn't mound up olives like a four-year-old! I sometimes wonder where you were brought up, Albia . . ." While I let her quips slide over me, I managed to cram in food, at the same time keeping an intact apologetic face. I am an informer; I can eat and look humble at the same time.

"Finished, Ma?"

"Yes, that's enough. What do you have to say to me?"

I had to say thank you, thank you, O dearest, most tolerant, most put-upon of mothers. It might be over the top, but I needed to sound as if I meant it.

To emphasise how wise it had been to position Sabatina out of reach here, I quickly told how the men had broken into our house, searching for her, and nearly killed our nursemaid. That helped me. Glaphyra was a family treasure; I only had her on loan. I made the way Gallicus Tranquillinus had grappled her on the stairs sound like a near-death experience. In fact, looking back with more time to think about it, I was genuinely troubled by the memory. He had looked determined to harm her.

I explained the true motives of the Priscus men, with my exposure of said motives. I promised that I would take full responsibility for informing Sabatina today that the love she had found in the apricot orchard had been false; her trust had been betrayed; she would not marry Venuleius Junior. Dotty emperors might "marry" eunuchs to offend public morals, but for our young man and his friend Augustus romance would be discreetly veiled. Gaius Venuleius would end up with one of those obituaries that say *he never married* and leave you to understand the code.

Helena thought Sabatina would refuse to accept my version. She would prefer hysterics; she had already tried it, until she saw it wasn't working. My parents had meanly left her to it. My father had growled he had to meet a man in a bar; my mother made the same excuse, then rushed out to meet up secretly with Father. Helena claimed no one would have believed her if she had merely pretended she was behind with her loom work. There wasn't a loom in the house.

As soon as Sabatina stopped bawling and faced the truth, we prophesied she would turn venomous and threaten to expose the two young men for unnatural activities. I would advise them to stand up to her. They were both so wealthy they saw themselves as free to live quietly out of Rome as a twosome. Perhaps they were right. Being stunningly rich makes the unconventional feel they can do as they want. They were handsome and friendly. If they gave enough temple donations and never let their sheep break into neighbours' gardens, they would be accepted. People liked them. I had liked Gaius Venuleius myself. Community support might rally behind them.

My mother enquired coolly what, if anything, were the girl's family doing in all this? I described the Tranquilli. Their crises were scandalous, their reactions inappropriate; their only method of coping was to call in lawyers, lawyers who then conspired with the opposition over lunches fuelled by indecent amounts of drink, while being entertained by very expensive dancers. I detailed the sparkly shoe, adorned with its faux-precious stones, that I had picked up at the Comet while the waiters were floor-washing. I assumed that, when performing, the shoe's owner had been wearing little else. "Maybe a ring through her belly-button?" suggested Helena, knowingly. Not for the first time I wondered about my parents' unseen lives.

She had a solution. Somebody sensible must have "a little talk" with Sabatina's uncles. Helena Justina was a good practitioner of "little talks" so she volunteered to go. Even though the two Cosconii were intimidating, she would speak to them, suggesting they take over and act as guardians for their dear niece. She reasoned that they would listen to her, because commerce was commerce, and she was a long-time customer of their loaves and rolls.

I approved. The brothers would either knead my brave mama into a very refined flatbread, or they would do whatever she said. My bet was on compliance.

Meanwhile, I rescued my exhausted sisters from Cosca Sabatina. As expected, my conversation with her began as difficult and turned worse. No young girl can relish hearing she has been publicly shamed by a failed elopement, let alone that the marriage she was relying on for her future independence and even perhaps happiness will never take place. Negotiations are terminated. There will be no floral headdresses, no gifts of redware dinner bowls and absolutely no sex. The beloved never wanted it. He has slid off to reside with his sheep-rearing lawyer boyfriend, while his relatives are revealed as lying connivers, no better than a bunch of hole-in-the-fence soft-fruit raiders.

In the end, this conversation did improve from my standpoint. Soon, Cosca Sabatina was no longer talking to me.

XLIX

I took the girl back to Sidewind Passage. Initially, the Tranquilli would
have charge of her. My sisters had exclaimed that Sabatina could not
walk up the Aventine in her best shoes, so we were lent Mother's carrying chair; Julia and Favonia would tell Helena, who would have to go
on foot to the Cosconius bakery. Fortunately, being cramped in a se-
dan with someone who thought me a monster held no terrors for me. I
hummed a little song and braced myself as we lurched uphill.

Rather than depositing Sabatina with her father, I dropped her off
at the lower apartment where Tranquilla Euhodia reigned. Paris had
escorted us, but I sent him home. I warned the matriarch it was now her
responsibility not to let the girl abscond again. "Don't worry. She knows
Venuleius is a dead duck. At least it means no randy male has spoiled
her purity so she's still saleable in the marriage market. The love of her
life has romantic good looks but they are committed elsewhere." I could
have specified that was with Euhodia's nephew's boy, but she probably
knew; after all, the family reputedly helped fund that tasteful hutment
with its silver taps.

Euhodia asked the crucial question: "Has she brought back her jewellery?"

"Yes. She is heartbroken, but still has her priorities."

No wine was served while I retold my evidence against the Priscus
family. "I am sorry, Euhodia. This was not what you were hoping when
you hired me, but it would be wrong to enable the wedding as you asked.
That marriage stood no chance. All the male Prisci ever wanted was the
orchard, and what Junior hankers for is not your skinny niece but your

hunky nephew. We can't begin to imagine what unhappiness would have ensued if the ceremony had gone ahead."

"She's blarting enough now!" her aunt commented. We could hear Sabatina in another room, crying again. Now she was back at home, her despair seemed real enough. Euhodia had declined to mop her up, but instead sent upstairs for the maid to do it.

"She will get over things," I promised.

"And one day will thank you?" Euhodia jeered grimly.

"I doubt that. With due respect to her upbringing, she does not seem the grateful type."

"Agreed. I am none too pleased myself with how your intervention has turned out, Flavia Albia. Can I ask for a refund?"

Euhodia was a typical client, but after many of those I had a riposte: "I had to impose your niece on my noble mother overnight so, no, you can't, I'm afraid."

"Give your mother my compliments!" It was said without malice.

"Thank you." I kept quiet about Helena intending to have the girl reassigned to other guardians. "In case you wonder," I reported professionally, "this is not case-closed for me. My commission was to show whether Postuminus had been emancipated—and I will still find you proof if I can."

Euhodia seemed impressed, not so much by my dedication as by the hope of value-for-money. She asked how I meant to tackle the problem now. This was my cue to enlighten her that I knew much more about Tranquillus Surus than anyone connected with him had previously said.

"He was a man. He had a dark side," Euhodia conceded.

"A dark side—and a large, light-filled house on the leafy Caelian!"

She refused to show surprise. "He was pally with property managers. They own houses everywhere."

"This one was his own. He lived there."

"Did he?"

"You must know!"

"We never talk about it."

"Secrets can be a big mistake. You assured me he never married, but that was untrue. Who was the woman who turned up and battered him?" I demanded.

"I wouldn't know."

"No? She ripped off part of his ear."

Euhodia gave me one of her straight looks. "Then she cannot have been very nice!" That was rich, from a parent of Mardiana.

"Wasn't it your mother?" I prodded Euhodia relentlessly. "Surus threatened to punish her for the attack. I wonder if he ever did?" I supplied a straighter look to inform her I had been working things out. "Tell me the truth!"

Tranquilla Euhodia took a long breath. Acknowledging that she had heard about the attack, she confessed slowly, "Yes, it was Hedylla. It was a long time ago. Aprilis and I were still on the farm then. I know Surus did have a piece of ear gone later, but we hardly saw him again. He stopped coming to the Campagna. He passed away—it was only a couple of months afterwards."

"Because of the attack?"

"I doubt it. Nobody said so."

"Attacking a master is a serious offence for a slave. Hedylla must have been extremely angry. I think you ought to tell me why."

Euhodia sighed. Her resistance completely collapsed. "It was in this apartment. She had come to Rome to see him. First he wasn't here, where she expected. Then when someone ran out quietly to fetch him, nothing went the way she wanted. She lost her temper with him and naturally he wasn't having that."

"What occurred? Did she tell you?"

Reluctantly Euhodia nodded. "I saw her by chance when they brought her back on a cart to the farm. I could tell at once something had badly upset her. She burst out with it, perhaps because, after all, I was her daughter. Nobody else knows, though. Once she calmed down, she never spoke about it. My brothers would be so upset to hear this. Don't tell them."

I agreed, though against my principles. Euhodia was looking her age today. We were talking about her mother, however distant they had been. She was my client, and now I felt for her. "All right. Only because I can see you have been keeping the secret for a long time, and it has done you no good, Euhodia."

This had altered our relationship. When she hired me to validate Postuminus, she must have known the reasons for that attack and what its results had been, so the commission she gave me could never succeed. All the talk of her brother being born unexpectedly was nonsense: Hedylla knew she was pregnant. That was what had caused her to up and leave the farm. She had journeyed to Rome, full of joy and hope, because she wanted to tell Surus her news: news that even though she had presumed she was past the age, she was carrying again. She, who believed herself a favourite, had come unasked to where she thought the father lived. Perhaps she had even hoped this child might make him grant her liberty and marry her.

Instead apartment slaves, probably unsympathetic snooty townees, revealed to her what nobody at the rabbit farm had known: the master normally lived somewhere else. There would have been a reason for that, and no doubt the reason was cruelly spelled out to Hedylla.

When he was summoned to the apartment that day, Surus was furious. Perhaps he even ranted that the unborn child would be sold, one of his young slave "investments." Hedylla became mad with rage, the worst possible outcome for her. Through her physical attack on Surus, she must have lost any hope of freedom. That meant the son who was eventually born had never been freed either. When Euhodia hired me to prove otherwise, she must have known. Postuminus was a slave to this day. His sister looked stricken now, as she had to admit the truth.

Hiring an informer to investigate cannot have been her real plan. Obviously she had wanted me to fake manumission documents. When I laid down that I would not create a forgery, she was lost on how to back out of hiring me. As I remembered, she acted well, but I had her on the run now.

After Hedylla attacked her owner and master, I imagined there were further consequences. He must have grown ever more furious as he tried to staunch his gnawed earlobe. Not only did he have bloodshed and pain, but he knew there would also be domestic upset of the kind most men hate. Surus had to go home sooner or later, home to his grand house on the Caelian Hill—with part of his ear permanently missing. He couldn't have hidden that. He'd had to explain it to whomever he really lived with.

I knew where his house was. I had been inside it. I now recognised who the people there must be—and what they were to him. Appius Tranquillus Surus had had family: legitimate children and a freeborn wealthy wife.

Hedylla had been fooled about the situation for years. Any hope for her own future was always pointless. Nobody at the rabbit farm had known the truth and the Tranquillus freedmen to this day avoided acknowledging it: Surus had long been a married man. The Caelian house had been built for his wife; perhaps her money paid for it. They had had two children, or at least two who survived to adulthood. When Hedylla visited Rome, the son was already eighteen and joining the army; the daughter would have been slightly older.

Those children were Ursulina Prisca and Gallicus Priscus, the cat lady and the centurion.

L

I decided to revisit the house.

In a city of hills, up on the tops you feel close to the weather. For a January day this was typical. Its breeziness was nothing particular, like a slightly unsatisfactory lover. One you cannot complain about but who can't be bothered to come up with any act you might find remarkable.

On the Aventine it blew harder. Down in the valley of the Circus Max it felt muggier. Up on the Caelian, that midmorning was dry, cool, cloudy, but bearable. Only senior citizens felt the wind whistle through their bones. One such venerable person was being led by the hand by a young slave-boy just as I approached where he lived. Wavering on a knobbly stick, he was managing to totter out of doors, but had to call on all his determination. He had enough of it, fortunately. He wobbled disturbingly but kept going. The boy went very slowly with him, patiently, as if used to the task.

This was an unexpected stroke of luck, but I had not prepared for it and needed to choose what to do next. I hung back. They could not be going far.

Around a corner stood a small street bar. This was the Little Caelian Caupona; it must have been used mainly for takeaways. Inside, it was empty of customers. It had a single table, at which the old man aimed himself rather wildly; he sank onto a gnarled bench with a gasp of triumph. Perhaps each time he managed to reach it, he thought it might be his last visit. The boy tucked a rug over his knees, then left him. I guessed he would return later to collect his master. Their visit seemed to be routine.

A waiter came through from the back area. He saw who his customer was, so began preparations without waiting for an order. I almost expected the old fellow to call out, "Do you have any of your excellent shrimps today, my lad?" like Surus at Nobilo's. However, I knew this could not be Surus.

They served only small plates and snack bowls. He was being given tapenade. The waiter actually spread the bread, then placed a board in front of the customer, saying, "Apple at the top, cheese on the right," as if the old man had limited eyesight.

He had shrunk to no more than a light-boned skeleton, loosely covered with skin, which wrinkled into furrows, like a lonely desert sand dune, minutely rippled by timeless winds; all his skin carried brown blotches, some large. He took his time, approaching the platter tremulously, with fragile hands that shook. I could not say how many years he had chalked up, but it must have been over ninety. His life had been easy; like many of the wealthy, he had lasted far beyond the average span.

His walking stick clattered to the floor. I went into the bar and picked it up for him. I leaned it against his table where he could reach it. He looked up with watery eyes and thanked me.

"Do you mind if I join you?"

Across at the counter, the waiter laughed gently at my question; he joked with the old fellow that it must be a long time since a good-looking woman had sidled up and asked him that. "Good job your wife is no longer around!" I sensed that the waiter was keeping an eye, being protective of his vulnerable customer. I was meant to know he was watching, although it looked as if he had decided I was not there to bamboozle or steal.

I laughed quietly with them. "I hope you don't mind, sir. This is a lucky meeting. My name is Flavia Albia. I am doing some work for a family you know. I really would like to talk to you about my findings."

I let it sink in. The old man seemed to absorb it. After a moment I sat down with him, taking the opposite bench so we could look at each other, though I was not sure he could really see me.

The waiter categorised me as harmless; he kinked up an eyebrow, but

I told him I had breakfasted earlier. He brought a water jug and poured for the old fellow in silence; he did provide two cups but, being a city waiter on one of the old Roman hills, he left me to serve myself. Women counted for nothing with him. He returned to the back haunts, perhaps glad that, although he had to tolerate me in his bar, for once he did not have to entertain the old one.

As an approach, I said, "If you had been having green olive tapenade instead of black, I would have thought Tranquillus Surus never died after all. And did you share his love of potted shrimps?"

"He was a right old beggar for those shrimps."

"So I heard."

"They don't have them. We often came for breakfast together at this place and here I am, still doing it. What do you think he would have made of that?"

I smiled. "I think he would have been envious that you held on for so long. You've beaten him by forty years! Were you younger?"

"A few years."

"Did you used to go with him to Nobilo's on the Aventine?"

"No. I was never over there. That was where he went when he was getting up to naughtiness. He never took me. It would not have been right."

"Why was that?"

"Well, you know . . ." He succumbed to vagueness.

I could cope with him being vague. All I needed was his existence. Smiling, I basked in this new turn: at last I had found the will's executor.

After a time, I said, "You must be a well-known character here, but everyone has been telling me they have no idea where you are. The majority verdict was that you had died."

He let out a cackle of laughter. "That didn't stop you finding me!"

"No! I am very persistent. I was about to ask a sybil how I could come after you down into the Underworld, but this is a better meeting place. Did people tell you I was asking?"

"They never tell me anything. They all pretend I've lost my wits."

"Oh dear! And have you?"

He gave this careful consideration, wondering. I worried over it, too, because I needed anything he told me to be accurate.

While he was considering, he took a bite of his olive bread. Then he laid it down again. I guessed that now he was so old, he had very little appetite. The waiter would serve up what he had always liked, but nowadays would have to throw away most of it.

"I only remember the old days. I can't tell you," admitted the old fellow, chewing slowly, "whether I came here yesterday. I can't remember how to go home again. They have to send a boy for me."

"Yes, I saw him. He'll be back. No need to be anxious."

"No," he answered, very thoughtfully. "No, I won't worry. Somebody will come for me. If they forget, you'll take me, won't you?" That was not said to me; he called it over one skinny shoulder, though the waiter was invisible. "He is a good lad. He looks after me." Slowly, he picked up his loaf segment, took another bite, then placed it down again. "I'll give him a reward one day." He chewed, almost maddeningly slowly. "What were you saying, young lady?"

"I believe, sir, you were the best friend of Appius Tranquillus Surus."

He nodded. That was very vigorous.

"And in his will, he named you as his executor."

More nodding.

"Can you remember anything about the will?"

He sat up straight. "Every word!" He became thoroughly animated. Given what I knew about that will and its endless consequences, excitement was understandable. He set off merrily, leaving me no chance to ask questions of my own: "Dear gods in Olympus, I had to go over the clauses enough times with daft people afterwards. I used to think those scrapping young scamps would never give up asking, as if that was going to change anything—it did them no good, of course. He wrote it plainly enough, and if anyone convinced themselves it said something different, they were stuck. I just brought out the scroll and showed them. What he said was what he meant. He was a bloody good businessman, you know, the best of the best. He really thought of everything. The younger generations always hated that."

"You had kept the scroll?" I queried, feeling breathless. He gave me a sharp look, so I cried, "Oh! You still have it today?"

"Of course," he replied complaisantly. "I never let it go. Even if one of their fancy-boots lawyers asked for a look-see, I made them come and inspect it while I stood over them. I let them take notes if they wanted, but I stayed right there, counting the moth-holes in their togas while they read. I never had a copy made. I just stuck with his original."

I chuckled. "I'm glad I never spent hours looking for it at the Atrium of Liberty! Is it at the house?"

"It's in a box."

"A box at your house?"

Now he looked uncertain. Even so, he confirmed his answer: "Yes, it is there. It's there somewhere. People want to make me hand it over. They are constantly at it, torturing me, but I won't surrender it to anyone, not even after all this time. I haven't had it out to look at for a few years. I hid it."

Obviously he had forgotten where, and that troubled him. I told him I often searched for lost documents so, if he wanted, I could help him try to find it again. Wrong move. That made him regard me as a schemer who was after his scroll for evil reasons. Playing the honest informer, I had to settle him down.

He seemed frightened by the people harrying him for the will. Either his terror was imaginary, or he was a helpless ancient citizen being victimised by scoundrels, his person bullied and his valuables stolen. The old are at risk from those who care for them. As so often in these situations, it was difficult to tell whether anyone was really abusing him. And you always have to consider that you might be reading too much into things. Remembering how Ursula, her mother and aunt, and his attendant had all spoken about looking after him, I decided he was safe.

"They are waiting for me to die!" he exclaimed, though he seemed easy with it. I commented that from what I had seen they were taking excellent care of him in the interim, feeding him custards, reading to him, letting him come out on his own for lunch . . .

"Oh, I am not supposed to run off!" he confided, giggling. "Young Ursula knows I come here but it drives the others mad when they think I am out on the loose."

"They worry about you? So, tell me, that is not your house?"

"My sister's. I lived with her after we had both been widowed. She left me the right to stay there. Be fair—I suppose the rest would have kept me on anyway."

"They all seem to think a lot of you. They have never said," I tried gently, "where you fit into the family?"

He looked confused. "Blow me if I know!" He thought about it.

"Can I help to work it out? For instance, how did Ursulina Prisca and the centurion fit? What was your connection to them?"

He was still thinking, with his worried frown. When I had almost given up on him, he sat up abruptly and shouted, "Uncle!"

"Good! And—forgive me for not knowing—what is your own name, sir?"

He paused, as if that was beyond him, but a gleam told me he was being mischievous. He liked to be playful with a strange young woman, but he still knew exactly who he was. "Gallus Ursulinus."

"Greeting, Gallus Ursulinus!"

"Greetings . . ."

"Flavia Albia. Daughter of Falco, wife to Faustus." He nodded but did not feel confident to say my name back. I slipped in another question: "And what about Tranquillus Surus? Why were you his executor? Why didn't he choose his son, the centurion?"

"Abroad." After this curt answer, the old one added suddenly, "And even his father thought he was a brute—without knowing any of what Priscus did after he came back to Rome."

"I see. Was there a strong connection between you and Surus then?"

"Old mates." He had regained his confidence. "When we were lads, we did business together. Old mates. Truest of old mates all our lives, that is until the silly duffer went and died."

"He died of a cold?" I checked.

"He did. Who gets a chill and croaks?"

"Someone suggested to me it was more than a chill. Perhaps he was murdered by his slaves, wanting his money?"

This old man simply stared at me. He sat in silence, staring, until I gave in and gently accepted that Tranquillus Surus had died of a cold.

I forced myself not to speculate that while he was sniffing and bedridden someone had helped him on his way. A poisoned lozenge. A pillow on the face. Windows left open. A freezing bed bath. It happens . . .

"If you are looking for a murder," Gallus Ursulinus instructed me, in a colder, sterner voice, as if he had read my thoughts, "you are looking in the wrong place!"

Naturally I pressed him to know what he meant. He would not say.

The slave came back to collect him. While the boy and the waiter were gathering him together, standing him up on his feet, tidying a cloak around him, the old fellow joked with me that nobody wanted him to stay out so long he might catch a fatal cold himself, like Surus. He was ready for his afternoon nap; that would use up the rest of his day.

Ignoring any impatience in his helpers, he kept chattering on. I was a new audience; he now seemed unwilling to part from me. "You asked me what he was to me, that daft man with his potted shrimps. Those shrimps! Jupiter, he brought some for me once and they were awful. Tasteless and watery. I told him, I said, 'Appius, you nutter, don't you bring me any more of your horrible pots.' The only surprise is, he never died of poisoning from those shrimps. I'll tell you, I can tell you right now. What were we to each other? We were mates and he married my sister. Galla Priscilla, she was not a bad woman, though I say so myself. She reminded me of Ursula. So, young lady, it is easy enough. Surus and I, we were brothers-in-law!"

LI

I let Gallus Ursulinus go off by himself. It was better not to let his relatives accuse me of preying on a helpless old codger. I realised they had
been hiding him away from me; even Julia Laronia, despite gossiping
so freely, had fudged her reply when I asked about him. The Tranquilli
didn't want me to find out Surus had been married; the Prisci may have
just wanted Ursulinus left alone.

I knew now that he still possessed the will. Finding it should be
possible. Whatever the will said, I believed that this man would have
carried out its instructions properly. I was determined to see it, and find
out what it contained that might affect Postuminus.

He had tottered a few yards, but then slowly revolved on the spot so
he could stagger back again towards the Little Caelian Caupona. The
boy looked annoyed, but could not refuse the turnaround.

"You're a daft lump!" the master cried to the waiter, who was standing with me. "You'll never be rich at this rate. Why didn't you tell me I
haven't paid my reckoning?"

"That's all right!" The waiter smiled. He was in his thirties. Lean,
mildly depressed by his situation, tolerant. I wouldn't want to raise
the subject of politics here; he would probably be a hard-line throw-
back: anti-barbarian, bring-back-Nero, woman-hating, what this city
needs is strong government, lower taxes and get rid of the no-weapons
regulations . . .

"I may have no money with me," fretted the oldster.

"Don't worry. I'll pop along to Philodamus later."

"He's a good man," Gallus Ursulinus patted his shoulder and praised him to me. "He always looks after me. Don't tell them at the house, but I'm leaving him a good present when I pass away."

The waiter smiled again, as if he appreciated the generosity, yet knew the old fellow might make similar promises to his boot-maker and barber, never actually arranging anything.

Suddenly Gallus rounded on me. "You forgot to ask your question, lady! Go on."

It was my turn to smile. "All right. If you don't mind. You were the executor, so you must know. In fact, I have two questions."

"I'll know. You ask me."

"I have to do something for Tranquillus Postuminus. He wasn't born when your old crony died. So, first, is there anything in the will about his mother, a slave called Hedylla?"

The old fellow narrowed his eyes. "Oh, I can tell you about her."

"Well, then?"

Gallus Ursulinus adopted a pedantic look, the one he must have used to irritate people for at least forty years. "I'll need to show you. I need to find what he wrote."

"Can't you say from memory? Please help me to help her son."

"Her son isn't mentioned, that's for sure. I must dig out that will. Then I shall show you, young lady."

I decided I had to accept this. "I shall be very grateful. And tell me about the orchard, please. The one all the trouble has always been about. Postuminus believes that he now owns it."

"Not possible!"

"I wondered that. But he says it was given to him."

"I told Surus not to buy it. He wasn't listening." Ursulinus had jumped back into older layers of memory. "He didn't know anything about land. It was cherries," the old fellow specified. "Cherries. They were never any good. Then apricots. His son planted those, without a by-your-leave. Now his grandson, Tranquillinus, chip off the proverbial block, he wants to dig them up and plant again with almond trees. Nobody ever asks me, of course."

"Nobody seems to be asking Postuminus either," I said. "Everyone seems to treat him as if he wasn't there. But he absolutely insists that the orchard has been given to him because of his mother."

"I know about his mother," the old man repeated, in a hard voice. "I heard what happened. I had to climb off my couch and sort out that mess—" Still standing on the pavement, swaying in his uncoordinated way, yet somehow keeping himself upright, Gallus Ursulinus fiercely shook his head.

"Even other people do seem clear Postuminus had the orchard as a gift after his mother died."

"Oh, yes, they all thought he deserved something for his mother," answered Ursulinus, dismissively.

"Why? What happened to her? Was there a tragedy?"

"We don't talk about it."

"Tell me, please."

"No. Ask them. Ask him. Though he won't want to remember, and I don't blame him. If you rake it all up, he will be upset."

"I don't want to upset him, I just want to know. Please, sir, you tell me. When Tranquillus Surus died, he left the land in trust for his son and daughter. Now his children have both died. Has Postuminus any real claim or does the orchard pass to their heirs?"

"Neither," butted in the old fellow impatiently. "He wrote this precisely. Aprilis and Euhodia could pick the cherries but the land stayed in trust. Of course the centurion replanted and tried to evict them. Well, that ended badly!"

"The poisoned rabbits?"

"He was a liability. Surus's precious rabbits? Should never have done that! When his apricot trees grew, he kept on trying to stop those people taking the new fruit. Half the time, if he managed to pick it himself, he took it too early. Then he wanted to put up new fences so they had no access—"

"Broken shoulder, sudden collapse." I tried to hurry him. "What was the trustee doing?"

"Being told he was an old man and need not concern himself. Whenever trouble bubbled up, usually caused by Priscus, Priscus would sort it with violence. Later on, he took his son to help him in the same style. I mean Tranquillinus, not the intellectual."

"Priscus thought he could do things with the orchard because he and his sister expected to own it eventually? After the trustee died?"

"No use if they died first. The trustee could keep it. The will said so."

"Surus had left their uncle as trustee," I recapped. "That was you?"

"Now you're getting there!" he cried triumphantly.

"So I am," I agreed, letting him have his moment.

"That land lies next to some I own myself. My walnut orchard. So it was my little thank-you from Surus, for being his executor. If I died, his children from his marriage to my sister would have it but here I am, still alive," crowed Gallus Ursulinus.

"So only you could have given it away?" I kept badgering.

"Only me. They asked me for it, during all that trouble over the dead mother, but I never agreed. Postuminus needs to be compensated in some other way, if people think that's right. Because *Who owns the orchard?* I do, Flavia Albia. The orchard is mine!"

LII

The old fellow was much too tired to stay longer. The waiter and his boy urged me to let him go home.

"We shall meet again!" he cried gallantly, stopping in his tracks once more. "We need to combine forces, young woman. This needs a peace treaty. You . . ." He meant to say my name, but obviously could not remember it. "Your task shall be to bring all these quarrellers to negotiate and knock their heads together."

"Thanks!" I said none too warmly. "You are talking about people who have forty years of never being sensible if something ridiculous presents itself! Put them in a meeting? Back off, oldie, it's my case."

"Show some respect for age! I shall support your endeavours. They will all be very surprised if I start throwing my weight around."

"Gallus Ursulinus, I myself will be surprised if you have enough body mass!"

"We can do it. You have that air about you," he assured me, as the slave-boy tried to lead him off. "This young boy will hold me upright, won't you? Pick a place, *Domina*, pick a time, set up a meeting. Tell them, no lawyers. I want to be there myself, though. I want to see you sort them out."

I chuckled. "I believe you are right. A full family council is called for. I shall invite you, sir, depend on it. Will they let you come?"

"This boy will bring me. He belongs to me. His father was left to me by my old mate. I freed his father, gave him his new life, years ago. He keeps a little hole-in-the-wall where he sells clothes baskets, I'm told. The boy stayed. He knows he has to look after me."

"I look forward to it. But everything will be much simpler, sir, if you can bring that will along. The will and, of course, any codicil."

Shaking off his young helper, my fellow conspirator remained on the spot, swaying. "Ohoho! You know about the codicil!"

It had been a guess, but I agreed one must exist: not the forgery that Tranquillus Julius had tried to pass off until Honorius stopped him but, surely, attached to any testament of standing there had to be a genuine codicil.

Ursulinus promised that if he could remember where he had hidden it, he would bring the will and any addition. He was dithering about whether he could find it; he mentioned that once the house had possessed a library slave, a neat scrollbox organiser who could pick out anything. I asked if his name by any chance was Erotillus.

"That's the boy! He was another of mine."

"Your relatives have given him to the Tranquilli."

"Oh, have they? What was that for? I wonder. Priscus doing damage no doubt, Priscus or Tranquillinus . . . Never asked me, of course." A memory came back to him. "Compensation. Broken step. Should have been mended, landlord's liability. Someone had an accident, that's the story." Ursulinus's voice might quaver, yet he could grasp the facts and be cynical about how they had been portrayed. "Erotillus?" He stiffened and looked pained. "He used to read to me . . . I had had him trained to look after documents. He was worth a lot of money. I miss him. He was a boy of mine. Tranquillinus should never have taken him. When you are old, no one listens . . ." Another gleam of truth returned. "They said he was sent to spy on those marriage negotiations."

"Well, the marriage will not be happening now! I'll see what can be done about him," I promised. "What happened on the stairs, please?"

"What stairs?" He had lost it.

Ursulinus was finally fading. The caupona waiter decided to weigh in. He and the young boy stationed themselves at either side of the old man, as if they had done this before; they turned him for home, lifted him off his feet and shuffled him forwards each time he needed to take a new step. They both shot me reproving glances as they danced him away.

LIII

I found a way down from the Caelian that brought me past the station house of the Fifth Cohort of Vigiles, one of the few with whom I had never had real dealings. Then on to the Street of Honour and Virtue. Cousin Marcia had lived there with her mother, causing many a joke that the name was incongruous, even though we knew that, by a process of scatty neglect, the free-loving Marina had brought up a child whose worst trait was being rudely outspoken. Among the Didii, that was standard.

Marcia was born to a soldier who never knew of her existence. Frontier provinces must be stuffed with others in the same position. I wondered whether the centurion, Gallicus Priscus, had left his own clutch of tousled orphans in Alexandria, or even some turbaned tot in Armenia, and whether that respectable family on the Caelian would one day open their door to find a hopeful visitor claiming a blood relationship, plus of course a share in their wealth . . .

As I walked, I readjusted. If Surus was married, there were not two opposing households, but one shambling family tree, with its halves unbalanced by social position and embedded feuds. Tensions rose on the Tranquillus side, not only because the Prisci were their landlords but because the Prisci had, and would always have, natural legitimacy. While some of the Prisci had clearly been antagonistic to the freedmen all along, others seemed more good-natured. Aurelia Priscilla was friends with Tranquilla Euhodia. Marriages had been arranged. Even secret relationships occurred. I could almost see a mood of wanting to enfold the freed slaves and their offspring into the main family, though perhaps that was a fantasy. Some in the male line persevered in hostility like picnickers swatting wasps. For some, resentment was a way of life: Gallicus Priscus had always been objectionable even with his full-blood sister.

I reached the Porta Capena, where my own relatives lurked. Passing under the aqueduct, I called in to leave word for the Camilli about my plan for my meeting tomorrow. Both uncles were out, so although I was invited in for domestic chat with their womenfolk, I pleaded work and did not stay. So we had our own tensions. Neither Claudia nor Meline was ever really delighted to see me, yet they would now believe they had offered a welcome, which I had spurned, so they would call me peculiar and standoffish. Neither could comprehend why a woman would work. They had borne it at one time, thinking that because of my background I might have no choice, but now I had married a man with a position in society. Why would I need independence, let alone my famously sordid occupation?

I couldn't help that. I was polite to them, but my heart was never in it. All three of us had come to Rome as outsiders, yet that never helped me pretend I had bonds with my theoretical aunts. Their concerns were not mine, nor mine theirs. Forget chat. I was tired and wanting to go home to my very different household.

Escaping them gave me a sense of freedom. My grumpiness lightened as I neared the Aventine. For a change I went up on the southern side. Walking along the Vicus Piscinae Publicae, I cut up opposite the north-west corner of the Fourth Cohort's station house. They were much more familiar to me than the Fifth, but not a group I would visit for casual gossip. Anything could happen inside those enormous barrack gates. Without a glance, I crossed into Greater Laurel Street, then straight past the grand Temples of Diana Aventina and Minerva into our own road.

It was now late afternoon. Grey and sombre. Foodstalls were reduced to selling limp greens at half price or dumping dry cakes in the gutter for the pigeons. Beggars were cold. Dogs on doorsteps that had looked quiet suddenly grew tetchy and went for other dogs they hated. Anyone who had come out for a tryst was now scuttling for home before anybody missed them, with a good chance they were heading into trouble anyway. If they were at a bar, perhaps in their haste they forgot to pay the bill. Either way waiters, longing for a break before the evening rush, gave people the evil eye, cursed openly, lost their chances of a tip and flicked cloths along counters angrily. If any new customer turned up wanting refreshments, the staff hid out of sight until the idiot accepted the lack of service and left, feeling like a rejected tourist.

At our house, I did not try knocking for the porter but let myself in. As I'd thought, Rodan was nowhere to be seen. Who knew why?

The boys were playing with their automaton again. They had broken off the little man who held the crocodile's food bowl, so he was now the meal. They had a new script by Corellius: "Do as I say! Guts on the grit! Nobody move or the croc gets him! You moved! Aaargh!" With lip-smacking jaw snaps and hideous screams, this scenario was keeping those innocents happy for hours. I waved. They merely looked up before continuing the urgent business of having the wooden man repeatedly eaten.

I washed my face and changed my shoes. Suza came hanging around, but I shunned her fiddling. My working day was not yet over; if I wanted to change my outfit it would be at dinner time.

I rooted out Paris. At dusk it was sensible to take an escort. "It's a bit late," he growled.

"I'll look after you. Informers can see in the dark."

I needed to find somewhere that would be a neutral space for bringing the families together. My first thought had been the big, barely used Temple of Claudius. As it was not far beyond the end of the Circus, I had stopped on my way home to ask whether I could hold a resolution council with a large family. Unfortunately I had used the temple premises before on a case, only last year. I had forgotten but they still remembered. I was now viewed as a bringer of scandal and discord so this time I was seen off.

There was one certain place for a bringer of scandal and discord: I trekked down the Forum Romanum, always a buffeting experience. With an angry glow and a fast-boiling personality, I marched Paris with me into the Basilica Julia.

"Are you serious, Flavia Albia?"

"Watch me! The people in my case are belligerent litigators. They will feel right at home here."

It was an assemblies-allowed day but not one assigned to legal action. There were a few togate men milling around the half-deserted spaces, but they were hopefully wondering how to meet a big rissole with money who would invite them to dinner.

I knew one man who was bound to be there. Since he had no wife or mother at home to organise meals, and he worked too hard to make real friends, I found Honorius by his usual snack stall, mournfully trying to decide between a cabbage parcel and a garlic squid, while he yearned for work to toddle along and attach itself to him. He looked nervous that only I came by.

"I have a meeting, Albia." He ran his fingers through his crinkled hair, as if that was his gesture when making excuses.

"No, you haven't."

"It's a Black Day in the calendar."

"Just right for a lawyer, then. Everyone sensible has already gone home. Listen! Honorius, you are a man-about-the-basilica. I need you to bribe an usher to book a spot here for me."

"Who is paying?"

"Surely justice is free?" I joked.

Honorius squared up professionally. "Flavia Albia, those things that are fair, moral, decent, deserved and legal have no price. Persuading an usher to erect barriers will cost you."

"My clients will pay."

He looked askance. "Have you told them?"

"Leave the invoicing to me. I have neat handwriting and a forceful manner. Don't be shocked, Honorius, but I want to use a courtroom for a reconciliation."

With his odd streak of innocence, he did look shocked. He fired up and told me it was a hideous suggestion: courts were for woeful litigants to be driven even further apart. "You may as well tell me you are seeking to end bitterness between the parties!"

I chortled. "*In re Prisci Tranquillique*? I wouldn't go that far."

"If those are the parties, I am not interested."

"You will be. I found out who really owns the orchard."

"Don't tell me, Albia. I would rather enjoy the warm thrill of being tantalised by endless doubt."

"Sounds like inadvertently peeing yourself! Won't you want to watch me announcing how the damned trees are not and were never theirs?"

"After all these years, I do not care."

"Yes, you do. Look, I'll buy you some stuffed cabbage—with a side of snails."

"Snails are off." Honorius had already asked. But he caved in when offered dinner at our house; he agreed to find space in the public rooms for a private gathering.

After he fetched out his pocket calendar, he said time was tight. This was Rome. Rome yearned for processions and sacrifice, not regular business. What was the point of running the biggest and best empire in the world, if you had to get up and go to work? Both the next day and two days later were public holidays when all work was forbidden. The day in between was a possibility. I said it was just my informer's luck to want a crucial denouement now. Half of my witnesses and suspects would wrongly turn up on a festival day. The people involved were not on good enough terms for me to bring them all together to an evening *convivium* privately: I would end up with victims being thrust head-down into tureens. "What festivals am I dodging?"

"Tomorrow is an Agonalia," said Honorius. "You know—the celebration that is so ancient nobody can remember what it is for."

"So why do they keep having it?"

"Nobody can remember, either, what penalty the gods will impose if they don't."

"I do love obscure archaic rites! Will it cause obstructions? What's the form, Honorius?"

"As far as I remember, they sacrifice the biggest ram they can find, for the well-being of Rome. He'll be led around with flowers in his horns, bleating ramfully, before he goes under the knife. That will cause a few traffic snarl-ups. Don't organise anything that brings people to the Forum, because the main site is at the Regia along the Sacred Way. You won't catch me anywhere near—my nerves can't cope. I panic if I'm caught up in a pavement blockage."

He was right. The Regia buildings were poked into an odd triangle, close to the Vestal Virgins' haunts and the new Arch of Titus. The area was gridlocked even on a normal day. The road, being so ancient, was a regular ankle-buster.

"What is the other festival?"

"Carmentalia. Nymph in a grove. Thanksgiving for agriculture, poetry, music."

"Midwifery." I groaned, remembering. "I can't be doing with that. Whole area from the river to the Palatine will be filled with women extolling their ancient rights. Absolutely maddening. They come to Rome from everywhere so they will be spilling about like barmy chaff, with no idea where they are or where they want to be. Why don't they decide one girl in every group will bring a map?"

"Can't read?" suggested Honorius.

"Don't be daft. They are dancing for the busy nymph who invented the Latin alphabet. She knew what a system needs: crops, poems, songs—and women who can write their own love-letters."

"Don't women always hold a map upside down?" If that was his notion of satire, I made short work of disabusing him. No wonder his wife left him.

We settled on the in-between day. Snagged between two different public holidays, we relied on the basilica being fairly quiet.

"Maybe the staff will let us slide in for free."

"Are you joking?"

"Right, bring on the bribery."

Then I, Flavia Albia, would attempt to effect a reconciliation where forty years of legal effort had failed.

LIV

As I had promised, I took Honorius home to eat with us. He seemed surprised by the size of my household and the quality of our life. Tiberius had been on site all day; he looked tired and I wanted to have a free mind for planning, so I made sure that everyone ate up and drank up, no messing about with stories of their day or other useless small-talk. Then I kicked out the lawyer and sent everyone to bed early.

Next day I summoned Paris again.

"Work two days running?"

"And more tomorrow. Get used to it!" Outlining my plan, I said today he was to go over to the Caelian to invite the Priscus family to meet. "Invite" was a cover for "order." Paris should not actually suggest arrests might happen, since I could bring no charges, but he should imply that key figures ought to come since, of course, they would want to put their point of view. "Pretend to confide that you have never known me use the Basilica Julia before."

"Isn't that because you are a woman so you can't appear in trials?" asked Paris, grinning.

"Yes, but subtly imply a trial may follow."

"Will it?"

"Might do."

"I'll take that as 'no chance'!" As an assistant Paris needed his rough edges filed off. "So, Albia, what are you up to now?"

"Similar. I shall take the dog for a walk over to Sidewind Passage and 'invite' the freedmen. Come with me first instance, because I'm hoping to retrieve something—well, someone—to send over to the Prisci. You can suggest to them that the Tranquilli will be rushing in droves tomorrow, while I'll convince the Tranquilli that the Prisci have already made advance bookings. They will all be afraid of missing something."

"Is this all about an orchard?" Paris marvelled, as we set off.

"It's about what the orchard represents."

It would be more than that.

On our way, we passed Fountain Court. In this filthy alley my father had sold a tenement to the senator from Spain. Ulpius Trajanus might turn up his noble nose at farming rabbits, taking the cleaner route of generalship, which involved nicer outfits, but the sale made me think about this old place, where I had lived for years whilst establishing myself. On a whim, I walked down, dodging the same old potholes of unpleasant black grease, listening to the ominous silence, keeping an eye out for muggers. I did have Barley on a lead, but she was no protection; she leant against my skirt, fretfully whining.

Paris was no happier. "This place stinks—literally!"

"You get used to it. I had a lovely little apartment here with hardly any mould or cockroaches."

The nightmare hulk of the existing building was being used to support a wonky scaffold. It was an invitation to agile cat-burglars who wanted to commit suicide. No one lived inside now. Even the people who had lived there before had had nothing worth stealing. Of course that never stopped burglars with no brains, which was most of them.

Outside, a man I took to be Trajan's agent was bidding farewell to another who had the unmistakable look of a contractor: broad in the beam, layered up with dusty clothes in indefinable colours, followed around by a thin, spotty lad, with a bored expression, who was dragging a short ladder. The agent shook hands, though I decided it was "I'll be in touch" rather than a done deal. Tiberius had told me he couldn't tell whether the agent was impressed with his own approach either.

I waited until the other builders left, then walked up and introduced myself, not as Falco's daughter but the wife of Manlius Faustus. "He comes across as diffident, but he'll see you right. Ancestors in the marble industry, so he has a wide trade inheritance. And anyone at the

Temple of Ceres will tell you, as a magistrate, they found him a pleasure to deal with."

I pushed it no more, merely made out I was interested in the fate of the Eagle Laundry for old times' sake. "Your senator is still abroad? Are you stuck in Rome on your own? It must be lonely," I sympathised. "Would you like to drop in for supper with us tonight? Corner of the Vicus Loretti Minor. I'm not sure what we'll be having—something simple, just pot luck. Nothing formal."

It sounded like a routine family meal, not the venal side of commerce. The man would come. By the time he had enjoyed himself with us, the chances were the demolition contract would be ours.

I felt no shame. I had lived in Rome long enough to know that in business much hangs on unspoken understanding. This was a kindness to a stranger, hardly a bribe. A good wife helping out her husband could invite a key figure. That was a social duty for her, so for him virtually honest . . .

After we parted from the agent, Paris was smirking. "Bringing men home two nights running? What's the aedile going to think?"

I mildly ordered him to settle down, then to warn Fornix later on his way back past our house. "Tell him simple but delicious. He'll know. The aedile helps nudge my work along, Paris—and I do likewise."

"Oh, you and Tiberius Manlius are as bad as each other!" Paris agreed.

"Yes, he's coming tomorrow, so I'm in for heckling."

At the Tranquillus building, where I was sure they also understood the wheels and deals of commerce, I called at both apartments. I made my pitch firmly and, as far as I could tell, secured all main parties to attend a council tomorrow. Perhaps, I thought wryly, they looked forward to punching up the Prisci.

I decided not to rely on the basilica staff to handle any uproar. I did remember how they had dealt cleanly with the man who had attacked his lawyer with a knife, but he was a regular offender: they knew him. I ought to take security to keep order.

Before I left Tranquilla Euhodia, I asked her to summon Erotillus. Once he was present, I said, "I am on a mission from a very old man called Gallus Ursulinus. Let's stop pretending, Euhodia. You must know he was the brother-in-law of Tranquillus Surus, also his executor. He owns this slave, Erotillus. I understand that the Prisci passed Erotillus to you without the owner's permission. I am asking you to release him back to his master."

Euhodia bridled. "You are working for me, Flavia Albia!" she protested.

"I am, until it interferes with my civic duties. A frail old man has been deprived of his property—in fact, he has a specific need of Erotillus right now. Ursulinus had paid for him to be trained as an archivist. This slave may be able to help him find an important missing document. You'll have a day for the task, Erotillus."

"What document?" interrogated the matriarch, suspiciously.

I saw no need for secrecy. "The will of Tranquillus Surus, which has been misplaced."

Erotillus nodded vigorously. He had brightened already at the thought of being returned to Ursulinus, the gentle, pleasant soul who enjoyed being read to. "Yes, I have seen it in the past," he confirmed. "I used to know the kind of places where he squirrelled it away. I'll give it a try."

I gave him a reproving look, to let him know I remembered us discussing the will before. Then he had staunchly pretended to know nothing about it. He stared back, a brazen slave, who had little to lose in defying me.

I told Euhodia we could either go through the legal procedures for Gallus Ursulinus to prove his ownership of the slave, or she could simply accept that he would succeed in a suit, and comply now. If the Tranquilli felt this left them out of pocket, they could ask for repayment after the meeting. Sighing grumpily, she agreed. I gathered up Erotillus to go with Paris. My runabout was to make sure the old fellow knew his slave had been returned through my intervention, and that Erotillus was primed to hunt out the will and its codicil.

I took them down from the apartment to the street before despatching them. When we reached the pavement by the basket shop, I looked back at the gloomy steps by which we had descended. "Erotillus, your old master mentioned a bad accident on this staircase. He is fragile and was tiring, so I did not pursue it. Was it something to do with a broken step?"

As far as I could tell, Erotillus did not look shifty, but his answer was oblique. "I don't know about the step."

"What do you know?"

He pulled a face. "Someone fell."

"Were you here then?"

"No. I heard about it afterwards. I was bound to, because sending me here was part of the Prisci paying out to cover the accident."

"What was that?" Paris joined in chirpily. "Somebody hurt? Bruises? Broken ankle?"

A slave who had been trained in librarianship and archive-keeping was excessive recompense for a bruised leg. Erotillus seemed reluctant, but confirmed how serious it had been. "None of us were supposed to talk about it. A person had died."

Paris was bouncing. "Oho! Who was it?"

"A woman."

"What woman?" Paris kept up his cross-examination, firing off fast in case I decided to stop him.

"A woman who lived here."

"Pot-washer? Salver-server? *Important?*"

Now Erotillus looked decidedly uncomfortable. "She was somebody's mother."

"*Hedylla?* Hedylla died in a fall on the stairs?" I waited. Paris now followed my lead.

Erotillus became more willing to gossip. The parties involved might want discretion but for him their secret was not worth keeping. "She lived in the upstairs apartment—with Postuminus and his daughter," he continued. "The wife had passed away just before. That was why his mother came. The centurion had always hated her, because of the orchard. He had tried to evict her from his land on the Campagna. Then he came after her again, after he found out she was here. Having her in one of their Rome properties drove him mad. He stormed in with his son—Tranquillinus, not the other one, not Turbo." At this point, Erotillus did look downcast again. He knew the significance of what he was saying. "They ordered her to leave, she refused to go. They tried to force her out. Somehow she fell down the stairs."

I pronounced it again: "Hedylla."

"Yes, Flavia Albia."

She had been involved in fights before. She would not obey enforcement attempts. This time, the centurion had gone too far. He had caused a serious accident, in which Hedylla died.

I finally understood why the Priscus family had caved in, given up their legal claims, paid off Honorius, then handed over the orchard to her favourite son as compensation.

LV

Paris left to go on his errands, meekly followed by Erotillus. After they were gone, I stood thinking, arms folded tightly under my cloak. The narrow street had little sign of life, though the man who ran the basket shop was out on the pavement, fiddling with his roped-together items. The Emperor had issued an edict to stop blocking streets with products, but in this kind of back alley nobody paid attention to it.

I stepped back to the staircase, looking up. It was one in thousands of ordinary household entrances to upper storeys. The opening led straight from the street, with no pillars or arch to mark it. By day it was acceptable but in the dark it would be uninviting.

The treads were wide enough for all but enormous feet. They rose very steeply between walls of indoor premises: squared stone, mainly with one slab, or less often two or three, to each riser. Their condition was unexceptional. A few lower steps, perhaps fielding bad weather and boot-grit, were the most worn. The rest had had occasional new stone pieced in, but were solid. Stone is often slippery, particularly when wet or dusty, but in Rome this was a normal building entrance. No one would call it a death-trap. Nor today could I see any reason to petition the landlords over maintenance. Fountain Court, with its ever-crumbling fabric, had always been far more dangerous.

Typically, there was no rail. If you needed support, you had to put a hand on the wall. Anyone with poor balance or weak eyesight was probably fine going up, but might hesitate on the way down. There was nothing to grab. Anyone who began tipping over would have to lean on a wall to recover their balance, but the width was narrow enough for one side always to be in reach. Carrying things might be a struggle. Still, they had slaves to do that. People who regularly used this route would be more comfortable than strangers.

Anyone engaged in a physical struggle would be at risk, especially if they toppled backwards. I had seen that, when Lucius Cosconius took his tumble, dragging Postuminus with him. They, too, racketed down from the apartment where Hedylla had been living; it was the same distance, the same fall. But even if he was concussed, Cosconius had survived.

"You want to know about that woman dying."

I started. The voice had come from the basket-seller. I could tell from his manner he was taking it upon himself to correct any nonsense other people might have palmed off on me.

He was skinny, and dressed only in a tunic despite the winter. No longer young, he had a full, curly mouth, almost like a woman's. His eyes wandered upwards, almost as if he might be blind. He wasn't, because I knew he had been watching my conversation and now he was closely observing what I did on my own.

I turned to him. "You were here?"

"Right where you were standing. When I saw the men arrive, I made sure I came out. I started bringing in my stock for safety straight away, if those bad boyos were around."

"You knew them?"

"From the landlords. Priscus and Tranquillinus," he spelled out, making it plain he was being patient with a woman he assumed was stupid. I ignored the routine prejudice to let him carry on bitterly. "That sick centurion from Egypt and his rotten apprentice. I had always known Priscus. Well, it was him who bought this shop and stuck me in it. He said he would make me a freedman, but he's never done it. I always thought I belonged to the old fellow, but that didn't stop Priscus poaching me. Jupiter's jockstrap, he was a vicious pig to everyone. I'm glad he's dead now, and his son won't follow him into Hades soon enough for me. He's a blight, too. I suppose you know Tranquillinus has had a long affair with one of the women from upstairs?"

I could not help a smile. "I do!" I realised something else too. "Yours was the shop that the soldier bequeathed to his sister, so she would always have cat baskets!"

"Correct! Pet beds are my strongest-selling line."

"What happens now the old sister is dead too?"

"Passed it on. She left it to the girl."

"Ursula? She seems a reasonable young woman."

His gaze wandered upwards again. "Not reasonable enough to drop the rent!"

"I'm sorry . . . So did you personally witness the accident?"

"I saw the end. When she came off the steps and out into the street."

"Forwards?"

"Half backwards, half sideways."

"Trying to stop herself?"

"No. Fell out like a wool sack, twisting. Dead weight. Just dropped."

"Did you know her?"

"I knew who she was. The old mother of that half-baked one."

"Was he there?"

"Down the street. They had him working in the garum shop in those days."

"Anyone come down from upstairs?"

"Not until it was well over. Their slaves must have all hidden in cupboards when the men arrived shouting. I don't know where the young daughter was."

"Cosca Sabatina?" She must have been a child, barely into her teens, if that. "So Hedylla took a tumble, then what?"

"Out they came after her, the cursed soldier and his son. Walking normally. Laughing, even. Neither of them stopped to check if she was breathing. She was in the gutter. I heard Priscus shout, as if he was joking, 'Disgrace! Someone has left a bundle of their rubbish!' That was what she looked like, lying there. They just stepped right over her, and went off back to where they came from."

"Not calling for help after the accident?"

"Accident?" The basket-seller used a mocking tone. "Oh, that was an accident, was it?"

The man was turning away. I stopped him. "What's your name?"

"Dindius."

"Dindius, will you come to the Forum tomorrow, to the Basilica Julia, and repeat this information? I can probably fix an honorarium to cover your loss of profit if you have to close your shop."

"I'd better not." He told me that all the commercial premises where witnesses had seen the incident had already been paid sweeteners.

"Recompense for the shock?"

"I don't know about any recompense. The cash was to keep us quiet."

"A cash gift from the Priscus family? The centurion and his son?"

"Those two were too brazen to admit they had done anything. The old man fixed it, with his womenfolk urging him, we were told. They were due to have a wedding for Tranquillinus, so they wanted to look good, with no scandal. They gave the family upstairs whatever they wanted because they had lost her, then everyone in the street took their share too and we kept our mouths shut."

"The old man who organised the hush-up is Gallus Ursulinus? He's still alive but very frail."

Dindius nodded. "They tend to treat him as past it, but he was—and still is, if he's lasted this long—the head of the family."

"I suppose he must be. I take it he didn't come in person?"

"Sent a deputy. That Venuleius. Relative by marriage. He's not bad. Once the old man had stepped in, things for tenants got more comfortable. We never had to deal with the bully-boys again—apart from us all looking the other way and grinning when Mardiana skips out with a smile on her face, off to a sly appointment with the younger one. Tranquillinus hasn't been here himself for years. Now Venuleius comes on a donkey whenever there is rent to fetch."

"Venuleius Senior? I met him. Brash and bad-tempered. Lunches with lawyers, but seemed straight otherwise. Still, not my type."

"Good for you!" sneered the basket-seller. "You wouldn't want a rent collector! Even the ones who don't chuck people down staircases are horrible."

"Who can blame them?" I sympathised. "To do that work, they have to be. But I might invite one home—if I could glaze his cinnamon cake with fatal poison!"

The basket man looked nervous. Teasingly mentioning that some people thought I was a druid, I offered to swap some good news if he reconsidered coming to the basilica for me. He said he'd think about it. I told him Gallus Ursulinus really had been his master. "He calls you one of his boys. What's more, he told me he *had* awarded you your freedom. Come tomorrow and I'll ask him to verify it."

Dindius growled, "The centurion lied to me? Then I shall be there for you—and they can forget their hush money. I'm going to tell the whole story!"

I gave him instructions for the meeting, then left.

That was murder. Hedylla was a slave, or her death would have had much more serious consequences for the Prisci.

To stumble down steep steps then collapse in a gutter while laughing men simply stepped over her corpse was a dreadful fate. It sickened me. I dropped into the black hole where informers punish themselves as they philosophise about injustice. Society is trash, morality is dead, the rich can cover up any crime they want. What is the point of law when it is codified by the privileged, for the benefit of villains, policed by the corrupt and operated by inefficient wimps?

This concept led to the usual conclusion: there was no way I could effect change, so I needed a drink. I was on my way home, where an elegant flagon could have been brought to me on a salver. Since a decent household matron was not supposed to indulge in bleak philosophical moods, let alone drink, I felt it more appropriate to take my grief elsewhere. I now understood why my father, who had a comfortable home waiting with Helena, would nevertheless sometimes swallow down beakers of liquor so raw it would crack lime scale off drains, knocking it back solo at some bar where sick rats went to die.

He took me to one once, in the curious period years ago when he was training me. It is inevitable that after two drinks in a place like that, you cannot remember where it is. This definitely applies when, afterwards, you can't find your purse and think you must have left it there.

I had an excuse. When we were joshing as a family, Helena Justina had suggested I ought to ask Rumpus and the skivvy whether Tranquillus Surus had bequeathed a large legacy to the bar-keeper he was so friendly with. Since my mother had told me to do it, I went to Nobilo's.

LVI

The copper shop was silent, but that was because the two metal-beaters had closed up for the evening, locked away their stock and tools, then moved along the pavement to the bar next door. They were both at the counter. There was space for three, but you needed to feel friendly; they parked themselves one either side, right next to me. I ignored them but was constantly aware they were not ignoring me. Luckily I was so wrapped up for winter they could not stare down my cleavage, but they kept up an unnerving fixation. The smell of sweat, lust and molten metal cooling on their ancient leather aprons was almost unbearable. Their dank garlicky breath was making loose strands of my hair curl.

There was no possibility of me ordering wine now. Still, I was used to being forced to ignore the need when out on duty.

Otherwise it went well. Rumpus called out the skivvy. I asked my questions. They knew the answers. That was completely unexpected. When suitably leaned on, they even had explanations. To find witnesses of this calibre at the end of a long, troubling day is a treat. It was worth being hopelessly squashed between strong-smelling men of massive muscle, who thought I could be there only for them to grope.

To the question, did Nobilo receive a legacy from Appius Tranquillus Surus forty years ago, the answer was: yes.

To: was the gift substantial, the answer was: Nobilo thought it good enough!

To: why did Surus do that? There at first seemed to be no answer.

Hoping to oil tongues, I joked about Helena Justina's theory that if Nobilo believed he was due to inherit money from Surus, then to help things along, he might have poisoned a portion of the much-loved potted shrimps. Rumpus and the skivvy conjectured that, if so, his old woman would not have liked that.

Whose old woman? Nobilo's?

No: Felicula.

Who was Felicula?

Nobilo's daughter.

And why wouldn't Felicula have liked having Surus poisoned?

Because Felicula had always thought she was his wife.

LVII

Next day it was raining hard. This heightened the smell of oily wool when a man strolled past leading a goat.

It was an extremely handsome male whose wet hoofs clicked loudly on the coloured marble slabs of the basilica's three-storey main hall. Someone said he had taken it to the Regia yesterday to be assessed for the Agonalia altar, not knowing that a ram was needed. He had cursed, apparently, because he did have rams at home. He was a vague personality and other, younger, sheep-breeders had pipped him.

I had no time to wonder how this goat's owner had managed to lead his rejected animal into the great Basilica Julia without being stopped, nor why he would do so today.

The public, even humans, were discouraged from using this mighty seat of Roman justice as a place where they could shelter from rain. Since we were between two big festivals, tourists did come in to shake off their sodden clothes and stare around. When ushers left stools and benches for my meeting, tired sightseers immediately sat on them. I left them temporarily, chomping leaden snacks and holding their guidebooks the wrong way up. Visitors are always a hazard of using an ancient monument for routine business but, as they rested, it stopped anyone walking off with our stools.

Honorius brought a head usher along. Managing to remain pleasant, I paid out a huge contribution to the ushers' funeral fund.

As I had hoped, the basilica was quieter than usual, though people did pass through, workers and customers of the shops and banks. There may have been civil actions in progress. The Court of One Hundred, which ironically handled inheritance issues, appeared not to be functioning; there is a reason why probate problems take so long.

Footsteps echoed: people were in winter shoes, some with hobnails to give them a grip out of doors, though in here they were prone to skidding. In the central space and the two side aisles, a haze of damp had arisen from wet cloaks, seeming to fuzz the view of the high roof. I could hear a lot of coughing from the spectators' balconies above.

I stood sentinel, ready to count my people in. There was a seat I hoped I could sink onto later, though it was a heavy folding X-frame item with ivory ornaments, one of those reserved for men of extreme rank. Since the Romans are a practical people, curule seats are extremely uncomfortable, even when cushioned; this encourages generals and dictators to carry out their duties fast, due to the proverbial ache in the tailbone.

"I've put a praetor on standby," Honorius whispered, when he joined me, signalling the curule stool. Praetors are the most senior magistrates. They are not supposed to make new laws; their role is to interpret the Senate's statutes. Sometimes they get out of hand and think "interpret" is a transitive verb meaning "change." Apparently none own dictionaries.

"Whatever for?"

"Anything that crops up."

Honorius sounded hopeful. I was horrified. I could not imagine a praetor's contribution being on a *pro bono* basis. The fee scale attached to a stool that hurt his coccyx would be steep. Honorius breezed off to buy himself a snack. I saw him bump into the Camillus brothers, so, with barely a casual wave to me, all three disappeared together.

I had Suza beside me as chaperone; she had imagined the basilica would be full of new fashions, not wet cloaks and old togas. Paris was informal security; Gratus my steward had come with him out of interest. They were currently dissuading gawkers, saying this was a private party. Justice should not be a secret affair, but I anticipated enough trouble, without total strangers offering numbskull contributions.

Gratus had shooed off several salesmen with trays of hot pies and one or two togaed toffs, who were crudely munching their produce.

Paris sternly shooed the goatherd when he rambled past again. Lawyers stared. A woman in charge piqued their interest, though I knew it was for all the wrong reasons.

The oldest widow ever had been brought by her relatives for a tour of the law courts, perhaps as her last request. Clad in black from her veiled head to sensibly shod toes, the stout great-grandmother wore her best jet necklace and had dragged along younger descendants, one of whom must be her son, on two sticks as he was more fragile than her. Like all heritage-hunters they seemed out of place in this working environment. Paris tried to steer the uneasy collection upstairs, where balconies served as viewing galleries.

At last my invited guests began to trickle in. First came the Prisci. They organised a cluster of seats where they could sit together but keep apart from other people, especially any who might be their tenants. Their configuration automatically split into male and female subgroups: Aurelia Priscilla and Julia Laronia sat with young Ursula, all silent, then Venuleius Senior snuggled alongside Gallicus Tranquillinus, occasionally muttering. The men were togate, under heavy cloaks. The women wore fine gowns and stoles over other layers, keeping their heads covered decorously by pulling up their stoles. Suza spotted twinkles of tasteful jewellery.

The old fellow had not arrived with them. Afraid he might have been left at home against his will, I sent Suza to ask the women, who told her he should be brought here soon.

The main parties in the freedmen's group arrived together: Tranquillus Aprilis and Marcella Maura were with Tranquilla Euhodia, all now looking distinctly elderly as if this investigation had taken its toll, then Tranquillus Postuminus, still looking bruised, and Cosca Sabatina, still downcast. The family must have managed to send messages to the Campagna because following them came Mardiana and her husband. Mardiana appeared to have squeezed in a beauty parlour for a quick smarten-up—well, yesterday had been Mercury day, her usual for pampering. She shamelessly nodded across to her lover, despite his wife and her husband being both present.

Gallicus Tranquillinus stood and walked over, not to her but to his brother. He and Turbo embraced with obvious affection on both sides.

While they clinched and then talked to each other, Mardiana coyly arranged herself beside her mother, putting down a hand to neaten her gown flounce and making sure her necklace showed. While Euhodia and Marcella Maura were rather stiffly wearing outfits they might not have tried on for a long time, Mardiana made much of smoothing down the rich sheen of her skirts with a practised hand. Eventually Tranquillinus smiled over at the women, using what passed for his charm, before he rejoined his brother-in-law, Venuleius. Tranquilla Euhodia glared. So did his wife, poor Julia Laronia.

Turbo ostentatiously picked up a stool which he carried right to the back alone. There he brought out a leather scroll case and began studiously reading.

The Cosconius brothers must have heard of this event. They came in dark cloaks instead of togas, and had not thought it necessary to be shaved. Although the Basilica Julia was scrupulously conscious of its importance, no one intercepted these large plodding men. They remained standing, on one side. They were in trade so they spoke to nobody and no one spoke to them. Only I smiled. They nodded back pleasantly.

Anxious about my aged co-conspirator, I went to look out through an arch into the main hall. I could see a litter being carried towards us very slowly; either side of it walked the helpful waiter from the Little Caelian Caupona and the young slave, though I saw no sign of Erotillus, which was troubling. Relieved that Gallus Ursulinus was able to put in an appearance, I was about to glide over to welcome him when someone else caught my eye.

Tranquillus Januarius was walking through the main hall. People were greeting him; he must have been well known here as a litigant. Surprisingly, he hurried up to the man I had previously seen leading his goat. The animal was being handed over to public slaves; the big stunning bleater was putting up a fight about being passed around. His owner looked anxious. I could tell intense husbandry instructions were being given. I even noticed a small shovel change hands, presumably in case anything pungent soiled the antique marble. Shears were passed over, too, with the loving owner first tidying his goat's beard. Then the goat, who had ideas of his own, headed off across the main hall, dragging his new custodians behind him.

Januarius and the dejected herdsman embraced, much like Tranquillinus and Turbo earlier. They were of the same age and stature, with matched receding hairlines. The goatherd was in a long tunic, not togate. Januarius looked to be urging him to join us. Before I could cross the hall to find out, they ran into the ex-bridegroom Gaius Venuleius; he arrived with another muscular young man of similar age and rich-boy appearance. Their togas had brilliant white naps and they were both growing spidery moustaches. I identified this as the special friend, which made him Januarius's son Augustus. In confirmation, Augustus embraced his father in greeting, after which each of the younger men gave a subdued nod to the goat-owner.

His response seemed standoffish. Then I remembered that up by Lake Albanus, Augustus bred sheep; I had imagined it as a dilettante hobby but perhaps he was serious. If one of his rams had been chosen as the Agonalia sacrifice yesterday, ruminant rivalry would explain any coldness. But who was the man who owned the goat?

I soon found out. All four men entered our side aisle together: the two in their forties and the two in their twenties. I saw a stir among the Tranquilli. Euhodia stood up; she approached the new man, the goatherd, and with matriarchal formality made him kiss her cheek. Marcella Maura pushed Euhodia aside and actually hugged him before more kissing. Then she brushed dust from his toga folds. She might have been a mother fussing over a fourteen-year-old on his first day in adult dress. Although Aprilis remained seated, he mimed a gruff nod; it was returned with all the nonchalance of any disgraced son encountering his parents after a long time. So! Never mind Belgica. Hot in from the Campagna, this was Tranquillus Julius. I hoped none of the clients whose money he had stolen had heard he was back in the basilica. My agenda had no scope for settling old scores of that type.

Just then, the Camilli returned with Honorius, who called out rudely, "Io, Julius! Long time no see. Have you brought another forged codicil for Flavia Albia?" Julius pretended he needed to refasten his shoe.

Ushers began tying ropes to the engaged marble-faced pillars on the side-aisle arches, probably not for privacy but to corral off my meeting from the main hall. Back came the Camillus brothers, who had rounded up dubious spectators: my family. I had known Tiberius was coming; he was attended by his body-slave, Dromo, who soon became bored and began flicking nuts around as if it was still Saturnalia. Here, too, were my parents. "We thought we must back you up, Tiddles!" I might have been arraigned for felonious kidnap or even on trial for making spells.

Helena whispered that my sisters would arrive in their own time since the basilica possessed shops. They regarded it as a sacred duty to inspect anything being offered for sale, especially in a building where wealthy men bought glittery presents for wives and mistresses.

My brother was in tow, accepting the outing placidly and clutching a waxed board to take notes. I hoped he had not brought his ferret, in case it scampered off, causing a commotion. To keep him busy, I sent Postumus to ask what Aurelius Turbo was reading. Neither of them thought it odd that a twelve-year-old boy should march up to a stranger with what both clearly saw as an intelligent question. Answer, unsurprisingly: Livy on the Samnite Wars. My brother then without reference to anyone took another stool for himself, which he placed alongside Turbo; they were kindred souls. Our lad fetched out a scroll of his own, turning the back of my space into an oddballs' quiet room.

Those two were peaceful. Everyone else was beginning to grow restless.

LVIII

Gallus Ursulinus had creakily emerged from his litter and made it across the hall to sit among his family. I stepped over to ask quickly whether he had had any success in finding the old will. He replied in the negative, but said Erotillus had remained in the house to have one last search in likely places.

I would have to improvise. Today would be a failure unless I produced some entertainment fast. Walking over to where my husband was standing with my uncles, I explained that we had to start and they must help. While Aulus and Quintus put their heads together for ideas, Tiberius called for quiet. When his efforts failed to achieve much, Dromo picked up the curule stool and clacked its two heavy halves together loudly. That worked just fine.

The seating had been arranged in a loose arc. I stood at the front. It was no worse than running an auction for Father, though I'd be lucky if I sold anything here, especially that sought-after speciality, domestic accord. I muttered to Tiberius that it felt like a wedding that was going to end up in the *Daily Gazette*.

"What's wrong with that?" he twinkled back, looking boyish. "Ours did!"

After greeting everyone and thanking them for their presence, I set out my objectives. Privately, I aimed to get through the morning without looking stupid, then shed the lot of them. In progressing from one minor debt, I had pieced together an intricate artefact that seemed to contain every conceivable family or business disaster; normally, even in the wild days after Saturnalia, clients only brought them one at a time.

In the realms of betrayal, stress and madness, the saga of Prisci and Tranquilli had everything.

Aloud, I admitted we were still hoping to produce the original will of Tranquillus Surus. Even without it, I hoped to bring about a more harmonious relationship between the discrete branches of his family. I would be addressing two major issues: was Tranquillus Postuminus a freedman as he had always believed, and what was the current position with their disputed cherry or apricot orchard?

"Almonds!" shouted Gallicus Tranquillinus, being objectionable on purpose. "I'm tearing it up and replanting! Is that current enough?"

The meeting might have ended right then as people took offence at him, but male associates of mine moved in swiftly, with firm hands pushing down would-be combatants, so they sank back onto their benches, merely seething. I saw Tiberius say something sharp to Tranquillinus; it looked like "Either shut up or leave." Positioning himself close by with his arms folded, Tiberius Manlius wore the same expression as when he had ordered our staff to hog-tie the man and throw him out of our house.

Smoothly providing a diversion, up came the Camillus brothers.

"I am Camillus Aelianus and this is my brother Justinus," announced Aulus, with no sign of deference for the place or the people he was talking to. "Flavia Albia, before you delve into the factual evidence, we suggest a brief summation of the legalities of ownership." He did not wait for me to agree. He had never been the kind of barrister who flattered colleagues by showing respect. It was my meeting—but I was only a woman and moreover his niece.

He gave us a measured résumé. When Aulus talked about the law, he was generally convincing. "The question is, who owns the orchard? It was set out simply in early Roman law that two years of continuous possession established title in the case of land, or one year of possession in the case of movables. Harvestable fruit may not be defined as a 'movable' but I understand there is a usufruct that requires additional consideration anyway. And we are discussing title going back how long?"

"About forty years," I told him glumly.

"The beneficiaries were?" I could tell Aulus was stringing this out for me to gain time.

"Gallicus Priscus, an ex-legionary of the Third Cyrenaica, and his sister, Ursulina Prisca. They both departed from life around four years ago."

"Whoever inherited from them will meet the criteria," said Aelianus, solemnly.

"There is a trustee."

"Ah! All the law requires, however, is, first, that possession was acquired in good faith."

"We hope the will proves that, Camillus Aelianus."

"Good. And, second, that the property has not been stolen or acquired by violence."

"There have been attempts at violence," I replied. "Accusations of theft have been levelled too. None of those involved the original trustee."

"What is at issue, then?"

"Possession."

Uncle Quintus moved his brother aside, using one hand to do it. The action looked polite, but might not have been. "Ownership and possession," stated Quintus, as if in a seminar, though he had more charisma than most lecturers I'd ever heard, "are separate and distinct in law. Ownership has protection whereas possession does not. However, if an owner seeks to remove a possessor, he must first prove his own title to the satisfaction of a sitting praetor."

Honorius stepped into the arena. "We do have a praetor on call, Justinus."

"Such forethought!" Honorius had indicated the curule stool. Justinus, being a maverick, sat down on it. Honorius, who was much more traditional, looked shocked. "The only aspect to examine," Justinus went on thoughtfully, as he spread himself on the cushioned stool as if born to it, "is whether at some point in its history the landowner, being the trustee in this case—or persons acting for him—has attempted to interfere with a possessor who rightly or wrongly claims title."

I intervened: "When you say persons acting for him, you mean with his permission to do so?"

"Oh, yes. If not, they are thieves and vagabonds! He would have a suit against them for misrepresentation and thus dishonouring his name."

Should the ancient Gallus Ursulinus now announce that he had never approved the attempts at eviction, this was a threat. I looked at Gallicus Tranquillinus who was yawning, as if that couldn't possibly mean him. "Assume the possessor has been interfered with. The praetor," concluded Justinus, "would insist that everything reverts to the status quo. *Then* he would adjudicate the title. If you do produce a will, it may render official adjudication unnecessary."

Unfortunately, we still had no will—but as we readdressed this problem, I noticed a murmur of voices. An usher was opening the ropes alongside our meeting to let other people in. One was the basket-seller from Sidewind Passage, my witness. He followed a despondent slave: in his usual unbleached tunic under a skimpy hooded cloak, but without his normal bright-eyed perkiness, it was Erotillus. He shook his head at us gloomily.

The old man struggled off his seat and tottered as fast as he could towards the despondent archivist. I scurried forward to help him. The news was hopeless. Erotillus had searched every scroll case in the family library, because that was where Ursulinus was convinced he had secreted his old crony's document on the last occasion he had handled it. He was sure he had pushed it in amongst the scrolls in a large set. Despite fetching out every individual item on shelves and in boxes, and even searching in other likely places all yesterday and for as long as he dared this morning, Erotillus had still not found the will.

LIX

Deep consternation struck me. Despite its age, this testament had acquired such notoriety that losing it might put its terms in doubt. Gallus Ursulinus knew its original contents but his frailty nowadays could make him subject to pressure from anyone who disagreed, in particular the aggressive Tranquillinus. People jumped up, exclaiming. Only with difficulty did we calm the noise and persuade them all to be seated again. Old Ursulinus slumped miserably, being fussed over tenderly by Julia Laronia and Ursula. He looked to have finally given up.

At that point, someone took a hand. Right at the back, Aurelius Turbo stood.

Looking in his direction, I saw him at once; others only became aware of him as he passed though the audience, but he made sure he advanced slowly so he gained everyone's attention. As the noise dropped around him, his pace was steady, his attitude pompous. When he reached me, his expression was so supercilious I could have stepped on his toe and ground into his foot with all my weight.

This was a man so foolish he had declared irresistible attraction to a wife who was at that moment publicly making eyes at her lover—his own brother—in Turbo's direct line of sight. Nevertheless, he had the gall to sneer at me. He used the mock-helpful tone people adopt when they are suggesting *You only had to ask!* "Could this be what you have been looking for?"

Juno and Minerva. I might have been grateful, but I am Flavia Albia: I hated him, him with his long face, high forehead and his sickening air of being so much better and wiser than the rest of us. To me, he was no better than his bullying brother.

Turbo was holding the index fingers of both hands apart with his elbows bent, like someone helping to wind wool. Between the two fingers he supported a slim, slightly battered scroll.

I understood immediately. "Thank you!"

So did Erotillus. "Oh, shit! It was in with his bloody Samnite Wars!"

Erotillus had once told me that after Turbo married, he brought to the Sidewind Passage apartment his personal copy of Livy. The *Ab Urbe Condita* trawls at great length through innumerable legends from the founding of Rome to now. Squashed among these notoriously numerous scrolls of history, Turbo must have found an extra. For more than ten years, he had been harbouring the will of Appius Tranquillus Surus.

LX

Honorius snatched it. This was a document he had wanted to see for more than a decade. He might groan that he wanted no more of this case, but he had worked hard for Ursulina Prisca, so he could not now contain his curiosity. He was fast. After a lightning perusal, he nodded to tell me it was the right will, the original, and its provisions were what we had been told.

It was his turn to take up a stance at the front of the meeting. This time silence fell abruptly with no need for curule clacking.

"According to his will," Honorius confirmed, "Appius Tranquillus Surus left his cherry orchard to be held in trust by his executor Gallus Ursulinus, that is, in trust for the two children of his marriage. If Gallicus Priscus and Ursulina Prisca predeceased the trustee, then the trustee would keep the land in his own right. It is a gift to repay him for his trouble as the testator's representative. So, the owner of the orchard is Gallus Ursulinus."

"I told you!" rapped the old man. Struggling upright, he pulled the scroll from Honorius and started rereading it. "The orchard is mine. I never agreed to have it given away. I've put the orchard in my own will and, Great-nephew," he addressed the fuming Tranquillinus, "you cannot alter that. I spelled out that your brutal father must never have it—and I have specified the same for you. When I pass on, I am leaving it to someone who rightly deserves a nest-egg from me."

"To whom?" boomed Gallicus Tranquillinus. He would not accept that his plans for a future almond orchard were dead.

"To Thymellus."

"Who in Hades is that?"

I answered him myself, smiling as I wished that Junillus and Apollonius from the Stargazer were there to see a colleague win out. "I believe he is standing over there. Thymellus is the waiter at the Little Caelian Caupona."

Tranquillinus might have physically gone for him, but Ursulinus had his own agenda. He was shaking the scroll as if looking for something. "Where is it? What have you done with it?" he demanded of Aurelius Turbo. When his great-nephew looked studiously bemused, the old man made himself hoarse, shouting, "It was here. It was wrapped up inside the scroll. Where is it?"

Whatever he meant was missing.

I sighed gently. I was hardly surprised.

"It's gone!" the old fellow wailed. "The codicil!"

I noticed glances pass between Tranquillus Aprilis and his sister Euhodia. Whatever addition had been made to the will, I felt certain they knew all about it. Perhaps they would be happier if its provision was never revealed. I was about to ask the old man, since presumably he remembered. Hearsay would suffice. He had shown himself to be an accurate, knowledgeable executor so he could be relied on.

But that was unnecessary. Another figure now approached from the back of our meeting space: my own young brother, shyer and less dramatic than Turbo previously, yet definitely up to something. Ignoring our parents' gestures for him to go to sit with them, he strolled forwards as if wandering down a country lane, but I recognised his secret air of purpose. His own reading material must have been put away in the satchel over his shoulder. He was holding something else.

This was my brother all over. As a master of innocent-seeming nosiness, as soon as he was left alone, Postumus must have looked inside Turbo's scroll container. It was not a full-size silver or wooden box, big enough for a whole collection of a long literary work. Today the historian had brought a cylindrical leather case, the kind used for travelling. It had room for a couple of scrolls. I had seen him take this or something similar when he rushed off to the Campagna in hopeless pursuit of Mardiana.

My stolid, single-minded brother reached the front. He applied his special sickly grin, the expression he used when he had been annoyingly a good boy. He gave the leather case to Tiberius, then passed me a single sheet of papyrus. Whether Turbo had known it was there and whether he had deliberately left it hidden remained in doubt. His expression was inscrutable. Now I had the crucial page, and after a nod to gain permission from the old man, I held up a hand for silence. Then I read it out loud.

This was a genuine codicil, written in obvious fury by Surus. It had been sealed and witnessed. The date showed he had organised it shortly before he caught his chill and died. It must immediately have followed the incident when his slave Hedylla came to Rome and discovered he was a married man. Her punishment for attacking him was that Surus wrote this, a new instruction that specifically concerned her.

Surus had bequeathed Hedylla to his brother-in-law. He made a provision that Gallus Ursulinus must never sell her. The reason was explained precisely. It spelled out that because of her vicious attack on Surus and the physical damage she had done to him, she must remain a slave for life. This codicil was an unbreakable prescript that Hedylla could never be freed.

LXI

Two questions and now two answers. Hedylla had lived and died a slave. "Appius Tranquillus Postuminus" might have used a *tria nomina* all his life, but he was a slave, too, because his mother had been. So even if Ursulinus had agreed to the gift, Postuminus could never have owned the orchard. However, his situation was much worse than that.

I felt profoundly depressed. I had fulfilled my commission to clarify his status, though this result was a disaster. His brother and sister must have known the truth all along; Euhodia and Aprilis were now slumped, heads down. Marcella Maura had dropped arms around both, while her two sons, Januarius and Julius, looked bemused and kept close to each other. Julius, with his legal training, spoke under his breath to his brother, perhaps outlining what might happen now to the man who, freed or not, was by birth their uncle.

I call him a man. That was my personal act of charity. Postuminus was a non-person. He had no rights; he was a piece of property. Where he had previously engaged in commerce, from now on he could do that only with permission and trust; he could own nothing, especially money, of his own. His orchard was gone. His right to sell those expensive little loaves of digestive bread would be rescinded by his one-time wife's relations. Some bathhouses would refuse him entry. He could be sold naked in the slave market. He could be raped and beaten half to death. He could be killed, and nobody would protest. He was as much an object as any item of furniture or a sack of some commodity; a value, a price, would be assigned to him. He was not credited with a soul.

Postuminus had probably known what he was but he must have

hoped never to be found out. All his life he had managed to persuade himself and others that he was a free citizen; now as he heard the truth given in public, without prompting, he stood up so he could carefully unwind the swathes of his classic heavy woollen toga. He folded the garment, as best he could because the shape of a Roman toga does not lend itself to making a neat parcel. He placed it on the bench beside him, took off and put his Alexander the Great ring on top, then sat, awaiting his fate.

He had made a slight gesture, as if in apology, to his daughter. Cosca Sabatina was beginning to realise what was happening and what it implied for his future. Stunned, she was not even crying. At that point, she seemed completely alone. She must have felt the other Tranquilli would have nothing for her. Did she even realise that, because of her late mother, she herself was not a slave?

It turned out she did. She went over to Postuminus and surprisingly it was she who apologised: "Gaius and I should never have threatened to expose you in order to take the orchard. I am sorry."

He stood up and embraced her, but then he put her away from him. He was a slave and she was free: she needed to be rid of him.

For her at least there was to be a future. Her two uncles from the bakery walked over and, quite gently for such big heavy men, led her away between them. The elder gave Postuminus a sociable nod, as if in thanks for her upbringing. Euhodia had half risen, with a hand outstretched, but the young girl had passed her before she could decide whether to finish the gesture.

So Cosca Sabatina went, with those uncles who had cared about her mother, into a new life. She would be rich. She would be spoiled. More than that, she would be loved. I hoped what had happened recently might make her appreciate the luxury she would have, including the genuine devotion of those two Cosconii.

That left the man who had been her father. He had sunk back onto his seat. I went to him as he was still waiting to be told what to do. I apologised. He was gracious: "My situation is not your fault."

"Nevertheless, I am sorry to have revealed it."

Postuminus looked up. A purist might have said that I should be seated while he humbly stood. In his quiet resignation he had even become a stronger personality. "Don't worry, Flavia Albia. This is what I deserve. I shall take it as my punishment."

He was the subject of my investigation, but I had brought him to this. My sense of failure was as great as any I had ever felt. I had viewed him as a limp dandelion, but all I could see now was his tragedy.

His contrition, which was heartfelt, made no sense. Trying to rouse him out of it, I snapped, "Why—what have you done, man?"

False confessions are traditional, yet this one shook even me. "I killed my mother," stated Postuminus.

LXII

Everyone seemed to have heard him. That's the trouble with dramatic confessions: people never make them in decent privacy. Before a good informer can cry, *Oh, no, you didn't!*—based on carefully gathered evidence and intelligently assessed likelihood—a roomful of people have accepted what was said. Whatever lunacy is placed in front of the public, most will love it.

I knew what had happened to his mother. I squared up to Hedylla's son and gave him the classic question: "Thank you, Postuminus. Just for the record, how exactly did you do that?"

"I ran her over with the garum cart." He could hardly bear to say it. There was no doubt he was reliving in his mind some horrific incident, something worse even than I already knew about. I needed this to be explained. We all did.

"Were there witnesses?"

"Everyone in Sidewind Passage."

"We shall see." I began to look around for the basket-seller.

This was not something Postuminus could have faked, but if he was mistaken, I had my witness ready. Dindius the basket-seller had been let in by ushers at the same time as Erotillus. Since he had arrived he had been talking to Gallus Ursulinus, his old master. I had seen them, heads together very happily, so they must have established that Dindius had been lied to and that he really had been awarded his freedom long ago.

I signalled him. The audience eagerly resumed their seats. I took charge.

"Dindius, you sell baskets in Sidewind Passage. You have a shop established for you by the late centurion, Gallicus Priscus, but in fact you are the freedman of Gallus Ursulinus, who is here today. I am just establishing that you are trustworthy, and that you were familiar with the people in this story. I want to hear about when the slave woman, Hedylla, died. That tragedy began when you saw the centurion and his son, Gallicus Tranquillinus, who acted as rent collectors and eviction enforcers, turn up at the building where Hedylla was living. She was staying at her son's apartment, this man here, Postuminus."

"That's right. His mother had come after his wife died."

"Thank you. So when you saw the collectors, you started putting your stock away, because you were apprehensive that they would cause trouble?"

"Those two were a couple of brutes." Dindius spoke firmly and forcefully. "We all knew they wanted to get the freedmen out of an orchard they owned and it had led to fights. Tranquillinus had been wounded on one occasion. So when Hedylla came to live at the apartment, we reckoned the centurion would soon go for her. We knew the Prisci, or the centurion at least, had wanted the freedmen out of that building for a long time."

"So he came to effect it?"

"That's right," confirmed the basket-seller. "Him and his son, over there, turned up, full of how they were going to shove her out. They went upstairs to do it. We all waited for the worst."

"And what happened?" I asked gently.

"Hedylla was the only one at home. First we heard a lot of screaming upstairs, then silence. After that there were some noises. Hedylla tumbled off the bottom of the steps, and lay senseless in the street."

"Was she alive?"

"No."

"How do you know?"

"She never moved and she made no sound. Even when the pair of them came out and stepped over her, she never budged. They had killed her."

"*They* had killed her upstairs in the apartment?"

"We thought so."

"No one actually saw it. You didn't think it could have been an accident?" I demanded.

"Of course not. It was on purpose. When they came out, they were boasting and congratulating each other. That was what they were like."

Jeering at that suggestion, Tranquillinus guffawed. His wife and sister both dug him with their elbows. Old Gallus Ursulinus looked disgusted.

"Then what happened?" I continued.

"So next thing, it was horrible. There is never enough room for vehicles—there had already been arguments. The big garum cart was being brought along, taking amphorae from the fish-pickle shop to one of their big retailers, so it was laden. It was so heavy with those giant pots, it could hardly move, or when it did, it couldn't stop. When people began shouting, the driver must've thought they were complaining at him again. He hadn't seen Hedylla. He was looking out to the other side, in case the cart hit the pottery stall. The ox missed, but before we stopped him, poor Postuminus drove the wheels right over her."

"He thinks he killed her."

"Not true."

"Can you be sure?"

Dindius fired up: "What do people take us for? We didn't all just stand there, leaving her. The lad who sells the kitchen pots had got to her first, but I went too. She had a mark on her neck as if somebody had strangled her. They must have done her in before they shoved her dead body down the stairs. She had definitely stopped breathing. It was horrible that her son drove over her, but she had already gone and it was never his fault."

"So why," I asked, "did people who knew that allow Postuminus to think he had killed her?"

"Because," said the basket-seller, with faultless logic, "that family is big on compensation claims. The pots fellow and I looked at each other quick, then we never told anyone. If those swines had made the son believe he killed his mother, he might be upset but he would be able to get more out of them."

That was true. The Priscus family had given him their apricot orchard.

Dindius said when the old man found out what had happened at the apartment he owned, he had paid off the whole street to keep quiet. He must have realised there was a good case to answer that Gallicus Priscus and his son, one or both, had committed murder. Ursulinus was sitting very quiet now, but he did not dispute the facts.

Tranquillinus jumped up and alleged, as he was bound to do, that it was his father who actually strangled the dead woman. Priscus was dead so could never be brought to justice for it. The son bragged to us, what did it matter? Hedylla was a slave in any case.

"She was *my* slave!" roared the old fellow, in protest. "Surus had given her to me."

Perhaps fearing that his great-uncle might come at him to redeem her value, Tranquillinus blustered: he had been a legitimate evictor in an incident that by mischance had ended in an accident. Ursulinus told him to sit down and shut up.

Euhodia and Aprilis had lost their mother, too, but they were looking completely crushed by hearing the details. The fact remained: Hedylla was a slave. Tranquillinus must believe the chance was slim that anyone would formally accuse him of this crime. Gallus Ursulinus, who had a right to recompense, had made it clear by his actions at the time that instead he would protect his own family.

Now events had been set out in public, he could have made demands after all, but clearly he would not do so. I would not advise him to take action. As an informer I saw no profit there. I glanced at the Camilli, who confirmed my view. So long as he blamed his father, Tranquillinus would get away with it.

Tranquillinus did lose something at the basilica: his lover. Mardiana left the seat she had occupied. She moved away from her mother and took herself closer to her husband, Turbo. They even held hands. It would not last. They were made to quarrel with each other. But in that moment at least, she showed some feeling for her murdered grandmother.

I still had my commission.

I could see a way for Postuminus to gain something. I had once asked, if he *were* a slave, after Surus died who would have become his owner? I checked quickly with the lawyers present. The Camilli and Honorius were of one mind: since he was born later, he would have gone with his mother into the ownership of Gallus Ursulinus. However, the codicil saying Hedylla could never be freed would not apply to him.

I walked across to Ursulinus. I was determined to achieve a good end if I could. "Sir, you can do some good here. Postuminus was your old crony's child. The life he has always known seems to have ended today—but you are able, if you will, to give him rebirth. It is not normally my role to beg, but I shall do it. Please, Gallus Ursulinus, give this unlucky slave his liberty, then be his patron. I believe he will make you a loyal freedman."

To my relief, Ursulinus nodded.

There was a scramble for action. Everyone wanted to be part of this. Honorius sent for his primed praetor. While we waited for this personage, the Camillus brothers and Honorius delighted themselves by expounding that the coming ceremony counted as a fictitious action in law. It was a way to pretend there was a dispute where none existed, they said, in order to obtain legal sanction for what was proposed . . .

After that lecture, the magistrate might have been startled by how eagerly his arrival was greeted. He applied his important backside to his curule chair. Unaware why he was needed, he had failed to bring with him the necessary special rod; his lictors, with their *fasces*, which we could have used, were lounging elsewhere in the basilica. Quick thinking, Tiberius commandeered the old man's walking stick.

Gallus Ursulinus firmly took hold of Postuminus. My husband volunteered to act as the necessary third party. He laid the rod upon the slave and pronounced him a free man. Next, Ursulinus took the rod and made the same pronouncement. He then turned Postuminus around and, with a little push, let go of him, symbolising his release into freedom. From now on he was Ursulinus Postuminus, *libertus*. My job was done.

The praetor said he would authorise adding the new citizen to the censor's lists though he hoped someone intended to pay the five per cent liberation tax. He also looked around to see whether anybody might give him an attendance fee. Since all he had done was sit upon his stool and watch, there was a general move to disperse as quickly as possible without noticing the request.

I was not having that. I stopped them all and gleefully cried, "Gallicus Tranquillinus will put his hand in his purse. But, sir," this to the magistrate, and I made sure it was obvious that I was not joking, "Tranquillinus has a reputation. Do not let him palm you off with a handful of military rivets."

We made Tranquillinus cough up. Honorius, to his credit, then took the praetor for a drink.

My husband winked and whispered to me, "Fancy an assignation with your handsome lover at a little place I know on the Aventine?"

"Have you brought any money?" I chortled.

"No, but the Stargazer will give us credit!"

Today seemed finally to have brought together both sides of that troubled family. The Tranquilli and Prisci were even arranging that, since Januarius had a birthday later in the month, they would meet up for a celebration.

As they were heading off, I spotted that the elderly black-clad woman, who had been looking at us earlier, was back, surrounded by her relatives. I saw her ask Aulus something, after which he gestured to the departing groups. The determined lady said something else. Aulus shook his head. But Quintus, who had overheard, looked more interested.

"What's that?" murmured Tiberius.

"Looks like a suit one or other of the Camilli may take on. Tell you later."

"Who is she?"

"I think her name may be Felicula."

That's right: Nobilo's daughter.

If I was right and Felicula was looking for a lawyer, there would be repercussions from Surus still to follow for his surviving family . . .

Otherwise, today we all thought everything was over. I had signalled to court officials that we were returning their space and their seating.

My own staff had already gone ahead, to avoid being asked to help clear the meeting place. My family were waiting for Tiberius and me, intending to muscle in on our quiet lunch together. Julius retrieved his goat.

It would have been a day to remember, even without what happened next. Tiberius suddenly caught my arm to hold me back from a disturbance. A man I recognised had begun screaming that he had been ruined. Ushers, with their arms full of benches and stools, were for once slow to react, even though I knew they intervened in his craziness all the time. With what sounded like triumph, this time he ran up to the departing group from my meeting. Among them was Tranquillus Julius.

Had Julius been wearing a toga, its full woollen folds might have partially intercepted the blow. His narrow goat-herding tunic gave him no such protection. The basilica maniac whipped out a dagger and struck him hard. For a moment, Julius seemed to experience the classic surprise, as if he thought somebody had unexpectedly punched him. Someone knocked the dagger from the madman's hands but as it clattered to the floor, he somehow acquired the goat-trimming shears and began viciously stabbing Julius, using both blades.

"Nincundio," I gasped. "Dear gods, he has really done it this time!"

People began hurrying towards us. Basilica staff seized and dragged away Nincundio. Januarius had cried out in horror. Julius staggered, fell and started fitting. Blood was soaking his clothes now. Then more blood was pooling across the ancient marble floor slabs.

The basilica maniac had finally killed someone. He had plunged his knife into Tranquillus Julius, right there in front of all his relatives. Although the men of my own family, who knew how to staunch wounds, tried to give him aid, it was too late. The tragedy was over. Julius, who was supposed to be hiding in Belgica, had foolishly reappeared in public, where he had been murdered.

LXIII

Nincundio was taken away and would be thrown to the arena beasts. Everyone assumed it had been a random act. Some did question whether he had been one of the clients who had once lost money to Julius, although this was eventually disproved. It turned out that all those clients had been repaid years earlier, by conscientious members of the Tranquillus family. His father, Aprilis, and brother, Januarius, had bailed out Julius at the time, then insisted he should remain in disgrace at their farm, running their programme for sheep to be used in sacrifices.

For my own satisfaction I did burrow around at the Basilica until I found out the true story. Nincundio was born in Iberia. He had owned a large herd of rough-terrain mountain goats. A reliable informant told me he then came to Italy in the hope of a lucrative future.

Before Julius had had his breakdown, then run off with his clients' money, an incident occurred that had left the Iberian bitterly distressed. There were rumours of unsavoury behaviour. No one seemed to know if that was true, but certainly Tranquillus Julius had persuaded Nincundio to sell him the pride of his flock. He was supposed to be buying the bellwether from which Nincundio had otherwise hoped to breed many generations of sturdy animals: his most handsome Spanish goat.

But then Julius had gone off and failed to pay for it.

SPOILER
WARNING

DO NOT TURN
THE PAGE
UNLESS YOU
HAVE FINISHED
THE NOVEL.

YOU HAVE BEEN
WARNED . . .

Family tree of the Tranquilli and Prisci/Venuleii

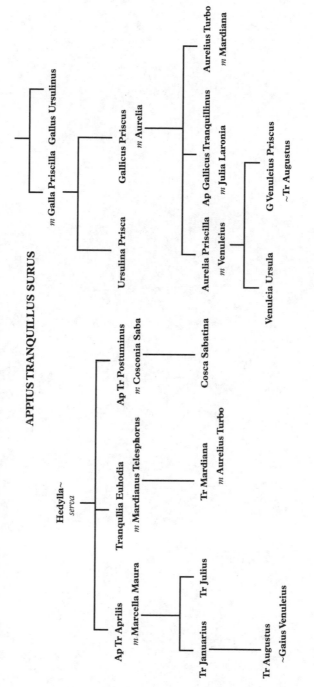

APPIUS TRANQUILLUS SURUS

Hedylla~
serva

Ap Tr Aprilis
m Marcella Maura

Tr Januarius

Tr Julius

Tr Augustus
~Gaius Venuleius

Tranqullia Euhodia
m Mardianus Telesphorus

Tr Mardiana
m Aurelius Turbo

Ap Tr Postuminus
m Cosconia Saba

Cosca Sabatina

m Galla Priscilla Gallus Ursulinus

Ursulina Prisca

Gallicus Priscus
m Aurelia

Aurelia Priscilla
m Venuleius

Venuleia Ursula

Ap Gallicus Tranquillinus
m Julia Laronia

G Venuleius Priscus
~ Tr Augustus

Aurelius Turbo
m Mardiana